AFGHAN HORSE

Robert A. Coryell

To Jimmy and Tod, my inspirations for writing this novel.
And to Nancy for suffering through its birth.

ACKNOWLEDGEMENTS

A most special thanks to Nancy Marsden for tolerating me during this long and often arduous process and, just as especially, for providing her editorial expertise.

Special recognition is in order to those that most inspired my confidence to continue on this journey. Thank you to my favorite daughter and son-in-law, Kanda and Patrick McMullen and my grandkids Riley and Evan, for allowing me to hide in their basement for months on end, away from civilization and the distractions of social contact. Thanks to my son, Kevin, for his knowledge of Coast Guard operations and procedures. A special thank you to my favorite daughter-in-law, his wife Ashley and my other two grandsons, Cooper and Carter, whom I love dearly and apologize for forgetting their birthdays and not being around as much as I should have.

Thank you to those that took time early-on to provide constructive criticism, feedback and support: Patrick Reynolds, Tom Delaney, Claire Nass, Kathleen McMullen, Lynn Johnson, Joyce Murphy, Rob Levin, Lori Wodrich and Diane Fitzgerald.

And finally, thank you to those that read and critiqued various parts and editions of my work along the way and provided helpful and much appreciated feedback: Donna and Tom Shafer, Janie Copeland, Maureen and J. J. Collins, Marjorie and Abbott Morgan, Terrie Gonzalez, Bonnie Brooks, Dick Morgan, Loise DiPalma, Susan Green and Bill Thorn.

"There are known knowns, things we know that we know; and there are known unknowns, things that we know we don't know. But there are also unknown unknowns, things we do not know we don't know."

— Donald Rumsfeld

PROLOGUE

At first he thought he was dreaming. He was waking but in a painful and unfamiliar way. The ringing in his ears was so loud he could hear nothing else. Every joint in his body ached and, for a few moments, moving was impossible.

He had found himself lying on his left side, his head awkwardly cocked against a solid wall. A crushing numbness made it difficult to assess the pain he felt, difficult to grasp what had happened to him. How had he gotten this way?

In survival training he had been taught to take inventory of his wounds, self-triage. But his jumbled thoughts made it difficult to focus. A throbbing in his left elbow made his fingers twitch uncontrollably and through the tear in his pants he could see his left leg had been cut about two inches above his knee. The wound appeared wide but not terribly deep. An uncomfortably numb warmth enveloped the right side of his face and he reached up to feel a loose flap of skin below a gash on his temple that was bleeding profusely.

Shifting himself, he reached out and tore a large scrap of cloth from the ragged, bloody shirt of the corpse beside him and wrapped half of it as a tourniquet around his knee. The rest he folded into a compress for his temple, holding it in place with the man's neck tie.

Shock would soon set in and he knew it. He could not allow himself to lose consciousness again. No doubt his subconscious was telling him to be still, relax. But consciously, his training urged him to fight against his desire to rest.

The scene around him was eerily still but chaotic. Smoke hung in the air filled with soot and ash. His eyes stung and he could see barely six feet in any direction, but it was evident the air was quickly beginning to clear of the heavier smoke and debris. There had to have been an explosion of some kind, though not a large one. Most of the destruction appeared concentrated in one corner of the small café where he remembered he had come to meet someone, a contact who had information of great importance to him. This was Paris, he recalled, near the center, the Charonne district.

The corpse lying beside him was unrecognizable. It appeared to be male by the way it was dressed, but the face was completely annihilated as if smashed by a large sledge hammer. Its legs were missing from the knees down. Atop a lone upright table several feet away, a foot, presumably from one of the missing legs, slowly dripped a trail of scarlet into a small congealing pool on the floor below.

The pain had begun to subside but the discomfort of the contorted position had grown unbearable. He shifted his body away from the wall behind him and brushed away the shards and broken pieces of glass nearby. Lifting his head, he looked over at the area where he and his contact had been seated. The wall that had been behind the man was partially gone, the man's bloody signature spattered around a gaping hole. On the sidewalk in front of the café, a severed head and torso smoldered, all that was left of what had once been the ill-fated gentleman with whom he had talked.

Habitually, he glanced at his watch. The crystal on the face was broken, the hands stopped at 11:31 p.m. Their meeting had lasted about 30 minutes. It wasn't clear what time it was now or how long he had been unconscious, but since no one had responded to the scene yet, he knew he hadn't been out very long.

The ringing in his ears was diminishing. He needed to get to his feet. He rolled onto his stomach and raised his upper body by pushing up with his arms until he managed to get his knees underneath him. Then he grasped what was left of a door jamb and used it to pull himself to his feet. His legs were wobbly but it was evident they would support him. He shifted his weight from side to side to be sure.

Standing over the corpse below him, he could see the cell phone and wallet of the man had fallen from his coat pocket. He held onto the jamb as he leaned down and picked them up noticing he was using his left arm. His elbow seemed to be okay although it hurt to move it quickly. The jamb offered support to lean back, freeing both hands to peruse the wallet. It was a small leather tri-fold, western style. The identification inside revealed the man was a French citizen, a Parisian resident who just happened to be in the wrong place at the wrong time.

A photo of the man's wife and children was tucked neatly into one of the plastic sleeves. The realization struck him that the man's family would never again see him. He said a short prayer for them. The pain of the loss of family is a universal one and though he had no immediate family himself he took a moment to grieve for them before he forced himself back to the present.

Given the proximity and size of the blast, it could only be assumed the bomb had been meant for him and perhaps his contact. If so, he was still in great danger. Events were moving slowly in his mind, as they often do in traumatic situations. But he was finally wresting control from the concussive confusion. What should he do now? Where should he go to seek safety?

It occurred to him to change places with the dead man at his feet, at least temporarily. They were about the same size. The man's face was obliterated, unrecognizable. The switch would probably fool authorities long enough to gather his wits, tend to his wounds, and put together some sort of plan for how to proceed. Certainly, going to the police was out. That was precisely what they would expect of him.

He pulled out his own wallet and passport, soaked them in the dead man's blood, and placed them in the man's coat pocket. He put his cell phone in the man's front pants pocket, or what was left of it, where he usually kept his when travelling. Then he removed his watch and placed it on the dead man's wrist. It didn't appear the man had been wearing a watch of his own, unless it flew off in the explosion. It would be good if he hadn't, one less piece of evidence to give him away. He kept the dead man's phone and wallet, putting them in his jacket pocket. What he would do with them later he wasn't sure, but he couldn't risk leaving them there.

He had begun to think more clearly. There was a place where he could go, an apartment that belonged to someone he knew. It would be too dangerous to try to go back to his hotel. Whoever tried to kill him would certainly be watching it. He struggled unsuccessfully to remember the address of the apartment but he knew approximately where it was. Perhaps when he got near he would recognize something that would jog his memory. In any event, it wasn't possible to stay here. He had to get moving.

Time had begun to accelerate. The experience was no longer in slow-motion which meant enough time had probably passed that the authorities would be descending on the café at any moment. His attempted killers might also return looking to assess their handiwork.

He turned and started up the main boulevard, du Charonne, from the direction he had earlier come, limping slightly from the pain. His knee had begun to swell and he would need to get it treated soon. His temple still throbbed but the bleeding had slowed. He wrung out the bloody compress then pressed it back into place as he walked. Despite his wounds, he was incredibly lucky to be alive. How he had survived was a mystery.

When he reached the end of the first block he turned and looked back at where the café had once been. From the scattering of the debris it appeared the blast must have come from inside the café. There were tables and chairs in the middle of the street and the glass from the large front window appeared to have been blown outward. Perhaps one of the men inside had placed the bomb, or maybe it had been a suicide bomber. It was doubtful he would ever know. But he was alive. That was all that was important at the moment.

3

The wailing of sirens was close by, coming closer. People had started to gather in front of the café, their anxious voices pierced the cool night air. For the first time he noticed the mixed acrid odors of spent explosives and burnt flesh, smells seared into his memory from time in Afghanistan. Unmistakable smells, acerbic odors of death.

His torn and bloody clothing would attract attention. It would be better to zigzag along the back streets rather than stay on the main boulevard. He turned the corner and started down a small one-way street barely wide enough for the compact vehicles prevalent in Paris. There was a walking path along one edge of the street next to a long three-story building that stretched well into the distance. He kept as close to the wall as possible, as much in the shadows as he could, the less conspicuous the better. As he walked, the voice of his contact began to speak again in his head.

CHAPTER ONE

Six Months Earlier

Eddie began to feel the warmth creep up from his toes and feet. For some reason, he always felt it first in his feet. He had friends who felt it first in their thighs, in their stomachs, others in their chest. But for Eddie Manson, decorated war veteran and heroin addict, the beautiful waves always started in his feet.

The euphoric swelling washed upward through his body slowing only briefly at the base of his neck before it rushed into his head with a mellow roar. At that moment all was right with the world. Trials, tribulations, hardships, pain, depression... all gone, purged in an instant by a simple tool filled with liquid paradise. That's how it always was for Eddie. He looked forward to each opportunity to shoot up these days.

Eddie had lost count of the trips to the VA Hospital. Everyone there was nice, well, mostly everyone, but they were only able to help so much. His wounds were horribly severe and it had taken almost two years to perform the nine surgeries needed to repair his upper spine and shoulder. The bullet that caught him in the back just missed his body armor, tearing through his shoulder and ricocheting around his upper back before finally coming to rest near the spine in his neck.

It had been a year since Eddie's last surgery. Living on the streets was difficult, but not as hard as looking into a mirror. Three years ago Eddie had the body of a warrior, six feet tall, one hundred ninety pounds, chiseled. Now his emaciated 146 pounds made him sick to his stomach every time he saw it. Mirrors were the enemy. By avoiding them he could also ignore the disheveled look of his unwashed raggedness and the dirty nastiness of his matted hair and beard. Most people walked by him as if he wasn't there. It used to bother him but not anymore. He didn't want to see himself either.

Eddie had no idea what it felt like to think clearly. Thirty-three months of pain killers clouding every thought made it almost impossible to comprehend the world rationally. When the meds wore off it was easier, but the pain would become too much to bear in no time. He was addicted to his medications and his tolerance had grown so great that the monthly allotment from the VA was no longer enough. His doctors refused to increase his dosages telling him he needed to work harder at managing his medication schedule and pain tolerance. He had tried, he tried hard, but then he found that heroin was cheap and an easy way to fill the gap between prescriptions. The VA knew he was addicted. They offered him group counseling meetings but he stopped going after a few months. He couldn't remember to go to half of them. The other half he was so high he couldn't make it there.

Eddie had been mustered out of the Army on a medical discharge when it was evident he would never be able to fight again. Sergeant First Class Eddie Manson was of no more use to them, so they patched him up and sent him home. He had commanded four tanks and seventeen men in Iraq, but today he couldn't find a simple job. The few he had found in the past he couldn't hold.

He had been twice arrested for vagrancy and once for shoplifting a sandwich at a 7-Eleven. But the most serious offence was a felony charge for the possession and sale of heroin. Eddie wasn't a dealer. He just happened to sell a couple of caps to one of his buddies in need. His buddy got busted and rolled on him. His brother being a Senator kept him out of jail. But after that it got harder to find a good source, most thought he was probably being watched and kept their distance. There was nothing about his life Eddie liked anymore. As sad as it was, his addiction was his life now.

The feeling was wonderful, as usual. This time was even more so because Eddie had finally made the decision to give up hope for a return to a normal life. That was never going to happen. With a simple needle full of joy juice, Eddie would end the pain, the sadness, the misery of his pathetic existence. He wasn't sure what lie beyond his consciousness but, whatever it was, it couldn't be worse than the way he was living.

The needle was still stuck in his arm. He hadn't had time to remove it before the rush overcame him. He was unable to move at all, every muscle in his body limp from the catastrophic effect of the huge dose he had injected for this final voyage into oblivion.

Dying under a bridge overpass would seem tragic to most people. He knew that. But he had picked this bridge for his ultimate experience because it felt friendly. He had played here with his big brother and his buddies as a kid. He had lived here as a homeless vagrant for the past few months, protected from the rain and the cold. It was comfortable, it was secluded, and it was unlikely anyone would find him in time to Narcan him back into the misery he had suffered for so long. His only regret was that he hadn't called his brother to let him know.

Eddie's brother, Gavin, had also been in the military, an investigations officer for the Air Force. He was smart and everybody liked him. Eddie looked up to his brother. He kept in touch with him, calling him every month from the free phones at the VA, but he had never told him how bad things had gotten lately. Gavin was busy, he was a Senator, and Eddie was proud to be his brother. Their parents had been proud too, before they died in a car accident in south Tampa a year ago. It was after their passing that things had started to spiral out of control. Gavin was all the family he had left now, and he felt terrible about leaving Gavin with no family at all. But not terrible enough to change his mind.

There wasn't much about the effects of "H" that Eddie didn't know. He had overdosed himself a few times, waking up in contorted positions, often with the stench of vomit all over him. He had been lucky, if you want to call it that, he hadn't choked on his own puke like so many people he knew had. A terrible way to die he supposed. Horrifying probably. Somehow, he had survived his past ODs. But he was pretty sure, and hopeful, this time that wouldn't be the case.

Eddie could tell his breathing was labored. The autonomic response which caused him to breathe subconsciously had failed, as it always does with an overdose. He had to consciously force himself to take breaths. Still he was curiously calm. He knew his last breath would be the one just before he fell asleep. The thought didn't bother him. All he felt was a contented peace wrapped gently around him. He had no regrets about his decision. In a strange way it was exhilarating. He was about to find out if anything lie beyond this earthly existence. After suffering so much in his wretched world, letting go of it was easy.

Eddie closed his eyes. Moments later the world had one less soul.

* * *

It was a hectic Monday morning. The phones were ringing non-stop in Senator Gavin J. Manson's office. Dozens of calls per hour were coming in with condolences and well wishes, not just from his home state of Florida, but from all over the country. The Senate switchboard was inundated. A few people complained about how the cops were hand-cuffed and should be let loose like feral dogs to purge our communities of the scourge of drugs. A smattering of others thought the Senator's brother got what he deserved, if you're addicted to drugs you're a drag on society.

"You'll need to make a statement, Senator. What time would you like me to set something up?"

Cynthia Lockhart had only known Gavin for a brief two years. The fact that he had chosen the young 29-year-old as his Chief of Staff was as surprising to her as it had been to his colleagues. For Gavin it was a no-brainer. With a BA degree in psychology and a PHD in Constitutional Law, Cynthia had made a name for herself in a town full of lawyers, not an easy feat. Her direct style and in-your-face confidence around some of the biggest egos in the world earned her kudos over and above her obvious brilliance. She knew how to work people and how to play them if they couldn't be worked. And it didn't hurt that she was a pretty black woman who loved cameras as much as they loved her. She always dressed impeccably, suit dresses, rarely pants. She kept her hair short, a straight dark bob style that was both chic and stylish.

Like Gavin, Cynthia hailed from the Tampa Bay area on the gulf coast of Florida. She grew up in Tarpon Springs, a small Greek community established in the late 1800s which became the premier sponge harvesting market in North America around the turn of the twentieth century. It was, for decades, the "Sponge Capital of the World", and still, the largest Greek community in the United States.

Cynthia was an athlete at Tarpon Springs High School, home of the "Spongers". She was a track star who ran cross-country, played soccer, and lettered in both. Her African-American heritage was barely noticed among a population of predominately white students, perhaps due in large part to the fact that, academically, she was the smartest kid in school. Her bubbly personality and innate ability to ignore resentment and prejudice made her one of the popular kids, and she relished the role. In her mind, there was nothing she had to prove to anyone, and nothing she couldn't accomplish. She loved working for Senator Gavin Manson and looked forward to getting up every morning.

"Make it eleven-thirty, Cynthia. And have somebody draft a statement for me. I'll tweak it before I go out there. Boiler plate stuff."

"Yes sir. Do you need anything else, Gavin? A hug maybe?"

Gavin stood up from his desk and walked around to embrace her. He had to bend his six-one, two-hundred-pound frame well over to touch faces. He dwarfed her petite five-feet-four slim athleticism, but the awkwardness was barely noticed.

"Cynthia, I screwed up. I screwed up so bad", he said as he released her embrace. "I should have kept a better watch on him."

"It's not your fault, Gavin. The system failed him, not you. Lord knows you tried to get him into the right programs and you practically browbeat the VA down there."

"Maybe. Then why do I feel so guilty?"

Gavin's voice was cracking. Cynthia sensed it was time to leave him to himself. "I'll come and get you when the mikes are set up. We'll do it in the hall outside, just a small handpicked group. I'll screen them myself."

"Thank you, Chief." Gavin often called her Chief when she was acting in her capacity as his top surrogate. "Ask Monica to come in, would you?" he said, just as Monica was coming through the door.

"Sure thing, boss." Cynthia had an equally irreverent sense of humor that Gavin admired and appreciated more than she knew. Monica held the door for her as she left.

Monica Sandoval was Gavin's secretary slash travel agent slash gal Friday. Radar O'Reilly had nothing on her, plus she was as sexy as the day was long. Her long jet-black hair hung in naturally smooth, tight ringlets when she let it down. But most of the time she kept it in a sexy updo, a restive bun held low on the back of her head with sparkly hair pins or colorful tiaras depending on her mood. She was a little taller than Cynthia with wider than normal hips and a buxomness that she wasn't hesitant to flaunt when it was advantageous. She was not only the definition of beautiful, but a Latin bombshell with a feisty personality and a sharp-witted tongue.

More importantly to Gavin, she was a dynamo, a perpetual motion machine that made things happen. And, like all the women Gavin kept around him, she was smart. Not brilliant like Cynthia, but street-wise.

"What do you need, Senator?" she inquired with a Spanish accent that Gavin never grew tired of hearing.

"See if you can get the Tampa mayor on the line and then later some funeral homes I can interview for Eddie's memorial service."

"Ms. Ortorio's secretary is on line one. They are waiting for you, sir. Why don't you let me take care of setting up the memorial service and the funeral arrangements? I'll keep you apprised, I promise."

"Thank you, Monica. And arrange for my flight to Tampa? Samantha will be travelling with me, of course."

"Of course, Senator." Monica had already started the flight and hotel arrangements and contacted the Tampa mayor's office. But Gavin didn't need to know that. She was good at letting him think he was in charge. It was one of the secrets to her success.

Gavin picked up the phone. "Mayor Ortorio, please."

Mayor Victoria Ortorio was only the second female mayor Tampa had ever had. She governed with a sensitive brand of populism that garnered her many fans in the growing metropolitan community. But the economic collapse in 2008 hurt her ability to grow her favorite cultural projects, like museums, a riverwalk along the Hillsborough, and parks which she cultivated like a political gardener. Philanthropic money ran dry and a shrinking tax base limited her ability to adequately maintain general operations like bus services, road maintenance and storm drainage. Her conservative rivals would likely oust her in the next election. Still, she was proud of the work she had accomplished.

A few moments later a female voice emerged from the silence, "Senator, I am so sorry for your loss."

"Thank you, Madam Mayor. I need a favor."

"Anything. How can I help?" The mayor's tone was genuine.

"I want to hold the memorial service in south Tampa, but I will bury him in Bay Pines. Can you arrange an escort for the procession across Gandy Bridge? I'll have St. Pete escort the rest of the way."

Gavin wanted his brother buried at Bay Pines National Cemetery in St. Petersburg. He had thought about Arlington, Eddie was certainly eligible, but he and Eddie had lived in the Tampa Bay area all their lives. It just felt like the right thing to do was to bury him at home with his parents who were also buried there.

"Of course, Senator. Your secretary has already been in contact with my staff. She said to coordinate all logistical efforts through her. Is that your wish?"

Gavin smiled. "Yes it is, Madam Mayor. And thank you for your gracious cooperation. I appreciate it very much."

Victoria dropped the pretense of protocol. "Gavin, I'd like to be there, the memorial that is. Not for a photo op, but to sincerely pay my respects. I didn't know Eddie but I'm aware of what he did for our country. I'd like to honor that."

"I'd like that, too, Vickie. Of course you're welcome. See you soon."

"You too, Gavin."

Gavin hung up the phone and leaned back in his chair. It was barely 9:00 a.m. but it felt like he had worked all day. He closed his eyes and pictured his younger brother, the whole one, not the broken one.

* * *

Behind the bank of microphones and recording devices Gavin stood alone, staring out with disdain at the paparazzi of reporters gathered for his statement. He hated talking to the press these days. Regardless of what he actually said, he knew his words would be parsed and spun to fit into whatever agenda the media determined their bosses and fans wanted them to say. He thought of the public as fans of the paparazzi press because the polarization of modern media coverage had become the norm, each fan base choosing to faithfully believe the propaganda of their favorite news outlet to the exclusion of all others. Somewhere in the middle lie the truth, but no one seemed much interested in it.

He dutifully read his statement to the small group of major network and newspaper reporters, asked them for as much privacy as they would allow him during this difficult time, and thanked them for their understanding. Then he turned and left without answering any questions. He knew the kind they would ask and he wasn't interested in contributing further to the fourth estate's feeding frenzy.

As he walked away he could hear them barking over each other like a pack of dingoes, clamoring for a controversial snippet, "Do you think he suffered, Senator?" "How long have you known Eddie was a drug addict?" "Where did he get the heroin?" "Was your brother a drug dealer?"

What had happened to the press? It was hard to believe this was how the public really wanted their news outlets to behave. Gavin never liked to think condescendingly of the public, especially his own electorate, but they obviously tolerated and apparently welcomed this kind of behavior from their criers or they would have demanded something different. Cronkite must be rolling over in his grave, he thought.

Cynthia gave the reporters a hand gesture that said "that's all" and followed Gavin back toward his office. "Monica has your flight and hotel arrangements ready. You'll leave Thursday afternoon. The services will be held on Friday. Samantha will pick you up at the Hart building's Constitution Avenue exit at 2:00pm."

"Thanks, Cynthia. Are you coming with us?" Gavin asked.

"No sir. I'll be taking a later flight. I have things to take care of before I can leave." Cynthia hesitated then added, "You know you can stay with my mom and me at her condo in Dunedin if you want. It's on the beach. Hotels are pretty lonely places. It's not that much of a drive to south Tampa."

"I know", he said. "And it's nice of you to offer. But I'll be fine."

* * *

Senator Samantha Lawrence was waiting outside the Hart Senate Office Building in her little red Miata, engine running, double parked next to a small VW bug on Constitution Avenue. Gavin spotted her car immediately as he exited the building. He chuckled to himself wondering why a woman nearly six feet tall would buy a Miata. It never ceased to amuse him when he watched her get into or out of it. It was a process more akin to putting it on and taking it off than getting in and out. But it was a process she didn't seem to mind at all.

She was standing outside of the car with the driver's door open, waving to him. He thought it odd she felt it necessary to wave, or even get out of the car - as if he might be confused by all the other candy apple red Miatas parked along the street. In any case, it was always nice to see her when she wasn't dressed for work, a sight he had only seen on rare occasion even though they worked together so often.

She was only a couple of inches shorter than him, with dark red hair and green eyes accentuated by high cheek bones and immaculately applied black mascara. She was thin but moderately endowed, and she usually wore her hair in one of several imaginatively coiffed fashions. But when she wasn't working, like today, she wore her hair silky-straight, parted in the middle and streaming down well beyond her shoulders, feathering out at the ends. She would sometimes pull the right side forward over her shoulder. It was a sexy look for a Senator. But then she was unmarried and it was nobody's business how she rolled after hours.

"No luggage?" she asked.

"Monica said she sent it to the hotel already. It will be there when I arrive."

Samantha's jealousy was evident as she started the entry process to the Miata. "I wish I had a Monica! I don't think you know how lucky you are, Gavin."

Samantha was a first-term Senator from Worcester, Massachusetts. She spoke with a Boston-like accent, which meant there were only 25 letters in her alphabet. She had had the good fortune to meet Gavin on her induction day, though she didn't realize it at the time. He had seen her wandering the halls of the Dirksen Building in wide-eyed awe and offered to show her around. She warily accepted, having heard about his reputation as the most eligible bachelor in the Senate and, at 36 years old, something of an experienced lady's man. But to her surprise, she found him to be a perfect gentleman, bright, contemplative and very good looking.

They belonged to opposite parties which she thought might be problematic for the future. But as it turned out, two years later they were very close friends, confidants in many areas, and she found it easy to work across the aisle on partisan and non-partisan issues. It never occurred to her not to accompany him to his brother's funeral.

She noticed Gavin appeared tired and sluggish. "Did you remember your ticket?" she asked, a question she wouldn't have felt necessary under different circumstances.

"Yes, Mother", he mocked with a grin.

"Okay, I'll stop", she laughed. "Can we both agree that no business will be spoken on this trip?"

"Fine by me", he agreed. "Sam, do you know much about the heroin epidemic in New England? I see stuff on the news all the time but I admit I never pay much attention to it."

"It's not just New England, Gavin. It's almost everywhere, small towns to big cities. They pass out free Naloxone in several states now. My state was first to recognize the size of the problem, but others are quickly coming on board. It's pretty ugly."

Gavin reclined his seat so he could lie back. The seat was surprisingly comfortable for such a small car. He closed his eyes and asked, "Where does it come from? Mexico? Seems like we should be able to get a handle on it somehow." He was almost ashamed he didn't know more about the drug that killed his brother.

"Mexico is one source, South America also. I read in the Globe that Afghanistan is also a source, a growing source." Samantha wasn't sure how much more Gavin really wanted to know. Massachusetts overdoses were twice the national average and the epidemic in her state was a full-blown crisis. She knew quite a bit about it because she had to deal with the ugly reality of it every time she went home on break. It was a major concern to her constituency but she had no idea how to begin to address it at the federal level.

"What do you feel about the War on Drugs, Sam? Apparently, we're not winning it."

"We never will", Samantha said matter-of-factly.

"Huh?" he muttered. "I want to pick your brain more later. But right now I just want to nap if you don't mind. I didn't sleep much last night."

"You have about 50 minutes to BWI", she calculated. "Sleep tight."

A car pulled up behind Samantha's double-parked Miata and honked with purpose, apparently not willing to go around even though there was plenty of room. In her unambiguously Boston accent she yelled back at the driver "Screw off!", flipped him a middle finger, then pulled away and made a tight U-turn doubling back onto Maryland Avenue, a feat her Miata performed with great ease. She followed the road around Stanton Park then onto "C" Street NE toward 295 and the Baltimore-Washington Parkway.

"Why didn't we fly out of Reagan?" she asked but got no answer. Gavin had been lightly snoring since Stanton Park.

CHAPTER 2

The flight from BWI to Tampa International took two hours and twenty minutes. Gavin managed to sleep for most of the trip. Flying first-class made it easier, something he didn't realize Monica had arranged until he reached the security lines at the airport. He rarely flew first-class on short trips unless he qualified for an upgrade. He felt it was taking advantage of the public's tax dollars. Many of his colleagues had no such compunction, he noticed.

Gavin was waiting curbside in the arrival pickup zone just outside of the baggage claim area for Kevin Falk to pick him up.

Samantha had already left the airport for the hotel. He and Samantha would be staying at the Marriott on Kennedy Boulevard, an easy location from which to attend his brother's memorial and visit with his old friend Kevin, a former Air Force buddy stationed at nearby MacDill AFB.

Gavin had joined the Air Force in 2002, straight out of college, less than a year after the twin towers came down. He was just sixteen when he entered college. Six years later he had a BA in Criminal Justice and a Masters in Criminology. The Air Force recruiter was licking his chops to get him into the Air Force's investigative arm, the Air Force Office of Special Investigation, AFOSI, and Gavin obliged with one caveat. He wanted to enter with the rank of Captain.

It was rare for a recruit to be accepted into the military without starting at the bottom and working his way up. Gavin never liked the bottom much and he knew there were exceptions, particularly for fields like doctors, lawyers and chaplains. So why not try? But the Air Force wanted nothing to do with a twenty-two-year old Captain who barely shaved. They offered him, instead, the rank of First Lieutenant with the promise of Captain in two years if he passed his proficiency tests. By the age of twenty-four, Captain Gavin J. Manson was headed to Afghanistan to conduct CTOs, Counter-Threat Operations, "outside the wire", an Air Force euphemism for deployment. That's where he first met then First Lieutenant, now Major Kevin Falk.

"You're still the best wing man I've ever had, but geez, you've gotten uglier. Time isn't treating you worth a shit, man!" It was the same old Kevin, gauche and irreverent.

Gavin turned around to see his old friend coming out of the baggage claim doors. His blond, military style buzz cut was straight out of the manual, high and tight. He was wearing a Hawaiian shirt and baggy shorts, sandals and reflective sunglasses that hid his dark blue eyes. Kevin was slightly shorter than Gavin but stockier. He apparently still worked out, his biceps and quads were pumped. And he still had the same wry smile and sauntering swagger. After seven years, not much had changed.

Kevin had joined the Air Force just a week after Gavin graduated from Officer Training School at Maxwell Air Force Base in Montgomery, Alabama. Their paths didn't cross until three years later when Kevin was deployed to Afghanistan. First Lieutenant Kevin Falk was a junior investigative officer for the AFOSI reporting to Captain Gavin Manson. Gavin's unit provided intel for the CTO field officers whose mission was to ID threats, develop target packages for kill or capture, confiscate and remove weapons from the enemy, and to seize drugs, especially hashish and opium, from the black marketers.

In almost no time, Kevin had become adept at recruiting resources, that is, snitches. And he was especially good at locating and planning drug busts. Nobody knew more about the Afghan drug world than he did. He and Gavin became a formidable team, fast friends, and brothers in a place where you're forced to put your life in your buddy's hands and his in yours. They worked hard together, and sometimes they played together just as hard.

"Yeah, well you look like you've been sitting behind a desk for a while. Is that a pooch I see growing down there?" The two embraced with a strong hug and laughs that reconnected seven years of separation in less than a minute.

"So, where's your car?" Gavin asked. "I thought you were picking me up?"

"I'm parked in short term. Got here a little early to meet someone. She's staying at the hotel here."

Gavin shook his head. "You're a dog, you know that?"

"But I'm a happy dog! So, let's go get a drink! We've got a lot to catch up on." Kevin put his arm around Gavin's shoulders as they walked toward the parking garage elevators. "Oh man! I'm sorry about your brother. I had no idea he was here or in the kind of trouble he was. I would've let you know, man."

"Yeah, I know." Gavin tried to shake off the maudlin feeling and distance the subject. "Let's go get that drink. Is Hooters still open on Gandy Boulevard?"

"You bet your ass! New crop of ladies, too. They might just find a Senator appealing."

Gavin needed a distraction and there was a day when hitting on a Hooters girl might have provided one. But a sitting Senator can't afford to be too loose with his behavior, especially in his own district, not to mention he was getting too old for most of the young women there. He would have to be satisfied with wings and beer tonight, and maybe a dozen oysters. It was good to see Kevin again, almost like they were never apart.

* * *

It had been a while since Gavin had been to south Tampa. It was a special place for him. He grew up there and went to school from sixth grade to twelfth. Every time he returned, something new was being built: a cluster of condos, a new Walmart, and many of the older homes were being razed to put up more modern ones. Old neighborhoods were being erased, replaced by newer versions.

As a kid he remembered all the empty lots and fields of palmettos south of Gandy Boulevard. The area was called Rattlesnake in the thirties and forties, and for good reason. The abundance of palmetto bushes was the perfect breeding ground for them. But snakes didn't stop him and his brother and their friends from building forts in them. Palmettos built great forts. Not many palmettos were left today. Tract homes, condos, apartments and businesses crowded them all out.

South Tampa was just a typical middle-class community of mostly single-family homes back when he was growing up. Many of the older homes were built in the fifties, after World War II, for all the returning Air Force GIs stationed at MacDill Air Force Base at the southern end of the south Tampa peninsula. But in the early eighties progress visited the sleepy community south of Gandy, SOG, the real estate people began to call it, and it became a mecca for young professional couples and the businesses that catered to them. Home prices soared and so, too, the taxes on them. The city loved that part and thus eagerly supported almost any business proposal that added to its revenue base, with only a basic regard for the long-term consequences on the utility infrastructure and traffic conditions. But, you could get to downtown Tampa in fifteen minutes on the Leroy Selmon Expressway, to St. Petersburg in thirty minutes, and the airport in twenty-five. SOG was the perfect location for modern day yuppies and they were drawn to it like hippies to Haight-Ashbury.

Gavin didn't like many of the changes to his home town, but he accepted them as inevitable. One change which did suit his culinary cravings was the addition of Hooters to the plethora of restaurants along Gandy. He had an affinity for chicken wings and raw oysters and nobody did them better. That pretty young women in short shorts and tight t-shirts served them up, made the experience that much tastier.

Gavin followed Kevin through the Hooters entrance and over to a table in the corner that was unoccupied, despite a large crowd milling around outside. The two girls holding the doors had smiled and greeted Kevin. "Hi, Major." Apparently, they knew him well enough to know his rank without a uniform.

Kevin motioned for Gavin to sit first. "God, it's good to see you again. I wasn't kidding when I said you were the best wing man I ever had. Between your good looks and my irresistible charm we were killer. I still dream about the leave we took to Sydney."

"Yeah, well mine are nightmares", Gavin joked. "I hope you're not going to be as obnoxious tonight".

"You got laid, didn't you?" Kevin grinned.

"Yeah, but it would have been nice not to have had to cold cock her boyfriend." Gavin was only half joking.

Kevin slapped the table and laughed out loud. "Hands of stone, mi hermano! I thought you killed him."

"Well, if I had I could kiss this Senator gig goodbye. Don't put me in that situation again. I swear I'll leave you to get your ass beat without so much as a thought. In fact, I'll help the guy." Gavin picked up a menu and tried to hold a straight face. Then they busted out laughing until they were holding their sides.

Kevin gathered himself. "So what made you want to be a politician? I never pictured you as the baby-kissing type."

"You know I've always had trouble with authority", Gavin said reflectively. "I figured I could be my own boss, not have to answer to a chain of command. And I wanted to serve the country. 911 got to me, I guess. It seemed like a better way to go than to try to claw my way up in the Air Force. Plus I was tired of being deployed, stuck in shit holes on the other side of the world with assholes like you."

Gavin paused to think about what he had just shared. He hadn't been honest with anyone like that since he had become a Senator. Something about Kevin allowed him to open up.

Kevin smiled. "Well, it seems to be working for you, man. You're only into your second term and I hear they might ask you to be Vice Chair of Intelligence? Youngest senator ever in that position."

"It's being kicked around", Gavin acknowledged. "So, when did you make Major? I thought the Air Force only promoted the best and the brightest."

"A couple of months ago. They're shipping me up to Langley next month. I'll be working with Selbourne. Remember him?"

"Not Colonel Jacob Selbourne?" Gavin was taken aback. "He's CIA! You're going to work for the Company?"

"As soon as they can arrange the clearances, yeah. I'm packed and loaded, just waiting on orders."

Gavin was troubled with Kevin's new assignment. "You do remember he was the son-of-a-bitch who kept us from making half a dozen busts in Afghanistan? He and his hired mercenaries protected poppy fields like they were gold. Said the reason was 'intelligence gathering'. If that was the reason I'll eat my shorts. Hell, I'll eat your shorts. I don't know what that bastard was doing, but it wasn't intelligence."

Gavin's voice had risen. The tables next to them were staring. He lowered his voice, "Look Kevin, be careful. That guy has no friends. No matter how friendly he gets with you, don't turn your back on him. I don't trust him. I'm advising you not to either." As his heart rate returned to normal, he sat back and asked in a hushed voice, "What the hell are you going to be doing for him?"

Kevin looked at his menu again, then lowered it and said calmly, "I don't know. They haven't discussed responsibilities with me yet. I'll probably find out more in a few weeks. Hey, maybe we can get together more often up there. Langley's not that far from you."

Gavin knew Kevin too well. He was obviously lying, but why? There was no point in pressing. Maybe he couldn't say. Maybe he didn't want to say. It didn't matter.

A tall, cute blond wearing painted-on orange shorts and a low-cut, sleeveless white t-shirt, with an owl peeking through the OO's in Hooter's, strolled up to the table and strategically positioned herself. She laid the order pad down on the table and sensually leaned over, her ample cleavage prominently displayed.

"What can I get you, guys?"

"Dos cervesas, Señorita!" Kevin answered, never looking up at her face. "And my amigo will have one, too."

* * *

Eddie's memorial service was small. Gavin didn't want the press to know where it would be held so he had Monica reserve a small building on Oklahoma Avenue, just off Manhattan, a half mile south of Gandy. The hall was located in a residential neighborhood. It belonged to the Lion's Club and they rented it out for things like weddings, square dances and today, a memorial service. Their staff must have done a good job of keeping the service secret, not a single reporter showed up until the procession formed for the trip to the cemetery. Apparently, a neighbor must have called in to one of the local TV stations.

There were only six cars in the procession to the cemetery, but with press coverage it grew to five TV trucks and several other vehicles that tagged along. Kevin was unable to make the memorial service but arrived in time to join the procession. Mayor Ortorio had attended the memorial service but she didn't make the trip to the cemetery. Neither did she make a statement to the press, apparently a woman of her word.

* * *

It was early afternoon when the procession carrying Eddie's cremated remains wound its way into Bay Pines National Cemetery, on the grounds of the Veterans Administration Center. During the early part of the Great Depression, Bay Pines veteran's hospital and domiciliary was built with federal funds appropriated by Congress for an old soldiers' home. Originally called the National Home for Disabled Volunteer Soldiers, the home lacked a place to inter patients who died. But not long thereafter, a twenty-one-acre burial ground was set aside and the first interment occurred in the spring of 1933.

By 1964, all the original grave sites had been used. In 1984, the Veteran's Administration transferred responsibility to the National Cemetery System which cleared out a large hedgerow dividing the grounds and made room for more plots. But today there were no more large sites left for coffins. Eddie's remains had to be cremated and buried on a smaller plot. He was buried with his dad, a Vietnam War veteran, and his mother, killed together in a car accident barely a year earlier.

The ceremony was not as somber as Gavin had imagined it would be. The chaplain had obviously performed many of them, his words meaningful, not trite or superficial. His message celebrated Eddie's life and accomplishments, barely mentioning the tragedy that befell him in the end.

Gavin had ordered just a small honor guard, so he was surprised when three of Eddie's buddies from his old unit attended in full dress uniforms and provided a three-volley rifle salute in Eddie's honor. His former unit commander came also. Obviously, Eddie was liked much more than he knew.

Everyone stood as a lone bugler played Taps, twenty-four haunting notes that nearly always brought tears to those attending. Civilians held their hands over their hearts, military removed their covers with their left hands, holding them below their right shoulders as they saluted at attention. One of the honor guardsmen collected three of the expended shells from the rifle salute and presented them to Gavin along with the U.S. burial flag which had accompanied Eddie's urn.

Gavin had held it together fairly well until he was presented the flag. As a homeless vagrant, Eddie had left no mementos or memorabilia, just a shopping cart full of junk collected for reasons only he knew. Other than some family photos Gavin had taken from his parent's house after they died, Eddie's flag would be all that he had left to remember his little brother. That, and the grave marker here at Bay Pines.

The chaplain approached Gavin and extended his personal condolences. Gavin stood and thanked him as the cemetery representative announced that the ceremony was concluded.

"That was nice, Gavin", Samantha said as she hugged him. "There is something important about military funerals. Thank you for letting me share this time with you." Gavin said nothing but hugged her a little closer. Her embrace felt especially comforting because he knew she meant it.

Kevin was next to approach Gavin. He had a completely different demeanor from the Kevin who had picked him up at the airport. He was wearing his officer service dress, dress blues most Air Force officers called them, with full regalia - badges, ribbons and medals displayed - hat, belt and shoes spit-shined. Like most military officers when in dress uniform, he carried himself with a confident stride and an air of authority that was impossible to ignore.

Samantha didn't wait for Gavin to introduce them. "Hi, I'm Samantha" she said, reaching across Gavin to offer her hand to Kevin.

Kevin's military bearing faltered briefly as he reconnoitered the situation. Samantha was stunning, dark red hair, ruby-red lipstick with matching nails, and a sleek black dress that hid nothing it wasn't supposed to hide. He recovered quickly, "Major Kevin Falk, ma'am", he offered, removing his hat and putting it under his arm before shaking her hand. "It's a pleasure to meet you. Of course, I know who you are... Senator."

"Don't call me ma'am. My name is Samantha, or Senator", she smiled with a come-hither grin.

Gavin noticed that neither had taken their eyes off of each other since they first locked. "Sam, I'd like to warn you off of this guy but I'm afraid you're on your own. Just don't let his charm disarm you, it's lethal. I know. I've seen it in action."

Cynthia motioned for Gavin's attention. He excused himself from the conversation he wasn't really a part of anyway and made his way over to her. She hugged him without words then asked, "Do you think Sam and Kevin might want to come to my mom's place for lunch and drinks? She lives just up Alternate 19 a few miles. We could pick up whatever we need on the way."

"You don't think she would mind?" he asked.

"Not at all", Cynthia assured him. "In fact, she would love to have company, especially two Senators. She's wanted to meet you since I started to work for you. It would make her day, I'm sure."

"Then I'm in." He turned to Samantha and Kevin whose eyes had yet to unlock, "Cynthia has invited us to her mother's for lunch. Either of you interested? I'm going."

Samantha confirmed, "Sure, I'd love to go."

"Sorry, Captain," Kevin lamented. "No can do. I have to get back to base. Duty calls." Gavin had noticed Kevin's phone had rung toward the end of the service and he had gotten up to take the call. It must have been important. He had hoped Kevin could join them at Cynthia's mom's house but he understood all too well your time is not your own in the military.

Kevin walked over to Gavin and hugged him. "Rough day, buddy."

Gavin agreed, putting his arm around Kevin's shoulder, "Thanks for being here."

"You bet", Kevin whispered, then turned toward the parking lot. He looked back, "Samantha, I look forward to seeing you again when I get to Virginia. Cynthia, it was a pleasure to meet you. Take care of my old compadre. He needs all the help he can get. I've seen him try to take care of himself, not a pretty sight."

Gavin noticed Samantha watching Kevin until his car exited the cemetery parking lot. He had never seen her drawn to a man before, but then he'd never spent much time with her, except at work. It seemed Major Kevin Falk had made a first-class first impression.

CHAPTER 3

Five miles southwest of Everglades City, Florida, just west of Ten Thousand Islands, sea captain Thomas Grogan was anchored in 28 feet of crystal blue water. Accompanying him were his wife, Mary Ann, his fifteen-year-old daughter, Lucy, and twelve-year-old son, Tod. The four were relaxing on a long weekend aboard the family's new Meridian 391 Sedan, a 41-foot luxury yacht which he had named the TICA, 'This I Can't Afford', in homage to another self-made man he admired greatly, Jim Walter.

Jim Walter was the inventor of pre-fabricated homes, precursor to modern day modular homes, and had owned a yacht, though much bigger, by the same name. Their stories, his and Walter's, were similar in many ways. Walter started with a thousand dollars borrowed from his father in 1946 and built two empires, Jim Walter Homes and Walter Industries. Thirty years later he sold them for two billion dollars. Tom had mortgaged his home in Palm Beach, Florida, to start a real estate investment company. Twenty-five years later he sold the firm for sixty-five million. Not quite the same scale as Walter, but an entrepreneurial success all the same.

Of course, Tom was not a real sea captain. The Coast Guard refers to every boat owner as 'captain'. It is a courtesy they bestow on sea-going vessel operators although 'skipper' is probably a more appropriate address. Tom took pleasure in the idea of being the captain of his own ship, believing himself the master of his own fate. But today that belief was being put to the test.

"Lucy! Mary Ann!! Get below! NOW!!!" Tom was screaming as he descended the stairwell from the flybridge onto the cockpit then hurried through the door into the maindeck salon.

"Tod, trip the EPIRB and throw it in the sink. Hail Channel 16 with three sets of Maydays then get below with your mom!" Tod did exactly as he was told. Tom knew he would which is why he gave the order to him instead of Tod's mom. She could be too emotional sometimes and he couldn't take that chance. Tod was a veritable rock.

"Tom, what's going on?!" Mary Ann was heading below as Tom had instructed. He had made it clear to his family that there is only one captain on the boat and his orders are the only ones that count. They can neither be questioned, debated, nor countermanded. Lives could depend on obeying them quickly and efficiently. For the most part everyone accepted that, although 'Get me another beer' was debated once as to its legality.

"Pirates!" he yelled back. "The anchor is raising now, I'm going to try to outrun them. All of you stay in the master cabin until I give you the okay to come out. And hang onto something!"

"Pirates?" Mary Ann screamed. "How do you know?"

Tom never answered her. He had already pulled his 9mm Glock and an AR-15 with two 30 round clips of ammo from the gun cabinet and was headed back up the stairwell to the flybridge and the helm station.

The anchor had weighed by the time Tom got back to the helm. Crouched down behind the helm console, he started the two 420 horsepower Mercury inboard engines and let them idle as he raised his high-power binoculars over the console to check on the pirate boat. "Oh Shit!" he uttered to himself. Now he could see two boats headed his way and fast. He had suspected that the original boat he saw was a pirate boat, though he hadn't been positive, because from a distance it looked like one of the two occupants had a rifle. But now there were two boats, maybe 2500 yards out, and he could definitely make out two men in each boat and all of them had guns. No doubt they were pirates. No doubt they were headed directly for him.

Smugglers in the southern Gulf of Mexico tended to steal gofast boats to run drugs and contraband into the U.S. The problem with stealing a vessel capable of 85 knots was its profile. The Coast Guard was on constant lookout for any unusual behavior of boats with "forward leaning radar posts". But smaller boats with 50 to 70 knot speed barely got their attention. Somehow the pirates chasing the TICA apparently knew that the Coast Guard "never looked twice" at high-speed fishing boats.

The boats in pursuit of Tom Grogan were identically, and somewhat unusually, outfitted. Both were 28-foot Contenders, v-hull designs with twin 250 horsepower outboard engines. They were designed to carry 180 gallons of fuel but had enlarged gas tanks for longer ranges. They had been stripped down to bare essentials, no dead weight, and the center console had been modified for aerodynamics. These were not fishing boats or smuggling boats... these boats were designed for piracy.

Still crouched behind the console, Tom's hands were shaking as he plotted a course for Coon Key in the Gullivan Bay near Marco Island. If he could get within sight of the area around Coon Key perhaps the pirates would think better and turn away. Regardless, he thought the idea his only chance of escape. He throttled up and came about, setting the bow NNW towards the key, and then pushed the twin throttles max forward. The boat rose on plane and he set the auto-nav system to take control, steering him automatically to the way point just west of Coon Key. It was 16 miles of open gulf to the way point. At 26 knots it would take about 30 minutes. Could he fend them off that long? He had no choice but to try.

Maritime vessels use Emergency Position Indicating Radio Beacons to identify their location in an emergency. Tom knew enough about the Coast Guard's system to know an EPIRB signal alone would not be enough to mobilize an immediate search. Commercial vessels often set them off accidentally, so the Coast Guard usually waited a while to give the vessel a period of time to realize its mistake and shut the signal down before they would respond. A corroborating Mayday, however, evoked an immediate response.

Tod's Mayday call had been monitored by the radio watch stander at the Coast Guard Sector Miami Command Center in Miami Beach. The watch supervisor immediately notified Coast Guard Air Station Miami in Opa-locka to start a search and rescue mission, a SAR, to look for the TICA. Even though it was on the other side of the state, Air Station Miami was the closest air operations station to the vessel. It took about 10 minutes to rotor up helicopter RESCUE 64 and get airborne.

Simultaneously, Coast Guard Station Marathon was notified to launch a supporting sea rescue operation. The closest Coast Guard vessel was TALON 17, a 33-foot Special Purpose Craft on routine patrol near Everglades National Park, less than an hour away. Within minutes, the TICA was being searched for by air and by sea.

From the location of the TICA's emergency beacon, the pilot of RESCUE 64 estimated rendezvous would be roughly 20 minutes after liftoff. At its present rate of speed, the TICA would be almost to Coon Key before the helicopter could reach it. TALON 17 wouldn't arrive for another 25 minutes after that. It would be a while before Tom would receive any help.

Tom grabbed the binoculars again and raised himself high enough to see over the aft wall of the flybridge and sited in the boats - four hundred eighty yards and closing. He wished he had brought more ammunition with him. His AR-15 was a standard issue Colt, gas operated, .223 caliber. On semi-automatic it could shoot a lot of rounds per minute, but he only had 2 clips, 60 rounds. "Fuck me!" he thought. He would have to use single shots. The Glock would only be useful from close range. God help him if he had to use it.

The boats were close enough now he could use the rifle's scope. He was familiar with the AR-15 from his tour of duty in the Air Force where he had trained with military M-16s, a similar weapon. But he had only shot at targets shaped like the silhouettes of men from stationary positions, mostly at 100 yards. And the brief familiarization session he did at the gun range when he first bought it hardly prepared him for anything like this. Now he was looking at real men willing to shoot back, moving targets which would not be easy to hit. Nor would his racing heart and heavy breathing make it any easier.

Tom debated the best position to take up on the boat. Should he stay on the flybridge, near the helm, where he could take back control from the auto-nav and maybe do some evasive maneuvers, if necessary? Or should he move down to the cockpit below and try to hide behind the cockpit transom for cover? From the flybridge he could look down in all directions, he could see the whole boat. From the cockpit he would have only limited visibility if they opted to attack the bow, but he would be positioned between the bad guys and the door to his family. There were tradeoffs either way. He decided to keep the high ground and stay on the flybridge where he had the better vantage point.

Tom poked his head again over the aft wall of the flybridge. The pirates were only fifty yards away. They had begun to swing wide on each side of his boat. "One will try to distract me while the other tries to board" he thought to himself. He brought his rifle up and aimed at the driver on the starboard side, then fired three shots in succession. Pop! Pop! Pop! Then he ducked and waited for a response. Nothing came. Tom raised his head again to see the starboard boat had dropped back slightly and was cruising at the same speed as him but several yards behind his stern. The boat to port had maintained its relative position to his side but moved further out. He took aim at the driver of the port boat. Pop! Pop! Pop!

The port boat dropped back even with its companion and the two pirate boats came together directly behind him in the middle of the smooth wake of his boat. Tom could see them all talking with each other, gesturing in a manner he wished he could understand. One thing was obvious, the fact that he had a gun made little difference to them.

Tom watched the two boats move away from each other, wide of his boat, then speed up to put their bows even with the stern of his. And then it began... b-r-r-r-r-r--p! b-r-r-r-r-r--p! Rapid automatic fire from both boats. b-r-r-r-r-r--p! b-r-r-r-r-r--p! Bullets tore through the aft wall of the flybridge barely missing him. He dropped down onto the deck crawling forward toward the console, waiting for the cacophony to stop. The seat cushions on the aft of the flybridge spit foam and fiber. The windshield above him fell broken and splintered, riddled with holes. Pieces fell onto the deck around him, but most over onto the bow. Somehow the helm had not suffered enough destruction to alter the TICA's speed or direction. She was still on plane. With every minute he was getting closer to Coon Key.

The firing died down. Tom got up on his knees. He could see that one of the boats, the starboard, had come along side and one of the men had thrown a grappling hook over the starboard aft railing. He went to raise the barrel of his rifle at the boarder but the other boat began another hail of bullets. B-r-r-r-r--r-p! He dropped to the deck again. There was no way he could defend himself from here. It was almost assured the man with the grappling hook was now aboard.

Tom was grasping for any idea. He couldn't charge four men with guns like some kind of John Wayne character. That would be suicide. The only thought that made any sense was to dive over the helm onto the bow of the boat and slide down to one of the gunwales where he might get a shot at one or two of the pirates before they realized he was there. There was no more time to mull, he rose to his feet, rifle in both hands, arms outstretched, and dove over the helm console head first.

The forward sloping window of the maindeck salon broke his fall and he slid down ungracefully but hardly feeling the impact onto the bow. "Port" he decided randomly, choosing immediately which side he would attack first. Tom turned himself to face the stern of the boat then slid off the sloping bow onto the port gunwale landing in a prone position, a familiar position from small arms training in the military. And there they were. The two port pirates were aboard, guns ready, looking up at the flybridge from where he had just come. He pulled the trigger of his AR-15 as fast as it would operate. Pop!Pop!Pop! Pop!Pop! Pop!Pop!Pop! Both men fell to the deck. A third man looked around the corner of the rear wall of the salon. He fired at the man, Pop!Pop!Pop!Pop! Fiberglass from the salon wall splintered and flew in all directions but the man ducked back. He jumped up and crossed over the bow to the starboard side gunwale. This time he stood, like John Wayne would have, adrenalin raging, rifle held low at his hips, ready to engage without aiming. There was no sight of the two remaining pirates.

Tom ran down the thin gunwale and leaped into the cockpit falling back against the padded seating facing the salon door, this time with the rifle at his shoulder again. No sign of either man. The salon door was wide open, they were definitely inside. He moved quickly but cautiously toward the door, peering around the corner into the salon. One of the men was lying on the floor, still alive, but bleeding out from his neck. He must have hit the man peering around the corner! Three down.

Tom moved inside and kicked the rifle away from the dying pirate. The only good pirate is a dead pirate. He backed away a few feet and fired a single shot at the man's temple, then looked around for the last man. He was nowhere in sight.

"Mary Ann!" he yelled. "Are you alright?" No answer. "Mary Ann!" Louder this time. He moved toward the cabin door where his family was hiding. The door began to open and he saw his wife coming out. She was pale as a ghost. "Are you okay?" he asked again. She said nothing. Behind her, his daughter and son slowly emerged, neither of them seeming able to speak. All three were shaking uncontrollably. Then the fourth pirate emerged holding a rifle against his son's back.

Tom could see that all four pirates were Hispanic, probably from the Caribbean. Cuba? Mexico? Jamaica? Impossible to know. Why they wanted his boat was also a mystery. Perhaps to loot and salvage it, maybe to sell on the black market somewhere? It was not the kind of boat to go unnoticed if it was stolen. But none of that mattered right now.

"Let them go." Tom demanded, trying to act as if he was in charge. Three of the man's companions were dead. It was possible the lone survivor just wanted out of there now. "Get in your boat and leave." He gestured with the barrel of his rifle.

B-r-r-r-r-r--r-p! Tom watched as his son's chest exploded. Tod collapsed in front of him, dropping to his knees then forward onto his face, his arms dangling at his side as he fell. "NOOOOOOOO!" Tom screamed, knowing instantly his son was dead. Then he felt a burning sensation, extreme heat in his chest and stomach. He looked down to see his abdomen covered in red, and his chest spurting blood like a small geyser in perfect rhythm with his heartbeat. He had been shot with the same bullets that killed his son. He, too, collapsed, falling onto his side, still facing the pirate and his wife and his daughter. Mary Ann and Lucy were screaming, out of their minds. Lucy knelt beside her brother, crying uncontrollably. Mary Ann ran to her husband, screaming "Tom! Tom! Oh, Tom!" trying to hold back the geyser with her bare hands.

Lying there, Tom could hear the auto-nav up on the helm had started to beep, warning that the waypoint near Coon Key was approaching. The boat slowed to an idle as the auto-nav disengaged. He watched the pirate put a single bullet into the skull of his daughter while his wife stood up and bravely tried to tear the eyes out of the man who had taken her family's lives. The pirate pushed her away, fired a final shot to her forehead, and the tragic ordeal had come to an end. His family was dead.

The pirate kicked Tom's AR-15 out of reach and turned to leave. Tom could barely move. It took every ounce of anger he could summon to pull the Glock from his waist band and raise it just enough off the floor to get an angle from which to fire at the man who had killed him. As the room went dark he pulled the trigger. The last thing Tom Grogan heard was the sound of a helicopter hovering overhead.

* * *

What had begun as a search and rescue operation for the Coast Guard helicopter team from Opa-locka quickly took a different turn when they arrived at the TICA. The crew of RESCUE 64 circled the TICA which appeared to be idling, drifting slowly with the tide.

"Three dead bodies, port aft. No movement I can see, sir." Petty Officer 3rd class, Marisha Thompson, handed the binoculars to her immediate superior, Lieutenant Greg Banford, who confirmed the assessment.

"There are automatic weapons on the deck. Advise keeping our distance until TALON 17 gets here", Banford informed the pilot over the crew headset.

"Roger, that", the pilot concurred.

This was no longer a rescue operation; it was now a crime scene. When TALON 17 arrived, it would be assigned the responsibility to secure the TICA and have it towed back to Marathon where investigators from the DEA, Border Patrol, FBI, U.S. Customs and other law enforcement agencies would pour over it looking for answers. Why did four Hispanic pirates try to seize a 41-foot luxury yacht and what had they planned to do with it?

CHAPTER 4

On the 19th of October, 1921, a low pressure area began to form off the northern coast of Panama. By the following afternoon it had grown into a tropical depression, encouraged northward by a large high-pressure system hovered over the Bahamas. The warm waters of the western Caribbean fed its thirst for speed and power, and by the evening of the 22nd it was swiftly speeding through the Yucatan Strait, just west of Cuba. The next day it was a full-blown hurricane arcing north and eastward toward the gulf coast of Florida, packing catastrophic winds and rain. On the morning of the 25th, the enormous power of the Tarpon Springs hurricane had diminished only slightly as its raging eye made landfall just south of the Anclote River. On impact, it had sustained wind speeds in excess of 115 mph, a category 3 monster. Six miles to the south of Tarpon Springs, just off the coast of Dunedin, the once seven-mile long island of Caladesi had been sliced in two.

Samantha and Gavin stared out Cynthia's mother's picture window overlooking the Gulf of Mexico as Cynthia described the view. "That large channel between Caladesi straight out there, and Honeymoon Island over here, is called Hurricane Pass. Caladesi used to be one big long island, miles and miles. But the hurricane just ripped a big trough right through the middle of it."

"Wow!" Samantha looked at Cynthia. "You can't realize the power a hurricane must have until you see what one can do up close."

"That was the last major hurricane to hit this area", Cynthia informed the group. "And it was only a category 3. Eventually we're due for another one. We've had near misses like Charley about ten years ago, which landed south of here, and Donna in the early sixties. She came ashore north of us. My dad was a little boy then. He told us kids that his father had taken him and his brothers for a walk underneath the Gandy Bridge. The hurricane had sucked most of the water out of upper Tampa Bay."

"That's incredible! We just drove over that bridge this morning", Gavin pointed out. "I find it hard to believe that that much water could have been sucked out... that's half the bay!"

"Imagine what a huge hurricane like Andrew could do", Cynthia continued, "especially to the barrier islands all along this coast line. It's inevitable we'll get hit again. If you look down that way", she pointed across the coastal waters toward Clearwater to the southeast, "all those high rises, hotels, and office buildings are sitting on barrier islands. They could easily be washed away, just like the pass between the islands here. This pass is a quarter of a mile wide."

Samantha seemed the most inquisitive. "So why do they allow building on the barrier islands if it's so dangerous?"

"Because they won't all get washed away", Gavin chuckled. "That's a lot of property tax money out there. As long as insurance companies continue to pretend to insure them, local governments will gladly extract the revenue from them. It's a collusive game. If the damage is catastrophic the federal government, FEMA, steps in and pays for much of the damage, with your tax money, of course. Insurance companies will continue to insure as long as they believe the government has their backs. It's just another form of too big to fail."

"So why is it called Honeymoon Island?" Samantha was intrigued by the history.

"It used to be called Hog Island", came a new female voice from behind them all. "In the forties the Florida Park Service advertised it as a hidden vacation getaway. Newsreels and magazines promoted the island as having 'undiscovered pleasures for newlyweds'. They built thatched huts on the beach for vacationing lovebirds and called it Honeymoon Island. Unfortunately, WWII started and all the huts rotted away, but the name stuck. Now it's a state park."

"Is that true?" Samantha was slightly incredulous.

"It's true", Cynthia confirmed. "Alex! I'm so glad you could make it! Gavin, Samantha, this is Alexandra, my best friend since grade school."

Alexandra Katsaros was a Tarpon Springs native of Greek descent. Her parents, Christos and Helena, had vacationed from Greece in the mid-nineteen eighties. Christos had heard about the small city of Tarpon Springs and longed to visit. When he and Helena arrived, they fell immediately in love with the thriving little Greek community.

Tarpon Springs was originally settled in the late 1870s by A. W. Ormond and his daughter Mary. They built a house on the Anclote River. Not long thereafter, an adventurer from the Bahamas, Joshua Boyer, happened upon the river, met and married Mary. He recounted in a 1928 newspaper article, "I came up the Anclote River on a fishing trip and by chance stopped off at Mr. Ormond's residence. I built a residence there, and the same year Miss Mary Ormond and I were married. Everything there was ours. The land and the game and fish were as free as air."

Tarpon Springs was originally a working town, the largest sponge market in North America. Thousands of divers from all over came seeking to harvest one of the richest bounties of natural sponge species in the world. Blacks from the Caribbean and Key West, whites and blacks from Nassau, Bahamas, competed with the Greeks for control of the sponge industry in the Gulf of Mexico. The Greek divers with their superior technology and undaunted work ethic eventually won out.

But by the late 1930s, the once bountiful sponge beds were all but depleted by overharvesting. And after WWII, synthetics reduced the demand for natural sponges even more, although a diminutive sponge industry continued to exist. By the time Christos and Helena arrived, the small community prospered mainly on tourism. But Tarpon Springs was a most fascinating and wonderful place, with lively still-operating sponge docks, authentic Greek restaurants and shops along a picturesque waterfront, and a magnificent Greek church, St. Nicholas Greek Orthodox Cathedral. The community of Greek immigrants, some of whose families dated back to the 1880s, had made them feel welcomed from the moment they arrived.

Less than a year after returning to Greece, Christos and Helena said goodbye to their families and friends and moved to Tarpon Springs, Florida, with everything they could afford to bring to their new home in America. Christos had cooked and baked in the small town of Igoumenitsa, across the channel from the Island of Corfu in northern Greece. The couple's American dream was realized when, two years after arriving in America, Christos was able to afford a loan to buy a small restaurant on Dodecanese Boulevard, across the street from the sponge docks. Not long after, Helena gave birth to a beautiful baby girl they called Alexandra.

Alexandra's mother had fallen ill and died from pneumonia when she was just eleven. Alexandra took her mother's place in the restaurant waiting tables, cleaning, and taking orders in the bakery. She had grown up faster than most of her friends.

Gavin caught himself staring at Alexandra though she was unaware of his gaze. There was something about her that was incredibly appealing, enticing even. She was dressed quite casually in contrast to everyone else who were still wearing their dressier garb from earlier in the day, just a floppy white fuzzy tee top, one shoulder exposed, and black denim calf-length jeans, skin tight.

There was a subtle elegance about her. She had alluringly olive skin, facial features of a goddess, and she was tall. Gavin estimated five nine or so. Her soft brown hair was done up in a messy side bun, an ancient Greek hairstyle among slaves who had little time or options to tie up their hair. But the look was stunning, like something from a red-carpet gala. She wore no makeup today, she really didn't need any.

Gavin thought her voice had an unusual lilt, almost like listening to music. It fit her appearance perfectly. She was obviously physically fit, like Cynthia, though not quite as muscular. Standing next to each other, Alexandra was almost a head taller than Cynthia and quite a bit larger, with long legs, broad shoulders, a slight waistline and slim hips. She looked more like a runner than Cynthia except for her ample bust size. Transfixed, he couldn't stop himself from wondering aloud, "How did a tall white girl and a short black girl become best friends?"

Cynthia laughed, "The first week of fourth grade, I'm sitting by myself at lunch. I usually ate with another girl but she was out sick or something, I don't remember why. Alex came over and sat down by me and we started talking about who could run fastest. She didn't know me and I didn't know her so both of us thought we were the fastest. It was an immediate rivalry, and the beginning of an everlasting," she smiled at Alexandra, "sometimes competitive, friendship."

"So, who was the fastest?" Gavin asked.

"I was", Alexandra giggled, watching for Cynthia's reaction.

"I beg your pardon, missy! Who won the race at recess the next day?"

Alexandra snickered, "You won the race. But I let you win."

Cynthia chortled, "Girl! You are such a liar!"

The two girls hugged as Alexandra bemoaned, "I've missed you so much. You don't come home often enough. It's lonely around here without you."

Cynthia's mother, Olivia, agreed. "That's right! I tell her the same thing."

Olivia was a short portly woman with curly gray hair. She was no taller than Cynthia and waddled a little as she walked. She had had four children, Cynthia was the second youngest. All of her children except Cynthia still lived in the area. Her husband, Sanford, had died of sickle cell anemia when the kids were still little. She had raised the kids as a single mother. Cynthia was her pride and joy.

"You can blame it on me", Gavin apologized. "I keep her awfully busy these days. For what it's worth, Olivia, your daughter is the smartest woman in Washington, D.C."

Olivia smiled broadly, accepting the hyperbole as fact. "She was always the smartest kid in her class. Takes after her father, God rest his soul. She just always knew what was what about everything."

"Mama! Are you saying I was a know-it-all?" Cynthia jested with a laugh.

Olivia was still beaming at Gavin's compliment. Of her four children, Cynthia was her favorite, even though mothers weren't supposed to have favorites.

"Mike didn't come with you?" her mother inquired.

"No", Cynthia replied, "He had things to do. Plus, this wasn't exactly a pleasure trip, Mama."

"Oh, that's right. Senator Gavin, I was so sorry to hear about your brother. It was truly awful what happened. I said a prayer for him, and you, too."

"It truly was, Olivia. Thank you for that." Gavin hoped that would end any further discussion of his brother. He had thought about it enough for one day.

"So, who is Mike?" Alexandra beseeched with palpable curiosity.

"Cynthia's new beau!" Olivia chimed in. "His name is Miguel Angel Ramirez."

"Cynthia Lockhart! I can't believe you haven't called me with the lowdown!" Alexandra pretended to be offended.

Cynthia pretended to be apologetic. "I just haven't had time to tell you the whole story. We've only been seeing each other for a month. I didn't want to call you and say, 'Hi, Alex, I'm seeing a new guy' and then hang up. Grab a glass of wine, girlfriend, and follow me. I'll tell you all about him."

"Excuse us." Cynthia smiled at the group who were all staring, mesmerized at the two girlfriends' humorous re-connection ritual. "We're going to take a walk on the beach. You're welcome to come", she offered Samantha and Gavin.

"No, you guys go ahead", Samantha said. Gavin deferred as well.

"Excuse me, too", said Olivia. "I usually take a nap in the afternoon. I hope you don't mind if I go lie down a spell."

"Of course not", Samantha said. "Gavin and I can look after ourselves until the chatty Cathies get back."

"We'll be fine, Olivia", Gavin added.

* * *

The girls exited Olivia's condo, wine in hand, and sauntered east across a small bridge connecting Honeymoon Island to the Dunedin Causeway and the beach beyond. They removed their shoes to sift the warm, soft sand through their toes as they strolled. The air was thick with salt and a light breeze from the south made a warm spring afternoon seem even warmer. The mile-long manmade causeway joined the Dunedin mainland to Honeymoon Island and welcomed tourists and locals alike. It was a popular spot for sun bathers, beach combers, fishermen, kayakers and paddle boarders, sunset watchers, sea birds of every kind, and an occasional otter.

"Alright, give it up. Who is he? What does he do? How did you meet him?" Alexandra was having fun with her best friend. They shared everything as young girls, and now they had another life experience, one of the best kinds, to share.

"His name is Miguel Angel. He calls himself Mike. I really like the name Miguel but he says people respond better in Washington if he goes by Mike." Cynthia was glowing as she talked about him, and Alexandra was deeply happy for her.

"Nothing wrong with Mike. It's a strong name. I like it!"

Cynthia knew Alexandra would approve. But to hear her express her supportiveness made the expose so much more fun. "I met him at a presser for one of Gavin's town hall meetings in Ocala. He's a reporter for the Post, mostly political reporting these days. But he's amazingly intelligent. Anyway, he asked me a question and I went limp. I just stared at him. I never heard the question. I mean, I collected myself but we both could sense there was something there. When we got back to D.C. he called me and asked me out. It was wonderful!"

"So, has your mom met him?"

"No, not yet. But he called her on the phone and talked with her for over an hour. I think she's more in love with him than I am!"

Alexandra was impressed. "Who does that? He sounds astonishing! Okay, cut to the chase, woman. Is he sexy?"

"Yes, he's sexy. Incredibly so."

"Incredibly? Oooooh. Keep going."

"And he's very intelligent."

"That's it? That's your idea of sharing?" Alexandra probed, laughingly.

"Did I mention he was intelligent?" Cynthia snickered.

"I'm so happy for you." Alexandra hugged her best friend with a closeness reserved only for cherished soulmates.

"So happy!"

The two had ventured almost to the end of the causeway before they realized it. Cynthia was the first to notice, "We'd better head back."

"Oh, my goodness! Yes." As they turned around Alexandra implored, "So tell me about Gavin. He seems awfully nice. I feel terrible for him."

Cynthia was quick to offer, "I'll introduce you two a little more when we get back."

"It was just a question, Cynthia. Not a request for a setup." But Alexandra was secretly hoping Cynthia would follow through with her offer.

"Well, he's thirty-eight, never been married, a former Air Force officer, like a spy guy, sort of. He works out at the gym almost every day. He jogs three times a week, and he's very good looking."

Alexandra quipped, "Well, I can see that! Tell me something I can't see."

"He likes cats."

"He has a cat?" asked Alexandra.

"No. I said he likes cats."

"Well, how do you know if he doesn't have a cat?" Alexandra liked the idea that he might be a cat lover. She loved cats. Not so much dogs, but cats were perfect for her life.

"I've seen him around people's cats. They seem to take to him and he picks them up and strokes them. He talked once about having cats as a kid, particularly a big yellow tabby named Big Fat Kitty. I guess they overfed him. I don't know."

"That's so cool! Big Fat Kitty. Silly name", Alexandra chuckled.

"Well, is Percy Sledge any less silly?" Cynthia chided.

"Hah! I suppose not", Alexandra agreed with a laugh. "Percy just seemed like the right name when I got him home. He loved listening to 'When a Man Loves a Woman'. He would cuddle up on my chest in a tiny furry purr ball and fall fast asleep whenever I played the CD. Tiny little motor running."

"I remember", Cynthia acknowledged.

"He's still my best buddy. So, how's Speedy?"

Speedy Gonzalez was Cynthia's Chihuahua. "Oh, he's fine. Feisty as ever. He doesn't like Mike, though. Can you believe it? A Mexican dog that can't stand my Mexican boy friend! It's hilarious. Mike's watching him while I'm gone. Maybe they'll bond", she laughed, "But I'm not holding my breath."

"Oh! Cynthia, look!" Alexandra pointed to a wedding party gathering along the west end of the beach. Several rows of white wooden chairs were arranged in the sand in two sections, with a dividing aisle between them. The aisle was strewn with hibiscus pedals and led to a beautifully arranged palm wedding arch. Below the arch was an adorable altar draped with white gardenias or cape jasmines as the locals called them.

"I've always dreamed of a beach wedding. I'm a little jealous of you and Mike", Alexandra sighed wistfully.

"I know you'll find the right guy one day", Cynthia assured supportively. "A relationship was the furthest thing from my mind when I met Mike. I know it's only been a month but I can't help thinking about a future together."

The girls hugged again and started back across the little bridge to the island condo, holding hands as they walked, wine glasses swinging empty at their sides.

* * *

Samantha and Gavin sat across from each other in Olivia's living room. Samantha had parked herself on the plush couch which practically swallowed her thin frame with its overstuffed cushions and pillows. Gavin sank into a matching recliner that he thought was, maybe, the most comfortable chair he'd ever sat in.

Olivia's living room was the picture of comfort. Besides the couch and the recliner, she had another large matching chair, all of them a subdued mix of beige and brown cross-stripes. Color was added by some vases and a couple of throw rugs that pulled in ochre from accent wall. There was a pair of black African masks hanging on the wall behind the couch and a tall drum in one corner, testament to the family's African-American heritage. The rest of the furniture was a more traditional mix. Some of the end tables were strewn with sea shells Olivia had probably collected herself across the street.

None of the furniture in the room was very old, a couple of years at most. Gavin thought it likely Cynthia and her siblings had bought this place for their mother, well-deserved payback for an earlier life of sacrifice. It was hard to stay awake in such comfort. No wonder Olivia had to take naps, just sitting on the furniture put you to sleep.

"Gavin, I know I said we weren't going to talk shop but I can't help thinking about something I want to get off my mind." Samantha was leaning forward in a way that Gavin recognized as a serious entreat.

"Okay", he said cautiously.

Samantha leaned back, comfortable that she had his attention. "This experience has left me empty and angry that so little has really been done to help people like Eddie, to keep them from being treated as criminals. Don't get me wrong, you know I'm not an ideolog, but I think if we worked together we could do something to help other Eddies."

Gavin turned his gaze toward the picture window. Samantha watched his eyes glaze and wondered if maybe he hadn't really heard her. She leaned forward again putting her elbows on her knees, her hands cupped under her chin, and stared at his face. He said nothing for a long period. He just peered out the window with a blank look on his face. For a moment, Samantha feared she may have made a mistake in broaching this subject so soon after the funeral.

Finally, he turned to look at her. "You know I support legalization. Decriminalization is a half-step measure. It doesn't begin to address the real issues, the real and substantive problems of drug use."

"I know", she acknowledged. "But if we can craft the legislation the right way, I'm sure I can find a way to support it. I can't speak for others in my party but if you and I can agree, I'm willing to try to move them in your direction."

"Why the sudden interest, Sam?"

Samantha's eyes teared as she thought about Gavin's brother and the events of the day. "It's not that sudden, Gavin. Look at my state. You think I don't see the misery going on? The problems in western Mass are pervasive, approaching pandemic. Whatever we're doing now isn't working. I'm willing to try something different. I think my constituents will be willing, too."

"Our efforts will go nowhere without Hackart's support. Without the Speaker, it won't even get a vote in the House." Gavin returned to staring out the window.

"Leave Hackart to me", she insisted. "He doesn't care about this issue and I know plenty of people over there I can curry favors from. One thing about fat peepee touchers, they don't have any room for objections on moral grounds."

Gavin's head snapped around. He grinned broadly at his red-headed friend, the first term Senator from Massachusetts. "You learn quickly, Sam. You know, you're beautiful when you're conniving."

"It's called shrewd, Gavin. So, does that mean you're on board?"

"Okay, I'm in. Let's do this." Gavin reached over to shake hands to seal the deal. But Samantha stood and urged him to his feet. She wrapped her arms around him and they hugged a long sincere embrace.

"Are you ready to get back to the hotel?" he asked.

"Yes. I'm exhausted."

Gavin pulled out his cell phone. "I'll call an Uber. Looks like there's one right down the street, 8 minutes. We might as well go down and wait for it out front."

Cynthia and Alexandra returned just as Gavin and Samantha were about to leave. "You're leaving?" Cynthia asked.

Gavin hugged Cynthia. "It's been a long day, Chief. I need to get back to the hotel and get some rest. Thank you for inviting us. I surely needed the downtime."

"Tell your mom I really enjoyed everything. She has a beautiful home", Samantha concurred.

Gavin reached out and shook Alexandra's hand. "Alex, it was a pleasure to meet you. I'm sorry we didn't have more time to talk. Hopefully we'll meet again. Do you ever get up to Washington?"

"I keep threatening Cynthia but her schedule hasn't been cooperative so far", Alexandra said dejectedly.

"I'll see what I can do about lightening her load once in a while", he promised. "Maybe you'll allow me to show you some of the sights while you're there?"

"That would be wonderful!" she exclaimed, almost too giddy in her acceptance. She glanced at Cynthia who was smiling wide-eyed with lips pursed, as if saying "Oooohhh".

As Samantha and Gavin closed the door behind them, Cynthia looked at Alexandra, "He likes you, Alex. I can tell."

Alexandra wasn't sure how she felt about Gavin Manson. But one thing was for certain. She wouldn't pass up the chance to tour Washington with a handsome Senator if the opportunity presented itself.

* * *

Kevin stood on the seawall of Coast Guard Station Marathon, observing as the TICA was towed into port. The crew of TALON 17 helped the crime investigation unit moor the boat and setup a perimeter for investigators. Ingress and egress paths were established, a necessary step to protect the evidence from being destroyed, damaged or contaminated. The CSI agents from U.S. Customs Miami were the first on the scene and assumed jurisdiction. A short time later the FBI and Border Patrol arrived. The last to show up was the DEA. No evidence of drugs or drug related activity was found so they left almost immediately.

U.S. Customs Special Agent Omar Sickles was in charge of the crime scene, a short pot-bellied man with a gruff voice and a cigar hanging from one side of his mouth. Kevin recognized Sickles from the description one of the other agents had given him. He caught him as he was about to board the TICA. "Agent Sickles, I'm Major Falk, U.S. Air Force. I'm with the OSSI at MacDill. Got a minute?"

"Air Force?" Sickles looked puzzled. He put his cigar in his mouth as he shook hands with Kevin. "What the fuck does the Air Force want to know about a maritime crime?" bouncing the cigar up and down as he talked.

"Truthfully? I don't know, Agent. I was ordered to find out what I could about the incident. Grogan was ex-Air Force, retired reservist. Somebody above my pay grade is interested in whether or not he was involved in anything the Air Force should be concerned about."

"Like what?" Sickles queried.

"Probably won't know unless I see it." Kevin was trying to be as vague as possible and still get the Agent to keep him informed in the investigation.

"Too goddamned many chefs stirring this stew! Look, Major, I'll find you a liaison but keep your ass off this boat. I won't have you traipsing all over the place getting in the way, contaminating shit. Capiche?"

"Understood, Agent. I'll be in the mess hall. Just one question. Is anybody alive on the boat?"

"No. They're all dead", Sickles answered stiffly as he turned to go aboard.

"How many bad guys?" Kevin was probing for as much as he could get.

Sickles barked without looking back, "Four. Your liaison will answer any further questions, Major."

It was getting late in the day. The evening breeze felt nice, Kevin thought. He loved the Florida Keys; bikinis, beer, sunsets. He had turned to walk toward the mess hall when his phone rang. "This is Falk. --- Yes, sir. --- No, sir, they're all dead. All four. --- Not sure yet, sir. It looks like Grogan killed them all. --- I don't know, sir. Who knew he was that good? I don't think he ever had any training. Maybe he was just lucky. --- Yes, sir. I know how fucked up this is. --- I understand, Colonel. I'll be there at 0:900."

Kevin's liaison approached as he was finishing his call. "Major Falk?"

"Yes, I'm Falk."

"I'm Agent Carver. I'll be your liaison."

"Thanks, Carver, but something's come up. I won't need a liaison. But thank Sickles for me."

"Yes sir. Will do."

Kevin opened his phone and scrolled through his contacts. He dialed a recently added number, a new acquaintance, female with red hair. "Hello Senator. --- Yes, ma'am. I mean, yes, Senator. Turns out I'm going to be in Washington tomorrow. I was wondering if you might be available for dinner tomorrow night? --- Great! I'll call when I get into town."

CHAPTER 5

Gavin's office was located in the Russell Senate Office Building, the oldest of the three senate office buildings in Washington, D.C. He could have chosen to have his office in the Dirksen or Hart Buildings, more modern structures, but there was something about the Russell's Beaux-Arts style of architecture with its twin marble staircases, marble walls and columns, and glazed oculus which illuminated the rotunda with soft natural light, that drew him to the early 20th century design.

Gavin loved history and the Russell building had it: the 1912 hearings on the sinking of the Titanic; the Teapot Dome Scandal investigations in 1923; the 1954 hearings where U.S. Army counsel Joseph Welch ended Joe McCarthy's years of baselessly charging American citizens as Communists by asking him "Have you no sense of decency, sir?" Most famously, it was the venue for the 1973 Watergate hearings where a special committee established that President Richard Milhous Nixon participated in the cover up of the Watergate break-in and was eventually forced to resign.

The Russell Senate Office building had been named after Richard Brevard Russell, Senator from Georgia from 1933 until his death in 1971. He was widely admired and respected by his colleagues during his tenure. But, truth be told, he was a racist, unapologetically so. He wasn't a cross-burning racist, but a staunch segregationist none-the-less and did more to slow the advance of Civil Rights legislation than arguably any other man in Senate history. Gavin had once mentioned to a group of fellow senators that, perhaps, it was time to rethink the name of their building. No one seemed much interested in the idea. But Cynthia had heard about his comments from fellow staffers and it endeared him to her even more than he already was.

There was nothing fancy about Senator Gavin Manson's Washington D.C. office. He was a Scotsman and an avid golfer so there were plaques and trophies of some of his accomplishments on the mantel of his non-functional fireplace. He had hung a kilt, passed down to him by his father, on the wall beside his desk. It was made from the Manson Clan tartan, broad blue and red stripes alternating vertically and horizontally with a thin white line down the middle of each strip and two small parallel green stripes, evenly separated, along both edges of each blue and red stripe. He was proud to say the Manson tartan was registered in the Scottish Register of Tartans.

Next to the kilt he had hung a set of bagpipes and next to that, a picture of Old Tom Morris nestled between an antique pair of crisscrossed golf clubs, a mashie and a niblick. These were things of beauty in his eyes, ancestral heirlooms to be treasured.

The Manson family was originally from the city of Androssan, southwest of Glasgow. There was a high concentration of red hair in his family so it was a bit of a mystery why he had apparently not acquired that gene, although a tinge of red could be discovered amidst the dark brown on close inspection.

Gavin's desk was large with a rosewood top and plenty of room to spread out. The desk, he felt, was the most important piece of furniture in his office. In the military, his desks were always too small. Like everything else, desk size was 'by the book'. And besides, Captains weren't yet of sufficient rank to command offices large enough to accommodate a big desk, that is, if you wanted anything else in your office. And you certainly couldn't have a desk bigger than your superior officer's.

Behind the desk he had a high-back reclining leather chair with wide arm rests, not too comfortable, not too uncomfortable. A comfortable chair was a necessity he had learned. It shouldn't put you to sleep but if you wanted to rest it should be able to do the job. Two small oxblood leather guest chairs faced his desk for quick meetings with colleagues or constituents. And a hardwood coffee table, surrounded by an oxblood leather couch and two similar chairs, could accommodate up to six guests when the other two chairs were pulled over.

As a male with no sense of décor, Gavin was happy to let the women on his staff work out color schemes, accent pieces, rug colors and placements as well as the sizes and locations of pictures and floral arrangements. They must have done well. It seemed everyone who visited offered nothing but high praise and compliments. His office today looked a far cry better than it did his rookie year when he remembered someone telling him it resembled an 'early carport' motif.

Besides the nod to his heritage, the only other piece of furniture he contributed to his office was a small cherry wood liquor cabinet hidden tactfully behind the folding screen of the faux fireplace. He was proud it had been his idea to put it there and, the women agreed, it was the perfect addition to round out his workplace. After all, a shot or two of scotch at the end of a long day's work wasn't a luxury for a Scotsman in this business, but a downright necessity.

Gavin could hear Monica talking with someone in the outer office. It was a female voice and he immediately recognized the lack of R's in her speech.

The anteroom door opened and Monica ushered in Samantha. "Senator Lawrence is here to see you, sir."

"Good morning, Sam! You look more rested than the last time I saw you."

"I feel wonderful! It's amazing what a couple of days off can do for the soul." Samantha smiled widely as she took a seat on the leather couch, crossing her long legs at the knees. She removed the large tiger-striped sunglasses from the top of her head and put them in a similarly striped case, then set her purse, briefcase, and glasses under the coffee table and looked up at Gavin. "Let's fix this problem, Senator!"

"Well, you seem more energetic than usual", he said. "What has you so perky this morning?"

"Since you will find out sooner or later anyway, I had dinner with Kevin the other night. He took me to the zoo yesterday and I have to admit, I've never had so much fun spying on animals in my life. Your buddy is an adorable man."

"I thought I warned you about him? He can be terminally charming."

"Too late", she said with a smirk which made it clear the relationship was already more than platonic.

"Would you like some coffee before we get started? I can have Monica rustle us up some doughnuts or muffins if you want."

Monica knocked and entered carrying a silver tray with a small teapot, a coffee carafe and assorted pastries and buns, some jellied, some not. She set it on the end of the coffee table and left without interrupting.

Samantha poured some tea and reached to butter a small croissant. "I want a Monica, Gavin."

"Not this one" he assured her. "So, what kinds of ideas have you come up with. I thought we might just brainstorm today, hash out some differences and find a direction that makes us both comfortable."

Samantha pulled a notepad from her purse and a pair of ultra-thin reading glasses from the front of her bra. "You're reading my mind."

She opened with a few facts about the heroin epidemic in her state of Massachusetts. "We had almost 1800 opioid-related deaths by overdose last year. That's up from about 350 in 2000, a five hundred percent increase. That's about 26 deaths per 100,000 residents. Roughly 1575 of those were unintentional, preventable in my mind. Heroin alone constitutes over 50% of those deaths. Nationwide, we're talking about 90,000 deaths a year and growing with no end in sight. With that many deaths it's not hard to extrapolate how massive the addiction problem is."

Gavin found her statistics unsettling but not surprising. "Those kinds of numbers will make it difficult to sell legalization. But I'm convinced that's the only method that will work. Making drugs illegal has only inconvenienced addicts and turned them into criminals. It makes the problem so much worse than it was before we declared war on them. Legalizing drugs would enable us to address the problem for what it truly is - a mental health issue. Still, we'll need an incredibly convincing case to sell to the American people the idea of legally available drugs, much less the rest of Congress. Plus, I'm realizing there's a huge amount of money involved in the 'War on Drugs'. The DEA, for instance, isn't going to like the idea that their arch enemy, one of their major reasons for being, no longer exists."

"I agree." Samantha sipped her tea. "Decriminalization would make it seem like we were just forgiving someone for breaking the law because the possession amounts were small. But, it would keep the DEA in business which would be an easier political sell, I think. If we're going to try to dismantle the war on drugs after all these years we'll have to start with creating the perception that the war was wrong, it's not working, and bring the general public around to see the issues from that perspective. I'm still struggling with the idea myself. I'm sure the average American will struggle, too. Convince me you have some answers."

"I want to start with the premise that all drugs should be treated exactly like we treat alcohol. We don't arrest people for using alcohol. There's no law that says you have to be sober, ever. What you cannot do is be under the influence in situations where your actions put others at risk; driving, operating machinery, flying planes, public intoxication, etc."

"Gavin, alcohol laws don't measure the level of impairment, just the amount of alcohol in one's system, how much a person consumed. It's not exactly a fair test of sobriety. I have friends that can have four martinis and you would never know it. Then there's Anne who can get fall-down drunk on a single Mai Tai."

Gavin understood. "I know. But it's not possible to have a sliding scale to measure a person's tolerance to alcohol or any other drug. Every state has adopted .08 percent as the least common denominator for blood alcohol toxicity. I'm okay with that, but only because I don't know a better way to measure impairment."

"But that doesn't measure impairment, just the alcohol level."

"Right. Hence the least common denominator approach. I'm not saying it's the right way, I'm saying it's all we've got and we'll need to do something similar with all drugs if we legalize them."

"Alright, so the point is to treat all drugs the same as alcohol. Then how do you measure the level of intoxication of a heroin user, or cocaine, or marijuana? What about prescription drugs?" Samantha was high-lighting the complexity of the problem.

"I'm guessing those aren't going to be simple answers. But they're answers we have to come up with and clearly present in any legislation we put forward."

"Alright", Samantha agreed. "Let's say we've solved the problem of measuring impairment..."

"As opposed to level of intoxication?" Gavin asked.

"No, no. You're right. Level of intoxication."

Gavin interrupted again, "By the way, I don't think measurement will be a problem. The market will take care of that solution - eventually. There's a company in California in clinical trials for a device that measures someone's level of THC with a breathalyzer. Hospitals have tricology tests that screen for a whole range of drugs, legal and illegal. The science is there. It's the ability to extend the science to the field where law enforcement can access it in a timely fashion. That's the missing piece, Sam. But if there's a buck to be made somebody will find a way to make it. All those problems are solvable."

"Okay. We can find a way to make that case later," Samantha acknowledged. "So, the next hurdle is Federal versus States rights. We're proposing federal legislation to legalize drug use. Don't you think there will be push-back by the states? They're ultimately responsible for implementing whatever we come up with."

"States want our money, not our help. Remember what Reagan said, 'The nine most terrifying words in the English language are: I'm from the government and I'm here to help.' I think he's right, Sam."

"What kind of money?" Samantha probed. "Are we supposed to subsidize testing? What about drug dealers? Internet sales? Darkweb?"

"Most of that would diminish on its own if drugs were legal. How many black markets exist for alcohol in the U.S.?"

"None that I'm aware of", she granted.

"There are moonshiners in the south but that's more a cultural heritage than a black market. To your point, I don't know of any that exist today. Contrast that with the Prohibition Era when black market breweries, speakeasies, gin mills, sprang up everywhere and crime bosses like Al Capone ruled the industry with a violence that's still unparalleled in our history, but not unlike the seedy drug world today. Joe Kennedy made his fortune running Jamaican rum. But when Prohibition was repealed the black markets disappeared. Why? There was no reason to buy illegal alcohol of questionable content and integrity once alcohol became legal again and regulated for quality."

"And are you saying drug dealers will just disappear if drugs are legalized?"

"That's exactly what I'm saying, Sam. I believe people will prefer to buy from legitimate producers who are regulated and controlled like the alcohol industry."

"That doesn't seem to be happening in the marijuana industry", she observed. "There is still a huge black market for pot."

"The black market is across state lines where it's not yet legal. Eventually, assuming every state legalizes it, cross-state black markets will collapse, simply dry up."

"That could be a hard-sell, Gavin. Colorado is legal but pot is expensive there. It's taxed at 30%, more or less. The middle class there can afford the legal stuff, but the poorer people are still buying illegally from cheaper sources."

"That's a price-point issue, Sam. There is not enough competition yet to bring down the cost. If every state were legal the competition would lower the cost like any other product. States would compete with each other for the tax revenue; supply and demand."

Samantha was enjoying playing devil's advocate. So far, Gavin was doing a decent job of overcoming her objections. She was still personally skeptical but his arguments were sound and he was making a solid case for his proposition.

"What about the morality of it all? We've all been programmed for decades to believe that drug use is morally wrong. Just say no. How do you see that stigma being overcome?"

This was a subject for which Gavin had the fewest answers. "That issue may be the weak link in the chain, Sam. I don't have good ideas for countering an argument from a probity position. There are still plenty of people who believe drinking alcohol is morally wrong. But I think a case can be made for comparing other drugs to alcohol both practically and morally. Alcohol can kill you just as dead as most drugs, generally not as fast perhaps, but more people die every year from alcohol-related accidents and illnesses than drug-related. We'll need a strong campaign if we're going to keep our adversaries from pushing us over that slippery slope. Even so, I'm confident we'll find a means to present our position fairly and equitably to the public in a way that makes sense to them."

"So how do you see this legalized drug industry working? Do you have a model in mind?" Samantha had never really thought about how drugs would be sold in a free and open market. "Let's say the pricing, policy, and morality issues are solved. How does a person who wants heroin, for example, get access to it? Do they just go to a store and buy it?"

"Pretty much. I see a system of legal distributors not unlike the marijuana industry, similarly regulated. I think you need face to face sales to keep minors from being able to buy them unbeknownst to their parents. But just like you can have alcohol shipped to your house or you can pick it up from a brick and mortar, I don't see treating other drugs any differently. Young people like to do everything online today, so a pizza delivery model might be a likely acceptable one to them."

Gavin continued. "Remember the guy who ran Silk Road on the Dark Web, called himself DPR, Dread Pirate Roberts, after the hero in Princess Bride? His real name was Ross William Ulbricht and he was eventually busted in October

2013 by the FBI and sentenced to life for money laundering, computer hacking, conspiracy to traffic narcotics among other counts. It was a harsh sentence for the actual crime but the government was trying to send a message to future DPR's, don't try this. It didn't work, of course. There are dozens, if not hundreds, of darkweb operations now, better and more sophisticated, unstoppable really. Ulbricht was ahead of his time.

Ulbricht's Silk Road website had a comment and rating system for the sellers on the site. If you sold drugs, for instance, the quality of the product, the speed of shipment, etc., was rated by the buyers, the same as Amazon or Ebay or Walmart does. The market policed itself."

Samantha was coming around. "And I'm guessing you think the same kind of rating system should be implemented to help with the acceptance of legalization?"

"Why not?" Gavin affirmed. "Plus, I think death rates would plummet using such a model. If you have legitimate online vendors with consistent quality, consumer rated products, why would someone go to a back alley and take a chance on buying questionable product from a sketchy individual who may or may not be trustworthy?"

"Price?" she offered.

"Okay, you're right. If the black market dealers can undercut the legal market enough to justify the risk then that could be an issue. But I doubt black marketers would be able to compete. I just don't see that happening any more than an illegal beer brewer today would be able to undercut his local Budweiser distributor."

Samantha could see Gavin's arguments and they actually made sense, to her surprise. "But a system will have to be designed and put into place first. That process could be terribly long and painful."

Gavin knew she was right. "Painful, perhaps. But I think worth it in the long run. Sam, we've got to come up with a design and an architecture that works for everyone involved: consumers, producers, distributors, sales companies, healthcare, insurance companies, the gamut. Otherwise we're pissing into the wind."

"Europe is more liberal on this issue than we are", Samantha noted. "We need to study places like the Netherlands and Portugal which have already decriminalized most drugs, see what's working for them and what's not. We're going to need facts and figures to support any conclusions. Which means we need research, which means we need researchers. Do you have staff for this kind of project?"

"No", Gavin admitted. "But I can get Cynthia to look into finding someone to help us get started."

"And I'll see what I can do about finding sympathetic co-sponsors if you want", Samantha offered.

Gavin was hesitant. "Not yet, Sam. Let's build a framework first, before we try to bring anyone on board. We'll need something tangible, something credible, if we're going to convince others we're right on this issue. Let's keep this close to the vest for the time being. I don't want it to fall apart before we even have something to present."

Samantha picked up her tea and took a sip. It was cold, a sure sign it was time to go. "Nice session, Gavin. I think we accomplished a great deal this morning. It's a good start."

"I think we did", he said. "I'll let you know when I find a researcher and we can orient her together."

"Her?" Samantha laughed.

Gavin chuckled, "You don't think I'm going to hire a man to do important work like this do you?" He was joking but Samantha wasn't so sure.

Samantha put her readers back in her bra, gathered her purse and briefcase then reached out to shake Gavin's hand. She smiled and shook her head at the same time. "Of course not, Senator." Then she turned toward the door.

Monica opened the door before she reached it and held it for her. Samantha looked back at Gavin then at Monica. "Would you be interested in coming to work for me?"

"How much do you pay, Senator?" Monica played along with the gag.

"Name your price, Monica. I look forward to hearing from you soon."

Gavin stood speechless as Samantha left the room. Monica smiled at him as she cleared the coffee table. "It is comforting to have options, sir."

* * *

"Buenos tardes, Monica! Que tal? Como estas?" Cynthia was practicing her Spanish on Monica who seemed to relish her performance.

"Muy bien, Cynthia! You're getting better every day. Mike is amazed at your progress, no?" Monica was amazed as well. Cynthia was learning the language at an incredible pace.

"It's a beautiful language. I understand completely why it's a romance language. And, honestly, it's so much easier than English. Why didn't the world adopt Spanish as the international language?"

"Maybe they will", Monica grinned. "He's waiting for you. You may go on in."

Gavin was leaning back in his chair, feet on his desk, eyes closed as Cynthia entered. It was late in the afternoon and he had thought hard today about how to begin the undertaking ahead of him. It seemed daunting at the moment, convincing a nation that the effort it had put forth for decades to rid itself of drugs, drug related crime, and the associated public health problems, had been all for naught. That's a hard thing to admit in the first place, but then to turn around and suggest to the people that drugs should now be legal to purchase, possess, and consume could be political suicide. He had to be one hundred percent sure, himself, it was the right thing to do or how would he be able to convince anyone else?

That's why Cynthia was here. He needed facts, figures, and information on which to build a convincing case for legislation. He needed her to find someone capable of digging deep into the data mines, pulling together disparate pieces of information and correlating them in ways that made sense; someone who could develop coherent methods for presenting complex issues to an unsophisticated audience.

Cynthia sat for several moments waiting for Gavin to respond. His eyes were closed and he appeared lost in thought, but she knew he was awake. He had looked at her briefly when she first entered. "You look tired, sir. Long day?"

"Sort of", he said. Gavin sat up and faced her, his hands together in front of him, elbows resting on the desk. "I have an impossible task for you."

He explained what he needed, or what he thought he needed in a researcher. Cynthia took it all in. When he was done he apologized. "I hate to have to put this on you but I don't have anyone else I trust to do this."

Cynthia was unfazed. "I believe I have the perfect candidate, sir."

"Really? So quickly?" Gavin was truly surprised.

"I can tell you a little about her. She is a graduate of the University of Tampa, an International Studies major. She's also completed advanced studies and is certified in International Organization and Global Governance. Right now she does research for the Institute of International Education. She's published in several journals. If you would like to see some of her work I can arrange that."

"Sounds like she may be over-qualified. Are you sure she would want the job?"

"No. I'm not positive. Would it require her to move to Washington? Or could she work from home?"

Gavin thought for a minute, "I want someone here. I don't want to play phone tag or have to communicate complex issues by text or email. No, definitely here."

"Okay. I will talk to her. I can let you know in the morning. By the way, you've met her, sir."

"I have? Someone from the State Department?"

"No sir. Alex Katsaros. You met her at my mother's the other day."

"The Greek goddess! I'll be damned." Gavin flashed back to his first impression of the Aphrodite from Tarpon Springs he had met days before. She certainly hadn't impressed him as an intellectual. But then they hadn't talked either. "You're sure she's qualified to do this kind of research?"

"I'm positive she's qualified. I'm not positive she'll be motivated. I'll talk to her tonight and get back to you." Cynthia was secretly overjoyed that her best friend in the world might be coming to Washington to work with her. Hopefully Gavin couldn't see the elation bubbling inside her. She needed to get out of there before she exploded. She stood to go.

"Thank you, Cynthia. I hope this works out, for both our sakes. I know you'll be happy to have a friend from home so close by."

"Yes sir. That would be nice", she said stoically as she turned to the door. Monica was already there holding it open for her.

"Hasta lluego!" Monica smiled broadly.

"Hasta la vista, baby!" Cynthia retorted.

Gavin laughed out loud as the girls high-fived each other. The day was ending on a high note. It was time for a shot of single malt scotch.

* * *

Percy had finally found some peace, stretched out quietly on the window sill, soaking up the late afternoon sun. It had been annoying having to move from one piece of furniture to another, one room to another, to avoid the ungodly noise of the vacuum cleaner and the filthy feather duster that seemed to follow his every move. But the worst was over, it appeared. Only minor straightening was taking place at the moment, his chosen place of respite would be safe for a while. The warm sun felt good on his paws and Alexandra's soft strokes behind his ears and along his back were putting him to sleep... until the phone rang.

Alexandra left Percy in the window sill and found her phone on the dining room table. She flipped it over to see that her best friend was calling, a terrifically exciting and unusual event. "Is this the party to whom I am speaking?" she answered in her best Lily Tomlin voice.

"Sit down, Alex. I have a very important question to ask you."

Alexandra slid onto one of the dining chairs as she was asked. "Okay, mystery girl. What's the question?"

"Are you sitting?"

"I am."

"How would you like to come to work in Washington?"

Alexandra took a second to digest the strange query. "Doing what?"

"Senator Manson needs a researcher for a bill he's working on. I told him you'd be perfect for the job. I know he'll hire you on my recommendation if you want it." Cynthia's excitement was apparent.

"Slow down, Cynthia. I can't ask Percy to just up and move a thousand miles just like that!"

"You're kidding?"

"Of course, I'm kidding, girl! But you need to tell me more about what I'm getting myself into before I make a decision like that." Alexandra knew this was probably the opportunity of a lifetime. Cynthia would not have called her unless it was. But her nature was cautious even if it was her best friend's recommendation.

"Don't do that to me, Alex! You have no idea how excited I am that we could be working together." Cynthia was barely managing her enthusiasm.

"So what kind of research? And I would be working directly for the Senator?" Alexandra could feel her nerves tingling all over. She had a thousand questions but knew she could only ask them one at a time.

"This project is right up your alley, Alex. You would be gathering data on drug use, the impact of drugs on communities, cities, states. Investigative research on cartels, dealers, mafia, Russian mob behavior, even police and drug enforcement agencies, pharmaceutical companies... anything that relates to drugs or drug activity of any kind."

"For what purpose?" Alexandra wondered.

"Samantha and Gavin are co-authoring a bill to legalize drugs. The research is needed to confirm whether or not legalization will lower healthcare costs, crime rates, death rates, addiction rates, strengthen community involvement in drug use prevention, etc. They need real numbers, not the fake statistics being used by government agencies to justify the War on Drugs."

"The War on Drugs is a myth. I think that's pretty common knowledge these days." Alexandra was warming to the idea.

"So, Alex, are you interested? It would be so nice to have you up here. You will fall in love with Washington. There is so much history, so many things to see, so much to do. You would have a fabulous time! We would have a fabulous time." Cynthia's fingers had been crossed for several minutes and had begun to cramp.

"When would I start?" Alexandra asked.

"As soon as you want. They need somebody yesterday."

"I need to talk to Dad." Alexandra wanted to get her Dad's approval, more for his sake than hers. She had no doubt he would be okay with the idea, it was just a family formality. They had never been separated before, although she was often away for long periods while she was in college. She had her own apartment on the gulf but he lived close by and they saw each other often. It would be an adjustment for them both.

"And you should." Cynthia agreed. "Call me when you're ready. Gavin will want to interview you personally. That'll be just a formality, just don't say anything stupid!"

"I love you, sis!" Alexandra sniffled. "I'm so numb right now. I think I'm excited."

"Let it sink in, girlfriend. This will be a new chapter in your life, in our lives. I can't wait to get you up here!"

Alexandra hung up the phone wiping tears from her eyes as she looked for Percy. He was still sacked out on the window sill, his tail ticking, ears twitching, probably chasing lizards in his dreams. Florida lizards were easy prey for an expert hunter like Percy. From the lanai, he had brought in many mangled torsos and a few twitching tails, proud presents to assure his roommate of his remarkable prowess.

✳ ✳ ✳

There was not much Chuck McCrory couldn't do and little he didn't know. One of those rare individuals Earth produces just because it can. Hardly a saint, surely an honorable soul, he looked up to no man or down on any.

Few knew him, really. He was a mystery to most people, larger than life when he was around but he was away as much, perhaps more, than he was home. No one really knew what he did, other than he was an Army officer, and he never said. His wife, of course, knew that he was a Delta Force ranger, a black ops specialist. She was sworn to secrecy and had never told anyone, not even her best friends.

Chuck was an Army man through and through and he had the muscles and the tattoos to prove it. He ran 10 miles five days a week and worked out religiously. Most just knew him as the easy-going, friendly guy with a big heart. Perhaps because he had killed so many men in his life, or maybe just because he had a heart as big as Montana, something within him demanded he help people whenever he could. Not in large ways often, but in enough small ways that an inventory of his life's achievements was a mountain of good deeds. For Christos and Helena, his big heart was about to change their lives.

On the north bank of the Anclote River, tucked between a county park and a dry storage marina, a small tiki bar beckoned Chuck and his wife every Saturday afternoon when he was home. Miss Vicki's was a small-band venue with plastic tables and chairs sitting in the sand and adjustable umbrellas to keep the angry afternoon sun from baking the parched patrons.

Chuck liked music and he liked to drink. He was good at one of them. His wife, Vera, was as much a saint as he, not for any particularly philanthropic reasons, but simply for putting up with him the past 19 years. Sometimes it was easy, sometimes it wasn't. Today, it was very easy.

"Chuck McCrory" he declared, offering his hand to the man sitting at the plastic table beside him.

"Christos Katsaros", came the reply in a thick Greek accent.

"I heard you telling the waitress you were from Greece, visiting. Just wanted to welcome you to America, Christos!"

"Ef-hari-sto, Thank you! This is my wife, Helena."

"Vera." Chuck's wife leaned over to shake hands with them both. "How long are you here? You're on vacation?"

"Two weeks we are here", Helena said in the best English she could find. "Pardon my English, not so good."

"Your English is fine!" Chuck bellowed, changing his usual southern accent to a Scottish brogue any Scotsman would be proud to have. "I was born here and I still don't speak the language."

The ice had been broken and the two couples spent the rest of the afternoon becoming fast friends over several buckets of beer, blackened fish sandwiches and French fries. By sunset, Chuck had promised Christos that if he ever moved to America he would help him find a place to live and a car to get around in. Less than two years later Christos and Helena were living in a small house south of the river and driving a little Toyota Celica to work every day, thankful for their wonderful American friends.

It wasn't long before the Celica drove Helena to the maternity ward at Helen Ellis hospital where Alexandra first opened her eyes to the wide world that was about to get even wider today. Today, her Uncle Chuck was helping pack her new Toyota for the move to Washington, D.C.

"Chuck, I don't know how to thank you for driving my Alexandra to Washington." Christos had planned to drive her himself but the restaurant was short-staffed and four days away seemed impossible.

"Happy to do it, Christos. You know that."

Christos nodded appreciatively. "You did not know when you agreed to be her godfather it meant you would do work, no?"

Chuck just grinned. It wasn't work, far from it. His wife, Vera, was dead now. He was past sixty and starting to feel it. But he still ran 5 miles three days a week and worked out every day. He was retired from the Army and had little to do except for the occasional private investigative work he still did, mostly to have something to do. This trip to D.C. with his goddaughter was a welcomed distraction.

Alexandra walked out of her condo and locked the door behind her. Percy was in his cat carrier bemoaning his situation with combinations of low whiny growls interspersed with hisses. This kind of vehicle usually meant a trip to the vet where he would be unceremoniously poked, prodded, shot and clipped. Not once had it been an enjoyable experience.

"Let's go Allie!" Chuck yelled from the car. He had always called her Allie, since the day she was born.

"What's the rush?" she yelled back, hugging her dad with one arm, Percy dangling from the other. "I love you Dad! Come see me as soon as you can."

"I will" he vowed. "Just as soon as I can."

Alexandra put Percy in the back seat and buckled herself into the passenger seat. Chuck would drive the first shift.

"You're the best, Uncle Chuck!" Alexandra reached over and hugged him. He was not really her uncle, but she was closer to her godfather than any blood relative. "Make her smile!" she pleaded.

Chuck took his hands off the steering wheel and pulled the short sleeve up above his left bicep. Tattooed on the inside of his bicep was a picture of Mona Lisa, a somber scowl on her face. He flexed his muscle and her eyes widened, her lips curled upward at the edges and she began to grin with that unmistakable, mysterious smile. Of his many tattoos, Mona Lisa was her favorite. She had loved it since she was a little girl. She kissed her uncle on the cheek and settled into her seat. "Da Vinci would be proud, Uncle Chuck!"

CHAPTER 6

The past five months had flown by for Alexandra Katsaros. Never would she have expected the drug world to be so interesting, so filled with mystery and intrigue. The information she was compiling led her to believe the government's War on Drugs was a complete hoax, a fabrication of such immense proportion that even conspiracy theorists would have a difficult time with its believability. Before she accepted Senator Manson's offer she knew, or at least suspected, the war had little to do with eliminating drugs in America. But now she could see the proof. It was big business, and so much bigger than anyone would have ever imagined.

Gavin had been exceedingly helpful and supportive. Anything she wanted, anything she needed, he provided. Over hundreds of cups of coffee, countless work sessions, and many late evening dinners, they had worked out a game plan for amassing relevant data, organizing it and storing it for quick and easy reference when the time came. They had become a team, a single functioning unit. They thought alike, finished each other's sentences, and much to her surprise, they both loved learning from each other. She taught him how to search and investigate global electronic databases. He taught her how to file FOIAs, Freedom of Information Act requests, and how to submit backdoor requests for records from government agencies, even ones reluctant to cooperate. She was becoming a Washington insider, a bittersweet but exciting skill. *What* you know is directly linked to *who* you know inside the beltway, and she was starting to know plenty of people.

One of the things Gavin had provided was an office in the Russell Senate Office building just down the hall from his office. It wasn't spacious but it was more than adequate and he let her know she could put her touches on it in any way she pleased.

People work better when their environment is comfortable. She ordered an ergonomic chair for her computer desk and a couple of large high-back chairs for visitors. Her computer equipment was state-of-the-art and her internet connection was high-speed. She had a large white board that was always full of something, and after realizing it was easier to stay at the office sometimes than go home late, she ordered a cot to sleep on.

Gavin had installed cable TV for her, on which she mostly watched CNN even though he obviously despised it. "When Ted Turner first created it, people called it Chicken Noodle News", he would say. "Turned out to be a great network for a while. Now it's almost a joke. Should be called the Counterfeit News Network, they just make shit up sometimes." She was more tolerant of it than he was.

"Morning, Alex. You look exceptionally gorgeous this morning." Alexandra had slept in the office overnight. She sometimes did when she knew it would be necessary to maintain a long train of thought, the kind of thought process where it's necessary to start from scratch if the thread is broken before the mental process is completed. Last night had been one of those nights and she knew she must have looked quite haggard and disheveled. Gavin was good at putting her at ease. She loved that about him. She smiled at him, "Thank you, Gavin. I was hoping you would notice."

She poured a cup of coffee and handed it to him. Monica had come in early and brought her a breakfast sandwich and a pot of coffee.

"Thank you, ma'am." He held out his cup and gestured like a toast. "So, where are we?"

"What do you know about a guy named Gary Webb?" she asked.

"Nothing. Who is he?"

"More like 'Who was he?'" she replied. "Gary Webb was a controversial investigative reporter in southern California. In the nineteen eighties and nineties he investigated Iran-Contra. He was found dead after reporting that the CIA was responsible for cocaine being smuggled into California and sold on the black market. The coroner ruled his death a suicide, shot himself twice in the head."

"Twice? Shot himself twice? In the head?"

"That's what the coroner's report said."

"Are you kidding me, Alex? Who would believe a man would, or could shoot himself in the head twice?"

"The interesting thing is, the main stream media acted like this guy's reporting was conspiracy theory bunk, but totally bought into the two-bullet suicide theory."

Gavin's wheels were turning. "So, what did the CIA have to say about his accusations?"

"Nothing. They didn't have to. Webb had a history of wild investigative claims that often went unsubstantiated. He had a credibility problem. On this issue, however, he did have some hard evidence and some heavy supporters. Montel Williams had him on his show and he made the circuit on other talk shows. But most California newspapers like the L.A. Times and the Examiner gave him almost no coverage. When they did cover him, it was to further discredit him. Almost as if the CIA owned the California media. The whole period was a cake walk for the CIA. The government action was no reaction, obviously a careful strategy because nobody would believe them if they came right out and said "we didn't do it". They let the liberal press speak for them. It worked. They never had to defend themselves from his claims because the mainstream media never pressed them on the subject."

"And you think Webb might have been right?"

"Gavin, I'm almost sure he was right. There's no other explanation for the amount of cocaine that permeated California back then. The reigning cartel in Mexico was the Sinaloa. They are the only ones who could have supplied the quantity of drugs necessary to fit the statistics for overdoses, busts, and seizures at the time. Webb claimed that the CIA used the Sinaloa to generate a cash flow, similar to the Iran-Contra scandal."

"So, you've correlated assorted public records to calculate the amount of cocaine necessary to produce the statistical data?"

"Pretty much. A great many people would have had to look the other way to move the amount of cocaine the statistics indicate. The most plausible explanation is Webb's. The CIA had to be complicit. Not that their operatives actually participated in low-level smuggling or the sales, but they had to know what was going on and allowed it to happen, presumably for a fee. Webb claimed they were on the take and even provided protection for the cartel. I would bet money he was right."

Gavin shook his head. "So much for the credibility of Nixon's War on Drugs! I just hope this kind of information will resonate with people when we try to make our case to the public."

"This might help", Alexandra offered. "Harper's Magazine ran a story in 2016, a report actually, on an interview Dan Baum did with John Ehrlichman in 1994. Ehrlichman was chief of domestic policy for Nixon. Ehrlichman admitted that the War on Drugs was implemented to criminalize Nixon's enemies: Black people and anti-war hippies. Listen to this, Ehrlichman talking to Baum:"

You want to know what this was really all about?

The Nixon campaign in 1968, and the Nixon White House after that, had two enemies: the antiwar left and Black people. You understand what I'm saying? We knew we couldn't make it illegal to be either against the war or Black, but by getting the public to associate the hippies with marijuana and Blacks with heroin, and then criminalizing both heavily, we could disrupt those communities.

We could arrest their leaders, raid their homes, break up their meetings, and vilify them night after night on the evening news. Did we know we were lying about the drugs? Of course we did.'

"And every President since has used this fake war to his advantage one way or another", Gavin noted with disgust. "Even if we win the fight to change public perception we still have to defeat the machine that continues to wage this pointless war. I'm not sure this is a winnable battle, Alex."

"Maybe not, Gavin. But you're committed now. You can't give up."

"I'm going to order a safe for you, Alex. I'm uncomfortable with just a locked filing cabinet for this kind of information." Gavin was more than a little concerned about probing the CIA's checkered past, afraid it might rankle some feathers at the agency if what they were doing became known. "Are you sharing this with anybody?"

"No. Just you. But it gets worse. A safe is probably a good idea, but not for that information. That's old public record, anyone can just Google Gary Webb or Dan Baum for that. There's even YouTube video of Montel's TV show online."

"What do you mean *worse*?" Gavin sat down in one of the high-back chairs and listened intently.

"I did the same sort of analysis for Baltimore, Philly, New York and Boston - the I-95 corridor. I looked for spikes in drug arrests, overdoses, street supply estimates, large seizures, etc. Then I correlated those with stolen or missing truck shipments, air cargo, maritime shipping thefts, etc."

"And..." Gavin stood and walked over behind her to look at her computer screen.

"I've only gone back three years, but the statistical spikes correspond precisely with elevated theft reports of shipping containers at the Crimson Hook shipping terminal."

"New York Harbor, Crimson Hook?"

"Yes" she affirmed.

"You're saying what, Alex?"

"Guess where the missing containers came from?"

"I don't know, where?"

"Afghanistan via Yemen, Oman and Pakistan. Every four to six months there's a spike in the stats and in every case, a few weeks before, a number of Afghan shipping containers go missing."

Gavin drifted back over to the chair and sat down. He paused for several moments then looked at Alexandra. "There's only one company that can make that happen."

Alexandra understood the gravity of her discovery. "I know" she said. "I know."

"Have any of the containers ever shown back up?"

Alexandra shook her head. "And it gets worse yet, or at least more concerning."

"How?" Gavin asked.

"Ever heard of a Taliban drug kingpin named Khan?"

"Yeah. Wasn't he captured in 2010 or 2011?"

Alexandra brought up a picture of Haji Juma Khan onto her computer screen. "Then you know this guy is considered one of the world's top drug traffickers. He's from the Nimruz Province of Afghanistan. His empire traded tons of heroin and opium before he was lured into capture by the DEA in Jakarta in 2008."

"2008? Okay. Where is he now?" Gavin asked.

"Well, that's the big question, Gavin. He was taken into custody and held at Guantanamo for a while. Then he was moved to New York and brought to trial. But everything about his prosecution is shrouded in secrecy. His case was supposed to be a signature prosecution for 'narco-terrorism'. But it's been almost ten years and he hasn't been convicted of anything. Moreover, both the CIA and the DEA have paid him several times for services rendered. What those services were neither agency will say. But the CIA has lobbied hard against the DEA's desire to keep him locked up in the Federal Bureau of Prisons."

"They fought against the DEA? What's that about?"

"I don't know", Alexandra confessed. "If convicted, he was supposed to have served 20 years. But after less than 10 years they cut him loose last month from the Metropolitan Correctional Center in Lower Manhattan. They just let him go."

"So where is he now?" Gavin asked.

"No one knows. Whether he was deported or stayed in the states is anybody's guess. But he's back on the streets. The guy only has one skill. It's not hard to guess what he's doing. The biggest question is... who's he doing it for?"

"This is like Iran-Contra on steroids. This is really good work, Alex, but holy fucking shit! What in the hell are we up against?" The enormity of the problem gave Gavin the chills. Could their lives be in danger? Who do you report this kind of information to? Could this be sanctioned business by the CIA? Or was it a rogue operation, a black op? Even if it was rogue somebody had to know it was going on. The agency isn't stupid.

"Gavin, we have to assume there is the real possibility the CIA is partly, if not largely responsible for the heroin crisis in the northeast, maybe even nationally, but definitely the I-95 corridor. Oh, and I've started using a TOR browser for this kind of research. I use Chrome or Internet Explorer for most searches to keep up the appearance of business as usual. But I'm using TOR for anything remotely risky."

"Okay. But if anyone is watching they can tell if you're using TOR. They can't see your traffic but they can tell if you're using it." Gavin knew this was going to be a serious problem to overcome - how to continue working without setting off national security alarms. The NSA tracked everything in the U.S. If they wanted to know what his staff was doing, it was a simple matter for them. He could only hope that if they found out he was investigating potential CIA corruption they wouldn't share it with them. The two agencies really didn't like each other anyway. Maybe he was just being paranoid. Still, he had to protect Alex from any risky activity. This was going to take some thought. In the meantime, Alex had to stop internet searches and FOIA requests until he could come up with a way to ensure no one could identify what she was doing.

"Alex, I'm going to call Samantha and have you brief her on what you've told me. Can you be here this afternoon at, say 5:00 p.m.?"

"Sure. I need to go home and get some rest, take a shower. But I'll be here."

"Good. You are amazing, Ms. Katsaros. Amazing."

* * *

Colonel Craig Selbourne settled back in his chair then pressed a button on his phone for his secretary. "When Major Falk arrives, send him on in."

"Yes, Colonel", came the reply.

Twenty-five years in the Army and another thirteen in the CIA had left him almost humorless. He never told jokes, he never laughed at jokes, and he rarely smiled, especially since he had been assigned to black programs six years ago. Perhaps it was because he was no longer a fighting machine, overweight and out of shape, or maybe because his wife had divorced him fifteen years ago just before he retired from the Army, or maybe there just wasn't anything in his life left to smile about.

He had been married twenty-two years to a woman ten years younger. They never really knew each other, partly because he was always gone, partly because she was an artist and a musician with a set of friends he neither knew nor wanted to. They had had one child, a daughter. The last time he saw or spoke to her was at his ex-wife's funeral. Cancer had eaten away at her cervix. He had no idea until his daughter called and told him she had died.

His last assignment in the Army was Afghanistan. That's where he had run into Lieutenant Kevin Falk. Falk was working for a sorry-ass Air Force captain named Manson who had no fucking idea what 'back off' meant. Selbourne was on loan to the CIA which wanted certain poppy fields protected and, by God, he was going to protect them. Too often Manson made that mission difficult. It seemed like he was constantly crossing swords with the arrogant puke who appeared to think busting drug runners and destroying poppy fields actually helped the American cause there.

Falk, on the other hand, was less ideological, an easy man to talk to. Falk had even given him a heads-up several times when a major bust operation was about to go down. A few times he was able to stop the asshole Manson before he could make the bust. Falk was a good man.

When he retired from the Army in 2004 there wasn't much to do, what with a dead wife, no family that would speak to him, and no hobbies. He called a friend at the CIA and offered his services. A few months later he was being trained in covert operations. Seven years later he was assigned his current job. Now he was in charge of overseeing several black programs all over the world. And he was good at it.

To be good at running black operations you had to be a sociopath, better yet, a psychopath. You kill people and you get them killed and if you lose sleep over it you're in the wrong damn business. But at the same time, you have to be able to talk with, communicate with people who aren't. You have to know what to say, what they want to hear, and pretend their concerns are important to you also. It's hard sometimes. But Colonel Craig Selbourne had become a master, studying men like Cheney, Rumsfeld, Hayden, Brennan and Clapper. Like them, he could charm the press with witty aplomb and big smiles and chuckles at the appropriate times, all the while self-describing his actions and motives as those of a concerned patriot. He was even better in front of Congress when committees would grill him. He was unflappable no matter how far his answers strayed from the truth. Of course, in his current role, public appearances were rare to not at all. And that suited him just fine.

Selbourne had recruited Kevin Falk himself. He knew his father from years past. Kevin had been a disappointment to his father. General G.W. Falk had been career Army. When his only son, Kevin, wanted to join the Air Force it was as if his world had stopped turning. Goddamned pussies and pansies in the Air Force! If you're going to be a soldier at least join a real fighting service, Army or Marines, but for God's sake not the fucking boy scouts. It was a sad day when Kevin Falk was inducted into the Air Force. General Falk didn't bother attending Kevin's graduation from the Air Force Academy.

Selbourne recruited Falk because he was smart, he could work independently, and he would blindly follow orders without question. Major Kevin Falk was the perfect candidate for his next operation.

Colonel Selbourne's office was nothing fancy, a desk, two chairs, an American flag, and a picture of the Director on the wall behind his desk. It was sparse for a reason, no place to hide bugs. Even inside the CIA complex he had his office scanned once a week. Paranoia isn't if they're really trying to get you. Selbourne took no chances.

When Kevin arrived, he had to leave his wallet and his cell phone in the outer office. A guard posted in the corridor outside of Selbourne's office ran a wand over him before he could enter.

"You wanted to see me, Colonel?" Selbourne had been out of the Army for thirteen years but he still required subordinates to call him Colonel.

"I have a change in assignment for you, Major. Close the door."

"Yes sir. What sort of assignment?"

Selbourne leaned back in his chair. "Thirteen years ago I started this job. This is all I've ever wanted to do. Son, there is no greater calling than public service. Those of us who get up every morning and look out over the ramparts for the bad guys rarely get any credit. But it's not about credit."

"No sir."

"It's about protecting this nation from its enemies, within and without, enemies that want to see us dead, our institutions destroyed. That's not happening on my watch!"

"Nor mine, sir." Kevin felt like his boss was reading his mind.

"Good! This assignment won't be easy. You won't be able to share what you're doing with anyone, no family, no friends."

"Understood, sir. That won't be a problem."

"We've been forced to create this program because the goddamned sequester has killed our goddamned budget! There's no money for the things we have to do - and I mean have to do - for the security of this nation. Those piss ants in Washington can't get out of their own way. Well goddamnit, we're not going to let that stop us from getting the job done. Any idea what the fuck I'm talking about, Major?"

"I think I do, sir."

"Ollie North did what he had to do to raise money for the Contras. Kicked Boland right in the ass and he didn't apologize for it. I admire the shit out of that kind of leadership. Are you comfortable with where I'm going here?"

"Absolutely, sir. I assume you're talking about Green Valley?"

"I knew you were smart, Major. Absolutely, I am talking about Green Valley. The revenue from the Valley operation took care of that Venezuelan asshole a few years ago and the Ukrainian overthrow after that. Sent that fucking pinko faggot packing, turn tail to Moscow.

Son, I knew your father and he would be damned proud of you right now. This kind of thankless fucking work can only be done by those of us willing to take the risks, to break some goddamned eggs. Do you know why I hired you?"

"I assume because I know my way around Afghanistan, sir."

"That, and the fact that your test scores were through the roof, miles above every other candidate. You don't know, maybe you can't appreciate it, but your father's stern discipline is what made you the man you are."

"I loved my father, sir. And I respected him. But, in all honesty, Colonel, I don't believe he loved or respected me. He never once told me I was doing a good job."

"Well, I'm telling you, Kevin, you're doing a hell of a job. I couldn't be prouder."

Kevin was surprised to feel a tingle on the back of his neck, a sense of elation. It was an emotional feeling and his eyes teared slightly forcing him to buck up. "Thank you, Colonel. That means a great deal."

"Alright, Major. Enough bullshit. I'm sending you to take a look at Green Valley, see how it operates. You have three weeks to learn what you can then we have to expand. We've hit a wall in the northeast. I want to start a similar operation in Florida and you're going to head it up."

Kevin was ecstatic that the Colonel was assigning him a full-fledged program to develop from ground up. It was validation for all the hard work he had done. His chance encounter with Colonel Selbourne in Afghanistan all those years ago had come to this... a chance to do something important with his life, a chance to feel good about himself.

"By the way," the Colonel added, "you did a good job cleaning up the Grogan debacle. No one suspects that was our operation. Fernandez fucked that up and he paid the ultimate price. I don't want that to happen to you."

"No sir," Kevin assured him it wouldn't. "I don't think hijacking private vessels is the right approach, sir. Expendable accomplices are more reliable."

"You'd better be right, Major." The look in the Colonel's eyes told Kevin he was dead serious.

"Yes sir. When do I start?"

"I'll let you know. In the meantime, you can assemble a team. Take some of the Green Valley operatives to get you started. You'll need some experienced men. Use the list to back-fill both teams. Everyone on it has been vetted. We're going to call this one Afghan Horse. The mission is the same, the rules are the same. This is pure black, Major. Your head will be chopped off if you fuck this up."

"That won't happen, Colonel."

"Good. You're on your own, Major. You're dismissed."

Kevin stood to leave Selbourne's office. He wasn't sure what made him do it, but he came to attention and saluted the civilian Colonel. The Colonel appeared impressed and returned his salute.

Colonel Selbourne reminded Kevin of his father in many ways. He had always tried to make his father proud. That the Colonel knew his father would be proud of the work he was doing gave him extraordinary satisfaction. There had been a void in his heart since his father died. For some reason, he felt a kinship, an inexplicable bond with the Colonel. It bordered on love for the man. There was no way he would ever fail him, no way he would ever disappoint him.

* * *

Samantha arrived a few minutes early at Alexandra's office. She went to turn the handle to the office but the door was locked. She assumed no one else had arrived yet. Moments later the door opened and she could see both Gavin and Alexandra were there.

Gavin greeted her. "Come in, Sam! How was your day?"

Samantha entered and Gavin closed and locked the door behind her. She felt an unusual sense of anxiety in the room. "It was fine, Gavin. What's with the chariness?"

"I'll cut to the chase. Alex has discovered some concerning facts about the proliferation of heroin on the east coast. You need to see this. She'll give you a rundown. It will all make sense when she's done."

Gavin sat in one chair, Samantha in the other as Alexandra laid out the detailed facts of her investigation so far. As Gavin expected, Samantha was dumbstruck. When the presentation was complete Samantha sat silent for a few minutes. Then she opened up.

"We have to tell somebody about this, one of the committees. Your committee. Gavin we can't sit on this, there needs to be an investigation."

"No!" Gavin was emphatic. "At this point we can't talk to anyone. We need more information. We come forward with this and it looks like an accusation, an accusation without evidence or proof. It would be a simple task to cover up this trail. All we have is circumstantial evidence. We need cold hard facts or our careers, hell our lives, could be at risk. We don't know."

Samantha knew he was right. The circumstantial evidence was convincing but it wasn't proof. "So how do we proceed?"

"I'm working on that. We may have to move Alex to a more secure location where her computer system, electronic files and paper records aren't available to prying eyes. Someplace only we are aware of."

"I think you definitely have to move her." Samantha had come to the realization Gavin was right. "Any idea where?"

"Like I said, I'm working on it. I'll let you know when I have a solid answer. If you have any suggestions I'm all ears."

"At this point I don't have any ideas", Samantha admitted.

Alexandra had been silent while the Senators went back and forth but she had some ideas. "How about a van outfitted with wifi range extenders. The problem with using an office or a private location is that the ISP knows who you are. From a van I could park near free wifi sites, motels, campgrounds, coffee shops, the airport. Secure anonymous logins, anonymous TOR browser. To find me, they would have to know where I was, actually follow me."

"Sounds uncomfortable", Samantha remarked.

"But it's an option worth considering." There was merit to the idea and Gavin liked it more as he thought about it. "Any idea how we find a van without exposing any of our identities?"

"My Uncle Chuck may be able to help", Alexandra offered.

"How?" Samantha wanted to know.

"He was a spook, so to speak. Believe me, he would know what to do, how to do it, and how to cover our tracks."

"Sounds like our guy." Gavin approved of the idea but he wanted to talk with him first.

"Alright. Have him fly up here at my expense. Tell Monica to make the arrangements. He can stay at the Marriott."

"He can stay at my place", Alexandra suggested. "And he should make his own arrangements. Family staying with family would draw no suspicion."

"Good idea", Samantha agreed. "We can reimburse him anonymously for his expenses."

Gavin wanted to make sure everyone understood the need for absolute secrecy. "Need I say no part of this conversation leaves this room?"

Everyone concurred and Samantha gathered her things to leave. "I want to meet this Uncle Chuck. How old is he?"

"Sixty something", Alexandra replied.

Samantha opened the door to leave. "That's a shame." She smiled and closed the door behind her.

"Are you hungry?" Gavin asked. "Dinner's on me if you're interested."

Alexandra countered, "I have a different idea. How would you like to have an authentic Greek dinner, home cooked?"

"Home cooked, huh?" He loved Greek food. He had never been to her apartment. He was curious and hungry. "Sounds like a plan."

* * *

Alexandra's apartment was nothing like he had pictured. It was simple, unimaginative, and gray. Everything was gray. He was reluctant to comment but felt he had to, saying nothing felt awkward. Before he could say anything she piped up.

"Too gray for you?"

"No. I like gray", he claimed. But, in truth, he wasn't impressed.

"It's one of those student rental packages from Kord rentals. You know, a hundred and nineteen dollars a month? I wasn't sure how long I would be here. I wasn't going to spend money on furniture without knowing I would be here a while."

"You're going to be here a while", he assured her.

"Well, maybe I'll upgrade then", she tittered, knowing she probably wouldn't. "I did buy a decent mattress. The one that came with the package was as hard as a rock."

"Something to be said for a good night's rest", he quipped.

Alexandra poured him a scotch without asking, she knew he was a scotch man. Then she went into the bedroom to change into more comfortable clothes. Gavin looked around the apartment then wandered over and sat in the easy chair and briefly closed his eyes. When he opened them he could see her bedroom door was slightly ajar and beyond that she was undressing. She was facing away as she unsnapped her bra and laid it on the bed. Then she raised one leg then the other, removing her panties. Gavin was spellbound but he felt like a peeping Tom.

This was not a normal feeling for him. With any other woman he would be full-on voyeur, taking in as much of the scenery as he could observe. But Alexandra affected him differently somehow. He felt like a gawker, like he was being disrespectful. He watched as she opened a dresser drawer and pulled out a pair of sweat pants and a clingy tee, not unlike the one she wore down south. She was beautiful. He didn't want to stop watching her but he forced himself from the chair and walked over to the kitchen island where she had left the scotch bottle. He poured himself another one.

"Have you ever had dolmades?" she called from the bedroom.

65

"Lamb-stuffed grape leaves? I love them." They weren't really his favorite Greek food but he wasn't about to say so.

"How about tzatziki sauce?" Alexandra came out of the bedroom and turned on the sound bar by the TV. She set it on Bluetooth, then synced a favorite playlist from her cell phone. The list was laid-back jazz and cool blues, Luther Vandross, Van Morrison, Chick Corea. He was more than happy with her taste in music.

Percy had been hiding in the guest bedroom. Now that things had settled down he felt comfortable coming out and taking a look at the surprise visitor. He strolled over to Gavin and rubbed his head and neck against Gavin's leg. Gavin reached down and gently stroked along his neck and back then scratched his head. Percy gave him an approving purr and Gavin picked him up. The purr turned into a deep, murmuring motor.

"He likes you", Alexandra announced with apparent pleasure.

"Never met a cat I didn't like", he quipped, setting Percy back on the floor.

"I made the tzatziki this afternoon. I'm sure it's cool by now." She pulled the bowl of white sauce from the refrigerator and set it on the island along with a tray of sliced cucumbers, carrots, broccoli and cauliflower. "It's hard to find good Greek bread in D.C.", she said as she sliced a loaf of Psomi and arranged it on a small plate.

"This is excellent", he fawned, as the two of them dipped and ate standing together at the small island.

Alexandra dipped a cucumber slice in the sauce and hand-fed it to him. Gavin smiled and returned the favor with a piece of cauliflower. There was anticipatory tension in the air and they could both feel it. Alexandra reached over with her finger and wiped some sauce from the corner of Gavin's lips. He gripped her finger and licked the sauce from it. She pulled herself closer putting her hands on his cheeks, her soft breasts firmly touching his chest. Then she wrapped her arms around his neck and they kissed, a long and sensual kiss neither wanted to end.

"This probably isn't a good idea", he cautioned.

"Too late", she said as she took his hands and moved them inside her soft tee-top. Gavin gently continued the motion, softly brushing his fingers across her pert nipples. She kissed him with a passion she had never felt with other men, excitedly scary. Had she fallen in love? She couldn't be sure. There were so many emotions to sort out. But she had never met a more perfect man. She took his hand and led him to the guest bedroom. "If this doesn't work out", she thought, "I'd rather not have these memories in my own bed."

Gavin knew they were both about to cross a line beyond which neither could ever return. There was commitment implied in their union tonight. He was ready to make it. He realized he was in love with her and she with him, he was sure of it.

Gavin began to lift her tee and she raised her arms in cooperation. She helped him remove his shirt then wrapped her arms around him, pulling herself close. He moved his hands behind her and inside her sweat pants as they kissed, a long passionate kiss. Then they laid down side by side, tenderly touching and exploring each other for the first time. Neither had ever felt so comfortable in another's embrace, so wonderfully one, the world a universe away.

Alexandra could feel the strength in his arms as he gently moved above her, and in them she felt safe and unafraid. She gasped in hushed breath as he tenderly encouraged her hips to join his. In the soft milieu, a dulcet Percy Sledge, his heart bleeding melody, desperately expressed what it's like 'When a Man Loves a Woman'.

CHAPTER 7

C huck McCrory was a man's man. At five feet nine he was never an intimidating figure, but he carried himself with a strong, confident stride, his presence always acknowledged. Nor was he shy, quite the opposite, he was outgoing and gregarious but never obnoxiously so. He loved learning but not the stuff they taught in school. A voracious reader, he devoured books about physics, philosophy, science fiction and, in particular, military history. He was a mechanical genius. He could make or repair almost anything. As a teenager he rebuilt car engines in the back yard. His father urged him to think about unconventional solutions when conventional ones eluded him. "Son," he would say, "anyone can work with tools. It takes a real mechanic to work without 'em."

Chuck also liked electronics. He learned radio and TV repair from little notebooks he would buy at Radio Shack. He hand-built his first computer with a machine language kit from Franklin Electronics. A conversation with Chuck could leave the other person scratching their head. Who is this guy?

As a child he was on the thin side but that thinness was all muscle, pure sinew. His parents started him in martial arts at the age of eight. He immediately excelled and was competing as a black belt by the age of thirteen against kids much older and bigger. His sensei was a humble and honorable man who instilled in him all the right virtues: humility, respect, self-discipline, self-confidence, concentration, sportsmanship. And Chuck was an excellent student.

The Vietnam War was all but over when Chuck turned nineteen. There was no longer a military draft but he enlisted in the Army anyway. His father had been in the Army, served in WWII and Korea, but never pushed him to volunteer. His dad never talked much about his service, few soldiers of that era did. It seemed most people had become disillusioned with the war in Southeast Asia and detested anything that had to do with the military by the time Nixon declared "Peace with Honor". But there was something that fascinated Chuck about the military. The history, strategy, and discipline sucked him in like an irresistible vortex. It seemed his destiny was to be a soldier.

Chuck was a pacifist at heart but he didn't resist the call to serve like so many of his friends. Pacifism and military service weren't mutually exclusive in his mind. Indeed, they had a great deal in common. His study of Buddhism shaped much of his thought about the way to live life and helped him see the compatibility of things that appeared contradictory to more rigid western minds.

His physical abilities didn't go unnoticed and his calm confidence in boot camp caught the attention of his DI who recommended him to the Special Forces unit commander of the Green Berets. Green Berets were unconventional warfare forces who undertook clandestine guerilla operations wherever they were required. They could be dropped into a hot zone anywhere in the world and needed to be able to speak the language and understand the local culture. Their missions could range from hostage rescue to manhunts, reconnaissance, counter-terrorism, even psychological operations. Army Special Forces members were a rare breed that Chuck McCrory fit into perfectly.

For Chuck, one of the best things about being a Green Beret was that he rarely had to take any crap from local ground commanders. He belonged to the 1st Special Forces Command, an airborne unit that usually reported directly to the United States Special Operations Command, USSOCOM. The Green Berets were an elite team and nobody outside of their own chain of command could give them orders.

His mentor was a man named Charlie Beckwith, a Vietnam veteran and former Green Beret officer. Beckwith was largely credited with convincing the Pentagon high command that the Army's Special Forces needed small, adaptable and autonomous teams with a broad array of specialized skills who could take direct action and perform covert counter-terrorism missions. It was Beckwith who created the Army's Delta Force and Chuck was an original team member.

Chuck had only a high-school diploma when he enlisted, but he was urged by his superiors to go to college and apply to Officer Candidate School. He was widely read for his young years and excelled at physics and math, which he had learned mostly on his own, so his foray with institutionalism was a dicey one. He had no problem challenging or correcting his instructors. Eventually, his superiors decided his services were needed more than his formal education and they shipped him off to OCS with the promise he could complete school later, but he never did. He had no problem completing the Army's grueling tactical and leadership training program. Twelve weeks later, Second Lieutenant Chuck McCrory graduated OCS with honors.

Chuck grew up on the tail-end of the hippie movement and carried with him much of the laid-back attitude of the sixties. If you could get him to talk about politics or government he sounded anti-establishment. He had nothing good to say about either subject, including the military-industrial complex. His buddies would often ask him why he ever joined the Army. He never answered them and thus remained an enigma even to those closest to him. But none of his Delta Force buddies ever questioned his ability or loyalty or patriotism.

Chuck had a stellar reputation for intellect and bravery with both his peers and commanding officers, and he rose quickly through the ranks. He was a Colonel when he retired from the Army in 1998, at the young but seasoned age of 44. Before he retired, he had thought about a brotherhood of allies, a team of specialists who would keep in touch, as long as they lived, if possible. He had approached four of his closest comrades with the idea. They all agreed to a musketeer's credo - all for one and one for all. If one of them needed the team, they would all help. It was Jimmy 'Nunchucks' who came up with their name... Delta 5.

In and out of the military, Chuck was everybody's friend, and genuinely so. One of the best friends he had made in his life was Christos Katsaros, a gentle restaurateur who had asked him to be the godfather to his only daughter, an honor that humbled and elated him.

When little Alexandra was born, he and Vera had visited Helena in the hospital. By any honest account, Alexandra was truly an ugly baby. She had been delivered by forceps, her head was lopsided and she was as wrinkled as a bloodhound's jowls. Still, he told Helena and Christos how beautiful their newborn was.

What a difference a year made. On her first birthday, Alexandra wasn't just a cute little girl, she was strikingly beautiful. A year before, he had thought she looked like a little pink lizard. Twelve months later she had the visage of an angel.

Chuck knocked and rang the door bell to the angel's apartment and stepped back to wait for her to open the door. He was both curious and anxious to know why she had called him to come and visit 'as soon as possible'. She wouldn't say over the phone and he naturally wondered if something might be wrong. She had assured him she was fine but insisted she wanted to see him right away if he could make it. Twenty-four hours later, she answered his knock.

"Uncle Chuck!" Alexandra hugged her uncle who reciprocated with one arm, the other holding a hastily packed duffel bag with three days of clothes and personal items. "How was your flight?"

"No fights broke out if that's what you mean." Her uncle had a naturally sarcastic wit. "You look as beautiful as ever, Allie."

"Thank you, Uncle Chuck. Come in, come in."

Chuck's first impression of Alexandra's apartment wasn't unlike Gavin's. "What? They had a sale on gray that day?"

"It's a long story", she laughed. "This is your room." She guided him to the guest room. "You can settle in. I have to finish getting ready. By the way, we're going to dinner with Gavin at six."

"Hobnobbing with a Senator!" he cracked. "I'm moving up in the world."

"You'll like him, Uncle Chuck. He's an amazing man. He reminds me of you."

Chuck cringed at the idea. He had never liked much about politicians. Local politicians were okay sometimes; school board members, supervisor of elections, city council. But by the time a politician made the big show they were either a liar, a cheat, a thief, or some combination of the three. For Chuck, the definition of politician was '1. liar; 2. cheat; 3. thief;'. Political party was of no consequence. In his sixty plus years he had noticed, long ago, it made no difference which party was in power. His life never got any better or any worse because one or the other ran Congress or the White House. The only thing that changed was the rhetoric, and he could give two shits about that.

Chuck set his duffel bag on the dresser and zipped it open. That was all the 'settling in' he needed to do. He journeyed back out to the living room and did some reconnaissance. "Where's the bar?" he called toward the bedroom.

"Under the kitchen island", she reported back. "All I have is scotch and wine."

He opened the cabinet door and saw a bottle of 18-year-old Glenfiddich. "Someone has good taste!"

"Gavin only drinks scotch, and pretty much, only that one."

He found a glass in the cabinet behind him and poured a double shot. "Well, if you're only gonna drink one, this is a good one." Score one point for the Senator. Obviously, he spent some time here.

Alexandra came out of the bedroom adjusting a slinky, black knee-length dress and wearing a pearl necklace with matching ear rings. Chuck was wearing blue jeans with a reddish Hawaiian shirt and sneakers.

"I guess I'm over-dressed", he quipped.

"You look fine. Gavin will probably be dressed casually. I just don't get a chance to dress up much these days."

Chuck's first rodeo was years ago. It didn't take a genius to see his goddaughter was gussying up for a man... and it wasn't him.

"So, what do I call him? Senator? Your highness?"

"Stop it, Uncle Chuck! I'll introduce him as Gavin. After that you can call him Gavin."

"Okie doke, young lady."

Chuck didn't know much about Senator Manson except what he saw on TV. The Senator seemed like a decent guy from what little he could learn from thirty-second sound bites. It was no secret Alexandra was smitten with the man and it was a good bet the two had already attended a joint session of congress. A man don't leave his scotch where he can't get to it.

* * *

Alexandra had been happy to see a change of venue text message from Gavin on her cell phone. He had originally suggested a simple steakhouse in D.C. but changed the location to a fine dining Greek grill in Rockville. She assumed he made the change for her. In fact, he had thought better of conversing too close to the prying ears around the Capital.

Gavin was waiting at the bar when Alexandra and Chuck arrived. He paid his bar tab and the maître d' showed them to their table. He had tipped the maître d' to put them in a quiet corner far enough away from the nearest table that their conversation would be assured of privacy.

Gavin had come dressed in business attire, sans the tie. It was a Saturday evening and most people in the upscale eatery were similarly dressed. Alexandra had said Gavin would be dressed casually, and, for Gavin, that was casual. Chuck's red Hawaiian look was unique among the Saturday evening diners. A less secure man might have noticed the askant glances as the trio was led to their secluded table. Chuck didn't.

The dinner was exceptional everyone said. The waiter had talked them all into the house special, Moussaka, one of Greece's most famous dishes. It consisted of layers of fried aubergine, minced meat and potatoes, topped with a creamy béchamel sauce and then baked to a golden brown. Chuck hadn't realized it was eggplant until the dish arrived. He wasn't a big fan. But he ate it. A few coffees and a baklava later he was fine. Once the scotch began to flow all was right again with the universe.

Alexandra was both happy and relieved the two favorite men in her life were getting along so well. She could see they had a mutual respect that could only be shared by men like them, men who knew what it was like to be a warrior. That both men had grown up in Tampa, though a generation apart, added to a sense of community and trust, and bode well for a future alliance.

"So why am I here?" Chuck eventually broached the elephant.

Alexandra looked to Gavin who nodded.

"We need your advice and expertise, Uncle Chuck."

"You must be desperate, then", he chuckled. When neither of them shared his attempt at humor he took a more serious tone. "Whatever I can do, Allie. What is it you need?"

Again, she looked toward Gavin. "How much can I tell him?"

"Everything. But not here, not tonight. For now, let's concentrate on the van."

"I've been doing research for legislation Gavin wants to propose", she began, "and we have discovered some extremely sensitive information that we don't want anyone to know that we're aware of. We think it may be dangerous to continue researching on government networks. Our idea is to outfit a van with a high-tech computer system and internet equipment capable of moving around the D.C. area undetected. We want your advice and help procuring it and setting it up."

Alexandra could see the concerned look in her uncle's eyes.

"What the hell have you gotten my goddaughter into, Manson?" Chuck's voice bordered on livid as he stared red-faced at Gavin, the veins in his forehead protruding slightly.

"He didn't get me into anything", she interrupted. "In the course of what seemed like mundane research we discovered, I discovered, some disturbing information I will tell you about. But not here. For now, will you or won't you help us with a van I can do research in?"

"Allie, I swore to your father to protect and watch over you. I feel like I might be violating that oath, his trust."

"Uncle Chuck, first, you can't tell Dad. I forbid it." Alexandra was staring straight into her uncle's eyes. "Second, I'm not a child anymore. Will you help me or not?"

Chuck sat silent for what seemed like eternity to Alexandra. Gavin knew better than to put his two cents into what was essentially a family matter at this point.

"No, you're not a child anymore, Allie. I know that. It still doesn't make it any easier when I know you may be putting yourself at risk. I can guess what you're up against, but I'm not going to try to talk you out of it. I'll help you no matter what you need."

Alexandra leaned over and hugged her godfather uncle for all she was worth. "Thank you!" she said. "What we're doing is important, Uncle Chuck."

"I'm sure it is", he nodded, then glanced at Gavin. "I agree, no discussions tonight. I'll locate a place we can get together and talk safely. I'll let you know where in a day or two."

"You're a good man, Chuck." Gavin was relieved the tension had deescalated.

"Yeah," Chuck mused. "It's a shame there's so little demand for good men these days." He smiled and reached over the table to shake Gavin's hand, a firm, positive grip... the kind that tells you something about a man. "The van is a great idea. Who thought of it?"

"I did!" Alexandra beamed.

Chuck held up his empty scotch glass and studied it with a gimbaled hand. "I'll get a vehicle up here by next week. I know a guy in Tampa who owns an RV dealership. He can do conversions. I know exactly what you'll need." He looked at Gavin. "You'll need to give me a couple of days to train her how to use it."

"Done", Gavin confirmed as he raised his hand for the waiter's attention. "Two more scotches and a Shirley Temple for the lady."

Gavin grimaced from the pointy-toed kick to his ankle as Alexandra corrected him, "Another shiraz, please."

Chuck sat back amused, smiling inside and out. His goddaughter was happy and her choice of beau appeared to be a good one. If it hadn't been evident before, it certainly was now... congress was definitely in session.

CHAPTER 8

Alexandra's new van arrived the following Saturday. Chuck had asked Gavin to have anyone who would be using or interfacing with the van meet him at the Maryland House, a rest stop on I-95 a few miles north of Baltimore. The Maryland House was a travel plaza with a number of fast-food restaurants, ice cream shops, a kiddie play area, a gas station and, importantly, free wifi.

Chuck had chosen this particular place because it was well-traveled with thousands of people passing through every day. There was a constant stream of humanity: large busloads of tourists, families on their way to or from some gathering, traveling salesmen, vacationers, and travelers just needing a restroom or a bite to eat. Several people standing around a van, talking in a group or climbing in and out of a vehicle in a busy parking lot, would not seem unusual in this environment. He would be able to demonstrate the operation of the van with little worry about prying eyes or inquisitive ears.

Chuck had parked the van in an uncongested area far enough from the main traffic flow, but close enough to the hubbub, that its presence would easily blend in with the swirling mass of trekkers. He had asked that the attendees travel separately, and as each arrived, he strategically placed their cars around the van in a way that shielded it, as much as possible, from public view. Cynthia had brought along Speedy Gonzalez, a sight he welcomed, as the presence of pets lent a domestic air of family to the assembly.

Chuck had asked Gavin and Samantha not to attend the initial meeting. It was important that the group not be recognized and Gavin and Samantha's high-profile faces could jeopardize the operation if they were to be spotted, particularly by news reporters or enthusiastic supporters who might be inclined to post pictures on their social media pages. Chuck already knew Cynthia. Alexandra introduced him to Monica, and of course, Cynthia's Speedy.

"Welcome ladies... and gentleman." Chuck looked at Speedy who seemed oblivious to the proceedings, more interested in the van's tires than anything he was saying. "So, we're here to go over the operation and use of this vehicle", he began. "I'll be talking to Allie, primarily, but all of you should pay close attention and ask questions if you don't understand something."

Everyone nodded in acknowledgement.

He started with the outside of the van. "Techies ON CALL. The brand name is fictitious; the phone number resolves to a legitimate tech service company should anyone decide to call it. Looks like any other service company truck for computer help or technical support. And that's the point. It's obscure because there are so many of them around. Note the van is white, the colors are muted, indistinct and, hopefully, won't garner much attention."

He opened the sliding door on the driver's side. Inside, the layout looked like a rolling tech lab. There were two monitors mounted to a curved desk with a low-boy captain's chair bolted to the floor which could swivel between the two. Beside the desk was a work bench with a piece of disassembled equipment, its wiring laid open. A peg board organizer was mounted on the passenger side wall, full of tools typical of any geek-driven service vehicle.

A collective "Oooohh!" went up from the group.

"This is so cool!" Monica exclaimed. "I want one." Everyone laughed.

Chuck invited them into the van to look around. Alexandra sat in the captain's chair. Another, less comfortable chair, also permanently fixed, was positioned in front of the work bench. Monica sat in it. Cynthia could stand up with no problem as Chuck stood outside the door talking up to the group.

"The computer is located there", he pointed to a conspicuous box mounted underneath the desk. "But the hard drive is there", he pointed to another small rectangular box, less conspicuous, mounted to a vertical side panel separating the curved desk from the work bench area. "The top snaps open and the drive pulls out easily by grabbing the tab and pulling toward you. Try it."

Alexandra flipped the box open and tugged on the tab. The hard drive slid out into her hand. She pushed the drive back into the slot and snapped the box shut again. "That's convenient."

"Take it with you whenever you leave the van. Never leave it in the van alone, not even to visit the ladies' room."

Alexandra nodded with understanding.

"This power switch controls the monitors." Chuck flicked the switch and the monitors came on. "This one switches between the two. You can use either one. The one you're not using will be filled with random, meaningless data. It's just for show. You can also use them both if you want." He toggled a third position and both monitors were connected.

Monica spoke up. "Shouldn't you have killed the power to the computer before removing the hard drive?"

"Good point, Monica." Chuck was impressed with the knowledge of his students. It was making his job easy. "When the cover to the drive is opened it automatically kills power to the drive. Should it be necessary to make a quick exit, just flip the cover, grab the drive and go. If you have time", he pointed to a loose drive on the work bench, "insert that one. In fact, you should insert that one every time you pull the real one. Note they are color coded so you can't get them confused, green good, red bad."

Cynthia asked the obvious question. "What's on the bad one?"

"Just some basic operating system software, nothing of any value, no identifying information." Chuck pointed out other features of the van. "Refrigerator, microwave, short-wave radio, thermostat for the air conditioner, and this switch... the wifi extender. If you pull up some place and the signal is weak, you can try to use the extender to get a better signal. It's built into the carrier on top, not visible. This switch rotates the extender antenna 360 degrees. If you still can't get a signal, move to another location."

Chuck had Alexandra try to use the computer. It asked for her username and password, neither of which she knew yet. After three tries the system shut down and he handed her a cell phone, an old flip-style phone.

"Dial 911", he told her. When she dialed the number the computer came back to life, the screen again prompting her for the login information. "Don't lose this phone. There is no time out period for the lock out. If you screw up your login this phone will save you. If the computer is ever shut down when you enter the van - you've been compromised."

"What if I'm compromised? What should I do?" Alexandra wanted to know.

"Call me... immediately", he said. "That goes for the rest of you. Stay away from the van, wherever it is, and don't go near it until I've checked it out."

Suddenly the reality of what they were doing began to sink in. It was impossible to know if all the cloak and dagger was really necessary, but the thought that it might be gave them all pause.

"How many of you have used a TOR browser?" he asked. Only Alexandra had. "It's mysterious to most people but it's not complicated." He gave Alexandra her login and password and had her bring up the TOR browser.

"Most people don't know that the TOR Project is a 501-(c)(3), a non-profit online anonymity project for information privacy. It's free software, an open network designed to defend against traffic analysis. Who wants to analyze your traffic? Everyone from nefarious characters who want to steal your identity, to corporate espionage agents, to state security agencies - CIA, NSA, FBI, and their foreign nation equivalents. All of them are threats to your personal freedom and privacy. Too few people realize the dangers posed by these assaults on their privacy. Too many want to give the federal surveillance agencies the benefit of the doubt when it comes to who and what they surveil. That is a mistake."

Cynthia questioned Chuck's assertions. "If you can't trust the federal agencies to have the nation's best interests at heart, what is the point of having an agency?"

"We're not talking about FISA court warrants where someone is suspected of a crime and the court authorizes an agency to tap their phones or keep an eye on their activities for a while. We're talking about the illegal mass collection of data that simply gets housed in a server farm in perpetuity, for no specific reason other than they might be able to use it against you someday. Do you think they would ever collect it and hold it to one day exonerate you from something? I assure you that will never happen."

Cynthia continued, "But if you've done nothing wrong why should you care if the information exists in a server farm somewhere? What possible difference could it make?"

Chuck was adamant. "It should be enough to know that it is illegal for any federal agency to do mass surveillance without a court order. Yet they all do it. In and of itself, that is dishonest and speaks against any argument that they should be trusted to do the right thing. If they could be trusted to do the right thing, they would be advocating for the protection of your private information, not the compromise of it."

"Cynthia, leave him alone!" Alexandra admonished her friend. "Uncle Chuck, she's just pulling your chain. She knows better than any of us how much the assault on our personal privacy has challenged our Constitutional rights. She's a Constitutional lawyer for God's sake!"

Cynthia grinned at Chuck, "Just testing your resolve."

"As you should", he responded.

"So how does it work?" Monica asked.

"When you open the browser, your TOR browser, it begins to build a circuit of encrypted connections through relays run by volunteers on the network from all over the world. The circuit is built one hop at a time. Each relay only knows which relay fed it data and which relay it will feed data to. No individual relay ever knows the whole path the data will follow. Every hop has its own encryption keys which ensures the data can't be traced along the connections it passes through. That sounds complicated, and to some extent it is, but the idea is simple. If you're being tailed, you take a twisty, turney route, instead of a direct route to your destination. Along the way you cover up or erase your footprints to make it harder for the tail to follow you. For example, a typical route could take three hops, one through the Netherlands, then Canada, then France, then to the website you requested. That website then sends the information back in the opposite order, France, Canada, Netherlands, then you."

"Volunteers?" Monica was unaware the TOR network was a volunteer project.

Alexandra explained, "Yes, TOR depends on volunteers to maintain personal or even business computer systems as relays for the data passing through. They are growing in number but maybe not fast enough for the sophistication of the state actors who want to see the network compromised. Nobody hates TOR more than the NSA, CIA, FBI, MI6, GCHQ, FSB, MOSSAD. All of them want to be able to capture the passing information and trace it back to the source. They don't want the network destroyed because they use it too. In fact, it was developed for the U.S. Navy. Most governments run relays themselves so they can test ways to capture and decrypt the information flowing by. But the more people that volunteer to let their computers be used as relay stations for the network, the better the chances for TOR's success and survival."

Monica was curious. "What about bad guys, criminals using it. I've heard TOR is bad because law enforcement can't see their criminal activity."

Chuck assured her that was not a problem. "Criminals already break the law. They have many options for surreptitious communication, TOR is simply another one. They steal cell phones, use them a few times and trash them. They steal laptops and tablets all the while using the identity of the owner to do their dirty work. They buy burner phones for anonymity. On the flip side, someone in a country whose repressive government tries to control or block the internet can often use TOR to get around the blockades. Law enforcement uses it to anonymously surveil questionable websites like terrorist sites or even social media sites of suspected criminals. Every global military uses it. Reporters in foreign countries use it to send controversial or dangerous stories back to their home countries. It's used by human rights groups, whistle blowers, activists of all kinds. It's safe to say it has helped many more people than will ever be harmed by it. Anyone who tells you it's dangerous is either ignorant or trying to take advantage of your ignorance."

Alexandra brought up several websites and tested the speed of the equipment she had been handed. "It's not the fastest thing I've used but it will do. Thank you, Uncle Chuck."

"You be careful, Allie. All of you be careful. The fact that you feel the need to make yourselves this dark makes me nervous. None of you has experience in hiding from the kinds of people that this kind of operation implies. Do not communicate about this subject on the phone, only in person. Do so only in public places with plenty of ambient noise. Allie, never take this van anywhere near your apartment or the Senator's office or his home. I've arranged for you to use a parking garage near a hospital in Edgewood. Never fill up at the same gas station more than once every two months. Never talk to anyone when you do. Am I being scary enough?"

"I think so", she replied.

"Monica, it was nice to meet you. Cynthia, it was good to see you again. I see my next class has arrived." As they pulled into the parking area, he could see Samantha and Gavin arriving in her little red Miata. What the hell? Couldn't they have picked something a little more ostentatious? "Ladies, I have to ask you to leave quickly and quietly if you would. Allie, jump in the driver's seat and start her up."

Cynthia and Monica exited the van. Monica drove away immediately. Cynthia was detained slightly. As his paws hit the concrete, Speedy made a beeline for the adjacent wooded area two rows over. He had his own business to attend to and time was of the essence.

* * *

Samantha had picked Gavin up at his Chevy Chase apartment before heading north to I-495, the Washington Loop, and eventually I-95 to the Maryland House, about an hour and a half drive. Samantha's apartment, a small flat in Westboro near Bethesda, wasn't far from Gavin's so it was hardly out of the way.

Gavin's apartment was quite nice, fairly large but sparsely furnished. It was more of a bachelor pad - big screen TV, pool table, foosball, functional furniture but not fancy. As a first term Senator, Samantha couldn't afford big or luxurious. Even if she could, she wouldn't have leased either because of the many horror stories she had heard as a newbie. Constituents don't appreciate their representatives moving to Washington and setting up camp, rarely coming home to their districts. It was best to come home as often as possible your rookie term. The worst thing you could do was to alienate yourself from the people who sent you there. Still, she liked her place and her landlord, a middle-aged widow who kept her flowers watered when she was away.

Chuck had asked that she and Gavin meet him at 11:00 a.m. The other girls had arrived around 10:00 a.m. He wanted to work with each group separately, he had said. She wondered if that was the real reason but not enough to ask why. As she and Gavin made the turn onto I-95, Samantha anxiously admitted to having some recalcitrant thoughts about their bill's ultimate objectives, specifically full-blown legalization of all drugs.

"Gavin, I need to come clean. It's getting harder for me to embrace the full legalization aspect of this bill. Plus, I'm not sure I'll be able to pull in that many co-sponsors. I floated a couple of trial balloons the last few weeks and they went nowhere."

"Goddamnit, Sam! I thought we agreed you would keep this bill under wraps until we had sufficient architecture to present it to both sides of the aisle. Are you trying to subvert me?"

Samantha knew she was going to incur his Scottish ire, but he came out of the corner screaming at the top of his lungs. That, she hadn't expected.

"You don't have to yell, Gavin."

"I think I do. Have you forgotten this legislation was your idea? Why the cold feet now, Sam?"

"It's not cold feet. I've just had time to think about what we're proposing in some depth and I'm hesitant, reluctant to go against the established order of things so blatantly. I'll never get re-elected if this goes south."

"How is that different from cold feet, Sam? Look, we started this project together. You've been vital to its success so far. We have amassed an amazing amount of proof of concept, statistical and analytical data. The man-on-the-street feedback you've done in Worcester and Boston are phenomenal. How do you discount your own work like that?"

Samantha felt her chest tightening. Her eyes were tearing and she couldn't stop them. Damn him! He always knew what to say, how to negate her words and make them sound trite.

And he continued. "Sam, you're a good senator, a great senator. You will be re-elected. That's not going to be an issue. It sounds to me like you've been listening to your colleagues instead of your constituents. That's a fatal mistake, absolutely fatal. Your colleagues didn't elect you."

Samantha pulled a tissue from the door pocket and wiped her eyes, checking the rear-view mirror for smudges in her mascara. She didn't want to blow her nose but it couldn't be helped. A deep breath and she was back in control.

"Gavin, I'm struggling with this issue. You're right about my constituents. They almost unanimously support trying something different, even something as radical as legalization. Maybe it's me. Maybe I don't know how I really feel."

Gavin realized he had over-reacted. "Sam, I'm sorry I yelled at you. I feel so strongly about our project I can't understand how you don't. We've been working on this over six months now. Don't give up yet. Try to find a way to make it work in your mind. When we're near the end you can always walk away if you still have doubts. But don't abandon me now."

Samantha reached over and squeezed Gavin's hand. "Sorry I was so emotional. I know how hard you're working."

Gavin interrupted her, "And so are you."

"Thank you, Gavin, for understanding."

They both sat mostly silent for the rest of the trip, exchanging small talk, Samantha's thoughts leaning toward trying to understand why she was feeling so unsure of herself, his hoping her overly emotional state was biological and would diminish in a few days.

Samantha could see the exit coming up to the Maryland House. "Looks like we're here", she said.

As they entered the off ramp, Gavin began to look for Chuck and the girls. "It's a white van with 'Techies ON CALL' on the side. Shouldn't be hard to spot."

Samantha pulled into the parking area. "There it is", she pointed. Monica was pulling away as they drove up. She could see Cynthia walking her dog toward the shrubbery at the edge of the parking lot. "Chuck is motioning for us to hurry up, I think."

"Yeah," Gavin said, "Looks like he wants you to park on the other side of the van."

"Let's go, let's go", Chuck urged as Samantha and Gavin pulled up next to the van. Gavin exited almost immediately and walked around to wait next to Samantha's door while she gathered her purse, organized her belongings, and checked her makeup in the mirror one last time before exiting the car. Once she started to get out Chuck thought she would never stop standing up. He hadn't realized how tall she was. He smiled to himself thinking the little red Miata looked like a clown car next to her.

"Come, come! We have to go", he insisted. At Chuck's urging they quickly walked around to the driver's side of the van and in through the sliding door. Chuck closed the door and walked around to the passenger side front and hopped in. Samantha reached into her purse and clicked the lock button on her car key fob. The little red machine reacted twice with a wimpy beep-beep.

"Head north, Allie", Chuck instructed. "Take the first exit to the right and pull into the first motel on the right. Make a quick left and drive all the way to the end of the parking area. Park under the last tree on the right."

Alexandra wasn't sure if she could remember all the directions but the heading north part she got. She gave the van some gas in the acceleration lane and it pushed her back into her seat. Gavin nearly fell over grabbing the lab table for support. Samantha was quite comfortable in the captain's chair, impressed with the van's pep.

"Wow! This thing really moves!" Alexandra declared.

"Try not to get a ticket", Chuck warned her. "If you do, there's a record tying you to this vehicle. You don't want that."

"This is very impressive, Chuck. And you got it built in only a week. Good work!" Gavin was duly impressed.

"The hardest part is that I had to drive it up here myself. I'm not as young as I used to be." Chuck was serious but everyone else laughed.

"So why did you hustle us out of Maryland House?" Samantha asked.

"You both have familiar faces. I didn't want to take any chances that someone might recognize you and try to engage; a selfie, a photo posted on social media. You know."

"Sure", Samantha nodded. "I get it."

When they reached the parking area behind the motel, Chuck exited the passenger side and entered the side door of the van where Samantha and Gavin were seated. He began the same lecture he presented to the women earlier. This time the questions were different, as he had expected.

"So Chuck, if it becomes necessary to abandon the van, and Alex doesn't have time to insert the dummy drive, what happens when the computer is compromised?" Gavin was wondering if the bad guys would know there was a hard drive out there somewhere, one someone might want to look for.

Chuck explained. "The computer has an internal hard drive with bogus pre-loaded data which is constantly being time-stamped in real time. It becomes the primary drive when the green auxiliary is pulled. The auxiliary hard drive she is using, the one on the panel wall here, is wirelessly connected to the computer. When it is engaged it is the primary drive. When it is pulled, the computer automatically engages the internal hard drive. When the red drive is engaged it acts like a secondary drive. Making sure it is installed when the green drive is removed makes it harder to figure out how the system operates. It will take at least several hours, possibly days, before anyone would realize what the situation actually is. That should be plenty of time to get the real drive to a safe haven."

Samantha responded, "Ooh! This is like something out of a spy novel! I'm getting goose bumps."

Chuck was concerned with Samantha's whimsical attitude. This was not a game, the seriousness couldn't be overstated. "This is not a game, nor is it high-tech stuff, Senator. It doesn't get much lower tech than this. All this is is a shell game. When someone knows how the game works, hiding the pea from them is not as easy. The people you folks are trying to hide the pea from have seen this game before. Remember that."

Samantha felt another swell of emotion. For the second time in as many hours she had been chastised. Of course this is not a game! Of course it is serious business! She didn't need to be told that. Where did he get off talking to her like that!

"I understand it's not a game, Mr. McCrory", she shot back.

"I meant no disrespect. My people skills lack sometimes. My point was simply that you are attempting to play a game with the guys that invented it. You can never let your guard down. Your comment sounded like awe. If you are in awe you are not focused. That's all I was alluding to."

She knew he was right. She wasn't focused. Was it because she wasn't convinced of the need to do this kind of investigation? Or was she scared? Scared that she was in over her head? Everyone in the van was staring at her. She gathered herself.

"Okay", she said calmly. "If Alex is compromised, what are our options?"

Chuck reached into a satchel and pulled out two more cell phones. He passed one to each of them. Alexandra already had hers. "Gavin and I have worked out a plan for just such an event. If any of you believe you have been detected, use this phone to contact me. I may not answer, but you can leave a message and I will get back to you as soon as I have a plan of action."

"How long will that take?" Samantha asked.

"Minutes to hours", he replied.

CHAPTER 9

Alexandra parked her car on the third floor of the parking garage and took the elevator up to the fifth floor where Chuck had arranged a parking space for the Techie van. He had given her several pieces of advice for approaching the van, including instructions for losing a tail if she felt she was being followed from her apartment. While all good advice, truthfully, it was useless against professionals. But, he knew it would make her less paranoid and more cautious. Some precaution is better than none.

Today she was driving to a coffee shop in Silver Spring where she planned to do some in-depth research into the workings of the Crimson Hook container terminal where the Afghan shipping containers had gone missing. She parked under a shady oak, pulled the green hard drive from its mount, and went into the coffee shop to get a latte and a scone. Back at the van, she surveyed her surroundings then quickly entered the side door.

Alexandra was amazed and happy that her mobile office was so comfortable. The captain's chair was perfect for long hours of effort. It reclined and swiveled, the arm rests were adjustable, and a wireless keyboard allowed her to lean back and put her feet up when the mood struck. Chuck certainly knew what he was doing when he designed the work space. She brought up TOR and began to search for articles containing all the key words: Crimson Hook, heroin, shipping container, theft.

A few links showed up, some police blotter stuff, some ads for the terminal's services, a few news reports about DEA and NYPD busts at the docks -- nothing of great interest until page seven. A link to a short article in the Lakeville Press, a small Connecticut newspaper, titled "Lakeville man busted for heroin possession - says government agents set him up" caught her eye.

> "Leonard Loman of East Lakeville, Connecticut, was arrested
> on Saturday, allegedly in possession of an unspecified amount of
> heroin found in a shipping container stored in the field of a small

farm off Lime Rock Road. Sheriff's authorities haven't released the exact location of the bust nor how much heroin Loman had in his possession. But eyewitnesses say the amount appeared significant. Loman alleges government agents asked him to help with an on-going drug theft investigation, to which he agreed, but abandoned him when local law enforcement caught him checking on the security of the container holding the government's drugs. Sheriff Rick Staples stated that Loman was remanded to federal authorities on Tuesday. His office is no longer actively working the case. Loman's current whereabouts are unknown."

Alexandra stared at the article with intense interest wondering why it had showed up in her search results when she specifically asked for Crimson Hook references which apparently didn't exist in the article. Then it hit her. She clicked on the little green arrow, a link to the cached text of the original post. There, in the first sentence, was the original text,

"...found in a Crimson Hook Terminals shipping container stored in the field..."

Someone had edited the article and removed the Crimson Hook reference. But why? The cached version also contained the reporter's name, Jeremy Ballard. She searched the paper's website for the reporter's contact information. There was no mention of him. She wrote down the phone number of the news room editor and debated calling. But something told her it wasn't a good idea. Instead, she called Uncle Chuck.

* * *

Alexandra hadn't contemplated needing an anonymous way of communicating with potential informants. But her conversation with Chuck about the advisability of openly calling the editor of the Lakeville Press, to which he had staunchly objected, opened her eyes to a whole world she didn't know existed. She was aware of some social chatting apps that claimed to delete your communication once it was read. Their claims, however, were dubious at best, and outright dangerous to rely on at worst.

Chuck helped her set up an online dropbox for uploading and sharing files anonymously, and an anonymous email account to use for communicating with anyone with whom she would rather not divulge her identity. Both systems used encryption technology, meaning no one except the sender and the receiver could see the contents of the shared information.

The encryption method was old school but still amazingly effective. It had been developed by a computer scientist named Phil Zimmermann in 1991. He called it PGP, an acronym for 'Pretty Good Privacy'. But in reality, it was more than pretty good. Even the most sophisticated agencies, like the NSA and CIA, found it extremely difficult, more often than not, impossible to crack. Chuck explained to Alexandra that PGP didn't just encrypt a message, it authenticated the sender and verified the integrity of the data when it arrived. If anyone tampered with the information along the way, PGP would know and warn the recipient. If it wasn't sent by the person claiming to have sent it, PGP would know and warn the recipient.

Now Alexandra had a way to contact the Lakeville Press without telling them who she was. The next morning she fired off an email to the paper's editor, or whoever was monitoring the editor's email box, asking to talk with the author of the article about the drug bust of Leonard Loman. Within minutes she received a reply. It said only: "The reporter you are seeking is no longer employed here."

Okay. So where is he employed? She figured she would get more than that. She sent another message: "Can you put me in touch with him?" A few minutes later the reply shocked her: "I'm sorry, that won't be possible. Mr. Ballard is dead. He was killed in a car accident in New York City."

Alexandra leaned back from her computer terminal and took a deep breath. Maybe the accident was really an accident. But maybe it wasn't! The fact that the article had been modified was unsettling. Had Ballard modified it? Or someone else? She sent another message: "Can you tell me the circumstances surrounding Mr. Ballard's accident? Also, can you share any files or information he may have collected while working on this story?"

She included the link address to her anonymous dropbox with instructions for uploading to it. She included her PGP public key, a code phrase for the sender to use to encrypt any files uploaded to her dropbox, ensuring that only she would be able to read them. Almost instantly she received a reply: "I've shared as much as I'm comfortable with an anonymous contact. I have nothing further to say."

Somehow Alexandra knew there had to be more to this story than an edited article and a random car accident. Was the article edited before or after Ballard's demise? Was the newspaper aware that the article had been edited? She had to know. One last email: "Are you aware the article on your website has been edited, removing previous references to Crimson Hook Terminals and Mr. Ballard's name?" It was several hours before she received a reply. It simply said: "I was not aware. Crimson Hook is where Jeremy died. Check your dropbox."

Chuck had always told her, "There is no such thing as coincidence", and there were just too many coincidences in this story. References to Crimson Hook Terminals are mentioned then removed from an article about a drug bust written by a reporter who turns up dead near the same terminal a week later. Afghan shipping containers go missing from the terminal just before spikes in drug deaths, overdoses, street quantities, and busts. She was beginning to smell the odor of a small bucktooth rodent. No such thing as coincidence.

∗ ∗ ∗

Crimson Hook Terminals was a busy New York Harbor cargo operator and stevedore business which handled freight from all over the world. Alexandra found nothing suspicious about the Brooklyn-based company that would set off red flags in the death of Jeremy Ballard. So why had Ballard been killed there?

The dropbox files she had been sent by the Lakeville Press editor contained a police report and some photos of the accident. Ballard hadn't actually been killed on the terminal's property, but rather on a public road near the terminal entrance. The accident had been a head-on collision with a large 18-wheel container truck, supposedly driven by an illegal dock worker who ran from the scene and was never apprehended. More mysterious coincidence.

Adding to the mystery, the dropbox contained a copy of a set of hand-written notes with several references to missing manifests and the words "Green Valley" circled boldly multiple times. There was also a copy of a report by a New York Times investigative reporter whose article claimed that a drug bust by the NYPD was being covered up and the seized drug evidence never made it to the department's property section. The reporter didn't specify who was covering it up, but speculated either the DEA, Customs, or the FBI was involved. A call to the Times revealed the reporter, sadly, had a history of mental problems and later committed suicide. His story was dropped and never followed up.

Alexandra sat across from Gavin at a small barbeque joint in the Park View area near Edgewood where she kept the van. It was a warm July morning so they were sitting outside at one of the two tables on the sidewalk. Being a southern boy, Gavin loved good barbeque and had no problem getting his hands and face dirty on a short rack of pork ribs. She liked barbeque also but was a little more demure, preferring a knife and fork to Gavin's medieval methods. Her napkin got nowhere near the workout his did.

"Gavin, there's something there. I know it. But I've hit a dead end. There has to be a connection between the missing Crimson Hook containers, two dead journalists, and an NYPD cover up. I feel it in my bones."

"This is the best barbeque I've had since I've been in Washington!" Gavin proclaimed, talking with his mouth full. "How did you find this place?"

"Google", she replied. "Are you listening to me? There are dead people and missing drugs and I'm starting to get a little scared."

Gavin could see she was nervous. Her job was supposed to be data gathering and organizing, not an investigative probe into the underbelly of the drug world. That was more than he should have let her pursue.

"I don't want you going any further with this probe, Alex. I think we need to get some answers but it looks like professional experience is required. I've been thinking about your uncle. Would he be willing to help us? Would you be comfortable having him involved?"

Alexandra reached over and dipped her napkin into Gavin's water glass then began to rub the sauce out of a spot on the front his shirt. "You're hopeless. Why don't you eat like a civilized human being?"

Gavin took her hand and kissed it staring straight into her eyes. "I love you, Alex."

It wasn't the first time he had used the word, but there was something in his voice that assured her the words came from his heart. She could feel the tears slowly making rivulets down her cheeks. She smiled, "I love you, too, you messy person!"

He chuckled as she sat back and wiped away the tears with her napkin, then neatly folded and placed it next to her plate. "I don't know if he would be interested or not. He might. How would I feel? If he wants to do it I would feel good about it. I feel safe when he's around."

"So you'll call him?" Gavin solicited.

"Yes", she said. "This afternoon."

CHAPTER 10

On the 28th of July, 2016, a Washington, D.C., judge dismissed the charges against Ingmar Guandique, the convicted murderer of Chandra Levy, a 24 year old Bureau of Prisons intern from Modesto, California, who went missing in May 2001 and was found dead in Rock Creek Park outside Washington over a year later. The high-profile murder case was brought to national attention when it was discovered that Levy was having an affair with Gary Condit, a U.S. Congressman from her district in California. Condit was dismissed as a suspect early in the investigation of the case, but the negative notoriety cost him his re-election.

In 2009, Guandique, an illegal immigrant from El Salvador who had already spent time in prison for attacking two women in Rock Creek Park about the same time Levy went missing, was falsely convicted of her murder by the perjured testimony of a jail house snitch hired by federal prosecutors. He was granted a new trial in 2015, but when prosecutors had no evidence with which to retry him, he was released and deported to El Salvador.

"Levy's murderer has never been found", Samantha huffed, breathing hard from the uphill jaunt. She slowed to a stop and bent over putting her hands on her knees. "Probably never will. Let's take a break for a minute."

She and Kevin had jogged about two miles along the Western Ridge Trail and were near the location where Levy's remains had been discovered by a hiker and his dog out looking for turtles. Kevin was barely breathing, hardly breaking a sweat. Though he had had a desk job for the last seven years, he still ran 50 miles a week and prided himself on staying in 'fighting' shape. He motioned for Samantha to come sit next to him on a large, flat rock. "So, any chance Condit actually did it?"

"I don't think so", she judged still catching her breath. "They looked at him pretty hard back then. He had a rock-solid alibi for his time, but I think they believed he may have had her killed. Anyway, he lawyered up and refused to take a government-administered polygraph test. He had an independent examiner administer one and they claimed he was truthful. Down in that ravine over there is where they found her."

"You're not afraid to be alone in the park?" Kevin was curious why a sitting Senator felt so comfortable jogging by herself in a park with such a notorious reputation.

"Not that many people recognize me yet. I'm a first-termer so I can still fly under the radar most of the time. Right now, putting my hair in a pony tail and shoving it under a ball cap seems to be enough of a disguise. I'm sure there will come a time when I won't have that luxury. As for being assaulted or accosted, that can happen in front of the grocery store. I'm betting it's safer here than in the city."

"Do you come here much?" he inquired.

"More lately. I'm wrestling with some things Gavin and I are working on. Jogging helps me think, it centers me. There's something peaceful about this park, despite its reputation."

Kevin reached over and touched the underside of her chin, tugging her lips toward his. She put her hand on his cheek as they kissed. "What could possibly be bothering such a beautiful mind?"

"You wouldn't be interested", she averred. "Besides, it's not the work that's getting to me. I'm struggling with my own conscience. I find myself questioning principles I thought I had long ago set in stone."

"About what?" he asked.

"It seems silly when I talk about it. The legislation we're working on is about drug reform. Gavin wants to legalize all drugs. He believes it will stop the black marketing of drugs like the repeal of prohibition did to the black market for alcohol. He's of the opinion that legalization would eventually lead to fewer deaths and overdoses, lower healthcare costs, lower crime rates, addiction rates, more community involvement in prevention and rehabilitation, not to mention the cost savings of not putting users in jail."

"Yeah, we've talked about it. Gavin has always had a unique way of looking at the world. We busted a lot of drug dealers in Afghanistan. That he is pushing for legalization now is a one-eighty from the Gavin I knew back then."

Samantha shrugged. "I think what happened to his brother has changed him. He's convinced that his brother might still be alive if the law didn't make criminals out of addicts. Personally, I think the VA was more culpable than the law."

"So you're not convinced?"

"I thought I was", she admitted. "But my conscience keeps tugging at my objectivity. And our research seems to have taken a worrisome turn lately, some disturbing activity at Crimson Hook just adds to the stress of it all."

Red flags went up in Kevin's head. "What's a crimson hook?" he pumped delicately, trying not to appear overly interested as the first significant beads of sweat began to form on his brow.

"I can't really talk about it", she replied calmly, suddenly realizing she was talking to a man with ties to the CIA. Certainly Kevin couldn't be involved with anything sinister but the less said the better. She had already said too much. "Let's head back. I have a meeting at four o'clock, one I can't be late for."

Kevin stood up and wiped the sweat from his forehead with the sleeve of his shirt. "Then let's go", he urged, slapping her on the butt as she rose from the rock.

"That's no way to treat a Senator, Major!" she chided, attempting to slap him back in the same manner. He dodged her slap and laughed and danced in a circle around her, arms dangling at his side like Ali, floating like a butterfly. She gave up trying to make contact. He was too quick. She turned to jog back down the hill and felt his arms wrap around her from behind. He held her so tight she couldn't move, his strong arms pinning hers to her stomach. He kissed her on the neck and behind her ears, nibbling her ear lobes until she shivered with goose bumps. Then he let her loose, taking her gently by the hand and pulling her into a slow jog until their bodies were moving together in a synchronized rhythmic cadence. She was a little surprised and taken aback by his rough behavior but relieved he hadn't asked any more questions and glad he was apparently uninterested in her faux pas.

Kevin knew he couldn't dig any further right now. But he needed to know what she knew about Crimson Hook. The whole Green Valley operation depended on Crimson Hook, a potential single point failure. Maybe that's why Selbourne needed a second operation in Florida. Single point failures have a tendency to fail catastrophically. Until Florida could be made operational, he couldn't allow Crimson Hook to be compromised. He wouldn't allow Crimson Hook to be compromised.

* * *

Alexandra heard the ding of an incoming dropbox message on her computer. She hadn't communicated with anyone except the Lakeville Press editor. If there was something in her dropbox it had to have come from him, or her? She opened the box to reveal a folder titled 'Green Valley' and a note stating: "This is everything Jeremy had about Crimson Hook. You are the only person besides me that knows this exists. I don't know what to do with it. I am gambling you are trustworthy and that you can use it. Please do not try to contact me again. I cannot help you any further."

Alexandra closed the message and stared at the folder. Whoever sent it must have had an emotional connection to Jeremy Ballard, one strong enough that they were willing to risk everything, maybe even their life, to find out what happened to him. There was no way they could know who she was. They were gambling she wasn't the enemy, an act of desperation. But their bravery made her more determined than ever to get to the truth.

It was getting late in the day and Alexandra still hadn't called Uncle Chuck. Lunch with Gavin had been a wonderful reprieve from the loneliness of being trapped in a van by herself all day. At least when she was in the office she could walk over to the cafeteria or around the block to break the monotony. Her brain was fried for today. She decided to look at the folder in the morning. Right now, she would call Uncle Chuck and then head home.

* * *

Chuck McCrory didn't own much. After Vera died he had cleaned out his house in Tarpon Springs, keeping little that reminded him of the past. Vera had been the love of his life but had bore him no children due to a condition doctors called cervical stenosis. They had looked into intrauterine insemination and in vitro fertilization but she wasn't a candidate for either. In the end, they accepted that a child of their own wasn't an option and neither felt like adoption was right for their lives.

With Vera gone, it didn't make sense to keep living in a large house so he sold it and bought a small place on a canal. It was older, 1960s, with jalousie windows and a ballasted river-stone roof, but it was cheap and easy to maintain and relatively sequestered from nosey neighbors. Plus it had a dock with davits so he bought a small Boston Whaler and learned to fish.

Fishing was a great pastime. He could fish any time, day or night, plus he had a very good friend in the Florida Keys, a former military buddy, who also loved to fish and snorkel for lobster. Grady was every bit as good a friend as Christos but in a totally different way.

Grady White was five years his senior and had served in Vietnam, also a Green Beret. But Grady had been severely wounded by shrapnel, calling artillery fire in on himself to save his unit during a heavy firefight in Laos, a place his team wasn't supposed to be.

In the early days of the Vietnam War, reconnaissance teams used a scatter plan technique dubbed the 'quail tactic' when they would come in contact with superior enemy forces. Teams would disengage and disperse, rendezvousing later at a predetermined location. The tactic worked well during WWII and the Korean War. But it was not successful in the jungles of Southeast Asia against the North Vietnamese Army. It was eventually abandoned and replaced with a 'stingray' tactic where the unit would mutually concentrate their firepower to their rear as they attempted to rapidly escape while calling in artillery and air strike support behind them.

When the barrage was over Grady was missing and his team went back to look for him. He shot and killed the first man to locate him, believing him to be a Viet Cong soldier. His buddies never blamed him, but the guilt ate him from the inside and the shrapnel disabled him from the outside. Lieutenant Grady White, the only black soldier in his unit, never returned to duty and never received a medal for his courage and valor because he was officially never in the country where the firefight never happened.

Chuck met Grady at Walter Reed Army Medical Center in Bethesda, Maryland, in 1975. Chuck was there for a routine post-deployment physical and Grady was there for a psychological examination, which, if he passed, would get him sent home with a congratulations and thank you for your service.

Grady's physical wounds had long since healed, leaving him with a manageable but significant limp. But his invisible wounds never healed and he was being treated for what had historically been called "shell shock" in WWI and "battle fatigue" in WWII. In 1980 it would come be called PTSD, Post Traumatic Stress Disorder, but Grady's post-Vietnam War condition had no formal name and the treatment was poor, at best, however well-meant. He was eventually separated to fight his demons on his own.

It was in the cafeteria of the hospital that Chuck first met Grady, striking up a conversation with a fellow Green Beret. Grady shared his situation and told Chuck he planned to go to the Keys and be a beach bum when the Army cut him loose. The Army did and he did, living on a small disability payment that paid for his room and board and enough food to keep him amply sustained. Odd jobs earned him enough cash to be a regular at the local pub. Chuck came to visit many times over the years and the two became as close as battlefield buddies. Grady was not part of Chuck's Delta 5, but Chuck knew he could be counted on just as reliably, with one exception. Grady was repulsed by guns and never touched one after the Laos incident. The guilt of killing one of his own had given him recurring nightmares which had never gone away.

Grady eventually moved into a small duplex on the water. The building was old style Florida: flat roof, Miami windows and terrazzo floors. It had a window-shaker air conditioner but there was no such thing as air conditioning in the

Keys when the house was built in the 1950s. Most of the homes were constructed to take advantage of the morning and evening breezes to keep them cool. There was no breeze during the heat of the day. In the summer, doldrums settled over the keys and the water would become as flat as glass. Great for looking for lobster holes, not so great for sail boats stranded on the windless tides.

He had several landlords over the years. Today, he lived in one side of the duplex, his landlord, Muriel, in the other. He and Muriel had first met at the Tiki Pub down the street, an old watering hole on the bay side of the key overlooking the main channel. Lots of tourists passed through on their way to somewhere else. A few locals kept the place in business between waves of tourists. Grady was one of the regulars.

Grady was sipping on a Rum Runner one warm and lazy Saturday evening, something he had never drunk before but had decided to try just once, when Muriel and Agnes showed up on their way to Key West. The colorful concoction caught Muriel's eye and when she asked what he was drinking he pushed his glass toward her without a word. To the shock and chagrin of her friend, she took a sip. Muriel ordered one for herself and she and Grady spent the rest of the evening sipping umbrella drinks and sharing their histories while Agnes tried her best to fit into the conversation where she could.

Muriel had recently become a widow. Her husband of thirty-eight years had died suddenly of a heart attack only three weeks after retiring from one of the largest banks in Miami Beach. Muriel Goldman inherited their entire estate, including the 14-story apartment building where they had lived in the 6500 square foot penthouse.

Muriel had sold off everything, the apartment building being the last of the property to go. She had closed on its sale just days before, and she and Agnes were on a road trip, a trip to nowhere to think about nothing while doing as little as possible along the way. So far, the trip was right on schedule. Grady toasted her fortitude.

Grady could tell Muriel had once been quite beautiful. She was probably in her late fifties, best he could estimate, but she was well-preserved. She was average height, a few inches shorter than him, and on the thin side but definitely not skinny. She was dark, obviously a sun lover, with funny-looking eye sockets, lighter than the rest of her face from wearing sunglasses he assumed. Her makeup was fairly thick as was her New York accent. He could tell her thinning, white hair had been nicely coiffed earlier in the day, but now it looked like a lightly-used brillo pad. Still, her facial features were marvelous and he couldn't help staring at her constantly. This woman was out of his league, and he knew it, but he was happy to have been able to spend the last few hours with her. She was a wonderful conversationalist.

The trip was going so well, Muriel mentioned in passing, that she was thinking about trying to find an out-of-the-way place to stay for a month or two. Grady mentioned that the other side of his duplex was vacant and she was welcome to come take a look at his side if she wanted. At two o'clock in the morning she and Agnes were walking, more accurately, staggering, back to Grady's duplex where they all fell asleep, she and Agnes in his bed, he on the couch.

The following morning, at Grady's insistence, Muriel downed a vodka-laced can of V8 juice. Then she retrieved her car from the Tiki Pub and drove to the Key West Airport where she bought Agnes a ticket back to Miami. Muriel stayed Sunday night with Grady and Monday morning she contacted the owner offering him cash for the duplex. That afternoon she had her lawyer draft a check for $458,000 dollars. By Tuesday, noon, Grady had a new landlord.

Within a week Grady had new furniture and central air-conditioning. Muriel reduced his rent to a dollar a month in exchange for keeping the plants watered, the toilets working, and ensuring her two miniature Yorkshire Terriers, Winston and Sylvia, remained alive when she was away. So far, Grady had been able to accomplish his responsibilities without any major incidents.

Grady was excited because today his good friend Chuck was coming to visit. Lobster season had just opened and Grady had called him to come do some "tickling". Tickling lobster is a popular pastime in the shallow keys. There is a skill to it over and above being able to hold your breath for a minute or two. Grady made his own ticklers out of quarter inch aluminum rods cut to about three feet long with one end bent around to form a handle and the other bent so that about an inch of the rod created a ninety-degree spur, a tickle.

Lobsters like to hang around structure: rock holes, coral, and rocky crags and ledges. They back their way into their domiciles, facing outward, ever wary of the numerous creatures besides man that find them to be delicious, such as grouper, sharks, and moray eels. Florida lobsters aren't technically lobsters, though their hard exoskeleton resembles true lobsters. They are members of the crayfish family and, unfortunately for them, not very bright animals. A snorkeler with a hand net and a tickler can coax them out of their holes by pushing the tickler underneath them, turning the tickle end up and jiggling it behind them until they come out of their holes and turn around to see what manner of infestation has invaded their residence. It is not always a simple matter, but with practice a snorkeler can become adept at persuading lobster from their holes with a tickler in one hand and netting them with the other. Grady was something of an expert and Chuck was looking forward to a fresh lobster dinner.

Chuck had driven most of the day. It was a seven-and-a-half-hour drive from Tarpon Springs to Big Pine Key where Grady lived. He pulled into the driveway of Grady's duplex in the late afternoon and parked his 1962 metallic-blue Corvette next to Muriel's green 1986 Ford LTD Crown Victoria. Then he watched disgustedly as Fufu and Fifi, Chuck's sobriquets for Muriel's Yorkies, Winston and Sylvia, engaged in their usual greeting. The two bounded out of Muriel's apartment together, yapping with high-pitched attitudes and stopped as they approached the front of Chuck's car. Fifi stood up on her hind legs and performed continuous pirouettes, paws extended, still yapping, as Fufu raised his hind leg and signed his own personal signature on two of Chuck's tires. Then, the duo ran back into Muriel's place, Fufu strutting in the lead, Fifi prissily prancing behind him, until they disappeared from view.

Chuck got out and slammed his door. "God damn it! What the hell is wrong with those dogs?!"

"They like you!" came a reply from Grady's side of the duplex. "Not everyone is so warmly greeted."

"Son of a bitch, Grady! Don't they know this is a classic car? You don't piss on a classic!"

Grady ambled over on his gimp leg and handed Chuck a cold bottle of beer as the old friends hugged. "Leave that in the car, would ya?"

Chuck had forgotten to take his shoulder holster off. Grady had felt his gun as the two embraced.

"Sorry, my friend. No problem." Chuck removed his gun and put it in the glove compartment of his car before following Grady into his apartment. "How have you been, Grady?"

Grady continued walking through the apartment and out the back door into the rear yard. "Good", he said as he pointed to a camping chair next to a picnic table and a fire pit. Chuck sat down and Grady pulled up a plastic chair next to him as he extended his bottle toward Chuck's. "Nostrovia."

They clinked bottles. "Back at ya!" Chuck rejoined.

"I'm glad you could make it, man. It's been a while. I heard through the grapevine that Allie's up in Washington now."

"Yeah, she's working for a Senator up there. Seems like a decent guy. It appears they're dating. She seems happy."

"Boinkin' the boss?" Grady posed.

"Probably", Chuck concurred, adding "I know... don't say it".

Muriel came out of her apartment and waved at Chuck. He lifted his bottle, "You're lookin' more beautiful every time I see you, darlin'".

"Liar", she returned, and continued walking over to Grady's apartment. She was dressed only in a bathrobe and sandals carrying a small clutch with toiletries and a bath towel. She went inside and in a few moments Chuck could hear Grady's shower running. "She's showering at your place?" he asked.

"Technically, it's her place", Grady observed.

"You know what I mean! What's wrong with her shower?"

Grady appeared annoyed. "Are you the righteous police? Why do you care where she showers?"

Chuck smiled. "Ah hah! I have long suspected it!"

"Mind your own business!" Grady grinned.

Chuck looked around the back yard. It had changed since his last visit. A blue tarpaulin that Grady had hung between some palm trees to shade their conversation ring had been replaced by a king-sized bed sheet. Chuck looked up at the sheet, "What happened to the tarp?"

"It tore. I replaced it."

"With a sheet?"

"That's all I had", Grady shrugged.

"You can't afford a new one?" Chuck queried.

Grady shrugged again. "I'm on a fixed income."

"No. You're just a cheap bastard", Chuck laughed.

Muriel came out of Grady's apartment wearing only her bathrobe, the towel now wrapped around her head in a turban. Chuck noticed she was much more tan than he remembered. Grady pulled another plastic chair close and held it as Muriel came over and sat down. He pulled a beer from the ice chest for Muriel and opened it as she acknowledged his courteousness. "Thank you, dear".

"The tarp tore in the heavy winds yesterday", Muriel explained. "We put the sheet up this morning because you were coming. We're going to replace it with something more permanent eventually. Maybe we'll put a pavilion back here."

Chuck looked at Grady with a smirk. Grady just smiled.

Chuck couldn't help but notice that Muriel was no longer the up-tight, middle-aged socialite he had met a few years ago. To meet her today you would never suspect she was one of the wealthiest women in the Keys. She was relaxed, laid-back, and unpretentious to a fault, no doubt due to Grady's influence. "Life should be lived lazy" was Grady's motto. It appeared Muriel had adopted the philosophy well and easy.

The sun was beginning to set. The recycle bin was filling fast with empty bottles and their conversations had become more laugh-filled and bawdy the fuller the bin became. Muriel's robe kept falling open when she would lean forward to laugh but she didn't seem to mind. Sometimes she would re-wrap it herself, sometimes she let Grady help. Chuck was past the point of inebriated and thoroughly enjoyed the comedy duo.

"Looks like we're out of beer", Muriel noticed, as she raised the lid on the ice chest. "Should we make a beer run, sweetie?"

Chuck's phone rang and he pulled it out to see who was calling. He was in no shape to have a serious conversation but it was Allie and, as tight as he was, he felt like he had to answer.

"Hello, little Allie! To what do I owe this pleasure?" he slurred.

Alexandra recognized immediately that her uncle had been carousing with John Barleycorn. "If this is a bad time, Uncle Chuck, I can call back."

Chuck could tell from her tone that she was concerned about something. He sobered himself and covered the mouthpiece with his hand. "Excuse me for a minute, boys and girls, I have to take this call." He walked away from the group, took a deep breath and focused himself, "What's the matter, Allie?"

Alexandra explained the situation with the Leonard Loman article, Crimson Hook, and the mystery surrounding the Green Valley references. "Gavin would really like to hire you to help us Uncle Chuck. I think I'm in over my head."

Chuck knew that was an understatement. As impaired as he was he could sense that his goddaughter had stumbled onto something potentially perilous. It was impossible to say no to her request. The question was: was he putting himself in over his own head? "I'll come up in a couple days. We'll figure out what to do. If I can help, I will."

"Thank you, Uncle Chuck. I don't know what I would do without you. I really didn't want to drag you into all of this but neither Gavin nor I know anyone else we can trust."

"I understand. See you in a few days." Chuck hung up and walked back over to Grady.

"Allie alright?" Grady probed.

"She's fine", Chuck said. "Said to say Hi."

Grady knew Chuck well enough to know he wasn't being totally forthcoming. But he also knew him well enough not to pry. "We're out of beer. Me and Muriel are going to walk down to the pub and hang at the bar a while. She went inside for a minute, she'll be right back. You coming with us?"

"Absolutely!" Chuck agreed.

Chuck assumed Muriel had gone inside to get dressed before heading up the street but she returned still in her bathrobe and sandals, turban still affixed to her hair. "Sorry boys, I had to feed the dogs. Are we ready?"

In the distance they could hear a Bob Marley cover band working a pair of steel drums to 'Everything's Gonna Be Alright'. Grady and Muriel locked arms and headed toward the music doing a reggae two-step as they sang in harmony. Chuck lagged behind enjoying the show. He had no idea either of them could sing much less dance. Grady was pretty good for a guy with a gimp leg.

Muriel turned around, her robe falling open slightly as she grabbed the sashes and quickly re-tied them. "You should've been here Wednesday, Chuck. Buffett was here. Jimmy, not Warren."

CHAPTER 11

Cynthia Lockhart watched the digital display on her Honda CR-V flip to 4:30 a.m. as she pulled into the parking garage at the Russell Senate Office building. She had had a restless night, something unusual for her, and decided not to fight it. After waking Mike for the third time in three hours, coming into work seemed the sensible thing to do. Fighting insomnia had never been successful in the past, no reason to believe it would be any different this time.

As she turned the engine off and gathered her briefcase and purse, her private cell phone began to ring. She glanced to see a number she didn't recognize. Like many people in Washington, Cynthia carried both a personal and a business phone in order to keep her personal life as private as possible. If the caller had been anyone she knew their name should have come up on the screen. She let the call go to voicemail. No one she could think of would try to contact her at this hour. Besides, if it was important they would leave a message. She put the phone in her purse and made her way to her office.

As she set her belongings on her desk, the phone began to ring again. The number was from the same caller. No voicemail had been left the first call. She decided she wouldn't answer until she had had a cup of coffee. She let the call go to voicemail again.

It was a ten-minute round-trip to Monica's office. Monica always kept a K-cup coffee maker available stocked with pods of several brands of coffee and tea for anyone who stayed late or came in early. Cynthia liked Dunkin' Donuts the best, one cream, one sugar. When she returned to her office she heard her phone making the last ring of the third call since she had arrived. It appeared someone wanted to talk to her quite badly but didn't want to leave a message. She decided if the caller tried again, she would answer. She sat down at her desk and sipped on her coffee. Within minutes, her phone began to ring.

"Cynthia Lockhart", she answered in a matter-of-fact voice.

"Ms. Lockhart, this is Agent Smith with the CIA. It is my understanding you're the Chief of Staff to Senator Gavin Manson. Is that correct?"

Cynthia sensed immediately this was not Agent Smith and probably not the CIA. Her first instinct was to hang up but this was her private cell phone. Who was this? How did he get this number? She decided to play along. "Good morning, Agent Smith. Yes, I am Senator Manson's Chief of Staff. How may I help you?"

"You're smarter than I thought, Cynthia. I was expecting some resistance."

Cynthia felt a cold chill make its way down her spine. She could recognize potential trouble from the condescending tone of the caller. But it was too late to back up now.

"Not my style, Smith. State your business."

"I'll come right to the point. Someone from the Senator's office submitted a FOIA for information on CIA activity at Crimson Hook."

"So? That was months ago. As I remember, we received a notification that no records were responsive to our request. Obviously, that's false. Are you calling to inform us that you've now found some records, Agent?"

"On the contrary, Cynthia." The caller's voice was calm, deep, slow and deliberate. Cynthia suspected it may have been artificially disguised. "We've had indications that the Senator's investigations continue to include Crimson Hook. This is a courtesy call to inform him that it would be best for everyone involved if he curtailed any further probes into activities there until further notice."

Apparently, this was the CIA, or someone wanting her to believe it was the CIA. If it wasn't the CIA it was still someone with knowledge of the Senator's CIA FOIA requests.

"I'm not aware of any further investigation of the Crimson Hook terminals other than the initial FOIA. But I will inform the Senator of your concern."

"Warning, Cynthia, my warning. Not concern." Then the caller hung up.

Cynthia swiped the 'Call End' button on her phone and leaned back in her chair. Her heart was racing and her breathing had hastened. She took slow, deep breaths until it was back in control. It was obvious she wasn't aware of everything Samantha and Gavin were working on. Something they were doing prompted this call and if she was expected to be the liaison between Gavin and the CIA, he needed to keep her tighter in the loop.

But there was more to be concerned about. If this was the CIA, was she being watched? Did they know she was at work at 4:30 in the morning? Certainly, they had the capability to know. And now there was every reason to believe they were watching.

Cynthia flashed back to March 2016, when Wikileaks published more than 8,700 CIA whistleblower documents it called 'Vault 7'. The release revealed details of the CIA's global covert hacking programs, proof that the CIA was using weaponized exploits of Google Android and Apple products, Microsoft Windows, even Samsung TV's to spy on people, including people in the United States - a Constitutionally illegal act.

The exploits could turn on the cameras or microphones of anyone's phone or tablet anywhere in the world, even if the device was turned off. Using a device's Global Positioning Satellite capability, GPS, they could track the location of their targets as well. Perhaps that's how they knew she had come to work. She had to assume her phones had been hacked, which meant Gavin's devices likely were also, and who knows how many others on his staff.

Cynthia checked the clock. It was 5:02 a.m. Gavin wouldn't arrive until 7:30 or so. She needed to let him know about her conversation with the mysterious caller and her suspicions as soon as possible. But calling him on his phone was out of the question now. She gathered her briefcase and purse and headed back to her car.

*   *   *

Alexandra was both relieved and excited that her uncle had agreed to come to Washington to help her and Gavin look into the mystery of Jeremy Ballard's death. There were too many trails to follow and too few clues to solve the mystery herself. She wasn't a trained investigator. She couldn't go poking around Crimson Hook on her own. She knew she needed help and hoped the documents the Lakeville Press editor had left in her dropbox would add some clarity to the mystery.

Alexandra turned on the computer and adjusted the captain's chair. She opened the dropbox and clicked on the 'Green Valley' folder. The editor had said this was everything Jeremy Ballard had about his story on Leonard Loman. It wasn't much. The folder contained only three documents: a text memo with an address, a photocopy of a shipping container manifest from Crimson Hook, and a photo of the New York vehicle tag on a semi-trailer designed to transport shipping containers on land.

The address was in rural Massachusetts. She brought up a mapping program and used the satellite view to zoom into the area of the address. Once she found it, she zoomed further into street view and saw what appeared to be a hazardous waste transfer facility. The address was registered to a company called 'Green Valley Transfer and Storage'.

The satellite view of the ten-acre facility showed it was divided into three areas. One looked liked parking for about 10 large tractor-trailers lined up parallel to each other at an angle, like she had seen at rest stops along the Interstate highways. The second appeared to be stacks of containers, three, sometimes four containers high, and a crane, no doubt used to lift and move containers on and off trailer beds. The third area was a group of steel buildings, apparently warehouses and offices of some kind. Behind the buildings, bordering on a large wooded area along a railroad track, there was something funny-looking. It appeared to be several small shipping containers sitting on the ground, clustered haphazardly with tall grass and weeds growing around them as high as a man. From all appearances the containers hadn't been moved in some time.

It was likely the three documents in the folder were connected, it just wasn't clear how. Could the picture of the trailer tag have been taken at the facility? Or Crimson Hook? Perhaps the manifest was for a container that was brought there? Or maybe the Lakeville farm container? These were questions she would pose for Uncle Chuck when he arrived. In the mean time, she needed to call Gavin and tell him about the contents of the folder. She was about to call him when her cell phone rang.

"Hello?"

"Alex, it's me, Catherine." Catherine was her father's lawyer and closest confidant. She handled all of his business affairs and many of his personal ones. "Alex, honey, your dad died last night. The hospital said he had a heart attack. I am so sorry."

Alexandra lost her breath for a minute as she struggled to understand the news. Rarely was she overwhelmed by emotion but this news was devastating, completely unexpected. Her father was barely sixty. He couldn't be gone! He just couldn't!

She held herself together, trying to think through what she had just heard. "Oh, dear God. Oh, Catherine! I can't believe it!"

"I know, honey. It's a shock."

Alexandra knew Catherine must have been dragged out in the middle of the night. "How are you doing? Are you alright?"

"I'm fine, honey. I got the call from the hospital about 2:30 this morning. He had managed to call 911 but he was in cardiac arrest when paramedics got there. The paramedics said there was nothing they could do, it was quite massive. He never made it to the hospital, Alex. They said he died before they could get there."

Alexandra listened without responding for several moments. Catherine waited patiently then added, "They also said he probably went quickly, he didn't suffer long, if that's any consolation."

"It is, Catherine. Thank you. I can't believe it! He was so young." Tears began to flow more steadily as the realization of the news sank deeper. She reached for a tissue and tended to her eyes and makeup. "I'll catch a plane this afternoon", she said sniffling.

"Text me your flight number, sweetie. I'll pick you up."

"Thank you, Catherine. Thank you so much."

Alexandra hung up the phone. She leaned forward, her head in her hands, elbows leaning on the circular desk, and began to sob, deep convulsive sobs. She needed to call Gavin but she just couldn't right now. She would also need to let Uncle Chuck know. Her dad had always told her life wasn't fair. Until now, she hadn't truly understood what he meant.

When she was able, she drove the van back to the Edgewood parking lot. She removed the green hard drive and put it in her purse and replaced it with the red drive. She tried to call Gavin but got no answer. Then she drove her car back to her apartment and began making ready for the trip home.

* * *

Kevin drove up to the guard shack of the Green Valley Transfer and Storage facility. The young guard on duty asked for his identification and recorded his visit on the visitor's log: name, driver's license number, vehicle registration and time of day.

"Florida, huh? We don't get many visitors from Florida."

Kevin realized he hadn't yet transferred his driver's license or vehicle registration to Virginia because he planned to buy a new car. But he was amused by the guard's reaction.

"Oh, yeah? So how many do I make?"

"You're the first I seen, sir."

"Alright. Well, you keep countin'", Kevin laughed.

"Will do. The main office is to the right at the stop sign. Follow the road down to the last set of buildings and turn left. It'll be on your right. You can't miss it."

"Thanks", Kevin obliged, and made his way to the buildings where the young guard had told him to make a left turn. Colonel Selbourne had told him to skip the first left turn and proceed past the office buildings to a road leading behind the buildings, then left to the end of the drive where he would see a cluster of small shipping containers. As he approached the cluster, Kevin saw the Colonel waiting with another person. He parked and got out of the car.

"Major Falk, this is Dan Bemis. Bemis runs this place. He's the General Operations Manager."

Kevin shook hands with a man with a crushing handshake, a rotund and rather large fellow who could have been a lumberjack. "Good to meet you, Bemis."

"Likewise", Bemis returned.

Colonel Selbourne wasted no time. "Bemis is the only person I talk to here. He's the only person you'll talk to. Let's make that clear from the start."

"Yes sir", Kevin acknowledged.

Selbourne continued. "Major, this is where the rubber meets the road. This place was created to camouflage the movements of our Crimson Hook containers. Rest assured it is a legitimate business. It transfers and stores tens of thousands of tons of hazardous materials every year. Material flows in and out of here all day, every day. We meet all the requirements of the U.S. Department of Transportation's RCRA and our safety record is spotless, impeccable. Bemis sees to that."

Kevin looked at Bemis and gave an approving nod. Bemis nodded back.

The Colonel turned and began to walk toward the cluster of old rusted containers with weeds growing all around them. They were all small as shipping containers go, ten feet in length, about eight feet wide and tall. "If you ask anyone in any government agency whether Afghan heroin comes into the United States directly, they'll say 'no'. Why? Because we've trained them to say no. Where will they say it comes from, Major?"

Kevin felt like he was being tested. "Canada, sir?"

"That would be correct, Major. Canada. Much does come from Canada which has made it easy to convince the media to blame the Canucks, poor bastards. But most of it in the northeast comes from right here."

The Colonel had led Bemis and Kevin into the center of the cluster of containers where a small clearing opened up making visible a single set of container doors among the ring of container walls. He motioned to Bemis to unlock the doors.

Having opened the locks, Bemis backed away. The Colonel worked the handle and the latch on the right-hand door and pulled it firmly to swing it open with a loud creek and a groan from the hinges.

"Excellent!" the Colonel lauded as he peered inside.

Kevin moved to his right where he could get a better look inside. Bemis moved over to accommodate his view. "Whoa! I haven't seen this much shit since Afghanistan. What is this? Five tons? Six?"

"Six and a half", the Colonel affirmed. The Colonel looked at Bemis, "I assume this is going out tonight?"

Bemis acknowledged. "Affirmative. Vermont. Everything looks good so far. Of course, we won't have a rendezvous point until midnight but I've confirmed their truck is on the way down. ETA 1:00 a.m."

The Colonel nodded at Bemis, "Good", then he looked at Kevin. "No prearranged rendezvous locations, Major. We do it all by cell phone in real-time. GPS coordinates only. Their truck meets our truck in the middle of the night in the middle of nowhere, The Last Green Valley. The transfer takes less than thirty seconds. The vehicles just swap drivers."

"The Last Green Valley?" Kevin didn't know what that meant.

"Not familiar, huh?" the Colonel chuckled. "Well, neither was I, Major. There are 1,100 square miles that are still seventy-seven percent forests and farms running through south central Massachusetts and northwestern Connecticut. Small roads, a few small towns, but most importantly... no lights. Black as the ace of spades at night. Pilots say it's the last place on the east coast like it. Just a big black hole between Boston and New York."

Bemis spoke up for the first time. "So, no satellite images can be accidentally taken to compromise the exchange. Generally, no traffic to contend with that time of day. The drivers get out, swap trucks and go, less than thirty seconds to make the swap. If there's a vehicle following too close the drivers keep going then double back when it's clear. They have the option to exchange at an alternate location if they want."

"So, the customer's driver uses our truck?" Kevin wondered.

"Well, not exactly our truck, Major", the Colonel chuckled again. "Let's just say someone donates it, albeit unwillingly."

"And what about the money transfer?"

"Bitcoin", said Bemis. "Cash is trash these days. The funds are pure digital currency, anonymous and untraceable."

The Colonel closed the doors to the container and Bemis locked them. "Any more questions, Major?"

"None, sir." Kevin followed the Colonel out of the container cluster and back to his car. "This was helpful, Colonel. I have some wheels spinning already for the Florida operation. The team is headed down there now to scout out potential locations. We don't have anything quite as large as The Last Green Valley, but there is an area southeast of Tampa that looks promising. Not much there but farmland, orange groves, swamps, and fish farms."

"This area got a name?" the Colonel wondered.

"Wimauma."

"Never heard of it, Major." The Colonel was surprised there was an area of Florida of which he wasn't aware.

"Not many people have, Colonel. We plan to be able to access the location by land and water. We can bring shipments up the Little Manatee River from Tampa Bay, or down I-75."

"Sounds good, Major. Then I'll let you get back to work. Keep me posted." Colonel Selbourne smiled. It was an unusual occurrence and one that didn't go unnoticed as Kevin shook the Colonel's hand.

Kevin got into his car and returned the way he had come to the guard shack and the exit to the facility. His meeting with the Colonel had gone exceptionally well and he was looking forward to getting back to Virginia and finishing the assembly of his Florida team.

The young guard at the shack nodded and opened the exit gate as he waved Kevin through with a small hand gesture. He noted the time of the visitor's departure onto the log sheet on his clipboard and wondered, briefly, why the man from Florida had parked behind the office building instead of the main parking area. Some people just can't follow directions.

* * *

Cynthia entered Gavin's office where Monica greeted her with a broad smile. "Buenos dias, Cynthia."

"Buenos dias, Monica. Is he in? It's urgent." Cynthia tried hard not to show how nervous she was. By saying her business was urgent she hoped it would prevent Monica from asking any personal questions or starting a lengthy conversation.

"Yes, you may go right in", Monica gestured.

"Gracias!" Cynthia forced a smile and entered Gavin's door.

"Good morning, Chief! You're here early", Gavin said with a smile. "The sky must be falling. Have a seat." He motioned at one of the chairs in front of his desk.

"Thank you", she said, but remained standing. She pulled a notepad from her purse and wrote on the pad "Follow me!! Urgent! Say nothing." Gavin was shocked and confused but obeyed.

Cynthia led the way through Monica's office gesturing to Monica with a finger to her lips to be quiet. Gavin followed her down the hall to an exit door then outside and across the street to a small park area near the parking guard's entrance. Once they were alone Cynthia again pulled the notepad from her purse and wrote "Give me your cell phones". She presented him with a pouch to put them in and when he had done so and sealed the pouch she started to tell him of her earlier phone call.

"Gavin, I think our phones have been bugged by the CIA. This pouch is a little Faraday cage that will block any signals to or from the phones. I'm pretty sure they're trying to listen."

"I'm not surprised. But what gives you that idea?" he asked.

"I received a call this morning from Agent Smith who identified himself as CIA."

"Agent Smith, huh?" he laughed.

"Gavin, somehow he knows you're doing an investigation into something at Crimson Hook. He told me to 'warn you', those are his words, to stop snooping around there."

"Did he say what would happen if I didn't?"

"No", Cynthia said, "but he was insistent and mentioned that he knew you were still probing even after the denied FOIA request. Have you continued probing there?"

Gavin struggled to understand how the CIA could know that Crimson Hook was still on his radar. Alexandra was the only person looking into Crimson Hook. Could her operation have been compromised? Even after all the effort they had put into camouflaging her surveillance?

"Yes", he told her. "Alex is still investigating. But she's in over her head. I'm bringing in somebody to help but he's not here yet." Gavin was reluctant to tell her that Chuck was the investigator. He didn't like hiding information from his Chief of Staff but this development meant she was under scrutiny. The less she knew the less she could divulge.

"What do you mean 'in over her head'?" Cynthia wanted to know.

Gavin filled her in on the disappearance of Leonard Loman, the death of Jeremy Ballard, the altered newspaper article and the connection to Crimson Hook.

"Do you think they may have found out about Alex and the van?" Cynthia wondered.

Gavin shook his head. "I can't imagine how. She's as solid as a rock when it comes to protocol. Got that from Chuck probably. Even if they've followed her she's working one hundred percent encrypted." Gavin was eliminating all the possible leaks in his mind. The only person left was Samantha. But how could that be? He would have to speak with her later.

"I can keep this pouch?" Gavin assumed.

"Yes", Cynthia confirmed. "Here are more for Alex and Sam." She handed him a small stack of pouches. "You may want to back Alex off until we can understand more about what we're up against."

"I think you're right", he concurred. "I need to contact Alex asap and have her take some time away. We'll see what the investigator thinks when he gets here. I'm supposed to meet with them this morning."

Cynthia left the park first and walked back across the street toward the parking garage. Gavin removed his phones from the pouch and ambled back across the street to his office, checking his phone messages as he walked. One had just come in from Alexandra, another from Chuck. 'Good timing' he thought. He dialed Alexandra's number first and called her back.

* * *

Chuck McCrory lifted the cabin window shade of the Boeing 737 to feel the sun maul his face like an angry cat. He had just landed at Baltimore Washington International on Southwest flight 580, an early morning nonstop from Tampa International. He had read somewhere recently that hangovers became less painful the older you got. Bullshit! And damn Grady! And damn Muriel, too! Rum runners, beer, and margaritas for two days straight. How in the hell did they do it?

It was a little after 8:00 a.m. as he departed the terminal and made his way to the car rental desk. He was supposed to meet Alexandra and Gavin at her apartment at 10:00 a.m. His newly revised plan was to check into the hotel early and get some sleep before meeting them. He was about to call her when his phone rang. It was Alexandra calling him.

"Talk slow, Allie", he answered.

"Uncle Chuck", Alexandra managed through tears that told him something awful had happened. "Dad's gone. He died this morning, a massive heart attack."

"Oh, Allie. I am so sorry. I'm at BWI now. Are you at home?"

"Yes", she said.

"I'll be right there, honey. I'll be right there."

"Thank you, Uncle Chuck."

Suddenly Chuck's hangover was the least of his problems. He should have asked her if she had called Gavin yet. He decided to call Gavin himself and cancel their meeting. He dialed Gavin's number but it went straight to voicemail.

* * *

When Chuck arrived at Alexandra's apartment Gavin answered the door. Alexandra was sitting on the couch gently weeping, her eyes puffy from the ordeal. She rose as Chuck approached and hugged him with all her might. He was all the family she had in the States now. Everyone else was in Greece.

Chuck could tell Alexandra was obviously glad to have Gavin there. Gavin appeared to be both a comfort and a source of strength for her. He found himself liking the man more every time he met him. Chuck always felt he was good at reading people and what he read in Gavin made him comfortable.

"I have a plane to Tampa booked for this afternoon", she told Chuck.

"Good", he said. "How are you getting to Tarpon?"

"Catherine", she replied.

Chuck nodded.

"Is Catherine making the arrangements for the flight to Greece?" Chuck asked.

"Greece?" Gavin was surprised.

"I'm sorry, honey. I forgot to tell you. My Dad wanted to be buried with my Mom in Igoumenitsa. I have to take him there. I shouldn't be gone more than a week."

"No, no, no!" Gavin urged. "Take all the time you need. In fact, take some time off and visit with your family for a couple of weeks. Decompress. The work will still be here when you get back."

"Thank you", she said as she hugged him appreciatively.

With this turn of events, Gavin decided he wasn't going to tell her, yet, about Cynthia's phone call. She had enough to worry about and he had planned to pull her away from the investigation anyway. In the interim, maybe he and Chuck could figure out what the hell was going on and just how seriously to take Cynthia's mysterious call.

Alexandra went into the bedroom to finish packing. Gavin pulled Chuck out of earshot. "We need to talk as soon as possible. Will you be going back with her this afternoon?"

Chuck hadn't really thought that far ahead. "No, I don't think so. She has Catherine. Catherine can handle a situation like this better than I can. I'll call tomorrow and see if there's anything I can help with down there. But I doubt it."

"Then can you meet me at a little pub in Edgewood around 5:00 p.m.?" Gavin asked.

"Sure." Chuck calculated the amount of sleep he might be able to get between now and then. "Can we make it 6:00?"

"Not a problem", Gavin nodded. "I'll take Alex to the airport if you want. Give you time to get checked into your hotel and get some rest. By the way, you look like shit."

"Thanks", Chuck responded.

Alexandra came out of the bedroom pulling a rolling suitcase and carrying a back pack and a medium-sized hand bag. Both men rushed to help with the suitcase. Chuck quickly deferred to Gavin. It hurt to move that fast in his condition and younger men should do that kind of work anyway.

Alexandra had composed herself and she was feeling much better. For the first time she noticed the shape her uncle was in. "Uncle Chuck, would you like to stay here instead of the hotel?"

"You have a kind soul, sweetheart", Chuck said as he hugged her. "Tell Catherine to call me if there's anything I can do. I'll be down in a day or two to pay my respects to your dad. I'm gonna miss him, Allie."

"I know", she said. "We all will."

Gavin opened the door to exit Alexandra's apartment, pulling her suitcase with him. He turned to Alexandra, "I called Cynthia and told her about your dad. She wanted to accompany you to Greece. She'll meet you at the airport."

"You don't need her here?" Alexandra knew Cynthia was an integral part of Gavin's everyday business. "I can manage by myself. I really can."

"Nothing to discuss", he asserted. "I can manage by myself, too."

"Oh, here", Alexandra handed Chuck the hard drive from the van. "You need to look at the Green Valley folder in the dropbox."

Chuck took the drive and gave her a final hug before the door closed then went into the guest bedroom, removed his shoes, and stretched out on the bed. His head had begun to pound again and he was looking forward to the quiet. As he closed his eyes he heard an annoying motor purring not far away. He raised one eyelid to see Percy staring at him from the other pillow. He rolled over to face the other way, fluffing his pillow until it was as comfortable as he could get it.

"Shut up, Percy!"

CHAPTER 12

It was early afternoon on a dry but overcast day as Gavin pulled into the parking lot of the Beltway Gym, turned off the engine to his car, and sat in reflective silence assessing the situation into which he had put himself and his staff. Were they in any real danger? If so, what should he do to protect them? How should he proceed? He wasn't going to stop investigating and he wasn't going to be intimidated. Still, he needed to go forward with caution. He only knew one person who might know whether Cynthia's early morning phone call from the CIA was cause for alarm and could help him measure the risk if it was. Kevin would be here momentarily and Gavin was anxious to see if his old friend could give him any insight into how deeply his probing might have annoyed the powers that be.

Alexandra had been gone for four days and he missed her terribly. It was a strange new feeling and one that he wished he could shake. It messed with his focus. But the meeting he had with Chuck the day she left had been very positive and he felt much better now that Chuck was involved.

He also felt better knowing that Alexandra was doing better and had finished planning the itinerary for her trip to Greece to bury her father. She would be staying with her grandmother, her father's mother, who she called Yia Yia Illiana, and her Uncle Demetri, her father's older brother who lived with her grandmother. Gavin had never met Alexandra's father, Christos, and he regretted the fact.

After reviewing the information on Alexandra's hard drive, Chuck had suggested to Gavin that the perusal of Crimson Hook and the surrounding area was the most prudent and efficient way to begin investigating. Then he would move on to the Green Valley Transfer and Storage facility to see if he could learn anything there. Gavin agreed. Chuck was a secret weapon he knew he could keep under wraps. Only he and Alexandra knew that Chuck was onboard. And he planned to keep it that way.

Kevin arrived in his new Ford Mustang, barely a week old, a 5.0-liter V8 with 435 horses mightily straining to be let loose. Somehow Kevin had, so far, avoided a speeding ticket, perhaps by sheer luck, perhaps through law enforcement connections, but, Gavin was fairly sure, not because of any carefully self-imposed responsible driving habits. Kevin pulled up next to Gavin and revved the engine then shut it down and got out.

The two converged at the trunks of their cars where they shook hands with an urban grip and a shoulder hug. "I'm glad you called", Kevin said, as he removed his gym bag from the trunk. "We haven't worked out together since Afghanistan!"

"Glad you could make it", Gavin replied as he grabbed his bag and followed Kevin toward the gym entrance. "Nice ride."

"Always wanted one", Kevin beamed.

Gavin worried that if he started interrogating Kevin too quickly he might clam up. Better to let the endorphins kick in a while before pumping him for any information. "It's been a long time, my man. Should be fun if you can still keep up."

Kevin laughed and held the door as Gavin entered. "You're doing standup now. That's nice." Kevin knew there was more to this get-together than iron reps and sit ups. He was curious what his old buddy wanted, but he was also pretty sure he already knew what it was.

Gavin decided not to broach the subject of Crimson Hook or Cynthia's call during the hour and fifteen minutes the two worked out. It never felt right and it occurred to him that a conversation over a beer might prove more productive. Kevin wasn't surprised when Gavin eventually suggested, "I want to talk to you about something. Have you got time to get a beer across the street?"

"Sure. Just one though. I've got to get back to Langley this afternoon."

"One it is", Gavin accepted, as he held the door this time.

They stowed their gear back in their cars and moseyed across the road to the small Irish pub which was nearly empty after the lunch crowd had cleared out. As they entered, the female bartender pointed to a row of high top tables along the window in the front of the place. Gavin shook his head and pointed to a solitary table in the rear. She nodded and he and Kevin sat down as she came over and took their orders. Both men knew why they were there, although Gavin was not aware of Kevin's encounter with Samantha at Rock Creek Park.

"So, Sam keeps telling me what a gem you are", Gavin began. "How serious are you guys?"

Kevin smiled, lifted his glass and saluted his workout mate. "I owe you, man. She's crazy fun to be with. Feisty, but I can deal with that. She may be too smart for me, though. That woman's brain never shuts down."

"No it doesn't", Gavin affirmed. He shifted his chair back and smiled. "I'm happy for you guys. She seems quite enamored with you. Personally, I don't see it", he grinned, "but I'm glad for you both."

Kevin poked the elephant first. "Gracias, amigo. But I'm pretty sure you didn't ask me here to talk about Sam. What's on your mind, Gavin?"

"Nope, you're right. I need some advice, or at least some direction."

"Well, this is a twist", Kevin mused. "I'm usually the one picking your brain."

"I'm going to come straight out with it. Someone called Cynthia a few days ago, called himself Smith from the CIA, and told her to warn me to back off my investigation of suspicious activities at Crimson Hook Terminals."

"And you want me to tell you what?" Kevin asked.

"I want to know why they would do that. Is that common practice? It was an outright threat, which tells me I'm on to something. You're the only person I know who might be able to help me find out what that's all about."

Kevin could feel his throat tightening. This conversation was becoming increasingly uncomfortable and he needed to be sure of his words. One misstep and he could put the Crimson Hook operation in jeopardy. But, he needed to know more about how much his buddy knew and just what he was looking for. "What is it you're investigating there? Why do you believe the CIA is involved?"

Gavin sensed the need to be cautious. "There are drug operations going on there. I know that for a fact from other agencies' reports, DEA, NYPD, FBI. My initial FOIA to the CIA came back unresponsive yet Cynthia gets a phone call from them warning me to back off? It's too fishy, Kevin. If they have information that may be useful to me, I want it. I don't think they have the right to tell me not to investigate without telling me why. But I don't want to put my staff at risk either. The CIA is supposed to gather foreign, not domestic intelligence. So why would they behave this way?"

"I don't know anything about the terminals, or any CIA involvement, myself. That's not what I do. It sounds like you don't really know if it even was the CIA. I mean, I might be able to find out something for you, ask a few questions. But you know the Company doesn't take kindly to its operators sticking their noses into places it hasn't authorized nose-sticking. Besides, Gavin, I'm Air Force, and loosely tethered at that."

"I'm sure that's true. But there's something going on there, Kevin, and your company's fingerprints are all over it."

"What do you suspect is going on there?" Kevin saw his opportunity to learn what Gavin thought he knew.

"I'm not sure. But I'm aware of criminal activity, including drug smuggling and a murder that's damned suspicious. If they're investigating the same things it would have to be for national security reasons, right? So why not just tell me that? Why the threats?" Gavin thought it prudent not to make it obvious he suspected the CIA itself of being the smugglers. "If you're not comfortable helping me, that's fine. Maybe you can find a name, somebody I can talk with, somebody with some answers. I'm going to figure this thing out eventually. I was just hoping you might be able to ask some questions in the right places, maybe shorten my learning curve."

Kevin now realized that his friend was not going to back off. The phone call he had made to Cynthia had not done its job. In fact, it may have made matters worse. He chugged the last of his beer and stood.

"Gotta go, buddy. Look, I'll see what I can find out. But I make you no promises. I'm not risking my career on someone's hunch... not even yours, man."

"I understand", Gavin replied. "Whatever you can do."

Kevin knew Gavin's tenaciousness all too well. Gavin would not be letting go of this until he was satisfied he had exhausted every possible lead from every possible angle. It would be difficult, but Kevin knew that somehow he had to throw Gavin off track. He needed to send him chasing off someplace else, someplace away from Crimson Hook Terminals, some place where wild geese run amok.

CHAPTER 13

It was his third visit to Selbourne's office in as many days and Kevin had begun to feel micro-managed. But something was different about today's meeting. The Colonel was not asking questions about his plan status or operational progress. He was lecturing, like an academy professor, on the history of the CIA.

Kevin could only guess what kind of a place the CIA was in the past. Most of the high-level functionaries he came in contact with seemed schizophrenic, trapped between the legacy of the agency's glory years of the Cold War era and its failed role as modern-age terrorist hunters more reliant on digital signal interception than face-to-face communication with recruited enemy assets. The agency's primary mission was still 'stealing secrets', but modern methodologies were changing rapidly and the old school ways no longer worked, a fact the old guard found difficult to understand and hard to accept.

But Kevin realized that wasn't true of his boss. Colonel Selbourne knew exactly what he wanted to accomplish and exactly how to get it done. He was technologically savvy and not intimidated by the rapidly changing world of digital innovation. And he recognized that Langley, Virginia was a changed place since the end of the Cold War. The culture inside the institute had been slow to adjust, slow to adapt to its new role as a global terror thwarting, terrorist-hunting machine rather than its former single-minded purpose - to stop the spread of Communism by recruiting Soviet assets. As a result, morale on the 258-acre compound had suffered greatly over the years.

The collapse of the Soviet Union had ruined everything for the old school operatives. They were lost yet they remained in power, in charge of a business they no longer understood. They needed desperately to learn how to adapt to a new and different enemy, one whose top-level command was impossible to infiltrate, impenetrable. Nor could this enemy be bribed with money or honey pot sex, and it had no vulnerabilities to exploit by historical means.

The CIA simply wasn't able to function in the modern era and, instead, resorted to a sterile but blunt sword, a pseudo-technological approach: provide intel to track and kill the enemy with drones and missiles; describe the technology as 'cutting edge' warfare; stress the 'surgical' accuracy of the strikes; and never admit that the collateral damage being inflicted on the civilian population was horrific and did nothing to win their hearts and minds.

The 1990's had nearly decimated the CIA. Still reeling from its failure to recognize the fall of the Soviet Union before it happened in 1989, the agency was immediately thrust into the most humiliating and embarrassing scandal of its existence. One of its own, Aldrich Hazen Ames, was arrested by the Federal Bureau of Investigation in February 1994, on charges of conspiracy to commit espionage on behalf of Russia and the former Soviet Union.

Ames's arrest prompted outrage and alarm across a fearful country. How could the agency have not noticed that an employee of 31 years, making less than $70,000 a year, had bought a Jaguar and a $540,000 house... with cash? By the time the internal investigation concluded, it was determined that Ames had taken nearly $2.5 million over eight years for the information he had provided the Russian KGB and its successor, the SVR.

The 52-year-old employee of the Directorate of Operations, the CIA's most elite command of clandestine operatives and agents, had exposed and thus caused the death or imprisonment of at least 45 confirmed, and perhaps hundreds, of Soviet Union sources for the CIA and the FBI. The exact number was impossible to estimate. Clearly, the Russians had been better at turning our guys than we had been at turning theirs.

It would get worse. September 11, 2001, a date picked by the enemy to be symbolic of the United States' use of 911 in an emergency, caught the agency completely off guard. Worse still, the CIA subsequently provided counterfeit intelligence accusing Iraq of having weapons of mass destruction, WMD's, "to justify the President's desire to go to war with Saddam Hussein." The war lasted over a decade, killed thousands of American and coalition soldiers and tens of thousands of innocent civilians. So it came as no surprise to anyone when the agency failed to recognize the approach of the Arab Spring movement across northern Africa and the Middle East in 2010 and 2011.

"We're damned near useless these days, Major, and more and more people are catching on. Hell, even the goddamned media is turning on us, questioning our credibility, our need to exist. I don't want to see this agency destroyed. And by God I plan to do everything in my power to restore it to its former greatness. If killing a few junkies along the way is necessary, then so be it."

Kevin felt a sense of pride that the Colonel was including him in his plans. "I should have Florida operational shortly, sir."

"Still no blow back from the Grogan debacle, Major?" The Colonel was concerned that U.S. Customs or the FBI might find a link to his dead men, his hired mercenaries on the TICA.

"No, sir. I think we're in the clear there. I spoke with Agent Sickles earlier this week. He said they plan to clear the boat for release to Grogan's relatives who plan to sell it. I haven't heard anything about a prolonged investigation. As far as I can tell, they've assumed that pirates tried unsuccessfully to hijack it. Our covers for the men held up. Fernandez's identity was the only one I worried about. As we hoped, since he was a Cuban national there was little investigation of his background. That worked out well. The two Hondurans were basically criminals to begin with. Their presence was no surprise. Fernandez's brother, well, let's just say the time he spent in a Panamanian prison helped solidify the impression they were a ragtag group of criminals."

"That's fine, Major. Good work."

"Thank you, Colonel." Kevin was pleased the Colonel was happy with his work. Praise had come sparsely in his life. Even small doses felt wonderful.

"So I gather Fernandez's decision to take Grogan's boat wouldn't have been your first choice?"

"Nor my second, third, or fourth, Colonel. The yacht was big enough to stow five maybe six tons, but then you have the problem of navigating in shallow waters to get to a distribution point. Just too much draft with that much weight on that boat. The shallower the areas you can negotiate the more options for emergency contingencies."

"And your solution?" Selbourne wondered.

"Multiple smaller boats, fast like Fernandez's boats. At least four or five per shipment, more if necessary. They'll carry at least a ton each." Kevin explained, "If one or two are caught, maybe the others get away. We don't lose everything. They'll have shallow drafts able to make it far enough upriver to reach the distribution compound we've built in Wimauma."

"What about the containers coming in from Afghanistan? How are you going to handle those?"

"I want to use ignorant accomplices to get the cargo to Tampa. We'll hire space on small coastal cargo ships working out of Crimson Hook, ones already moving containers south along the east coast. There are owners who ask no questions about the cargo their ship is hauling, more than enough of them if you pay them well. Most of them only service down to Miami but they'll go to Tampa if the money is right. If their ship is searched or seized, the owner won't know anything of our operation except for what's on the manifest. Plausible deniability. The manifest is legitimate. All the paperwork will be in order... except for a single bill of lading... ours."

"What about the crew?" Selbourne was concerned someone from the crew might become suspicious.

"The captain belongs to us. He hires the crew. That won't be a problem."

"Alright, walk me through an operation starting from Crimson Hook."

Kevin could see the interest in Selbourne's eyes. This was his first chance to explain his strategic plans to the Colonel. He was nervous but ready for this moment. The plan was fool-proof and he knew the Colonel would approve when he was done.

"When the Afghan container ship docks at Crimson Hook our crane man pulls it off the ship and drops it in the usual location. Our longshoremen will move it to the designated holding area. We have 36 hours before it will arouse any suspicion."

"So nothing new there. Same as our current process?"

"Correct, sir. The small cargo ship docks within that window and we load the container on it for the trip to Tampa."

"And what happens if the small ship can't get a berth on time?" The Colonel knew that smaller ships might not be given adequate priority by the dock master.

"That's possible", Kevin acknowledged. "But not likely. Should that happen, I can have a truck from Green Valley pick it up within two hours. We'll take it back there and let Bemis deal with it until we can get it re-manifested."

"Any chance we can own the dock master, Major?"

"Not a good idea, Colonel. He already has owners."

"Right. Proceed."

"We can't control the number of ports-of-call the ship makes. It could be as much as seven or eight days before it makes Tampa Bay. That's not a concern, however. Our recovery boats are ready, docked in various locations around the bay area. As the cargo vessel approaches, the recovery boats will go out to meet it."

"What do our small boats look like?" the Colonel asked.

Kevin had been impressed with the boats the pirates had used to try to highjack the TICA. "Fernandez's design was exceedingly impressive. It was also easy to duplicate. Twenty-eight-foot Contenders rigged like fishing boats with twin 250 Yamahas. We can put those together or have them repaired almost anywhere without question or suspicion. The additional fuel tanks give us plenty of range to meet the cargo ship well offshore in the Gulf of Mexico and still make it back into Tampa Bay and up the Little Manatee River to the house."

"The Wimauma compound?"

"Yes, sir. It's tucked away on a small tributary, a creek on a secluded part the river. There's plenty of dock space and a boat ramp for bringing the incoming boats ashore. We're building a large metal building on site where we can offload the merchandise from the boats and load the transfer trucks which will rendezvous with the buyers. I plan to use the same strategy you introduced to me at Green Valley - middle of the night, middle of nowhere. Wimauma is perfect for that."

Selbourne was beginning to see the whole picture more clearly and he liked what he was seeing. "So how do you get the container off the boat?"

"We don't", Kevin explained. "Not necessary. Our Yemeni and Pakistani sources ship in two kilo bricks but we can handle any size up to five kilos. Unfortunately, the shape of the bricks isn't always uniformed after transport, but I've come up with a drift bag which can hold fifty kilos of any configuration. It seals itself and floats just below the surface of the water, indefinitely. It's camouflaged to reflect the color of the water around it - hard to spot from the air. Each bag has a rechargeable five-kilometer transmitter that lasts a minimum of 72 hours. Somewhere between Naples and Fort Myers, a Contender will come alongside the cargo vessel and handoff enough drift bags with active transponders for the size of the shipment onboard. It takes one crew member approximately one minute to fill and seal a fifty-kilo bag and toss it overboard. We'll have four crew members offloading this shipment. At four bags per minute, a six ton shipment can be offloaded in about thirty minutes."

Kevin noticed the Colonel smiling. He knew his plan was meeting with the Colonel's expectations and approval. "How many Contenders does it take for, say, a six ton shipment, Major?"

"At roughly a ton per boat, maybe a few pounds more if the loads need to be adjusted, it would take six boats to ferry the cargo to the house."

"And what becomes of the empty container?" the Colonel wanted to know. He trusted the Major but at this stage he felt details were important.

"We'll poke holes in it, leave the doors open and jettison it somewhere west of Sarasota. It should sink quickly."

"Should or will, Major?"

"Will, sir. I've thought about veering outside the shipping lanes for the jettison just to give some extra time for the container to take on enough water. But that's a trade-off. It could look suspicious."

"Agreed", the Colonel nodded. "Use your best discretion there."

"Yes, sir."

"Back to the Contenders. How many drift bags per boat?"

"Eighteen to twenty. Each boat will have a specific frequency receiver for the transponders it's responsible for. Follow the signals to the bags, pull the bags into the boat and stow them. One man per boat. Once he's loaded his bags he'll head for the Skyway Bridge at the mouth of the bay. Each boat driver will have a GPS and a navigational chart in case the GPS fails. The operation will take place under the cover of darkness. If one boat gets stopped by the Marine Patrol or Coast Guard the others can move away."

"And how do they know where they're going, where the house is located?"

"They don't, Colonel. These are Fernandez's men, which is perfect. They know nothing of our operation. If they're caught they can't divulge what they don't know. We just use them to shuttle the bags to the river rendezvous point. They'll follow the main channel to 6D then head due east to the mouth of the Little Manatee."

"6D?" The Colonel shook his head.

"That's a main channel marker buoy, sir. From there they bear east and stay north of Little Cockroach Bay until they reach the river mouth. The river channel is clearly marked. They follow the river upstream to Devil's Elbow, about two klicks. Our men will meet them there. They'll be blindfolded for the rest of the trip upriver."

"Let me get this straight. You're going to bring them to the house?"

"Yes, sir."

"For how long, Major?"

"We'll detain them as they arrive, roughly ten or fifteen minutes apart. When they've all arrived, they'll be shuttled to a motel in Tampa where their blindfolds will be removed. We'll pay them and give them plane tickets to Puerto Rico. They'll be instructed to leave immediately."

"Impressive, Major! Very impressive." Colonel Selbourne had always prided himself on being able to spot talent. Major Kevin Falk was, by far, his best recruitment to date.

Kevin basked in his mentor's praise for a few moments but he knew he had to tell the Colonel about his meeting with Gavin at the Irish pub. It was a subject he had been avoiding, hoping to think of a way to deal with the situation himself, but he knew that was going to be impossible.

"One other thing, Colonel. Gavin Manson asked me to meet with him the other day. I did."

"The Senator? About what?"

"He's been poking around Crimson Hook. Something there has piqued his interest. I'm not exactly sure what. But he knows about the dead reporter. I'm confident he has no idea about our operations but I'm concerned he might inadvertently stumble on something that puts us in a difficult position."

The smile the Colonel had worn for the last hour had disappeared. Kevin noticed his brow furrowing, a sure indication of irritation. He knew this wasn't something the Colonel wanted to hear.

"Major, I'm sitting on a FOIA I can't ignore for long. The Senator's office submitted one several months ago that I sent back saying there were no responses to our records check. It was narrow enough I could get away with saying that."

"Yes, sir, I'm aware of that", Kevin noted.

The Colonel held up the request form and shook it violently in the air. "But this one came just yesterday. This one is much broader and asks for any records we have containing information about drug busts in which the CIA has been involved or, problematically for us, informed. That's a problem, Major, because the NYPD and the DEA has 'informed' us of every stolen container that came from the middle-east." The Colonel's voice grew louder. "Some of our containers are in that lot. If I respond I'll be handing him a goddamned shopping list for investigation."

Kevin knew this was a serious problem. "He's a bulldog, sir. He won't let go."

Selbourne stared straight into Kevin's eyes. He leaned forward across his desk, stretched out his arms and put his fingers over the front edge of the desk. Then he raised his right arm and slammed his hand hard upon the desk, still glaring at Kevin. "Then we need to eliminate this problem at the source. Will you have a problem with that solution, Major?"

Kevin felt a lightning bolt of terror overcome him. There was no mistaking the Colonel's meaning. There would be no negotiating other solutions. He was being forced to make a choice, literally a life and death choice. A choice between the most important and meaningful work he had ever done with a mentor who was like a father to him... and the best and closest friend he had ever had.

"Major?" the Colonel implored.

Kevin felt his heart racing, his palms sweating as he weighed the conflicting options in his mind, options with no alternatives.

"Major?" the Colonel's voice grew louder.

Suddenly, Kevin's mind went blank as if in a trance. Everything around him ceased to exist, just a circumferential blur. He could see the Colonel's face, his furrowed brow compressing, the veins in his neck throbbing and his lips moving noiselessly until suddenly... he came awake.

Colonel Selbourne was screaming at the top his lungs, standing over his desk looking down at Kevin, "Will you have a problem with that solution, Major?"

"No, sir", Kevin heard himself say. "No sir. That won't be a problem."

The Colonel sat back down in his chair, a look of relief and satisfaction on his face. He had been worried the Major's allegiances, his loyalties, might lie elsewhere. But the affirmation of the Major's commitment to the mission was affirmation of the man's judgment and of his own judgment. The Colonel knew precisely how tough the man's decision had been. This man was protégé material. The next step would be to see if and how his protégé would carry out his assignment.

CHAPTER 14

Gavin met Chuck at Alexandra's apartment. It was the safest place to meet since Chuck had swept it for bugs and cameras. There were plans to be worked out for the investigation of Crimson Hook and Gavin had to be brought up to speed on Alexandra's dropbox information from the Lakeville Press editor.

With the possibility that the CIA had tapped Gavin's phones, Chuck thought it necessary to be able to communicate with Gavin surreptitiously. He had brought Gavin a crypto phone but he could see that Gavin's eyes had glazed over as he was explaining how crypto-communication worked. Perhaps he had taken his explanation of Boltzmann's H-theorem and Shannon's concept of information entropy a tad too far.

"Suffice it to say these phones are virtually unhackable. As long as both of them are in crypto mode, no one, not even the most sophisticated agencies in the world, can eavesdrop on our communications."

Chuck's last statement brought Gavin back into a world he could realize. "Good to know. So how do we do this?" Gavin had used crypto phones in Afghanistan but these were different from the military phones with which he was familiar.

"When one of us initiates a call", Chuck handed one of the phones to Gavin and dialed its number. Gavin answered it as Chuck continued, "notice the numbers displayed when you answer. That's your 'session' key. We both have the same one. It's arbitrarily generated and it's only good for this call. You read me the numbers you see on your phone, I read you the numbers I see. If the numbers are the same we have a secure connection. If the numbers are different, someone is trying to interfere with the signal."

Gavin shook his head. "I'm carrying around four phones now. This is ridiculous!"

Chuck laughed. "Welcome to my world, son."

"Not for long, I hope." Gavin turned off his phone and put it in the breast pocket of his jacket. "So, how was your trip to Florida?" Chuck had flown back to Tarpon Springs to pay his respects to Christos and to see if he could be of any help to Alexandra and Catherine.

"Good, good. Allie's doing much better. She's even looking forward to the trip to Igoumenitsa. She hasn't seen her family there in several years."

"I'm almost having second thoughts about letting Cynthia go with her."

"Yeah? That was a nice gesture, Gav. She needed somebody for sure." Chuck was appreciative of Gavin's compassion and generosity.

"Well, it wasn't all that magnanimous. I thought you might decide to go with her if she didn't have company. I needed you here, Chuck."

"I figured as much. At least you're honest about it. I really didn't want to go anyway. I'm happy to wait until they have him settled into his final resting place before I make the trip."

Chuck got down to business. "I took a look at the hard drive Allie gave me when she left. Did she have time to tell you about it?"

"No. Anything of value?"

Chuck explained the contents of the dropbox and brought Gavin up to speed. There was little to go on except for a new location to check out. "This Green Valley Transfer and Storage looks interesting. I'm gonna have to pay them a visit. Not much to go on right now but the pieces are interesting enough to warrant checking it out."

Gavin reached into his briefcase and pulled out an expanding folder of papers a couple of inches thick. "This is what I have on Crimson Hook: police reports, newspaper articles, agency reports for the DEA, Customs, FBI, etc. Alex gathered most of this. These are originals, I'll need them back."

Chuck opened the folder and looked at the stack. "You've been through this?"

"Several times", Gavin replied. "Nothing sticks out to me. I'm a trained investigator. I thought for certain something would eventually click but I've got nothing. Maybe another set of eyes can spot something."

As Chuck thumbed through the pages, the NYPD police report on Jeremy Ballard's death caught his attention. "They never caught the driver of the semi that hit him?"

"Not that I've been able to determine. NYPD investigators claimed he was illegal and ran from the scene. They also claim they did a dragnet but came up with nothing. Media reports assume he probably left the country, for reasons that aren't clear to me. There's a CCTV photo from a traffic camera in there if you want to see what he looks like."

Chuck was already looking at the photo. It was grainy but clearly showed the side of the man's face and his left arm hanging out of the truck window. A fuzzy tattoo on the man's forearm caught Chuck's attention. He pointed it out to Gavin. "What do you see?"

"A tattoo?"

"Of what?" Chuck asked.

"Hard to tell. Maybe an eagle and a flag?"

"That's what I saw. What kind of flag?"

Gavin looked more closely. "Could be an American flag. Tough to make out."

Chuck pulled the photo back and looked at it again. "Why would an illegal alien have a tattoo of an American flag on his forearm?"

Gavin looked at Chuck. "You know how many times I've looked at that picture?"

"This guy's no alien and he hasn't left the country", Chuck asserted. "If he's around I'll find him."

Chuck gathered the papers back into the folder. "I'll look through these and see if anything else sticks out. Right now my plan is to start at Crimson Hook. I have a sixth sense about that place. Keep that phone near you at all times."

"Will do", Gavin said, then added, "One more thing Chuck."

Gavin shifted in his seat. Chuck could sense he was nervous about something.

"I never got to meet Christos. I had plans to go down there with Alex soon. While we were there I was going to ask him for her hand in marriage."

Chuck smiled. He could see what was coming and it warmed his heart. This was a good man.

"Christos would have approved, I'm sure, Gav. And you have my blessing. That's where you were going, wasn't it?"

"Yeah. Thanks, Chuck. I love her so much. I wish she wasn't involved in all of this."

"She's a big girl", Chuck grinned.

The two men stood and hugged then Gavin left the apartment. Chuck sauntered over to the kitchen island and retrieved the bottle of Scotch from the cabinet underneath. He poured a double shot then made his way to the easy chair and turned on the TV which began broadcasting a CNN news station. "Why does Allie watch this shit?" he mumbled. He flipped through the channels until an old rerun of Gilligan's Island caught his attention.

Percy playfully sidled over and leapt into his lap. It appeared the neighbors were feeding him well in Allie's absence. Chuck tugged the handle and the chair reclined as Percy wriggled his way into a comfortable position.

"Be still if you're gonna sit with me!"

CHAPTER 15

As her father had done with her mother, Alexandra had her father cremated for the long journey back to Greece. Cremation had been a difficult decision for Alexandra because the Greek Orthodox Church insisted the body of the deceased must be buried so that the natural physical process of decomposition may take place. Cremation, the Church believed, was the deliberate desecration and destruction of the human temple of the Holy Spirit. Unless the body was buried whole, resurrection was not possible.

When her mother, Helena, had died, Alexandra's father had talked to her about the Church's position and how difficult and burdensome it was on the poor, and even the middle class in Greece. The Greek government, in deference to the Church, had made cremation illegal until 2006 when public opinion eventually forced the government to change the law and allow crematoria to operate. But to date, no company had actually built one in Greece. The pressure from the Church, even on the business world, was very powerful. Those who wanted to have their loved ones cremated were forced to make the long and arduous journey to Bulgaria or Germany, a cost few could afford.

"Why not just bury her?" the eleven-year-old Alexandra had asked her father. "If that's what the Church wants?"

Her father explained that land is a valuable resource in Greece and that the state required the recycling of cemetery space. To purchase a permanent site could cost more than one hundred thousand U.S. dollars. Only an elite few could afford that. He could not.

Those that could afford to could rent a grave. But graves could only be rented long enough for the decomposition process to take place, a maximum of three years. By law, once that time was up, a relative had to appear at the gravesite to witness a cemetery worker dig up the grave of their loved one. The body, which was sometimes not fully decomposed, would be exhumed and pried from the coffin, the bones then collected into a shoe-box sized container and taken to a communal ossuary for storage.

Even ossuaries cost money. The rental fee was not nearly as expensive as a gravesite but the cost was still above the affordability of many. Those who could not afford the ossuary fee, or whose payments lapsed, suffered the indignity of having the remains of their loved ones transported and unceremoniously dumped into a mass grave where chemicals would be used to dissolve the remains into nothing.

"Hypocrisy!" her father would say. "The Church will condemn cremation but allow the desecration of disinterment. It makes no sense!"

Thus, there would be no religious ceremony, no church-sanctioned funeral for Alexandra's father, as there had been none for her mother. Her mother's ashes had been spread in the field behind the house of Alexandra's grandmother, Yia Yia Illiana, overlooking the blue waters of the beautiful harbor of Igoumenitsa. She planned to do the same for her father whose request was to join his wife there.

Alexandra and Cynthia's flight to Istanbul had left Dulles Airport at 11:00 p.m. They were able to sleep on the overnight flight, so the ten hour and fifteen-minute ride hadn't seemed terribly long when they landed at Istanbul's Ataturk Airport at 4:30 p.m. local time. But the three-hour layover and one-and-a-half-hour flight from Istanbul to Thessaloniki had finally worn them out. They checked into a hotel near the airport and the next morning rented a car for the final leg to Igoumenitsa.

Igoumenitsa was a bustling tourist mecca with many maritime ferries to other parts of Greece as well as the island of Corfu and several cities in Italy. With two large seaports, called simply the Old Port and the New Port, Igoumenitsa also supported passenger cruise lines and commercial shipping. With a new major highway traversing northern Greece, the town was a perfect starting point for tourists arriving from Europe and ending point for trucks carrying commercial goods for export from Turkey.

The three-and-a-half-hour ride from Thessaloniki had gone by quickly, each of the girls taking turns driving while the other marveled at the beautifully scenic views along the Egnatia Highway.

Alexandra pulled into the short driveway of Yia Yia Illiana's small house tucked neatly into a hillside just south of Igoumenitsa. It was just as she remembered it from ten years earlier - a simple white concrete and stucco home with a red-orange terracotta roof and black wrought iron fencing atop a stone wall which butted right up to the road and surrounded the front of the house. The narrow road sloped uphill and the top of the wall was level, so the wall got shorter as the road traversed upward. The ironwork was not that fancy but the finials on the vertical pickets were shaped like arrowheads and every other picket was twisted several turns giving the fence uncommon character. Growing behind the wall and in and among the fencing were dark pink and lavender bougainvillea, their thick bracts and beautiful bouquets hiding their prickly nature.

"This is so beautiful!" Cynthia exclaimed.

"I told you. I almost wish I lived here", Alexandra sighed. "I have no idea how I would make a living though. But look at this view of the water!"

The girls stepped out of the car and stretched themselves. Yia Yia Illiana's house faced west toward the gulf waters. The town's waterfront ports and long crescent-shaped shoreline could be seen for miles wandering northward encircling the most crystal blue water Cynthia had ever seen. "I'm speechless."

"To the north, up there", Alexandra pointed to a sandy-beach area visible for miles beyond the town's ports, "is a seven-kilometer long beach, Drapanos, the longest one in this region. From there you can see Corfu and watch the ferries entering and leaving the harbor."

"How old is this place?" Cynthia asked.

"It's not very old. The Germans all but destroyed it in 1944 during the period they occupied Greece. So most of the town was rebuilt in the fifties and sixties after the new ferry terminal was constructed."

"I guess I was expecting a fascinating tale about an ancient and courageous Greek civilization", Cynthia laughed.

"Oh, this place has history", Alexandra assured her. "In ancient times it was called Titani, around the fourth century BC. The Romans conquered and destroyed it in the second century. When the Roman Empire collapsed, all of Greece eventually fell under the rule of the Ottomans, around 1300. They controlled Greece until the Greek Revolution in the 1820s. That's when Greece gained its independence. Actually, that's when it became Greece. It was always called something else before that. The Ottomans called it Grava, I think."

Cynthia was curious. "How big was the city then compared to now?"

"I wouldn't call it a city. For years, this was just a small fishing village, maybe five hundred inhabitants. Even after the revolution, the Ottomans still controlled this area until the Balkan Wars. Igoumenitsa was liberated from the Ottomans during the wars in 1913. Today, I think the permanent population is about twenty-five thousand. I have no idea how many people are here when it's packed with tourists."

Cynthia had travelled little so far in her life. This was the most fascinating place she had ever visited.

"Alexandra! Come here and hug your Yia Yia Illiana!" Alexandra turned around to see Illiana making her way toward the girls, her arms outstretched, the fingers on her hands making 'come here' motions. Her grandmother was smiling broadly as she slowly ambled across the drive, her feet making dragging noises as she stepped. She could still get around well for a woman of eighty-seven but Alexandra could see that the years had begun to take their toll.

Cynthia found Illiana's clothing fascinatingly lovely. Her dress was a simple one-piece garment that buttoned all the way down the front. It had a small, round collar, a colorful ribbon of roses wrapped around her neck. The high-waisted dress was navy blue, the upper half resembling a blouse with medium length sleeves, the cuffs tipped with the same ribboning as the collar. The skirt on the lower half was pleated, hanging over her protruding belly, draping nearly to the floor. The same ribbon of roses adorned the skirt's hem. Her thinning gray hair was covered with a light gray kerchief, tied in the back, festooned with a piece of the same rose ribbon as her dress. She was adorable, Cynthia thought. She could have been a model for a Grecian travel guide.

"Yia Yia Illiana!" Alexandra raced to hug her grandmother, stretching her arms wide as well. The two women embraced mightily, hugging and kissing each other's cheeks with smacking mats-muts for what seemed like eternity to Cynthia. It was a comedic embrace, Alexandra nearly a foot taller than her short, stout grandmother. But Cynthia could see the heartfelt emotion and the evident need for each other's comfort and support.

"I've missed you, Yia Yia? How are you holding up?"

"My heart breaks, Alexandra. But you are here and you have brought my Christos. There are brighter days ahead, I know."

Alexandra hugged her grandmother tightly as they wept together. Illiana eventually released her embrace and wiped her tears.

"Who is your friend?" she asked.

"Oh, my goodness!" Alexandra gasped, realizing she had left Cynthia just standing there. "Yia Yia Illiana, this is my best friend in the whole world, Cynthia."

"Ah, of course. Alexandra has talked of you. Welcome! It is so nice to meet you."

Cynthia hugged Illiana and kissed cheeks. "Illiana, I am so sorry for your loss. It is nice to meet you, too. Alex has talked so much about you I feel like I know you already."

Illiana smiled. "Please, girls, come inside." She turned and slowly led the way toward the house.

Alexandra had been here before but Cynthia was awestruck by the beauty of Illiana's patio. On either side of the entrance to the patio, two large clay pots stood waist high. Each contained a broad-leafed tree six or seven feet high which she recognized as Sweet Bays or Grecian Laurels, the source of bay leaves for cooking. A long simple trellis hung over the patio and extended from the door of the house to the front wall she had seen as they pulled up to the driveway. The bougainvillea visible along the fencing on the street also weaved its branches in and out of the trellis rafters and battens creating a wonderfully shaded sitting area.

Beneath the trellis was a long table with a wrought iron base and a rectangular wooden top. Six wooden chairs with lavender colored cushions surrounded the table, two length-wise on each side and one on each end. Beyond the far end of the table, along the side wall, was a red settee made of cast iron with cushions that matched the colors of the bougainvilleas. There were other pots and plants and knickknacks carefully placed and arranged.

Cynthia had never seen anything like it. "Illiana, this is so gorgeous. I would never want to leave it!"

"I sit here more as I grow older", she confessed. "I have tender memories of rocking my little Christos in the crib his father made for him."

Alexandra could see tears forming in her grandmother's eyes as she reminisced. She went over and put her arm around her grandmother and kissed her on the forehead.

Illiana put her arm around Alexandra's waist. "No mother should ever have to bury a child."

"I know, Yia Yia", Alexandra said softly. "It's not fair."

* * *

Cynthia awoke to the smell of baking bread. She looked over at Alexandra who was still sleeping, curled up on her side with a pillow in her midsection, her mouth agape, lightly snoring. She smiled at the image she had seen many times as a child when the two of them would have sleepovers. It was a good feeling. She quietly sat up, put on her robe and slippers, and went looking for the source of the bakery.

"Good morning", she said as she stood at the door of the kitchen waiting to be invited in. Illiana had made a loaf of olive bread and was preparing a large bowl of fruit and berries. In the breakfast nook, a small table with two chairs was already populated with yogurt and honey, Kaseri cheese, Greek butter, and Mandarin orange marmalade. "It smells so wonderful!"

"Come in, come in!" Illiana pointed to the table. "Sit. Would you like coffee?"

"Please", Cynthia replied.

"How do you take it?"

"A little cream, one sugar, please."

Illiana brought the coffee to the table along with the bread loaf and fruit bowl which she put in the middle. "Alexandra is still sleeping?"

Cynthia nodded, "Yes", as she spooned some fruit into a small bowl of yogurt. "She was always a late sleeper when we were kids."

"Here, also", Illiana laughed.

Cynthia sliced some bread and smeared it with marmalade and butter. "Illiana! This is so good!"

"It is favorite of Demetri", she said. "Christos much more liked croissants. I made for him when he would come home. Christos was baker but he would say he liked more my cooking." Illiana smiled at the thought.

"So who is older?" Cynthia wanted to know. "Demetri or Christos?"

"Demetri by four years. You will meet him in afternoon when we spread ashes. Christos and Demetri were not so close when they were young. Demetri was gone always, sometimes in trouble. But when they grew older they become very close."

Alexandra stumbled into the kitchen rubbing the sleep from her eyes. "Smells good, Yia Yia. Ah, you have marmalade!"

"Especially for you, Alexandra. Sit, sit!" Illiana got up from the table and made a cup of coffee for Alexandra. "Your uncle is in town to make plaque for grave. We will place it next to your mother in the afternoon."

"That's wonderful! I know that would make Dad happy."

Illiana left the room and Cynthia took the opportunity to ask Alexandra about her uncle. "Your grandmother said your Uncle Demetri was in trouble a lot. But she didn't say how."

Alexandra thought briefly about how much to share. But Cynthia was her best friend and the two of them had no real secrets.

"When Demetri was younger, in his thirties, I think, he used to work for the Mafia in Sicily."

"A Greek working for the Mafia?" Cynthia was a little surprised.

Alexandra looked around for her grandmother who was nowhere in sight. "Obviously, he wasn't family to them. He was a forger. He made licenses, travel papers, passports, fake receipts, whatever they needed. He was caught in the mid-nineties and the Italian courts sentenced him to 10 years in prison. They offered him a plea deal to rat on the crime bosses but he refused to cooperate so he served the entire sentence. Dad said he had no choice really. He had to keep his mouth shut or they would have killed him regardless."

"So does he still do that?" Cynthia asked.

"I don't think so. I think they take care of him somewhat for his loyalty. He doesn't talk about it and neither does Yia Yia. That's him standing next to Dad." Alexandra pointed to a picture of the two brothers hanging on the kitchen wall.

Cynthia could see he was tall and lanky with curly gray hair and a receding hairline.

"What happened to his ear?" she noticed.

"No one knows for sure. He claims he was tortured in prison. My Dad said he thinks it was probably bitten off by a hooker."

Cynthia laughed out loud.

"Every once in a while, you will see him reach up and scratch it. Except it's not there." Alexandra mimicked her uncle's motion with her fingers.

The two girls were rolling with laughter when Illiana came back into the kitchen. "What is so funny?"

"I was telling her about Demetri's ear", Alexandra snickered.

"Yes, that." Illiana shook her head and began cleaning off the table and the counter space where she had prepared the morning meal. Both Cynthia and Alexandra offered to help but Illiana refused. "No girls. You are guests today. Enjoy your coffee. So, Alexandra. I will need to go to market for some things for dinner. Can you take me there this morning? Demetri would take me but he is not here."

"Of course, Yia Yia. Whenever you like."

"Good." Illiana said, gesturing toward the clock on the wall. "We go at eleven."

* * *

Cynthia had stayed behind while Alexandra drove her grandmother into Igoumenitsa for groceries. On the way back they saw Demetri just ahead of them, apparently also headed back to the house. They followed him up the narrow road which serpentined back and forth up the steep hill.

Most of the houses along the road were built near the bottom and middle of the hill. A few houses had been constructed near the top, but not many. Illiana's small home had been purchased by her husband, Miko, in the late nineteen sixties. He had added a small one-car garage and built the patio area for Illiana. Both Alexandra's father and Demetri had been born in the house. Miko had died there ten years earlier. His death was the reason for Alexandra and her father's last trip to Greece. It seemed to Alexandra she only visited her native country when there was a death in the family.

Demetri pulled into the driveway in front of the small garage door of Illiana's house and got out to manually open it. He pulled the car inside and came back out carrying a small suitcase and a plastic grocery sack. He closed the garage door just as Alexandra and Illiana arrived.

Cynthia had been sitting on the patio and heard the commotion outside. She walked out to the drive to see if anyone needed help with the groceries. Alexandra saw Demetri for the first time since she arrived and went over to hug him.

"Uncle Demetri! How are you?" she asked, her arms spread wide.

Demetri seemed hesitant to put down his baggage but reluctantly set the suitcase and bag on the ground and wrapped his arms around Alexandra. Then he put his hands on her shoulders and pushed her to arms-length. "Let me look at you, little one. My God! You are an adult!"

Alexandra laughed. "Yes, Uncle Demetri, I am a grown woman. I want you to meet someone." She held out her hand to Cynthia and pulled her over. "This is my best friend, Cynthia."

Demetri nodded. Cynthia wasn't sure how to greet him properly but he was Alexandra's family and they all seemed to hug each other and kiss cheeks. So she hugged Demetri who seemed a little surprised but wrapped his arms around her mid-section then reached down and squeezed one of her butt cheeks.

"Demetri!" Illiana cried. "This is not Italy. Behave yourself! And apologize to Alexandra's friend."

Demetri seemed genuinely embarrassed, having been reprimanded by his mother. "My apologies", he said, as he picked up his belongings and headed into the house.

"He is harmless", Illiana assured Cynthia. "I don't know why he behaves so sometimes."

"He's done that before?" Cynthia questioned.

"Many times", Illiana confirmed. "He does not seem able to help himself."

"I should have warned you", Alexandra lamented.

The shock had worn off and Cynthia could see the humor in the old man's action. Illiana's allusion to it as rude Italian behavior made her smile. "It's okay" she snickered. "When in Rome, I suppose."

By mid-afternoon the sun was shining brightly and a few clouds had begun to form as the winds picked up. Illiana called for everyone to gather in the yard outside. It was time to spread the ashes of her beloved Christos.

Demetri had not been seen since the 'incident' in the morning and there was mild tension until he removed the marble plaque from the plastic bag he had been carrying earlier. The plaque was beautiful, a work of art, as was the other nearly identical plaque that had been placed twenty years earlier under the lone olive tree in Illiana's backyard in honor of Alexandra's mother, Helena.

"How were you able to have one made to match so well?" Alexandra asked.

"I simply carved one stone like the other", he replied.

"You carved these?" Alexandra had no idea Demetri had hand-made the plaques. "Oh my, Demetri! They are so much more special now. I didn't know."

Demetri smiled and scratched his missing ear piece.

The light wind was blowing in from the sea. Illiana opened the urn and began to slowly pour out the ashes of her son, Christos. She walked around in a small circle saying a quiet prayer as the winds carried the ashes away and up the hill. Everyone else stood silent saying their own prayers as they watched Illiana say goodbye to her youngest son. Her words to Alexandra the day before echoed in Alexandra's head... "No mother should ever have to bury a child."

When most of the ashes had been dispersed, Illiana sealed the urn leaving a small amount remaining and placed it into the hole that Demetri had dug next to the urn of Helena. It took only a few minutes for Demetri to fill the hole and place the plaque he had made for Christos next to the one he had long ago made for Helena.

Alexandra hugged her grandmother as they both wept. Demetri stood silent over his brother's grave, hands folded together in front, his head bowed in prayer. Cynthia rarely cried but she could feel the family's loss and it was emotional for her, too.

When Demetri had backed away from the grave, Cynthia came over and stood next to him. She reached around and pinched his butt cheek and smiled as he looked down at her. Demetri smiled as well. Apology accepted.

CHAPTER 16

Chuck's investigation at Crimson Hook Terminals turned up little. Some of the dock workers knew of the accident that had killed the Lakeville Press reporter, Jeremy Ballard. But no one had actually witnessed it. A couple of longshoremen had refused to answer any of his questions. It was hard to say whether they knew something and were covering it up or they just didn't want to get involved.

There had been one interesting lead, a conversation with an old stevedore, a crane operator who worked the midnight shift. One of the questions Chuck had routinely asked was if anyone remembered any containers going to, or coming from, a place called Green Valley Transfer and Storage. The old crane operator had. He remembered more than one occasion when Green Valley containers were moved, both on and off trucks. He specifically remembered because he wasn't allowed to operate the cranes that moved those containers. "Why not?" Chuck had asked. Because, he had been told by the superintendent, there were OSHA regulations governing the handling of this level of hazardous waste, and he wasn't certified. Hmmmm.

Chuck was headed to Green Valley anyway. But this new development put the trip into an entirely different light.

* * *

Following instructions, Kevin drove north on I-495. As he crossed over the Potomac River he bore to the right at Exit 41, toward the Clara Barton Parkway. At the first split in the off-ramp he kept to the right. As the ramp began to merge with the Clara Barton he quickly moved over to the far right lane and immediately exited into the entrance to the parking area for C&O Canal Lock 10.

Kevin drove to the far end of the parking area where he saw a small walking bridge over a drainage creek and a little park area with a single picnic table. He pulled into a parking space and walked the short distance over the bridge to the table where Colonel Jacob Selbourne sat waiting.

"Well, Major, this had better be important", the Colonel advised.

Kevin had called the Colonel to ask for this meeting. He suggested they not talk in the Colonel's office. Selbourne was pretty sure he knew what the meeting was about. He had agreed his office wasn't a good place, and had given Kevin instructions to meet him here, a secluded place where their clandestine meeting would not likely be observed.

Kevin sat down at the table and folded his hands. He took a moment to decide how to begin. "Colonel, I think I have a plan to eliminate our problem, but I will need your approval. There will be collateral damage, I'm afraid."

"What kind of damage, Major?"

"Perhaps a good kind, sir. We may be able to kill two birds with one stone, so to speak." He hesitated, "You tell me."

"What's your plan?"

"Our problem is exceptionally smart. He would immediately smell a rat unless we give him the truth. To lure the Senator into a trap, the bait will have to smell extraordinarily realistic."

"Go on", the Colonel urged.

"We have to give up Saffari, sir."

Kevin watched the Colonel's eyes narrow and his brow furrow. Those were never good cues. But he was ready for the Colonel's angry skepticism. In fact, he had prepared for it.

"Explain, Major. And it had better be good! Saffari is our most trusted and valuable asset. Without his Afghanistan connections the whole operation could fall apart."

"I agree, but I believe I've mitigated that, sir. Do you remember another war lord you met in Nimruz? His name was Abdul-Baser. As I remember, you thought quite highly of him."

"Abdalla." The Colonel's brow began to unfurrow.

"One and the same, Colonel. He is now the assistant Minister of Agriculture for the Nimruz province, Saffari's second in command. He would like to be first in command."

"Alright, son, you have my attention." The Colonel leaked a small but perceptible smile.

"The man you were able to get released from prison, Haji Juma Khan, has reestablished himself in the Nimruz province."

"As planned, Major. Get to the point?"

Kevin was hoping the successful release of Juma Khan, orchestrated by the Colonel months earlier, would help to convince him that the plan he was about to present was doable.

Juma Khan was the biggest drug trafficker in Afghanistan, the kingpin among a handful of lessers. Selbourne had been conspiring with the man almost since the day the U.S. invaded Afghanistan. With Selbourne's facilitation, Khan had become the CIA's greatest financial asset, controlling the bulk of Afghanistan's export of 5000 to 9000 metric tons of opium and heroin per year. When Khan was arrested in Jakarta, Indonesia, in a DEA sting operation in 2008, it became paramount for Colonel Selbourne to get him released, and to take control of his defense while he was in prison. Khan was, by far, the CIA's most prolific producer of heroin in the world and his incarceration severely hampered the agency's ability to generate clandestine income.

The battle had not been easy. Sen. Dianne Feinstein, co-chair of the Senate Caucus on International Narcotics Control, had described Khan as "one of the world's most significant heroin and opium traffickers, who provided direct support to the Taliban from his drug trafficking revenue." She and others in Congress had lauded the DEA's achievement making it extremely difficult for the Colonel to get the man exonerated. In a 2010 Senate report she had written:

> "Simply put: Narco-terrorism investigations have proven to be an effective tool in Afghanistan. So it should be a priority for funding and action."

Almost as quickly as Khan's case entered the court system in New York, it became evident that the DEA and the CIA were at odds with the man's fate. Selbourne and the CIA were not happy with his arrest and actively but quietly pursued his release. When Haji Juma Khan walked out of the Metropolitan Correctional Center in Lower Manhattan in the spring of 2018, his records had been sealed, the outcome of his cases were unknown, nor was anyone aware of where he had gone after his release... except the Colonel and a few close associates.

"Khan has formed close ties with Abdalla", Kevin continued. "We can take advantage of their close relationship. Saffari has been a concern for many months now. He's become too wealthy and too powerful and it's gotten harder to solicit his cooperation. In short, he just doesn't need us as badly as he once did. I know you've noticed that, I've heard you mention it."

"Okay." The Colonel was listening.

"I'm absolutely positive I can convince the Senator that Minister Habib Karim Saffari knows who the sources are for Afghanistan heroin in the U.S. and that if the Company is involved, he would have direct knowledge and information."

"Because he does", the Colonel interjected.

"Because he does", Kevin smiled. "The truth rings with authority and its siren song can be irresistible. The Senator will be on the first plane out if I tell him the Minister is willing to meet with him."

"And when they get together...", the Colonel began the sentence.

"...Abdul-Baser Abdalla will suddenly become the Minister of Agriculture for the Nimruz province."

The Colonel liked the idea very much. Major Falk was a brilliant tactician and his Afghanistan connections were extraordinary. But he was concerned about how the Major planned to carry out this delicate operation.

"Where do you plan to get these two together?" the Colonel asked.

"Paris, Charonne district."

"And how do you intend to neutralize the targets, Major?"

Kevin had a well thought out plan but he wasn't positive Colonel Selbourne was going to approve of it. He started slowly, watching the Colonel's expressions as he peeled the onion.

"Eliminating such a high-profile target will take planning and coordination. It can't look like an assassination. It must look like a tragic accident."

So far, the Colonel showed no sign of a negative response.

"The two men know each other. Not intimately, but Gavin, the Senator...", he corrected himself. It was hard to think about killing his friend Gavin. But this was business, not personal. It had to be done, and he had to work harder at keeping his frame of mind in check. It's business! It's just business. "... but the Senator worked with Saffari many times to help coordinate our operations when we were deployed there. He will trust that a meeting with Saffari is legitimate. There is a small café there where I will arrange for them to meet. A terrorist bomb will tragically take the lives of two old acquaintances who just happened to be talking about old times."

"And you don't think the press will come up with some kind of conspiracy theory when two high-profile government officials are murdered together?" Selbourne wasn't convinced. "The last thing we need is the press digging deeper into this."

"I've thought about that, sir." Kevin peeled off the last layer of the onion. "We will plant multiple false flags across Paris that night. Two bombs will go off in restaurants near Charles de Gaulle, which should close down the airport. The chaos there ought to get most of the press coverage. We'll plant another one near the Charlie Hebdo offices. That one will add to the confusion about who is responsible. It would be no surprise if ISIS took credit for the bombings. And, of course, the one in the café on Rue de Charonne. I am trusting the press will jump on some Muslim terrorist narrative as it always has in the past."

Colonel Selbourne was pleased. No plan is foolproof but this one sounded about as good as it gets. Sure, taking out the Senator would necessitate some collateral damage over and above the Afghan minister. Innocent lives would surely be lost and he would give them all medals for their sacrifice if he could. But there was a greater good to be considered and a pragmatism to the Major's strategy that outweighed any moral compunction. This was a mission that had to be accomplished, and its end, most assuredly, justified the means.

* * *

Gavin sat at his desk looking over a bill which held no interest to him and, he was pretty sure, none to his constituents. But he needed to be sure. One of the least satisfactory parts of his job as a senator was trying to read and understand the myriad pieces of legislation he had to vote on. Without Cynthia around to screen the important stuff and weed out the rubbish, he was mired in inexhaustible paperwork. It was a welcomed distraction when Monica knocked and entered with a surprise guest.

"Look what I found wandering the halls, Senator!"

"So this is what you do all day? Sit around pretending to be busy?" Kevin entered as Monica held the door for him then returned to her office.

Gavin got up from his desk. "Playing hooky? What brings you this far north?" Gavin hugged his good friend who seemed a bit stiff then sat back down motioning for Kevin to sit.

"It's not exactly a social call. Maybe we should take a walk."

"Yeah, sure." Gavin could tell whatever it was Kevin had to say was important. He wasn't the same laughing, smiling, joking Kevin this morning. "Where to?"

"Somewhere where we won't be overheard", Kevin said.

"Okay." Gavin got up from his desk, removed his cell phones from his jacket and put them in his top desk drawer. "Follow me."

Gavin guided Kevin to the Russell Senate Office Building's exit on the corner of Constitution and Delaware Avenue. They exchanged small talk as they shuffled down the steps and over the Delaware Ave crosswalk to the walkway into Upper Senate Park where they found an empty bench under the shade of a large tree.

Gavin motioned for Kevin to sit as he sat and opened the conversation. "What's up, Kev?"

Kevin bent over, his elbows on his knees, nervously rubbing his hands together, staring at the ground in front of him. Then he cocked his head toward Gavin and looked him in the eyes. "There may be something to what you asked me about at the bar. I think it's possible the Company, an element anyway, could be involved in a smuggling operation."

Gavin was already convinced that was the case. Now Kevin might be confirming his suspicions. "Do you have specific information? What makes you think so?"

"Look," Kevin said, "I don't want to know any more than what I'm telling you. Understand?"

Gavin stared at him in silence.

"I see things, you know. And I hear things. Things I'm not supposed to acknowledge or talk about. Things that can put me in real hot water if anyone even suspects I was the source of a leak."

"No, I get it", Gavin assured. "So how do we do this? Do I play twenty questions?"

Kevin sat up straight and looked around. Gavin assumed he was making sure there were no eavesdropping eyes or ears nearby. "I'm going to give you a name."

"A name that I can investigate or talk to?"

"Either or both", Kevin avowed.

"Do you remember the Nimruz government official that used to help us with bust operations? He's Minister of Agriculture now?"

"Saffari? Yeah, I remember him. Decent guy." Gavin had worked quite often with the man. He held him in fairly high regard.

"He's dirty. If anyone knows what the Company is doing over there and who's doing it, it's Saffari." Kevin could see Gavin was taking the bait. It must smell pretty good.

Any incredulity Gavin may have been feeling earlier was being slowly cleared away. "Who turned him?"

Kevin again stared directly into Gavin's eyes. When you tell the truth, even if it's for misleading purposes, the words will always ring credible. Here was the moment of truth... "Probably my boss." Kevin averted his eyes momentarily then relocked them with Gavins'.

"Whew! Oh, man." Gavin never saw that one coming. It wasn't really a surprise that Selbourne was involved. He had warned Kevin a long time ago not to trust the man. Nor was it any surprise that his close friend had made such a dangerous admission. But it was an incredibly brave act and Gavin was extremely appreciative.

"How do I contact Saffari without exposing your involvement?" Gavin asked.

"Saffari believes you have been recruited into the supply chain. I've seen to that. He will take a meeting with you whenever you want."

"The sooner the better", Gavin stressed.

Kevin stood up. "That's what I figured. I'll set up the meet for Friday evening, three days from today. What you're able to solicit from him is on you. There's no more I can do, nothing I can say to make this easier. You're on your own now, man."

There were tears in Kevin's eyes as he turned and walked away. This would probably be the last time he would see his friend again. He reminded himself: It's just business.

Gavin sat for a while, the gravity of the last few minutes weighing heavily on his mind. He wasn't sure how to go about the next few days. But he would wing it and hope for the best.

CHAPTER 17

Chuck McCrory drove up to the visitor's gate of the Green Valley Transfer and Storage Company. He had rented a flatbed truck, the kind capable of hauling small shipping containers. He had on a New York Yankees ball cap, blue jeans and a plaid shirt and it was his intention to try to convince the guard that he had business there. The young guard at the gate stepped out of the guard shack and approached his window.

"Good morning!" Chuck smiled and nodded.

"Good morning, sir." The guard walked around to the rear of the truck and noted the tag number on the visitor's log then returned to the driver's window. "Who are you here to see, sir?"

Chuck pretended to look through his paperwork. "Son-of-a-bitch! I had it here somewhere." He fumbled some more then looked at the young guard. "Raster, Rossen, Reemer?"

"Romero?" the guard volunteered.

"Romero!" Chuck said. "Thank you!"

"Is he expecting you, sir?" the guard asked.

Chuck pursed his lips and shook his head up and down and back and forth. "Not sure. The office just said to see him about a load going to Mass. I don't really know what or where. I just show up where I'm told."

"I'll try to call him", the guard offered.

The guard went back into the shack and Chuck could see him talking with someone on the phone. He hung up and came back out. "Mr. Romero isn't here today but Mr. Marsden said you can talk to him."

Chuck couldn't believe it was going be this easy to get into a hazardous waste storage facility. But there was no way he was going to try to talk with Romero or Marsden. It didn't seem likely he would learn anything from them, and his presence might alert the wrong person that he was there. Then again, accepting the offer would get him through the gate. He could see what happened after that.

"Marsden, huh? What does he do?" Chuck asked.

"Human resources, sir. Same as Mr. Romero."

"Human Resources?" Chuck said, puzzled.

Well, this was a fine how-do-you-do! He had just told the kid that he was here to pick up a load. Did he not make the connection? Why would he want to talk to Human Resources?

"Yes, sir", the guard offered. "All new drivers have to go through a background check. That's probably why they sent you to Mr. Romero."

Chuck could only smile. This really was too easy. Something was bound to go wrong. But, why not interview with the HR guy? He was feeling less concerned about being discovered since they would think he was a job applicant.

"I'll need to see some ID, sir."

Chuck opened his wallet and looked through the half dozen identification cards he carried. He pulled a driver's license from New York, Henry Clemson, and handed it to the guard.

The guard noted the name and time of entry on the visitor's log. "Thank you, Mr. Clemson." He handed the card back to Chuck. "Follow this road to the stop sign. Turn right and keep going until you reach the metal buildings on the left. Turn left into the parking area in front of the buildings. You can't miss it. Mr. Marsden's office is in the light blue building. It says Human Resources if you look close but the paint is fading on most of the buildings over there. People get confused all the time. Just remember it's the light blue building."

"Will do", Chuck said. "Thanks a lot."

Chuck made his way to the parking area as instructed. He pulled his truck into a pull-thru slot, parked and looked around. He had no idea what he was looking at or what to look for. He could wander around a little since the buildings weren't clearly marked and the kid had said people got confused here all the time. But would it be worth it if he got caught poking around in a sensitive area? Probably not. It was doubtful any information of value would be hiding in plain sight here anyway. Perhaps a chat with Mr. Marsden was the right way to go. Plus, it would give him an opportunity to do some reconnaissance.

Chuck entered thru the rusted steel door of the office of the Human Resources department. A receptionist with obviously little to do greeted him as he entered. She buzzed Mr. Marsden and told Chuck to take a seat in the two-chair waiting area. Chuck looked around the office but saw nothing that piqued his curiosity. He was hoping Marsden would be the talkative sort, the sort of person of whom he could ask some questions that might garner useful information.

Mr. Marsden entered from the same door he had. "Hank Marsden", claimed the owner of the extended hand.

"Hey, I'm Hank", chuck retorted with a chuckle and a big smile as he shook the man's hand firmly. "Henry Clemson. Good to meet you, sir."

"You're applying to be a driver?" Marsden asked.

"Yes sir."

Marsden gestured for Chuck to sit back down then pulled the other chair around to face him as he began what was obviously a canned series of questions.

"Have you filled out an employment application?"

Chuck shook his head, "No sir."

Marsden turned toward the receptionist, "Rosemary, bring Mr. Clemson an application, please." Then he returned his attention to Chuck. "You have a current CDL license, I assume."

"Yes sir."

"Are your OSHA certifications up to date?"

Chuck sensed this conversation would go nowhere unless he could control it, so he interrupted, "Can I ask a question, Mr. Marsden? If I get a job here will I get to go to New York City?"

Marsden was momentarily stumped as he thought about the question. With some annoyance he replied, "We go to New York City, yes. Whether or not you would be assigned any of those hauls I can't say. I need to ask..."

Chuck interrupted again before the man could finish his sentence. "Because I live in Brooklyn and if I could haul stuff to the docks down there, that would be great."

Marsden took a deep breath, obviously annoyed, and tried to finish the canned list of questions he had started. "OSHA certifications?"

"Oh, yeah, sure", Chuck replied.

Rosemary had brought the application over and was standing beside Marsden waiting for him to take the pen and clipboard from her.

"You will need to take a drug test pre-employment. Will that be a problem?" Marsden continued.

Chuck realized he wasn't going to learn anything from Hank Marsden and this was his opportunity to extricate himself. "I ain't peein' in no bottle. A man should be taken at his word. I ain't no druggie."

"I understand, Mr. Clemson. But it's the law, not just company policy."

Chuck stood up and offered his hand. Marsden stood with a perplexed look and shook Chuck's hand. "Thank you for your time, Mr. Marsden. Sorry to have bothered you."

Chuck noticed Marsden and the receptionist looking at each other with baffled stares as he exited the office. This had been a complete waste of time, not to mention potentially dangerous.

Chuck got back in his truck and sat there for a moment picturing in his mind the satellite photos he had seen on his computer. Behind this group of metal buildings had been a curious cluster of rusted old shipping containers. It was probably nothing, but if he made a wrong turn on his way out of the facility he could get close enough to see if anything suspicious caught his attention. He pulled out of his parking space and made a left turn past the metal buildings and then another left behind the buildings onto the short drive leading to the cluster. As he started down the drive he noticed two men in the distance standing together in conversation near the cluster, a large bulky man and a military officer. He stopped immediately and began to back up onto the main drive. "What the ...?" he said to himself.

Chuck shifted the truck out of reverse and into first gear and slowly headed back toward the exit to the facility. He glanced to see that the two men had paid little attention to his short presence, continuing their conversation as he pulled away. He didn't recognize either man. But what in the hell was an Air Force officer doing here?

Chuck drove to the guard shack at the exit and pulled into the small parking area off to the side. He got out and walked over to the guard who was standing there watching him.

"How'd it go?" the guard asked.

"Okay", Chuck said. "Hey, I met a guy in there in an Air Force uniform. Does he work here?"

"Major Falk? Oh, no, sir", the guard replied. "I think he's here to escort a truck going somewhere."

"Do you know where?" Chuck solicited.

"Not really, sir. They don't tell me."

Chuck half-saluted the young guard. "Alright. Well thanks. Have a great day!"

As Chuck turned to go to his truck the guard began to elaborate. "You know, I do remember hearing one of the other men say something about Florida. Something's going to a place, uh, the name reminded me of a dog."

"A dog?" Chuck turned and came back to the shack.

"Like a big mean dog. I can't think of it, sir."

"This place in Florida, so, what are they hauling there?" Chuck coaxed.

"I don't know, sir. This is a hazardous waste facility. That'd be my guess."

"A dog, huh? A place in Florida that sounds like a dog." Chuck was frustrated but he knew he couldn't press much more without drawing attention to his over interest. "Alright, take care, my man."

As he hopped back into the cab of the truck he heard the guard shout at him... "Weimaraner".

Chuck started the engine and put the truck in gear. The guard opened the gate and Chuck waved and yelled "Thanks!" as he pulled out of the facility. He would have to do some research. There couldn't be that many places in Florida that sounded like Weimaraner. And who was this Major Falk?

Maybe he was on to something, maybe he wasn't. But it was time to do some field reconnaissance. He hadn't camped out in a long while. He hoped his old bones could still bivouac.

* * *

Kevin's Florida team had been completed. He had just returned from Wimauma after inspecting the customizations to the house and the metal building at the property on the Little Manatee River. Everything was in order and he was satisfied that the team was as ready as it could be to begin operations.

He had trained seven lieutenants how he wanted them to assume command of the recovery boats as they arrived at Devil's Elbow. It was imperative they correctly blind-fold the incoming boat drivers and hide them from the view of any oncoming boaters or shoreline observers until they reached the distribution compound. The team had also practiced launching and trailering the boats at the boat ramp on the property. After weeks of drills and practice runs the team was ready and Kevin was comfortable they could do the job and do it well.

He was less comfortable with the team of recovery drivers that would pick up the flotation bags as they were dumped overboard from the cargo ship sailing up the Gulf of Mexico. In the beginning, he had over-estimated the skill of Fernandez' men and their training had taken longer than he had anticipated. Their work would be done at night, under the cover of darkness, with no running lights. In fact, there would be no lights of any kind. This had proven to be a problem for some of the men, unable to locate the floating satchels even with the aid of location transponders. He had gone through ten men to find six that were capable. But he was satisfied that the crew he now had was as ready as they could be.

His next step was to make a trial run and he had called the Colonel to inform him of the status of his team and his plan to execute a test operation. But Colonel Selbourne had had other plans, which is why Kevin was back at Green Valley Transfer and Storage talking with Dan Bemis.

"We go in seven days", he told Bemis. "I'll send you instructions for where and when to deliver the 'package'", a euphemism Kevin liked to use for the container of Afghan heroin. "I have two captains available but I haven't decided on one yet. Selbourne says you've worked with them both, Cox and McMullen?"

"McMullen for sure", Bemis assured him. "His crews are some of the best I've seen."

"McMullen it is then", Kevin affirmed.

Bemis glanced away as Kevin was talking. Something at the far end of the row of buildings had caught his attention. Kevin glanced to see a flatbed truck making the turn onto the drive that led back to the cluster of containers where he and Bemis stood conversing. The truck stopped just as it rounded the corner, then backed out of the drive and headed back in the direction of the facility exit.

"Happens all the time", Bemis said.

Kevin just shook his head. Everything made him nervous these days. And he was especially nervous as he waited for the squad leader of his Paris bomb team to confirm that the Charonne café bombing operation was a go. He still hadn't heard anything and there were only 36 hours to zero hour.

CHAPTER 18

It was "going to be amazing!" Monica had told her sister.

She was Senator Manson's Chief of Staff pro tem, along with her normal responsibilities, of course. In Cynthia's absence, the Senator needed a working surrogate for the trip to Paris that, yea!, she got to go on. That meant she would be able to spend time with her sister, Anita Sanchez-Montoya, and Anita's husband, Inigo, who had lived in Paris for the last four years.

Monica and Anita had seen each other only once since the couple left for Paris so that Inigo could take a job at the Spanish consulate there. Monica hadn't seen many sights in Paris and Anita had big plans to show her little sister some of the famous ones: the Eiffel Tower, the Arc de Triomphe, the Louvre. Senator Manson was going to fly back to Washington the morning after his meeting with an old acquaintance from Afghanistan. But he had told Monica she could stay a few days longer to spend time with her family.

Monica fastened her seat belt and slightly closed the window shade of the Boeing 787. The skies were clear and the late afternoon sun was a bit strong. "Thank you for allowing me to fly with you in first class, Senator. This is so nice!"

Monica had made arrangements for Gavin to fly first class on the trip to Paris. He had plenty of points, even enough for a swanky hotel room at the Maison Souguet, near the Moulin Rouge. She had initially arranged for herself to fly coach. But Gavin had insisted he didn't need a fancy hotel and instructed her to use the points, instead, to purchase a first-class ticket for herself. They would fly together.

"No thanks necessary" he insisted with a grin. "It's the least I can do for my Chief of Staff."

Monica smiled as she sorted through the papers and notes she had brought. "There will be a limo for you at the airport. It will take you to the hotel. The café where you are meeting the Minister Saffari is within walking distance. It is small and they did not take reservations but the person I spoke with said they are unnecessary at that time of night." She glanced at Gavin with a perplexed look. "Why was your meeting scheduled for so late in the evening? Eleven o'clock at night?"

"I wish I knew, Monica. It's going to seem a lot later than that, I'm afraid." Gavin had also wondered why the meeting was so late. Kevin had made the arrangements. Maybe Saffari had other business to attend to earlier in the evening. There was no way to know. But, there was an upside. At least he would be able to sleep through the afternoon and part of the evening before going to the café.

"So, you said your sister is picking you up from the airport?"

"Yes sir."

Gavin noticed Monica's Spanish accent had gotten stronger since she found out she would be travelling to Paris. He wondered if it had anything to do with the excitement and anticipation of seeing her sister. He had also noticed that Samantha's Boston accent would become more pronounced when she would head home to Massachusetts. Did his southern accent do the same on trips home? It was an interesting phenomenon.

Monica's excitement was apparent as she chattered away. Gavin didn't mind. "I went to visit my sister when she first moved to Paris. It was a wonderful trip. Her apartment is so beautiful. And the street where she lives is beautiful also. It has trees along both sides."

"What part of Paris is that?" he asked.

"It is called Saint-Fargeau, on Avenue Gambetta. It is not very far from where you will be in Charonne."

"Must be a nice area", Gavin said.

"Sí. Her apartment is on the fourth floor of a very fine brick building with a balcony overlooking the street. There are many shops and restaurants and quaint cafés, and a grocery nearby and a vegetable market. My sister's building has a pharmacy on the street."

"Sounds like the perfect place to live. You don't need much more than that", he laughed.

"No, Senator. It is perfect."

"Monica, you don't need to call me Senator or sir when we're having a personal conversation. Save the formalities for work."

"Yes sir", she replied.

Gavin shook his head. He was ready to put his phones in airplane mode when his work cell beeped. A text message had arrived and he saw that it was from Samantha. "Taking a couple days off while ur away. Recharge. Sam."

He replied to her text. "See you in few days. Enjoy." Then he switched the phone to airplane mode, closed his eyes, and waited for the plane to pull away from the gate.

* * *

"I'm glad you called", Samantha panted, as she jogged along the Rock Creek Park trail she and Kevin had been on a few months earlier. "I love it when the leaves start to change."

"It's beautiful!" Kevin said as he jogged alongside. "We don't get seasons in Florida. It's pretty much green all year, although a few deciduous trees will lose their leaves."

Samantha noticed the flat rock ahead that she and Kevin had sat on the last time they jogged the trail. She slowed and began to walk until she reached the rock then stopped and stood for a few moments with her hands on her hips, catching her breath. Kevin followed likewise.

"So, what would you do?" she began, pausing for a short while as she took one last deep breath. She walked over and sat down on the rock, facing the trail, legs dangling over the front edge, leaning back on both hands.

Kevin stood in front of her, facing her, waiting. Then he coaxed her to continue. "About what?"

"Do you know why Gavin's going to Paris?" she solicited.

"He is? I wasn't aware."

"Liar!!" she thought to herself. It made her angry that he would lie to her face.

"That's funny. Gavin told me you were the one that set up the meeting he's having there."

Kevin's heart rate began to rise. He didn't realize Gavin would have shared that information. Think fast!

"I told him not to tell anyone. Do you have any idea how much trouble I can get into if Selbourne finds out I am the source of Gavin's information? It could be career ending."

"Well, I guess he figured he could tell me. After all, he and I are partners in this adventure. We don't keep secrets. Not to mention you have a key to my apartment and we're swapping bodily fluids on a regular basis. Why are you keeping secrets from me?"

Samantha was livid. Kevin just stared at her. Where was this going?

"How married are you to that company, Kevin?"

"What are you asking me, Sam? And what would I do about what?"

Samantha sat up straight, hands resting on the rock beside her hips. "Your company's dirty and you know it. But instead of manning up and blowing the

150

whistle, you send your best friend to do the dirty work because you don't want to get into trouble!"

"I'm not the right one to blow the whistle, Sam. Gavin knows that. That's why he went. If he can get solid information from the guy he's talking to, he can come back and initiate an investigation. His word is a thousand times more powerful than mine."

Samantha just shook her head. Even if Kevin was telling the truth, even if he was right, he was a coward. At this moment he disgusted her.

She calmed herself and restated her question. "I was going to ask 'What would you do if you knew your boss was a criminal?' Well, you already answered it. Apparently nothing. Shamefully, nothing!"

Kevin was getting angry. This conversation was getting out of control. "What would you have me do, Sam?" his voice elevated from the heat of the moment.

Samantha got up from the rock. She straightened her clothes and brushed off her backside. "Well, I'll tell you what I'm going to do", she asserted. "I'm going to the Chairman of the Senate Intelligence committee, Gavin's committee, and tell him where Gavin is and what he's doing. If you had any balls you'd come with me!"

Kevin knew this was not a battle he could win but he needed to try to buy some time. "I wouldn't do that, Sam. At least wait until Gavin gets back and see what kind of information he's able to pull from the meeting. This is crazy talk, honey. It's too soon to open this can of worms."

Samantha turned toward the way they had come and began walking. "I'm heading back."

Kevin was not prepared for what had happened. It was not supposed to go down this way. This was not one of the carefully considered steps in his plan. Yes, he had known that Samantha would have to be dealt with eventually. But not now, not today! He hated the idea of making an uncalculated move. All his life he had been a chess player, at least one step ahead of his opponents. The risk was huge that someone had seen the two of them together today. If so, questions about his whereabouts would be dangerous to answer. Investigators would want a timeline of his movements for the day. He was going to need an alibi, a rock-solid alibi which he did not have and could not think of at the moment. What he was being forced to do now was incredibly dangerous, an act of desperation. But it could not be helped.

Kevin peered up and down the path. There were no joggers or hikers within eyesight. Sound can carry great distances in the quiet woods. This would have to be done quickly and silently. An errant scream or cry for help could bring concerned searchers. He called her name and begged her to wait. She stopped and turned to face him and he calmly walked up to her and pretended to try to give her a hug, knowing full well that she would pull away. When she had sufficiently turned away he reached around from behind her and grabbed the left side of her face with his right hand and the back of her head with the other. With every ounce of his strength in his shoulders and arms, he quickly and powerfully twisted her head around until he heard the bones in her neck shatter. She fell silently limp in his hands as he gently lowered her to the ground. In an instant she was dead.

Kevin picked her up and cradled her warm, dead body in his arms. He began to weep as he walked into the woods carrying Samantha toward the ravine where Levy's body had been found over a decade before. At the edge of a steep embankment he laid her down and searched her pockets for personal effects. She had only her cell phone with her. Unlike Levy, a cell tower nearby meant the discovery of her remains would be much easier to find. Samantha's body wouldn't stay hidden for very long.

Kevin opened her phone, searched through her contacts, and sent a text message to Gavin Manson: "Taking a couple days off while ur away. Recharge. Sam."

A few moments later Gavin's reply: "See you in few days. Enjoy."

Kevin hoped the fact that he and Samantha had been lovers would explain any of his DNA that investigators would surely find on and around her body. He removed the battery from her phone so it could no longer be pinged by cell towers. He wiped his fingerprints from the battery and phone with her jersey and placed her fingers and palm around the case. Then he used her hand to put the phone back into her pocket.

His tears were still flowing as he rolled her body over the edge of the embankment into the ravine below and watched it fall lifelessly to the bottom. It came to rest slumped over in a sitting position, leaning against a large bolder. She did not appear to be dead. He sat for several minutes sobbing as he stared at the woman he had begun to fall in love with, so beautiful, a beautiful redheaded rag doll.

He came to his feet and turned to walk away, still sobbing uncontrollably. Why had Sam been so impatient? Why had she made him do this? If she had only been reasonable he could have made her last moments so much more dignified.

CHAPTER 19

Chuck pulled up to the chain-link gate of the railroad service road behind the Green Valley Transfer and Storage Company. The dense woods growing up the hill behind the facility would offer cover and an elevated vantage point for a surveillance operation. From there he would stake out the activity in the transfer yard for the next few days. It was late in the afternoon and he wanted to get his bivouac site setup before dark.

After he had left the facility earlier in the day, Chuck had gone back to his motel and picked up the surveillance gear and supplies he would need for a two or three-day vigil. Then he had returned the large flat-bed truck to the truck rental company and walked across the road to a car rental agency where he rented a Jeep Wrangler, one with off-road four-wheel drive. Something was about to happen at Green Valley Transfer and Storage, he sensed it from the young guard he had talked with in the morning, and this was the best way he could think of to keep an eye on what was happening there.

The gate to the service road was locked and there was no way to drive around it. His Jeep could easily drive up onto the rail bed but a deep drainage ditch next to the tracks made crossing from the tracks to the service road impossible, even for a four-wheeler. He got out of the truck and looked at the padlock and heavy chain wrapped around the latch rails of the double swinging gate. The chain looked to be half-inch nickel plated steel. He retrieved a bolt cutter and a box of threaded quick links from the Wrangler and then cut off one of the links of the chain, carefully noticing how the chain had been wrapped.

There was no way to know when or how often a railroad security guard would make a cursory check of the gate's chain and lock. But Chuck had learned from past experience that a threaded quick link was almost never spotted by routine inspections if the quick link was the right size and matched the condition of the rest of the chain. He removed the broken chain, opened the gates, and drove inside. Then he closed the gates and rewrapped the chain as it had been before and installed the threaded link.

Chuck drove slowly up the service road looking for a place to turn uphill into the woods. He needed a place that would serve as both a vantage point where he could see the entire facility and had enough woods to camouflage the truck. He saw an opening in the tree line about 30 yards up which appeared to wind inside to a clearing. He pulled the Wrangler off the service road and its powerful four-wheel drive climbed the steep hill with ease. The clearing was perfect.

It took only minutes for Chuck to hide the truck with camouflage netting, shrubs and tree limbs. Then he built a blind further down the hill, just beyond the tree line, where he positioned high-power binoculars to overlook the facility. He liked these particular binoculars because they were digital, weather proof, had both day and night-vision capability, and they were WIFI enabled. In addition, the tripod he assembled them on could be controlled remotely. He would set up camp back by the truck, out of sight of anyone. From there he could control the azimuth and elevation of the tripod and watch the images being collected by the binoculars on his Android tablet in real-time. The tablet could even switch modes from night to day vision and control the zoom factor of the binoculars.

It had been a while since he had camped out like this. It brought back memories from years past, mostly good memories, of his time spent with the Green Berets and his buddies in the Delta 5. In those days, night vision technology was crude by current standards, relying on ambient light instead of generating an infrared light source. If there was no moonlight they often couldn't see at all. Sometimes they would take eye drops with them to dilate their pupils if there wasn't enough ambient light.

Chuck had made a small camp fire behind the truck to keep away animals, deter insects, and boil water for coffee. He'd also brought a three-day supply of MREs, military grade survival food. A modern 'Meal Ready to Eat' was much more tasty and satisfying than the ones he had eaten in the past. MREs didn't require water except to use with the accompanying heater pouch. You would put the meal bag in the pouch, pour in a little water, close the pouch, and the meal would be warm in about ten or twelve minutes, no fire necessary. Sometimes a small bag of salt water was included with the meal. If not, it was necessary to use water on hand. The meal itself was fully prepared. It required no water. You could eat it cold, if necessary.

MREs weren't meant to be eaten as a steady diet. The military designed them for eating quickly on the run in combat situations or when travelling fast. Chuck actually liked the taste of most MREs although they had nicknames like 'Meals Rarely Edible' and 'Massive Rectal Expulsions'. Tonight, his Chicken Fajita meal came with white meat chicken, refried beans, two tortillas, salt free seasoning, cheese sauce, a brownie for dessert, Irish cream instant powder, raspberry beverage base powder, a moist towelette, a spoon and a future necessity... toilet paper. Each meal was about 1200 calories. A couple a day would sustain him nicely. He'd also brought some apples and a banana.

It was nice to have the Wrangler to sleep in. He was short enough that he could put the rear seat down and stretch out completely in the cargo bay. He opened his thermal sleeping bag like a blanket, satisfied it would keep him warm enough. If the overnight temperature got too cold he could zip it closed and crawl in. Chuck was confident no one knew he was here so he didn't bother with any perimeter alarms.

It appeared that Green Valley Transfer and Storage closed up shop around 6:00 p.m. There hadn't been any movement inside the transfer yard since then. It seemed no work went on there overnight. That made monitoring the compound easy. He set a motion-detection alarm on the surveillance tablet to alert him and begin recording if the binoculars detected any movement. He plugged his tablet into a 12-volt power socket and snapped it into an adjustable mounting bracket he had hung from the Wrangler's cargo bay wall.

Chuck had been lying there watching the tablet do absolutely nothing for about an hour when his cell phone began to ring. It was Monica Sandoval. That's strange.

∗ ∗ ∗

"United States Senator, Gavin Manson, was found dead at the scene of one of Paris' three separate terrorist attacks this evening. His body was discovered among the victims of the Saint-Tropez Café in the Charonne district near the center of Paris. He was apparently having dinner there when a bomb exploded inside the café taking his life and the lives of several others, including passersby on the sidewalk outside the café. Again, this Breaking News, U.S. Senator Gavin Manson found dead at the scene of a terrible terrorist attack in Paris, France, earlier this evening."

It was all over the news around the world and on every evening news channel at 6:00 p.m. EST in the United States. Three separate terrorist attacks in Paris, probably executed by ISIS militants, had targeted Charles De Gaulle Airport, the Charlie Hebdo publishing offices and a Charonne café owned by a Hebdo employee's family. By 7:00 p.m., Breaking News had confirmed Senator Manson's body had been found among the dead at the café explosion.

Kevin sat waiting to make the phone call, a bittersweet call, to Colonel Jacob Selbourne. He had just received a call from the team leader of his field assets in Paris who confirmed that everything had gone to plan. Tears moistened his eyes as he sat alone, lonely on a Friday evening, phone in hand, forcing himself to get control of his emotions.

He pressed the call button on his phone and the Colonel's phone began to ring. "Selbourne."

"It's done, sir. Confirmed."

"Good. Good job, Major."

Kevin watched the news for a few more minutes, then showered and climbed into bed. His emotions were under control now. He had not yet told the Colonel that he had killed Samantha. He needed more time to work on his alibi and he knew the Colonel would question him about it. But he was confident he had left the park unseen. It had been two days and her body had not yet been discovered. The longer it took, the more likely he would get away with it. He consoled himself with the knowledge that he was very good at his job. Tonight's events were further confirmation of the fact. "Good job", the Colonel had said.

* * *

"Oh, mi Dios! Oh, mi Dios! Oh, mi Dios! You are alive!" Monica screamed. "They said you were killed at the café. ¡Alabado sea Dios!"

Gavin stood outside the door of Monica's sister's apartment in Saint-Fargeau. "Be quiet!" he told her as he walked in and shut the door behind him. He leaned against it and slumped to the floor, exhausted. His clothes were torn and his face and hands were covered in soot. "I need water", he pleaded.

Monica hurried for the first aid kit while her sister, Anita, ran to the kitchen and brought him a glass of ice water. Inigo bent over him, "How badly are you hurt, Senator?"

"Just my leg and my head" Gavin answered. "I think I'm alright. I made it all the way here."

The commotion woke the couple's two young children who came out to see what was happening. "Go back to bed Ernesto. Help your sister." Anita urged.

"Que pasó, mama?"

"Monica's friend has a boo-boo. He is fine. Go back to bed now", she urged, as she escorted the little ones back down the hall.

Monica returned with a wash cloth, gauze and bandages, tape, anti-bacterial cream, peroxide and isopropyl alcohol. She tore his pants leg open, removed the tourniquet he had applied, and began to clean the wound on his leg. "The news said you were dead. What happened, Senator?"

"I'm not sure, Monica. I think they tried to kill me and the man I was with at the café. He's dead. I saw his body as I was leaving. Somehow I was thrown clear of the worst of it."

"The news is reporting that the bombing was a terrorist act", Anita informed him.

"I don't think so." Gavin felt otherwise.

"Why would anyone want to kill you?" Anita asked.

Gavin suddenly realized, the less these people knew, the safer they would be. "I'm not sure, Anita. I'm still trying to figure that out. It's just a feeling."

The explosion had thrown Gavin up against a wall in the café and knocked him unconscious. He had come to before authorities arrived and had realized the bomb may have been intended for him. It could also have been intended to kill a man named Saffari, the Afghan minister Kevin had arranged for him to meet. The coincidence that he and Saffari would be together in a tiny café where · a random bombing took place seemed too unlikely. Was it possible Kevin was responsible for the blast? Had he been set up? For the moment, it was safer for Gavin to assume so.

There had been a dead body next to him when Gavin regained consciousness. It resembled him in weight and stature and the face had been so badly damaged it was unrecognizable. He had swapped identities with the man, leaving his wallet, passport, cell phone and watch for authorities to find on the dead man's body. It was Gavin's hope that authorities would assume the dead man's body was his, long enough to give him precious hours to recuperate and get as far away as possible from those trying to kill him before it was discovered the body was not his.

It had taken Gavin about forty-five minutes to walk to Anita and Inigo's apartment. From the café, he had zigzagged in and out of back streets to avoid the police, emergency responders and the public in general. Only a few people had seen him but he was worried someone may have either recognized him or, perhaps, thought him suspicious enough to contact the police. He was fairly certain no one had seen him come down Avenue Gambetta to Monica's sister's apartment building. He would rest here until morning then decide where to go.

"Inigo, how tall are you?" Gavin would need fresh clothing. He hoped Inigo's clothes might fit him.

"Five feet nine inches", Inigo responded.

"I'm going to need clothes...", Gavin began.

Monica interrupted, "I will go to your hotel and bring back your suitcase, sir."

"NO!" Gavin said emphatically. "Whoever did this could be watching the hotel. Besides, the police and other authorities have almost certainly converged on my hotel room. We can be sure of that." There was only one thing he could think to do. "Anita, would you go to a store in the morning and buy me some comfortable travelling clothes? I will also need a backpack, a ball cap and some tennis shoes. Oh, and some cash. Monica will give you a credit card to use at an ATM."

"Of course", she offered.

"I can go and get cash in the morning", Monica offered, realizing the business credit card she carried for him might be traced by the authorities. "It would be dangerous if I give her your credit card. They will know you are still alive. I can use my personal card."

"Using your credit card is a good idea. But you shouldn't go out, Monica. The police will know who you are. They may be looking for you by tomorrow morning. If not tomorrow, soon. They will come here when they realize you have relatives that live in Paris. You need to let Anita do it. She won't draw any suspicion in the morning."

"Gavin, do you think we are in any danger?" Inigo asked, obviously concerned for the safety of his wife and children.

Gavin couldn't be sure, but he thought it better to prevent panic right now than to give Inigo his honest assessment. "I don't believe so, Inigo. I'll leave here in the morning when Anita returns with my clothing. If the police contact you, just tell them the truth. You've done nothing illegal."

"Of course." Inigo nodded.

"You should get stitches, sir, for your leg and your head." Monica had finished cleaning the wound on his knee and started cleaning the gash above his temple.

"I can't go to a hospital", Gavin said. "One of you will have to sew me up. And stop calling me sir. Call me Gavin, all of you."

"Senator, I mean Gavin...", Monica struggled. "It is so hard to call you Gavin, sir."

"Keep working on it", he grinned.

"I want to go with you, Gavin. You will need help. And I can translate French and Spanish for you. You will stick out like a thumb which is sore if you travel alone."

Gavin knew she was right. But he resisted. "I'm not even sure where I'll go yet. I need to make a phone call first. Then I'll let you know if I need help. In fact, let me use your phone. It will call the States, right?"

"Yes sir. I mean, yes, it does", she smiled.

Gavin was kicking himself for not bringing his crypto-phone with him to the café. He had left it in the hotel and brought only his personal cell which he had placed in the pocket of the corpse at the café. Stupid! Stupid!

Monica located her phone and handed it to him. Anita had once been a nurse's assistant when she was young. She stood by with a curved upholstery needle and thread. It had been decided she would sew the stitches on the Senator.

Gavin noticed her readying the needle. "Slow down, there. Let me make this phone call first."

Anita smiled and backed away, nodding in the affirmative.

Gavin felt strong enough now to move to a chair in the kitchen where it would be easier for Anita to work on his wounds. But first he looked through Monica's contacts for Chuck's cell number then dialed it.

"Hello, Monica! What can I do for you today?" Chuck answered.

"Hey, Chuck, it's Gavin. I'm gonna need some help."

"Where the hell are you, Gav? I thought you went to Paris?" Chuck had not been keeping up with the news. His focus had been on setting up his bivouac site. He was unaware of the Paris bombings or that the major news outlets had been reporting on Gavin's death. Gavin brought him up to speed on his location and condition and his suspicion that he had been setup by his friend Kevin Falk.

"Major Kevin Falk? Is he Air Force?" Chuck inquired.

"Yeah, why?"

"Son of a bitch!" Chuck exclaimed. "I saw him here this morning. He was talking to somebody behind some office buildings. The guard said he was here to protect a shipment of some kind. His assumption was military grade hazardous material. My hunch was right. They're storing contraband here. I'm sure of it now. I'll be goddamned."

"This guy is CIA, Chuck. You need to be careful."

"That's what I do, Gav. I'll be fine. Are you going to be alright?"

"I was able to walk to Monica's sister's place after the explosion. That's where I am now. They're treating my wounds. Superficial. I'm okay."

"I assume you lost your crypto. This is not a secure phone. We need to limit our conversations. I know these guys", Chuck said. "They'll be all over this number by tomorrow."

"Yeah", Gavin concurred. "My crypto is at the hotel. Rookie mistake. I'll have a new burner in the morning. I'll call you with the number tomorrow."

"You can't stay there." Chuck advised. "You'll need to get moving as soon as possible. Paris is the last place you want to be right now."

"That's what I figured, too. I don't know where to go though. That's one reason I called you. Any ideas?"

"Give me some time to think, I'll get back to you early morning your time. Don't leave until we talk. Get as much rest as you can before you head out. It's hard to make good decisions when you're tired."

"Will do." Gavin assured. "Let me ask you... I'm not thinking straight yet. Should Monica come with me or stay here?"

"Definitely with you. She won't be safe there. Whoever did this will be just as interested in finding her as you, once they know you're still alive."

"Right." Gavin agreed.

"Hey Gav, don't call Allie. It's better right now if she thinks you're dead. She's flying back to Washington tomorrow. Her behavior may be critical to convincing the perps she believes you're dead. They may even want her dead. I'll hide her when she gets back and let her know you're okay when it's right."

"Thanks, Chuck. I know you're right", Gavin accepted.

"Just so you know, I've setup a stake out at Green Valley. I could be here a couple days assuming my assistance isn't required elsewhere. I'll get someone to pick up the girls at the airport tomorrow and keep them hidden until I can get there. I have a gut feeling about this place. I don't want to pull up stakes unless I'm forced to."

"Roger that." Gavin understood. "Be safe."

"You, as well."

Gavin ended the call and looked up to see Anita still hovering over him with the upholstery needle and thread.

"This will hurt a little", she warned.

Gavin grimaced as he watched her begin to work on his leg. She was actually enjoying this! She was also good at it which made it a little easier to tolerate the pain.

"What time is it?" he asked.

Monica glanced up at the clock. "Two-thirty."

Morning was going to come way too soon.

* * *

It was only seconds after hanging up with Gavin that Chuck's phone began to ring again. He held it up to see the call was from Alexandra. This was not going to be fun.

"Hello, Allie."

"Uncle Chuck, he's dead! Oh, dear god. He's dead."

Chuck needed to get a feel for Alexandra's mental state. He wanted her to be in control of her emotions for the trip home. If he said the wrong thing, gave the wrong advice, he could be putting her life in danger. He took a deep breath.

"I know, Allie. I saw it on the news a few minutes ago."

Alexandra was a strong woman but she had just lost the two most important men in her life, or at least she thought so. Perhaps not letting her know that

Gavin was alive wasn't the best way to handle this situation. He would relent if he had to but he would rather not tell her yet.

"I'm feeling so lost, Uncle Chuck. I can't stop crying. I want to, but I just can't."

He could hear her sobs and sniffles and it broke his heart.

"It's okay, Allie. Crying is a good thing. Don't fight it. What time does your flight arrive in Washington tomorrow?" Chuck knew her flight times but he needed to measure her ability to concentrate and think clearly.

"We land about four forty-five" she said.

Okay. That was good. No hesitation, instant recall. She was upset and distraught, but obviously in control of her faculties.

"All right, honey. I can't be there, I'm in Massachusetts. Grady will pick you guys up at the airport and take you home. You might want to think about staying with Cynthia for a few days."

"We've already talked about that. She's going to stay with me at my place."

"Good. Good." Chuck said. "I'll be down in a few days to help you get through this, figure out what you want to do."

"I love you, Uncle Chuck", Alexandra said.

"I love you to pieces, Allie. Be strong."

"I'll try", she said.

Chuck felt good about the conversation. His goddaughter had the strength of a lioness. He wished he could tell her and Cynthia that Gavin was still alive. But he was afraid their behavior might be too abnormal if anyone was watching them when they arrived at the airport tomorrow. For Gavin's sake, it would be better if no one even suspected he might be alive.

It was approaching ten o'clock at night. Grady might be asleep already, an early to bed - early to rise kind of guy. But that was too bad, he needed his help. Grady would have to take an early flight out of Key West to make it to Baltimore by 5:00 p.m. Chuck had specific instructions for what he wanted Grady to do when he picked up the girls. He knew he could count on Grady no matter the hour.

He dialed Grady's number and smiled as Grady answered, "You sorry son-of-a-bitch! You have any idea what time it is? A man needs his beauty sleep, you know!"

CHAPTER 20

Kevin stood well to the side of the U.S. Custom's exit doors on Concourse E where arriving International flight passengers debarked at Baltimore Washington International Airport. Cynthia and Alexandra would be coming through those doors soon. Their plane had touched down over fifty-five minutes ago. It was taking a while to get through customs apparently. He was in no hurry. He didn't have to be back to Green Valley until the following night.

Kevin was hoping the ladies would need a ride back to their apartments. He would offer to take them, it wasn't that far out of the way, he would say. I still don't believe what happened to Gavin. Alex, I'm so sorry. And, you, too, Cynthia.

If they accepted his offer, it would be the last time anyone saw them alive. There was a hole already dug and waiting for its occupants in the forest near the Pine Ridge Golf Club, next to the Loch Raven Reservoir north of Towson, Maryland. It didn't have to happen today. But the convenience of having both Alexandra and Cynthia together at such a vulnerable time was too much to pass up.

Kevin knew surveillance cameras could be problematic at the airport. But he had scrutinized their locations and carefully choreographed his movements to minimize any chance of being identified. Three-inch heels and jeans long enough to cover them made him appear taller. He wore a gray long sleeve shirt and sunglasses and a Baltimore Raven's ball cap. Not much to go on should anyone look for identifying features of the mystery man on surveillance film.

Alexandra and Cynthia exited the doors from the Custom's inspection area pulling their suitcases behind them. They immediately headed toward the ladies' restroom. Kevin kept his distance, not wanting to engage until it was certain they weren't being met by someone else. When they went into the restroom he changed locations, carefully avoiding exposing his face to the two cameras observing that area. When the girls came out of the restroom he followed them through the exit doors to the curbside pickup zone. He watched from a distance to see if anyone was waiting for them. They appeared to be looking for someone, so he waited, and watched.

Twenty minutes went by. If they were being picked up their ride was late. He would give it another ten minutes before he would approach them. As he waited, he carefully went over the steps he would take once they had accepted his offer of a ride:

- Take the shuttle to the remote parking area where his car was parked.
- Talk about his new Mustang and put on driving gloves to protect his hands from being exposed to the chemicals he was about to administer to them
- Once in the car, hand each of them Etophine-soaked tissues
- Bind and gag them when they passed out
- Drive them to the location that would be their final resting place

Etophine was a big-game anesthetic, elephant and rhinoceros tranquilizer. It was available only to registered veterinarians. Kevin had had no trouble obtaining some from a dark web seller using Bitcoins, so much easier and anonymous than stealing it from a veterinarian's office. Just getting a drop on your skin would incapacitate a person. Inhaling or injecting it is lethal.

Simply touching the tissues he would hand them would be enough to keep them from crying out until they were unconscious. He wasn't concerned with whether either of the girls died from the exposure to the tissues. They were going to die anyway. He would leave them on the floor board of the car, bound and gagged just in case, until he reached Loch Raven. If either was alive he would administer a final lethal dose before he dumped them into the hole he had already dug in a wooded area along the bank of the reservoir.

Thirty minutes and still no ride had arrived. It was time. Kevin approached the girls with a greeting of surprise. "Alex? I didn't expect to see you here! Hi, Cynthia."

Alexandra turned to see Kevin walking up. He began offering his condolences before he reached them. "Alex, I am so sorry. I saw the news last night and I was stunned. I can't believe he's gone, my best friend. Look at me. I'm still shaking." And he was... in anticipation.

Alexandra opened her arms and hugged him. "I can't believe it either. I'm a mess, Kevin. I have no idea how to keep going, or if I even want to."

"I know", he said. "It's all so surreal."

Cynthia stood by watching, saying nothing. Something about this situation just wasn't right. It was nothing she could put her finger on. Something just didn't feel right. "So why are you here, Kevin?"

Kevin looked at her with a forced friendly smile that bothered her further. It wasn't the right kind of smile. "I just flew in from Florida. I was down at MacDill for two days working with Customs and Border Patrol on a piracy case involving a former Air Force officer."

"They still have pirates in the Caribbean?" Alex said jokingly.

Her humor fell flat but Kevin acknowledged the attempt. "Yeah. They do. So, do you guys have a ride? I'm parked in long term. I'll be glad to take you home."

"Well, someone was supposed to pick us up but it's been quite a while. What do think, Cynthia? I don't know Grady's number. I don't know how to get in touch with him."

Cynthia felt uneasy but it had been almost forty minutes and Grady hadn't shown up. With no way to call him, maybe they should accept Kevin's offer. Kevin was here and a taxi ride all the way to the other side of D.C. would be expensive.

"I suppose", she said.

"Great!" Kevin said, in a manner too cheery for the situation. "Let me have those."

Kevin grabbed the handles of their suitcases. "We can catch a shuttle down this way." He began walking toward the remote parking shuttle stop, careful to avoid eye contact with a camera positioned just above the waiting area at the stop. A shuttle bus was pulling away as they approached. Kevin stepped out into the lane and waved at the driver who immediately stopped and pulled over to let them on.

The shuttle driver opened the door and got out to help with the bags. Kevin collapsed the handles on the suitcases and lifted them himself. "I've got it", he told the driver as he stepped up into the coach. The driver motioned for the girls to step aboard.

Cynthia stepped up into the coach. As Alexandra was about to board, a voice called from behind her.

"Allie! Allie! Hey, Allie!"

Alexandra turned to look behind her. It was Grady coming out of the terminal doors.

"Grady!" Alexandra called back. "Where have you been? We thought you weren't coming."

Grady limped over moving quickly, slightly out of breath. "I've been waiting for you guys to come out of the Custom's doors. You must have slipped by me."

"That's okay", Alexandra said, turning to Kevin. "Looks like our ride has arrived after all. But thank you so much for offering, Kevin."

Alexandra and Cynthia stepped down from the coach. Alexandra gave Grady a brief hug. "It's good to see you, Grady."

Cynthia hugged Grady tightly to his slight surprise. She wasn't sure why, but Grady somehow felt like a knight in shining armor. The anxious tension she had been feeling began to dissipate. Then she turned to Kevin, "Yes. Thank you, Kevin."

Kevin realized there was nothing more to be done here today. Mere seconds had thwarted his plans but there was no point in lamenting the fact. Adapt and overcome. He stepped off the coach and set the suitcases down on the sidewalk, pulling the handles to full extension.

Grady felt a bitter chill come over him. So, this was Kevin! He wanted to kill the son-of-a-bitch on the spot, with his bare hands! Chuck had told him last night that it was Kevin who had ordered the bomb planted that almost killed Gavin. Grady wasn't good at hiding his emotions. It was time to hightail it out of there before he got himself into trouble.

"Okay, ladies. We've been standing around here way too long. Let me have those." Grady grabbed the suitcase handles and began pulling them toward the elevators to the short-term parking garage, never acknowledging Kevin's presence. The girls said a quick goodbye to Kevin and turned to catch up with Grady who was already halfway to the elevators and moving away fast.

"Slow down, Grady. Where's the fire?" Alexandra implored.

Grady slowed as he realized he was moving at near light-speed. He had almost blown it! What if they had gotten on that shuttle? He didn't want to think about it. He was shaking as he loaded the girls' suitcases into the trunk of his rented Chrysler 300. He started the engine and sat there a few moments taking deep calming breaths as Alexandra strapped herself into the front seat beside him and Cynthia settled into the back.

"Nice ride, Grady!" Cynthia acclaimed.

"Buckle up ladies. We've got a long trip ahead. I wanted you to be comfortable for the duration." Grady exited the parking garage toll plaza and followed the signs toward I-195.

"Where are we going?" Alexandra asked. She was still in a daze. The fog of the last two days had kept the world from making much sense. Still, this wasn't the way to her apartment! Why wasn't he taking her home?

Grady turned off I-195 onto the BWI Parkway and headed south, then looked around at the girls. "We're going to Florida. You're going to stay with me for a while."

"Grady, wait!" Alexandra contested. "Why? Is this Uncle Chuck's idea?"

"You bet it is", Grady acknowledged. "I'll explain it all in due time, young lady. But let's start with some news I think you'll both like - Senator Gavin J. Manson is alive and well."

Crickets...

* * *

Anita returned from shopping with several bags containing the things Gavin had listed. As she set the bags on the kitchen table, Monica's cell phone began to ring. "Monica! Your phone."

Monica rushed from the living room where she and Gavin had slept overnight, he in a lazy-boy chair, she on the sofa. "Hello?"

"Buenos días, Monica."

"Good morning, Chuck."

"I need to speak with Gavin."

"Uno momento, he's still asleep, Chuck. I will wake him."

Gavin had heard the phone ring and the ensuing conversation. He was awake and sat up rubbing his eyes. He could see the clock in the kitchen, it was 10:30 a.m., almost seven and a half hours sleep. He hardly felt rested. His body hurt all over - even worse than last night. But he knew seven plus hours of sleep would get him through the day. He took the phone from Monica. "Good to hear your voice, Chuck!"

"Morning, Gav. Were you able to get a burner yet?"

"I don't know", Gavin replied, calling toward the kitchen. "Anita! Were you able to get a burner?"

"Yes." Anita came out of the kitchen carrying the phone still wrapped in the display packaging and handed it to Gavin.

"Yeah, I have it. It needs to be setup. Looks like it's international capable. This should work", Gavin affirmed.

"Good", Chuck said. "Get it set up and try to call me. If I don't hear from you in twenty minutes I'll call back."

"Alright. Sounds good." Gavin hung up and began tearing the packaging open. Within minutes he had the phone operating. He dialed Monica's phone. It rang. He hung up and dialed Chuck.

"Hello."

"Chuck, Gavin."

"Great! Okay I can see your number. I'll hang up and try to call you." Seconds later Gavin's phone rang.

"Looks like we're good. I'm putting you on speaker, Chuck. So, I have no papers. I had to leave them at the scene. I kept a dead guy's identification but it doesn't look much like me."

"Enough to fool a ticket agent?" Chuck asked.

"Maybe. But with the city on such high alert right now I don't know. They'll be looking more closely than usual."

"Probably", Chuck admitted. "Does Anita have a car?"

166

Gavin looked to Monica, "Does she?"

Chuck could hear Monica respond, "Yes."

"Good", he said. "Will she give you a ride out of Paris? Maybe sixty, seventy kilometers to a bus station in a smaller town where they won't be on such high alert?"

Monica was already headed for the kitchen to find Anita. Gavin heard her yell back. "Yes, no problem."

"Okay," Chuck advised, "Give me a second while I develop a plan here."

Chuck was on the internet using a French public transportation website. A minute later he was back. "Okay. It looks like there's a bus station in a small town about 70 kilometers from you. The place is called Mormant."

Monica had returned to the living room, Anita had followed. "I know Mormant", Anita nodded. "Perhaps an hour and one quarter, no more."

"Excellent! Gavin, get yourselves fed and packed. I'll put together an itinerant plan and get back to you in, say, thirty minutes."

"Got it." Gavin was anxious to get moving. "Anita can you be ready to take us there in thirty minutes?"

"Yes, Senator. With pleasure."

"Thanks, Chuck. I'm back in thirty."

"Roger, that."

Gavin sifted through the treasure trove Anita had bought. Pretty savvy woman, he thought, not unlike her sister. The bags not only contained the items he had asked for, she had bought a small flashlight and batteries, duct tape, a pocket knife, several yards of paracord, additional bandages and medicine for his wounds, some power bars, a small spiral ring notebook and a package of pens. She also contributed a couple of bottles of water for him and Monica.

Monica had gone into the kitchen and begun to prepare eggs and ham and toast. Gavin packed the backpack and got dressed in his new clothes. With the ball cap and sunglasses he looked like a typical American tourist. He strolled into the kitchen, "How do I look?"

Monica laughed. "Silly, but believable. Sit down and eat breakfast, sir. She put the meal on the table and left the kitchen.

"Are you going to eat?" Gavin called to her.

"I was eating while I cooked", she called back.

Gavin finished his breakfast and put his dishes in the sink. He checked the clock. He had about five minutes before he would call Chuck back. As he walked into the living room, Monica was coming down the hallway, a blonde, her long black ringlets gone, her eyebrows bleached to match her hair.

"What in the hell did you do?"

"How do I look as a blonde, honey?" She laughed at the words coming out of her mouth. "I think we should act like a couple on this journey. Do you think?"

"Did you cut your hair?"

"It will grow back." Monica modeled the wig doing a 360 for him.

"You look stunning as a blonde, and I suppose you're right, sweetheart." Gavin was constantly amazed at her ability to think street smart.

Gavin eased himself onto the couch, moaning as he did so. He was incredibly sore, still, and a little concerned it might hamper his ability to blend into crowds without drawing attention to himself. He would soldier through, but, damn, it hurt.

He reached for the burner phone, dialed Chuck and put the phone on speaker. Chuck answered immediately. "Get a pencil and paper, Gav."

Monica quickly located the spiral notebook in his backpack, removed one of the pens from its packaging and handed them to him.

"Go ahead, Chuck."

"This is the quickest, safest route I could come up with on short notice. But first..."

"Where am I going?" Gavin interrupted.

"Patience, grasshopper. Is anyone else in the room besides you and Monica?"

"Yes, Anita. Inigo took the kids to the park."

"Then take the phone off speaker and make sure Anita can't see or hear what we're discussing. The less she knows the better for her and her family. Also, the better for you and Monica."

Gavin looked at Anita who nodded and went to her bedroom in the back. He took the phone off speaker and handed it to Monica. She held it to his ear and listened in as Chuck explained his plan.

"Destination: Igoumenitsa", Chuck began.

Gavin was surprised and wondered why but remained silent and attentive as Chuck explained.

"To get you two out of Europe without anyone finding out, you will need new identities. I've contacted Allie's uncle, Demetri, in Igoumenitsa. He has agreed to make new passports for both of you."

"I have a passport", Monica insisted. "Why do I need a new one?"

"If you try to fly under your true name you will likely be flagged. If you're flagged it also gives away Gavin's location if you're together. You could travel separately but I wouldn't advise it."

"No", Monica said. "I want to travel with my lover."

"What?" Chuck asked.

"Nothing", Gavin deferred, as he shook his head at her admonishingly. "Go ahead."

"Your trip will be in four legs, all direct routes. Anita will take you to the bus station in Mormant. Buy two tickets to Lyon. That leg is a little over four hours by bus."

Chuck was scribbling, "Bus, Mormant to Lyon. 4 hrs. Okay."

"Make your way to the train station and buy tickets to Milan. This is a dangerous leg. You will be travelling across the Italian border and they may check your identification. The EU is supposed to support freedom of movement but cross-border is another animal. Sometimes you're checked, sometimes not. With the terrorist bombing last night, my guess is they'll be checking."

Gavin jotted down the information, Train, Lyon to Milan. "How long is that trip?"

"A little over 7 hours."

Gavin was curious. "What if I drive it? There are bound to be unguarded roads across the border."

"Yeah, yeah. Good thinking!" Chuck was embarrassed he hadn't thought of it himself. "Let Monica rent the car with her ID. Don't tell them where you're going. Car rentals check your ID but they don't report it to any international databases. Just leave the car in Milan...but not at the train station. Leaving it at the bus station would add some confusion if they find your trail."

Gavin recorded the trip details, Lyon to Milan, rent car... "How long is that trip?"

"Hang on..." Chuck quickly checked his maps program. "Five hours, plus or minus. Faster than the train!"

"Okay." Gavin pressed. "Where to next?"

"Make your way to the train station. You want to go to Bari on the southeast coast. Travel time about ten and a half hours."

"Got it."

"From Bari, take a high-speed ferry to Igoumenitsa. Make sure you take a direct one. Some stop on Corfu. Again, passports are hit or miss. It will be risky. That's about nine hours."

Gavin summed up the itinerary: "So, I have Mormant to Lyon by bus, four hours plus. Lyon to Milan by car, roughly five hours. Milan to Bari by train, ten and a half hours. Bari to Igoumenitsa, nine-hour ferry ride."

"You got it, man!" Demetri will meet you at the docks and take you to his house." Chuck sounded upbeat but he was secretly worried. This was not going to be an easy journey.

"Gracias, Carlos" Monica added.

"¡Vaya con Dios, Amiga!"

Gavin put the notes and pen into his backpack. Monica picked up her backpack, a gift from Anita, and called to her sister, "We're ready."

When Anita came out, Chuck handed her the wallet and cell phone of the dead man he had taken them from at the Charonne restaurant. He explained why he had them then told her, "If the authorities show up, give them these. If

169

they don't show within the next three or four days, take them to a police station and explain what happened."

Anita acknowledged.

Gavin looked at Monica, the blond woman who would accompany him across Europe for the next few days. He felt bad that he had gotten her into this mess. He hoped like hell he could get her out. He stood up from the couch and tried to stretch but couldn't. It was painful no matter how he moved. He just hoped it wouldn't get any worse.

CHAPTER 21

Chuck McCrory awoke to the buzz of the motion detection alarm on his Android tablet. The high-powered night-vision binoculars had detected movement in the transfer yard below him. He sat up in the Jeep Wrangler and tried to get his blood flowing by slapping his face and pinching himself to speed up the process. He detached the tablet from its mounting bracket and brought it close to see what had triggered the alarm. The clock on the tablet said 4:04 a.m.

This was the third night of his stakeout and it was going to be his last if something didn't happen soon. He zoomed in and panned around to see where the commotion was located. There was a truck and three people in the area near the lift crane where containers were loaded onto flatbeds. The yard lights had been turned on. It was difficult to see using night-vision with so much ambient light. He switched the binoculars to day-vision using the tablet's WIFI connection. The image became clearer, but not clear enough.

Chuck put on his shoes and climbed out the back of the Wrangler. The air was dry and the temperature chilly. He shouldered his police .38 Special and put on a lightweight black jacket and a ski mask. He decided to take along some GPS tracking darts and a slingshot. He put them in a jacket pocket and then started down the hill.

As he cleared the tree line he made his way over to the blind, detached the binoculars from the tripod, and put them in his other jacket pocket. He was wearing pitch black clothing but caution was still paramount in his mind. He carefully made his way down to the service road along the railroad tracks, jumped the ditch, and followed the tracks until he could see the open area where the crane and truck were located. He heard the crane motor start up.

The glow from the spotlights illuminated the crane and the loading zone area and extended out into the field beyond the fencing in the back. He wanted to get as close as possible to perhaps hear the conversation the men were having but the lights were hampering that idea. The fence was chain-link and offered no cover. There was one large oak tree to the side of a maintenance building that abutted the fence that would provide some cover. That appeared to be his best option.

Chuck stayed in the shadows as he moved further down the hill to a point where he could crawl through the brush on his stomach without being seen. He moved quickly on his belly using a weaponless leopard-crawl, a second nature technique he knew well from military training, until he reached the tree behind the maintenance shack. He was roughly twenty-five yards from the crane and he could easily make out what was happening. He could hear the voices of the men inside the fence, but with the noise of the crane motor, he still couldn't understand what they were saying.

There were three men communicating with each other. Two stood together by the bed of the truck, the other was the crane operator who sat up in the cab of the crane. Chuck took out the binoculars and focused on the two men standing together. He didn't recognize either man. He snapped a photo with the binoculars and took a short movie panning around the compound. He double checked to be sure the timestamp was on in case his recording could be used in court one day. Then he panned up to the crane operator. The face was familiar but he couldn't place it. He wracked his brain trying to get a synapse to fire. Nothing.

The crane operator rotated 180 degrees and began extending the boom over the top and beyond a metal building along the same row of office buildings Chuck had visited two days before. The two men went around the building following the boom and disappeared into the area where Chuck had seen the cluster of old rusted containers on satellite photos.

Chuck panned up to the crane operator and zoomed in on his face. It bothered him that he couldn't make the connection. He watched as the man, obviously skilled, manipulated the controls in the cab with expedience and efficiency. As the man reached for a lever above his head Chuck suddenly realized who he was. He snapped a quick photo before the man could lower his arm. Etched on the man's left forearm was a tattoo of an eagle and an American flag. He had just found Jeremy Ballard's killer. More than that, now there was no doubt that the CIA was involved in smuggling Afghan heroin into the United States and they weren't above killing people to do it. Gavin's hunch had been correct.

Minutes later the two men returned and the crane began to strain as it lifted a 10-foot ship container over the building and set it down on the bed of the awaiting truck. He watched as the two men returned to strap and secure the container to the truck bed.

Chuck was pretty sure he knew where this container was going but it would be nice if he could get a GPS tracking device on it. He had brought two with him but not the conventional kind of tracker. There were many kinds of civilian grade trackers available relatively cheaply. Most had to be magnetically or mechanically attached which required getting close enough to the vehicle to physically attach it to the underside of the body or chassis. That wasn't going to happen here.

Chuck had been experimenting with a different idea: there was a sticky dart being used experimentally by police departments to safely track vehicles fleeing pursuit rather than chase them at high-speed. High-speed police pursuits were extremely controversial in many communities nationwide as they often resulted in civilian casualties and, more often, damage to police cruisers and injuries to their drivers.

Typically, the experimental darts were shot from air pressure canons mounted in the grill of a cruiser. Law officers in pursuit of a fleeing motorist only had to get close enough to shoot a dart which would stick to the rear of the car with a specially developed super-sticky adhesive substance. A small GPS tracker in the body of the dart would allow police to then back off the dangerous high-speed chase and simply follow the GPS signal at a reasonably safe speed until the motorist was subsequently located, apprehended and arrested. One mid-west city had used the device eighteen times its first trial year and made eighteen arrests with no accidents and no civilian injuries.

Chuck didn't have a high-pressure canon but he didn't need one. His plan was to sneak around to the exit of the facility where the departing truck would have to stop, or at least slow down, before pulling out onto the main road. It was a low-tech solution, but he would use a slingshot he had specially designed for just this purpose, to propel the darts at the side of the container. Chuck's inspiration to use the darts came to him when his PI work had him once tracking a suspected cheating husband and he couldn't get close enough to attach a magnetic tracker to the man's car inside the walls of his opulent estate.

Optimally, Chuck would have liked to break camp and reposition himself and his vehicle closer to the front gate before setting up an ambush position. But that was not possible. Time was of the essence. He started back the same way he had come, crawling through the brush until he felt it safe to crouch and run along the edge of the railroad tracks toward the road that led downhill to the front entrance of the facility. The distance was a good quarter mile. When he made it to the road he kept low in the drainage ditch alongside, working his way toward the main entrance.

As he approached the entrance, he realized a street lamp made it impossible to get close enough to deploy the dart unseen from this side of the road. He looked around for options, any strategic position where he could hide undetected. There simply weren't any on this side of the entrance.

On the far side it was darker and there were trees he could use for cover. In fact, it was almost perfect. The problem was getting across to the other side without being seen by the guard at the gate or the attendant cameras. Chuck stared at the thirty-inch diameter culvert that crossed under the entrance road. He would have to crawl about fifty feet in the dark with no flashlight and who knows what kinds of creatures lived in there at night. This was a Shawshank decision he'd rather not have to make. But he crouched down in the ditch and made his way up to the culvert. Did it even go all the way across without obstruction?

Chuck set the binoculars to night-vision mode and peered inside the culvert. He could see a tree limb that had been washed in mid-way across. It was too large to crawl past. He would have to either push it out as he crawled forward or retrieve it and pull it back toward him. At the very far end he could see a pair of eyes intently watching him, probably a fox or coyote. It would run. He wasn't worried about that. He held the binoculars in front of him as he crawled inside.

Spider webs were everywhere. He couldn't see them but he could feel them sticking to his ski mask, brushing against his eyelids and lips, and wrapping around his hands and fingers as he moved forward feeling his way in the dark. Every once in a while he could feel a homeless spider scrambling for safety.

Chuck barely fit into the narrow tube and progress was slow. He couldn't turn his body around in such a way to get his hands beside or behind him, so he was unable to toss obstructions to his rear. He kept moving large rocks out of the way, grabbing them with one hand and tossing or pushing them forward until he would approach the same rock again and again, repeating the process. Every eight or ten feet he would stop to use the binoculars to assess his progress.

When he got to within ten feet of the tree limb he stopped and used the binoculars to figure out how best to tackle it. Once he got up close it would be pitch black and the binoculars would be useless at that range. It appeared the limb could be easily pulled out the way he had come but, at this point, he had no intention of going backwards. There were two branches that looked like they could be broken off at the trunk of the limb. If so, he should be able to push it out the other side. He memorized their locations and crawled forward in darkness until he reached it.

The branches broke easily. The rest of the way was much easier to traverse. He found that the limb acted like a broom. As he slid it forward, smaller rocks and debris collected in the branches and piled up in front of the limb. He still had to move the larger obstacles manually. A few feet from the other side he took a final look through the binoculars. The eyes he had seen earlier were now thirty yards down the ditch beyond the end of the culvert. In the distance he could hear a large motor vehicle gearing up, coming closer. He hurried to push his way out of the culvert and into the open ditch. The worst was over now. He was clear of the culvert.

Chuck crawled up the embankment into a thicket next to a clump of small trees and got down on one knee. He was less than 15 yards from the road bed the truck would have to pass. The slingshot would have no trouble propelling the tracker from this distance. He retrieved the slingshot and both tracker darts from his jacket pocket and laid them ready at his feet. He wanted both darts ready in case the first one missed or didn't stick to its mark. Then he raised the binoculars and looked for the oncoming truck. He wanted to make sure it was the right one. It was.

The truck made the turn from the Green Valley entrance onto the main road. Chuck took aim. As the truck passed in front of him he fired. The tiny missile flew straight and true, affixing itself almost noiselessly to the side of the container near the rear. He watched it dangle in the chaotic slipstream as the truck shifted gears and accelerated out of sight. He was fairly sure he knew where the truck was headed, but now he could know for certain.

It took Chuck almost thirty minutes to get back to his camp, break it down, stow everything, and get underway. He wasn't worried that the truck ahead of him had a head start. The driver would have to cautiously follow all the speed limits on the trip to New York harbor. Chuck calculated he could catch up to it well before it made Crimson Hook. When he initiated the GPS tracking app on his tablet, he was surprised to see the truck had not yet left northwest Connecticut. From the Green Valley facility it had made a beeline to Lakeville. Huh?

* * *

Leonard Loman awoke to hear Sonny and Cher intoning a familiar 'I Got You Babe' on the raspy motel clock radio. He debated hitting the snooze button as he rolled over and, instead, hit the off button. The blue digital display brightly broadcast 4:40 a.m. There was no time to dally. He had about twenty minutes to get the job done, then a few more to get to the cornfield.

Leonard hated this town. It had been nothing but a source of misery for him since the day he first set foot there. It had been his job several months ago to guard the container after it was delivered to the little corn farm off Lime Rock Road. He knew the drill: signal the truck's driver with the okay sign if the coast was clear; wave the truck onto the dirt road into the cornfield; lead it with his four-wheel ATV to a small clearing; camouflage it from aerial discovery where it would be left until nightfall; take the drivers to the motel where they would sleep for the majority of the day.

Leonard was familiar with the whole operation. The container would leave the Green Valley Transfer and Storage facility in the very early morning before any employees showed up for work. The truck would be driven here, to Lakeview, during the wee hours before the sun came up. It would remain here during the day until late evening when it would make the late night run to Crimson Hook. The idea was to travel at night and get to the docks between midnight and 2:00 a.m., just in time for the container to be loaded onto a freighter or cargo ship before the early morning shift clocked in.

The operation was usually as smooth as a baby's butt. But that morning, it wasn't. Perhaps it was just as well because the Florida operatives had failed to acquire the boat to which the cargo was supposed to have been transferred. The debacle would have been even worse had the container made it to Florida with no boat on which to offload it.

Leonard had learned a valuable lesson that he had paid only a small price to acquire. A local farmer had been on the road that morning and saw the Green Valley truck pulling into the cornfield. It was suspicious enough he made a call to the county sheriff who came out to investigate and arrested Leonard when the contents of the container were discovered. Leonard had spent four days in the sheriff's jail, a nasty puke-smelling cell block, before he was remanded to the DEA. Then he spent another three weeks in their custody before Selbourne managed to convince the DEA that Loman was an undercover investigative operative on a national security mission and they should cut him loose.

Leonard knew it was his own fault, he shouldn't have signaled the truck into the field when he saw the oncoming headlights, no matter how far off they appeared. He wouldn't make that mistake again. In fact, he wouldn't be here with the opportunity to make the same mistake again were it not for his other, more important skills, one of which he would be employing this morning.

Leonard washed his face and combed his hair, got dressed, and packed his small duffel bag. A glance at the clock noted the time was now 4:55 a.m. The Lakeville Press editor would arrive at her office in five minutes. He had watched her show up every morning, like clockwork, at precisely 5:00 a.m. for the past week. There was no reason to believe this morning would be any different.

The Lakeville Press publishing office was located in a small strip center directly across the street from the motel where Leonard was staying. The business had been started by Emily Ballard and her brother, Jeremy. They began as a local, two-person operation. Emily ran the office as editor and publisher. Jeremy was the reporter, investigator, and solicited ad revenue for the fledgling paper. By chance, he had been up early the morning of the Loman drug bust and heard the police scanner in his bedroom squawk with unusual activity for such a lazy, quiet community.

His heart raced as he rushed to the crime scene hoping to scoop the larger papers. It was hard to make sense of it all, but he gathered there was a great deal of drugs involved and one of the farmers at the scene said the truck had had magnetic signs on it which had been removed. "What did they say?" he had asked. "Crimson Hook something or other", the farmer had replied.

Leonard actually felt sorry for Ballard, young cub reporter with a real nose for investigative news. He had made it all the way to Crimson Hook and interviewed a number of dock workers and stevedores, piecing together the mystery of the Lakeville bust. No one could figure out how he had learned about Green Valley, but once he had, it was impossible to let him run with the story. Selbourne had had Jeremy Ballard killed at the docks. Now Leonard had to tie up a loose end, one that may or may not know what Jeremy knew. Why Selbourne had let her live this long was a mystery. But, it didn't matter to him. A loose end was a loose end.

Leonard left the motel room at 4:58 a.m. He walked across the street to see Emily getting out of her car and walking toward her office lugging a large briefcase and a macramé purse strung over her shoulder. She didn't see or hear him as she unlocked the door to the office and walked in. Leonard walked in behind her before she could close the door. She turned around startled to see him as he closed the door behind him with one hand and raised a silenced gun with the other. Two in the heart, one in the head and he was done with his first task of the morning.

Leonard looked around briefly, rummaging through a file cabinet and cursorily checking through piles of paperwork on the two desks in the office. He didn't expect to find anything. The effort was mostly so he could say he had done so with a credible voice. Then he peeked out the unopened blind making sure there was no one near before he walked back across the street, got into his car, and drove toward the cornfield on Lime Rock road. He had just enough time to hide the car and get the ATV out to the roadside before the Green Valley truck arrived.

* * *

The GPS tracker dart was doing its job and had, so far, gone undetected on the side of the container. Chuck could see from the map that the container was sitting in the middle of a field. As he followed the route the Green Valley truck had taken, he noticed it was starting to get light out. He wondered why the truck had come here. Maybe they just didn't like traveling during the day. Maybe they wanted to do the unloading at night. Either or both notions would make sense.

At the junction of U.S. 7 and County Road 112, Chuck turned onto Lime Rock Road and followed the GPS signal until he came to a dirt road into a corn field where, he could see on the GPS map, the container was now located. He slowed only slightly as he passed by, not wanting to arouse any suspicions were there guards posted inconspicuously. This was probably where the truck had entered the corn field.

It was nearly dawn now and Chuck surmised the container wasn't going anywhere for a while. He was tired, dirty and hungry. There was a motel on the map a few miles ahead. It had been four days since he had had a shower and a hot meal. He would eat and rest at the motel and wait for the container to begin moving again.

CHAPTER 22

H ow far from the border?" Gavin asked.

"Fifteen kilometers if we stay on A43. But there is a tunnel and a toll plaza before the tunnel entrance. Anita said they sometimes check for ID there."

"What's our alternative?"

Monica was navigating. She zoomed in on their location noticing Gavin's burner phone seemed to work great. "D 1006. It is forty-five minutes longer but the border looks completely unsecured."

"What's my exit?" The bus ride to Lyon had been uneventful and Monica had been able to rent a car without a hitch. Gavin wanted to drive the stretch to Milan, but he was beginning to get tired. He thought he could drive the entire leg from Lyon to Milan but his knee was already aching, as was much of the rest of his body, and he felt himself getting sleepy.

"Exit 30", Monica advised. "It's coming up. Follow the sign to Modane."

"What kind of road is this? Highway? Backwoods?"

Monica had rented a Mercedes C Class coupe at Gavin's suggestion, a 2.2-liter turbo diesel with a six-speed manual transmission. The manual transmission had seemed like a good idea at the time but now Gavin was realizing his right knee, even though it was primarily used for gas, was getting six times the workout it would have gotten with an automatic.

"It is very mountainous, especially once we reach Lanslebourg", she advised.

"Then I'm going to need you to drive", he said. "My knee just won't do it. It's killing me."

Monica actually looked forward to driving. A C class Mercedes wasn't near the top of the luxury models, but the two-hour drive, so far, had been amazingly smooth and comfortable from the passenger seat. "We should fill up in Lanslebourg before going into the mountains. Can you make it that far? Twenty minutes, maybe?"

"Oh, yeah. I can do another twenty minutes", he nodded.

As they drove into the little ski village, Gavin was singularly focused on finding a petrol station. Monica was absorbed in the beauty of the mountains and the quaintness of the little winter getaway called Lanslebourg, one of five villages which comprised the Val Cenis ski resort area.

It was too early for snow but she could still picture the hills and mountains dusted white with powder and drift covered trees. The main road through the village, Rue du Mont-Cenis, could have been one long postcard from the French Alps. Ahead of them was a peloton of twenty or more bike riders on a weekend run. Their presence pleased Monica because it forced Gavin to drive slowly behind them, allowing her to soak in the ambiance of the tiny retreat.

Monica was awed by her surroundings. Along both sides of the road were hotels and hostels, three and four stories high butted right up to the road edge. It was like driving in a canyon. The buildings were mostly empty now, but no doubt in the winter they would be filled with French and Italian vacationers who had come to get away for a week or enjoy a weekend away from the grind of the daily life wherever they lived.

Everywhere there were pastry shops, restaurants, sidewalk cafés, ski rental and sporting goods stores. The owners apparently lived above their shops. The balconies of their apartments had tables and chairs for lounging while they watched the humanity bustle on the sidewalks below. Many of the balconies were adorned with colorful laundry hung from the railings to dry in the cool, crisp autumn air. In the distance, the majestic Alps rose above the buildings, the higher peaks dolloped with snow year-round.

"There is the road we will take into Italy", Monica informed Gavin. She had pointed to a right-hand turn across a small bridge marked with a yellow arrow-shaped sign that said 'Italie'.

"How much further to the gas station?" Gavin groaned, as it appeared they were about to exit the far side of the little town. He was running out of patience and his knee was starting to throb.

"Just ahead", she said, regretting that her brief daydream had ended so abruptly.

"Have you driven stick shifts much?" Gavin asked, thinking maybe he should have had her rent a car with an automatic transmission. He hadn't planned on her driving any of this trip.

"My dad taught me to drive when I was twelve. He drove race cars in Mazatlán. He even drove in the Baja 1000 in the sixties. He was on TV with Jim McKay on Wide World of Sports. Have you ever heard of Mickey Thompson or Parnelli Jones?"

"Sure I have", Gavin avowed.

"My dad knew them all."

"Is your dad still living?" he wanted to know.

"Yes. He is still in Mazatlán. But he is very old. He lives with my brother now, after my mother died."

"When was the last time you saw him, or your brother?"

"It has been three years. Since I started to work for you", she stated.

"Why haven't you been home?" Gavin inquired.

"It is always so busy, sir. I didn't want to ask."

"Damn it, Monica! If you call me 'sir' again I'm going to fire you. And I'm sorry you feel so tethered to your job. That's my fault. I depend on you too much, I know. When we get through this you can take as much time as you want to see your family. If your dad can travel, bring him to Washington, show him around."

"Thank you, si.., thank you so much! Muchas gracias."

Gavin had no idea he was such a task master. But, apparently, he was. It was something he was going to have to work on. But right now the petrol station was in sight and he was relieved he would be able to relax and be a passenger for a while.

Gavin pulled up to the lone petrol pump and waited for the attendant to finish chatting with a visitor. It took several minutes before the attendant wandered over to help. Time means little in rural Europe. Even though he was in a hurry, being from the South, Gavin could appreciate the laid-back local attitude. The attendant eventually filled the car's tank and checked the fluid levels and tire pressures while he and Monica bought a snack and a soft drink from the vending machines.

Monica got into the driver's seat and adjusted her seat back and mirrors. She fastened her safety belt, started the engine and pulled away. As she drove out of the station she made a U-turn and doubled back the way they had come.

It was less than a kilometer until she made a left-hand turn across the small bridge they had passed earlier marked with a yellow arrow-shaped sign that said 'Italie'. Two other white arrow markers informed the distances to Mont Cenis and Suse, or Susa in Italian. It was ten kilometers to Mont Cenis, thirty-six to Susa, Italy.

From Susa it was just a short hop to Milan. The border crossing into Italy was high in the mountains and unguarded. Monica was looking forward to a pleasant and picturesque drive to Susa, especially the scenic drive along the French highland lake, Lac du Mont Cenis.

The first part of the drive was fun, six miles of serpentines back and forth through evergreen stands of Christmas tree shaped pines. The road was very narrow and it was probably a dangerous drive in the winter when the roads were frozen and the winds blew hard. Today it was just a lazy jaunt through a wooded wonderland.

Monica had cleared the last steep serpentine turn and the road had begun to shallow out when she glanced in the rearview mirror to see a car coming up behind her at a very high rate of speed. "Idiota!" she thought to herself, making tentative plans to move over as he passed, offering him plenty of room to blow by. The road was straight at this point. He should have no trouble getting around her.

As the car came closer it slowed and pulled in behind her. She watched in her rearview mirror as it pulled up directly behind her and inched closer with no obvious intention to pass her. "Senator!" she alerted. "The car behind us is behaving strangely."

Gavin was half sleeping, dozing off more as he had become comfortably convinced Monica could actually drive well enough for him to relax. "What?" He shook his head, clearing the light cobwebs.

He turned around in his seat and his heart nearly stopped. "How did they find us this quickly?" There were two men in a black BMW M6 behind them, less than a car length away, and the looks in their eyes told the story.

"Do you know who they are?" Monica asked.

"No", Gavin responded. "But they don't look too friendly."

"You think they mean us harm?" she asked, as the first tap to their rear bumper jolted their Mercedes forward with a lurch.

"Never mind", Monica said. "Sit back and hold on, sir."

Gavin looked at her then sat back in his seat, still staring over at her. "What do you have in mind, Monica?" Monica could tell he was concerned that the situation was out of his control. But there was nothing she could do about that at the moment.

"Hold on, sir!" she urged forcefully.

Monica accelerated to 120 kilometers per hour. The BMW behind followed suit. She could tell by the speed with which it had caught up to her that they had the faster, more powerful car. She wouldn't be able to outrun them. Ahead, she could see a right-hand turn, and in the turn on the left side, an empty graveled scenic overlook. As she entered the turn she spun the steering wheel hard to the left. The car whipped around and began sliding backwards. Monica jammed the emergency brake with her left foot, straightened the steering wheel and downshifted into second gear, then she released the emergency brake as the car slowed to a stop. She popped the clutch and gave the engine as much gas as it would take. The rear wheels fishtailed, throwing rocks and gravel and dust into a huge cloud behind her until the wheels finally caught hold. The car lunged forward onto the road, screeching as the tires left a pair of jet-black tread marks on the pavement. She was now headed in the opposite direction, the car's gas pedal to the floorboard, quickly shifting through the gears.

The black BMW had been caught off guard. She watched in the rearview as it locked the tires and did a U-turn. "I need to get back to the serpentines", she said calmly.

Gavin was dumbstruck. He had no idea she could drive like that. He was feeling much better about their chances now. Still, they had no weapons. If there was a gun battle it would be a one-sided affair. "That was an E-ticket ride, Monica!" he joked uncomfortably. "Why the serpentines?"

Monica shifted into sixth gear. Her speed was now in excess of 180 kilometers per hour. "Do you know about demolition derbies?"

"Yeah, where you run into each other and try to disable the other guy's car."

"Exactly!" she said.

They were quickly approaching the hairpin curve of the first serpentine. Monica looked at its shape and the view of the lower portion of the road from above as she descended into the sharp turn. Too exposed. She needed the trees inside the turn to obscure the visibility of the lower portion of the road for as long as possible. She would try the next hairpin.

Monica accelerated out of the apex of the curve and sped forward, watching the rearview mirror for the gaining chase car. The black BMW rounded the first serpentine turn still a quarter-mile behind. The next turn was coming up. She looked down at the lower road. It wasn't visible until well into the turn, the thick trees blocked the view of the road below. Perfect!

Monica slowed and negotiated the hairpin onto the lower portion of the road. She pulled a short way past the end of the turn and stopped, leaving the car sitting in the center of the road. Then she shifted into reverse and waited.

If the driver was a professional, the Beamer would slow only enough to make the turn into the apex of the curve, then it would begin to accelerate out of the turn, except by then it would see her sitting in the middle of the road. At that point, one of two things would happen. There was no room to go around her on the narrow stretch where she was parked. If the driver was any good he might have time to stop after he made the turn. That was the best-case scenario. If not, he would run into the back of her Mercedes, hopefully having slowed enough to keep from damaging the rear of the car too badly. She was going to need the back of her car intact for this plan to work. She hoped he was a better driver than that.

"Brace for impact, Gavin." This was the first time Monica had comfortably called him by name. The fact did not go unnoticed. Gavin had been in battle many times during his tour in Afghanistan. He recognized the calm authority in her voice. This woman was as competent and brave as any soldier he had ever fought beside.

"Yes ma'am", he verbally saluted.

The BMW spun around the narrow turn of the serpentine and immediately slammed on the brakes when it saw the parked Mercedes. Monica watched in the rearview mirror until the car had almost come to a stop just a few meters behind her. She was already in reverse. She revved the engine and popped the clutch accelerating backwards, never letting off the gas pedal.

Their Mercedes slammed into the black BMW, crumpling its front end, shoving the radiator and transverse engine deep into its fire wall. The hood of the BMW buckled on impact and steam began to shoot out of the cracks and open seams of the engine compartment, the radiator obviously punctured or dislodged. The air bags in the BMW deployed and a white corn starch cloud was being emitted from its shattered passenger windows. She kept her foot on the gas until both cars had come to a halt, her car no longer able to move the other any further.

Monica shifted into first gear and tried to pull away from the other car, dragging it several feet. The two cars were locked together, her wheels spinning, a cloud of black smoke billowing up from the burning rubber. She put the car into reverse and pushed the BMW backwards again for a few feet. Then she shifted into first gear again and the cars broke loose.

The Mercedes sprang forward, free of the entanglement. She drove ahead a few meters and stopped. She and Gavin both turned around in their seats watching the cloud of smoke disappear until they could see the BMW sitting cock-eyed, off to one side of the narrow road. Their vehicle disabled, the two henchmen inside were dazed but freeing themselves from the wreckage, drawing their guns as they did so.

"We've got to get through that gap", Gavin implored. "Do it!" he barked. She and Gavin could not go back the way they had come. It was mandatory they make it into Italy. Armed or not, Monica had to try to get past the gunmen.

"Yes sir!" she said with grit. She put the Mercedes into reverse and aligned the rear of the car to shoot the small gap between the disabled BMW and the rock barrier wall on the inside of the serpentine turn. She accelerated toward the gap. Both men were standing in the way, firing at them with rapid-fire handguns. Bullets shattered their rear window and tore through the front windshield. Two bullets ripped through Gavin's headrest. He heard the whistle of one of the projectiles as it whizzed by his ear. Monica plowed through the gap, brushing against the rock wall. Her side-view mirror was ripped from its mounts. Both men scrambled to jump out of the way, still firing as the Mercedes blew past them.

Once by the mangled black car, Monica turned the steering wheel hard to the right until the front end was pointed toward the upper road of the sharp serpentine hairpin. Simultaneously she slammed the shifter into first gear, and deftly let out the clutch until the rear tires took hold. She straightened the steering wheel and another billow of smoke trailed behind as she revved the engine and accelerated away. Gavin turned in his seat and watched as the frustrated assassins stood helplessly by their crippled machine, their empty guns now silent at their sides.

"Like watching a movie!" Gavin lauded. "That was as good as it gets, Monica. Your daddy taught you well. Was he a moonshiner? That first J-turn was right out of the Jimmy Johnson playbook!"

"A moonshiner?" Monica asked puzzled.

"A southern tradition", he laughed.

"What did you mean, E-ticket?" she asked.

"Ha!" Gavin chuckled. "Disneyland rides used to be priced by their popularity, the best being the most expensive. 'A' tickets were the cheap rides, 'E' tickets the most exciting and expensive."

"So E-ticket is good?"

"It's very good!" Gavin said, as the seriousness of the moment began to sober him. "But how in hell did they find us?"

"Maybe the rental agency told them?" she offered.

"Maybe. But I don't think so. I don't get it."

"We should pull over and make sure we are not leaking any gas", Monica suggested.

"Right", he agreed. "We're going to have to dump this car as soon as possible. I don't think we should try to take it all the way to Milan. Not as messed up as it is."

"We could leave it in Susa and catch a bus to the Milan train station", she suggested.

"That should work", Gavin concurred. "That's our plan, then."

Monica pulled to the side of the road and inspected the rear undercarriage of the Mercedes. It was fine. She pulled back onto the road, once again absorbing the picturesque beauty of Mont Cenis, especially the high mountain lake she had read froze solid in the winter. Several holes in the windshield whistled as the cool mountain air rushed through them, a tolerable annoyance given other less agreeable outcomes.

She had not been scared during the heat of the battle, but the adrenalin was wearing off and Monica could again feel her nerves, her hands lightly trembling on the steering wheel. Then she looked over at Gavin who had leaned back and was already dozing again. At that moment she realized something she had read about but never thought much about. Warriors rest at every opportunity, because they never know when the next opportunity will come. That Gavin had been so calm, so comfortable in the heat of battle, a battle where she, not he, had been in charge, made her feel special and proud. It made her feel like she, too, was a warrior, except she wouldn't get a chance to rest until they were on the bus to Milan.

Chuck had gambled the container wouldn't be moved before nightfall. He had set his alarm to awaken him at 5:00 p.m. It was a gamble, but his GPS app had no function for setting an alarm to alert him when the container began to move again. He awoke to see he had been correct. The container was still in the corn field, right where it was this morning.

It was roughly five miles from the motel to the location of the container. He could see no point in trying to visually keep an eye on it. Chuck ordered room service, propped up the tablet where he could see it, and turned on the television news.

"Where is Senator Gavin Manson?" the Breaking News was asking. It had now been discovered that the body originally thought to have been Gavin, wasn't. Chuck knew that was going to make Gavin and Monica's journey even more difficult. He wondered where they were and how they were doing.

The next few hours wore on, then, at precisely 10:30 p.m., Chuck saw the first movements of the container truck as it backed its way in a three-point turn to exit the corn field. He grabbed his gear, made his way to the Jeep, and mounted the GPS tablet to his dash. As he suspected it would, the truck pulled out of the corn field, made its way to White Hollow Road, and headed south toward New York City.

* * *

The three-hour ride to Crimson Hook Terminals had been about as boring as any three hours Chuck had ever spent. But the nice thing about the GPS tracker was that he had been able to be bored a half-mile behind the target, zero chance of being spotted tailing them.

As he rolled up to the terminal entrance, Chuck was trying to figure out how he would get into the yard this time of night. He had gotten past the gate guards during the day on his previous trip, saying he needed to talk to someone at the onsite truck rental company. It was 1:30 a.m. now, and he could come up with no plausible story. He slowly drove past the gated entrance and made a right turn onto the side street next to the terminal property.

The street stretched for a city block then curved to the left along the waterfront, property still owned by Crimson Hook Terminals. Chuck's first thought was to jump the fence somewhere along the property line. The problem was, the fencing along the property was wrought iron, like prison bars, nine or ten feet high, with the tops of the pickets sharpened to a point and curved outward, making it impossible to scale, the danger of impalement too great.

The further he drove down the dimly lit backstreet, the more secure the property became. Chain-link fencing was added to concrete walls, the top of the chain-link guarded by multiple strands of barbed wire. He had reached the end of the terminal property and was about to give up the idea of finding a breach along this side, when a small blue concrete structure caught his attention. It was the emergency pumping station for the fire hydrants and sprinkler systems for several buildings and piers along the wharf.

Chuck estimated the pump building to be about eight feet high and twenty feet square. More importantly, the street side of the building had an unguarded wall that stuck out nearly a foot past the Crimson Hook wrought iron fence which abutted it, a ledge he could use to step over the sharp tines of the iron fence. He turned left onto an adjoining street and parked the Wrangler under a street light, hoping to deter looters but knowing full-well it probably wouldn't. He changed into clothes that would pass for a dock worker, put on boots, grabbed a set of work gloves and headed back to the pump station.

Chuck scaled the concrete wall with ease, jumping to grab the chain link fence above it and pulling himself up onto the ledge. Then he shimmied along the edge of the ledge and around the corner, stepping over the tines of the iron fence. Once across, he dropped to the ground inside the Crimson Hook Terminals fencing. The easy part was over.

There didn't seem to be anyone near this area and he couldn't see any surveillance cameras nearby. Several yards away was a small tug master, a load moving vehicle used to haul containers and other cargo around on the docks. He casually walked over to check it out. Inside was a hard hat and somebody's badge hanging from the rearview mirror. The keys were in it. He wasn't sure this was a good idea but he had seen oodles of them running around the wharf the last time he was here. No one seemed to care much who was driving or where they were going. He put the man's badge around his neck and donned the hard hat, cranked the tug's engine and flipped on the yellow flashing caution light on the roof top. The best defense is a good offence, he figured.

When he had last checked the tablet the container had been on the south side of the basin area. That's where he would start looking first. He headed in the direction of the basin.

Chuck debated what he would say if asked what he was doing there. He had no good ideas until he saw a large portable generator sitting off to the side of a stack of large containers. He backed the tug up to the hitch and connected the generator to his tug. "Somebody over there needs a generator", he would say, if questioned. Better than nothing.

Chuck had no idea what kind of ship the container was going to be loaded onto. There were two very large container ships being serviced by the two main cargo gantries he could see as he approached the basin wharf. It was doubtful it would be on either one of those. As he got closer he saw the lights from a smaller cargo ship moored on the inside of the basin, against the south pier. Sitting on the pier was a truck that looked like the one at Green Valley. As he drove closer he recognized the container hanging from the level-luffing crane onboard the ship.

Chuck didn't want to get too close now that he had confirmed the container was being loaded onto a ship, the Maruska Alabama he could read along the side. But he needed to know, for sure, where it was headed. He could see two groups of men gathered along the pier. There were six men off by themselves, fifty or sixty yards from the ship. Another four or five were standing next to the ship observing the container being loaded. He decided to approach the men standing by themselves.

Chuck drove the tug up to the men, killed the engine and casually asked, "Anyone know where this generator is supposed to go?"

"Not me", one of the men responded. Others shook their heads.

Chuck recognized the old crane operator from his first trip to Crimson Hook. He would have liked to get him off to the side to question him but it didn't look like that was going to be possible. It was a gamble but he asked him anyway, "This another one of those special hazardous deals you're not qualified to load", then gave a sarcastic laugh.

The old stevedore looked at him funny. Chuck realized the man didn't remember who he was. He took off his hard hat hoping that would help. It didn't seem to. "Yeah", the old man answered. "Do I know you?"

Chuck wasn't sure whether or not to explain himself. He took a chance. "We shot the shit a couple weeks ago. You were mentioning it."

"Oh, yeah, yeah!" the man smiled. "I remember you. Yeah, this is one of them deals. Fucking bullshit, if you ask me."

Chuck saw his opportunity. "So where is this boat going?"

One of the men chimed in, "Don't call it a boat to McMullen's face. He'll string you from the yardarm!" The old stevedore laughed and made hangman motions. "That two-hundred-foot rust bucket is a ship, mind you! And you best not forget it."

All the men were now rolling with laughter. Apparently, that was funny. Chuck suspected the captain was not the most well-liked individual on the docks. He feigned laughter along with them.

One of the other men offered Chuck's answer. "Baltimore to Miami to Tampa if it can stay afloat that long!"

Again, the men all laughed and shook their heads.

In the distance a voice yelled across the basin, "Get your asses over here and get back to work." The men turned to leave, still chuckling together as they donned their hard hats and put their gloves back on. Chuck cranked the tug and watched momentarily as the Green Valley truck pulled away and headed back toward the terminal entrance. He memorized the name, Maruska Alabama. The name would be important. The battery in the GPS tracker would be dead long before McMullen's "ship" made the mouth of Tampa Bay.

CHAPTER 23

She's a goddamned secretary for Christ's sake!" Kevin Falk was screaming into the phone. "It's not possible... "

"Look, sir, we weren't expecting anyone in that car to be able to drive like that. No one gave us that kind of intel. All we have is what we're given and nowhere in their dossiers did it say one of them was a professional driver."

Kevin hadn't been aware Monica could drive like that either, but these guys were supposed to anticipate anything. "No one knew the woman had that kind of ability. But I pay you clowns to expect the unexpected. Obviously, you weren't up to the job."

"We'll catch them in Milan, Major. The signal is still strong. They're at the bus station in Susa. They must be headed for Milan."

Kevin wished he had time to replace the two ignoramuses who couldn't take down an unarmed Senator and his secretary, but time wasn't on his side. The longer that Gavin and Monica remained on the run, the more likely they might get away. "Fail again and I'll personally have your heads."

"That won't happen, Major."

"The copter's on its way. ETA eight minutes", Kevin informed the henchmen. "Make sure you don't leave anything in the car. You can do that, can't you?"

"Yes sir."

This was a distraction Kevin really didn't need right now. The 'package' had left Crimson Hook and was en route to Tampa. He needed to get to Florida where he could shepherd the green team of recruits that would be executing his Afghan Horse operation for the first time. He didn't want to be sitting at a desk in Langley, but Selbourne had insisted. "One mission at a time, Major."

* * *

Chuck pulled into the crushed oyster shell drive of Grady and Muriel's duplex. As quickly as he parked his vintage Stingray he jumped out of the car, stood in front of it, and waited for Fifi and Fufu to come waltzing out of Muriel's apartment. Nothing.

Confident he was in the clear, he made his way to Grady's door and knocked before going on in. He called and looked around. No one was there. There were two cars parked out front, Grady's and Muriel's. They couldn't be far, he thought. Maybe everyone was at the pub, except it was only eleven in the morning.

He ambled out the back door. The back yard looked different. The bed sheet was no longer hanging from the palm trees. It had only been a week, but apparently Muriel had had a pavilion built, a nice one, too. It had a raised bamboo floor, thatched roof, a small tiki bar at the far end and speakers all around. The furniture was bamboo with hand-woven rattan, weatherproof cushions, picnic table, chairs. The fire pit had coral-lined walls and a set of nice iron pokers. All this because Grady had decided to try a rumrunner. Who'da thunk it?

Chuck heard a commotion around front. He walked around the side of the duplex and saw Grady and the three girls getting out of the Chrysler 300 Grady had rented in Baltimore. The trunk was open and everyone was laughing and having a merry old time, grocery bags in hand.

"Hey, Chuck!" everyone said almost simultaneously.

"We figured we better stock up before you got here", Grady joked. "Grab that last bag."

Chuck walked over to the trunk of the Chrysler and picked up the remaining bag. As he closed the trunk lid he noticed the driver side tires on his Corvette were wet. He looked around but the little piddlers were nowhere in sight. "Goddamned stealth pissers!" he complained, his voice raised. The unsympathetic crowd just laughed. "It's not right, Muriel! I blame you. You're a lousy mother! You can't train your kids any better than that?"

The laughter continued into the house. Chuck was shaking his head, half laughing with them, half serious. He was going to have to stop bringing his Vette to the Keys, that's all there was to it.

"Have you heard from him?" Alexandra asked her uncle, as she set the groceries on the kitchen table.

"Not yet", Chuck said. "But I'm sure he's okay, Allie. If he wasn't we'd have heard something in the news. No news is good news in this case."

Alexandra hugged her uncle. "I'm so scared", she admitted. "I just want to hear his voice. You can't call him, Uncle Chuck?"

"No", Chuck insisted. "He probably doesn't have his phone on, but even if he does, he wouldn't want it to ring at an unexpected time. He'll call as soon as it's safe."

Cynthia was in the same situation. "I haven't called Mike since we got back. I wasn't sure what to do. He must be worried sick right now."

"I know", Chuck sympathized. "You've done the right thing. When this is all over, he'll understand."

Muriel was staring at Chuck with a puzzled look. "What's going on, Chuck? Grady won't say. But all of our lives are a little disrupted right now. And Grady's nightmares have gotten worse lately. I think we deserve some answers."

"Muriel!" Grady admonished.

"No, no. She's right", Chuck accorded. He addressed the group, "In a nutshell, Senator Manson thought he was meeting an informant in Paris who could tell him names and positions of CIA officers and operatives involved in a heroin smuggling ring. Instead, it was a setup to kill him and another man, the one with the knowledge. The other man is dead, killed in the café bombing that nearly killed the Senator. The other man was an Afghani minister. Before he died he confirmed the existence of a CIA funded and controlled operation and explained how the operation worked along with names of most of the principals. The Senator and I are working to get him out of Europe and back here where he'll be safe to expose the people and the operation we've uncovered. That's all I can tell you right now."

"Are we in any danger here?" Muriel wondered with concern.

"No", Chuck assured. "Grady's been off the grid over thirty years. That's why I sent him to pick you girls up at the airport." He looked at Alexandra and Cynthia. "Unless someone followed you, there was no way to know who Grady was or where he resided. No one knows you're here. Everyone is safe. I assure you."

Chuck looked at Grady. "I assume you had the GPS tracking disabled on that rental car."

"Our friend in Jacksonville", Grady concurred.

"Okay, then. I have to go to Miami for a few days. I'll be back when I'm done there. I have a job for Grady that will require him to leave the rest of you here for a day or two. Just stay out of trouble in the mean time." Again, Chuck looked at Alexandra and Cynthia. "No phone calls, no traffic tickets, no credit cards. If you win the lottery, keep it to yourself."

"We'll be fine", Muriel interjected. "The girls and I will embellish our tans and sip parasol cordials until you boys finish your business."

"Good", Chuck said. Chuck looked at Grady and tipped his head toward the door, "We need to talk a minute."

Grady followed Chuck out the front door as the girls headed out back for the chaise lounges. Chuck walked him to his Corvette and opened the trunk. "I think it's time you took some protection with you. What you're about to do could be dangerous, man. Really dangerous."

Grady observed a stash of weapons in the trunk of Chuck's car. Hand guns, a shotgun, and a couple of semi-automatic rifles lay neatly arranged in a pocketed blanket. Grady stared down at them for a long time before raising his eyes to look at Chuck. He reached up and closed the trunk of Chuck's car. "You keep 'em", he said, and turned back toward the house.

Chuck knew he had stepped over the line but he hoped Grady understood why. He worried about Grady not being able to protect himself on the assignment he was about to give him. Chuck wished he could ask somebody else to do it, but Grady was the only person he knew that had all the necessary skills.

Chuck walked back through the house to say his adieus to the girls before heading to Miami. As he exited the back door his phone started to ring. It was Gavin's burner number. He turned around and went back through the house and out the front door. "Tell me something good", he opened.

"So far so good", Gavin reported. "We had a little trouble in the mountains but we've made it to the train station in Milan. We have tickets to Bari. Our train leaves in about two hours. I'm sitting in a little café on the ticketing concourse."

Chuck looked at his watch, 11:30 a.m. That meant it was 5:30 p.m. in Milan. "What kind of trouble?"

"A couple of thugs chased us, but we got away." Gavin didn't go into detail, no time, he thought.

"No shit! How could they know where you were?" Chuck became extremely concerned. Something didn't add up.

"Racked my brain, Chuck. Must have been the car but I don't know how. It makes no sense. Anyway, the car's in Susa. They'll assume we came to Milan. But if we can get out of here unscathed it's doubtful they would think Bari would be a destination. From here, they would probably concentrate on Venice, Rome, Bologna, Florence, maybe Naples. Bari should be way down the list."

"I don't like that you have to sit there over two hours, Gav. That's too long in one place. Get out of the station. Walk around the square, hang around large groups of people, blend in. Make a beeline for your train just in time."

"Great advice, Chuck. But I'm still sore as hell. And I can't stand long on this knee."

"Okay. I get it. But move around as much as you can stand. How's Monica holding up?" Chuck was concerned she might be slowing Gavin down.

"Holding up? If it wasn't for her we wouldn't be having this conversation, Chuck." Gavin began to laugh. "Here she comes now. Oh my lord!"

"What's so funny?" Chuck asked.

"She's a redhead!" Gavin roared. "A latin redhead!"

"What?"

"Never mind, Chuck. I'll explain later. How's Alex doing?"

Chuck didn't want to let Gavin know that Alex was only yards away. Nor did he want Alex speaking to Gavin and possibly messing with his emotional focus. "Grady says she and Cynthia are fine. They were greatly relieved when he told them you were alive. Try to keep it that way, understood."

"My top priority!" Gavin assured him. "I'll call when we reach Igoumenitsa."

"Stay safe, Gav."

Gavin hung up smiling at the face of the former blonde. "The yellow eyebrows will give you away", he said, smiling.

She pulled a travel-sized bottle of hair dye from her purse and waved it at him in a pendulum motion. This woman thinks of everything!

Monica started toward the ladies' room. "I'll be back in a minute." She had barely turned around when her cell phone began to ring in her backpack.

"Gavin!" she exclaimed, as she opened her backpack, removed the phone and quickly lowered the volume to vibrate.

"You brought your phone?"

"No!" she assured him with a whisper. "I don't know how it got here. I left it at Anita's."

They both realized Anita must have put it in her backpack before they left, an honest mistake. Gavin looked around. "That's how they know where we are. Did you see who was calling?"

"Yes. I didn't recognize the number."

Gavin stood and took the phone from her and grabbed her hand. "Keep up with me. If I let go of your hand, grab my backpack. Do not lose touch with me."

Monica nodded.

Gavin moved swiftly to the doors of the café. He looked up and down the narrow concourse of shops and vendors. If they were out there it wasn't evident. The phone began to vibrate in his hand. He looked at the number. Same as before. It had to be them. But where were they?

They must have lost the GPS signal inside the train station and were trying to see if the phone would ring to get a location. Gavin let go of Monica's hand and motioned for her to go sit back down. He walked over to the café order line and asked the girl behind the counter for some aluminum foil. She returned shortly with a half dozen hot dog wrappers. That would probably work. He reached into his pocket and presented some coins in payment. She waved him off with a smile. He walked back over to their table.

"Change of plan..." he informed Monica. "Stay here until I come get you."

"Will you be long, dear?" she posed with a grin.

He just shook his head. Her nerves were obvious, but this woman was as cool as they come.

Gavin enclosed the phone in the tin foil wrappers. He hoped they were thick enough to keep both the phone's GPS satellite signal and wireless signal from broadcasting strongly enough to be discovered. The goons would probably be focused on locating two people together, perhaps looking hardest for a short blonde. If he moved from group to group alone he might be able to flush them out without being seen. That was the plan anyway.

Gavin stepped out into the concourse and merged into the first group passing by, a family of six which seemed to be making their way toward the boarding gate escalators. They walked past the red self-service ticket kiosks and stepped onto a people moving conveyer, an escalator up to the gate level. He followed them closely, trying not to invade their personal space so much they might say something, but close enough he would look like he belonged with them. The escalator dumped them off at the entrance to the B gate. There was a sea of humanity now. He felt much more comfortable milling around.

There was a long line of people in front of an ice cream and pastry vendor beside the gate. Many more people were hanging around enjoying their Italian ices and scones as they leaned against the station's marble walls or relaxed in the row of plastic bench seats along the edge of the escalators. This would be a good vantage point from which to keep a watchful eye out. He would return here when he finished with his plan.

Gavin walked down to the C gate, only thirty yards away. He looked around, comfortable he would be able to adequately observe any activity that went on here from the B gate pastry shop. He crossed over to the far wall of the concourse and strode toward to a set of stairs that rose from the ticketing level below. He walked half-way down the stairs then removed the tin foil from Monica's phone. He hoped whoever was watching wasn't close enough to spot him immediately. Regardless, it was a risk he had to take.

Gavin walked back up the stairs as nonchalantly as he could, trying not to limp although his knee was throbbing. He crossed over to the far side of the terminal concourse then sidled left toward the C gate. Once at the gate he moved into the shortest line, stood there for a few moments, then re-covered the phone with the tin foil wrappers. He slid the phone into his pocket, excused himself from the line, and made his way back down the concourse to the area in front of the pastry shop. Then he waited.

With any luck he would get a look at the men looking for him. If the men were monitoring the GPS signal, Monica's phone should have begun to broadcast half-way up the stairs and continued to broadcast over to the C gate entrance to the boarding area.

It didn't take long. He was only fifteen feet from two men quickly moving up the escalators. They passed right by him, briskly walking, just short of running. They made their way to the C gate and stopped, peering through the glass walls into the boarding area on the other side. Their frustration was evident. It was obvious they believed their mice to be on the other side of that wall.

There were twenty-four trains on the other side of the gate. Gavin knew that the pursuers knew that the odds of finding their prey, at this point, weren't great. They could buy tickets to get themselves into the boarding area, but that would make no sense unless they got another signal from the phone. They would be forced to monitor this gate, and probably the ones on either side, for a couple of hours with the hope they might get another signal or see their prey returning through the gates for some reason. Gavin watched for several minutes as the two men stood outside the C gate, discussing who knows what, befuddled as to what to do.

Confident he and Monica were now safe, Gavin got on the escalator and rode it down to the ticketing level where Monica was waiting in the little café. He and the little redhead sat there until ten minutes before boarding time, then made their way through the E gate and onto their train to Bari.

Before getting on their train to Bari, Gavin had removed the tinfoil from Monica's phone and casually dropped it into the large hand bag of a woman getting onto a train destined for Rome. He wondered if the would-be assassins were smart enough to realize they had been duped when they once again began to receive a signal from Monica's phone.

CHAPTER 24

The musty-smelling South Beach hotel room Chuck had rented was more than suitable for killing time watching television. The room needed to be aired out but he didn't really have any complaints. He had just spent three days in the woods sleeping in the back of a Jeep Wrangler. He tossed his duffle bag onto the queen-sized bed and opened the window overlooking the parking lot three stories below. Not much of a view. No matter, he wasn't going to be here long.

He grabbed the TV remote and hit the ON button as he collapsed heavily into the well-worn chair that could only be described as vintage. Chicken Noodle News was breaking a story on the disappearance of Senator Samantha Lawrence. Rumors had it she and Senator Manson had been working together on a piece of controversial drug reform legislation, legislation that might have incurred the ire of the Russian Mafia or perhaps Mexican drug cartels. Could their disappearances be linked to a hit squad that had been under investigative surveillance by the FBI and the DEA for many months? Stay tuned for the latest developments.

Chuck clicked the OFF button and tossed the remote onto the bed next to the unopened duffel. The CIA had apparently felt the heat from Gavin's disappearance, enough so, anyway, to start a disinformation campaign using their favorite international news tool. Although apparently uninterested in presenting any semblance of truth in their reporting, the network had inadvertently gotten part of the story right: both Senators had, indeed, disappeared. Chuck knew Samantha's disappearance did not bode well for her. It wasn't likely she was still alive. Neither was it likely Russian mobsters or Mexican drug lords were responsible for her death.

The Maruska Alabama was scheduled to dock soon at a small commercial wharf near the southern tip of Dodge Island, home to the Port of Miami. The good thing about this particular wharf was its proximity to all kinds of boating traffic. It was not unusual to see small fishing boats, recreational boats, even jet-skis, buzzing past freighters and commercial cargo ships in the busy channels around the port.

Chuck had rented a small fishing boat, a twenty-two-foot center console open fisherman, which would get him as close to the Maruska Alabama as he would need to be. He had seen where the container had been loaded onto the ship when he was in New York. He was confident he would be able to attach another GPS sticky dart to the container as the cargo vessel sat moored to the Miami dock overnight.

With a five-day battery charge, the GPS's tracking signal should last until Grady could get eyeballs on the ship as it sailed up the gulf coast of west Florida on its way to the Port of Tampa.

Chuck had originally planned to track the ship himself. That plan had been scuttled after he had discussed with Demetri how to get Gavin and Monica back into the U.S. from Igoumenitsa. Chuck's plan would necessitate some help from one of his Delta 5 brothers. He would give Nunchucks a call as soon as he could. But first, he had another tracker dart to slingshot.

* * *

Something didn't add up. This missing female Senator, what was her name? Lawrence. She was all over the news. Yet he hadn't heard a word from Falk. Why was that? Colonel Jacob Selbourne poured himself a second cup of coffee. One way or the other, Falk should have hummed a few bars of that little ditty.

Selbourne's Georgetown apartment was as sparse as his office, for exactly the same reasons. He rarely did business from home because it was too exposed to long-distance listening devices and potential video eavesdropping. But this latest news bothered him greatly, as did the fact that the Major hadn't felt it necessary to inform him about the disappearance of the woman he'd been seeing. She wasn't just any woman. And that fact made the Major's silence unacceptable.

It had taken three attempts over a three-hour period to make contact with Major Falk before Selbourne got the chance to raise his voice in anger. "Why the fuck did I learn about this on the six o'clock news, Major? The woman's been missing for a week and you didn't think that might be something I would want to know about?"

"I've had a number of things on my plate, Colonel. She told me she was taking some time away the last time I saw her. I didn't put a time limit on a general notice like that." Kevin was doing his best not to tell the Colonel he knew about her disappearance, much less that he was responsible. He had other bad news to relate. "Besides, I didn't keep up with her schedule. I wouldn't have known she missed an intelligence briefing. I found out the same way you did, sir."

Kevin was scrambling for words, hoping his arguments were making sense. He needed to dial down the tone of this conversation and deflect any suspicion the Colonel might have that he might be somehow involved. "I'm as worried as anyone, Colonel. It's not like Sam to not call or something. In retrospect, I should have informed you. But in my mind it was a personal matter, not something I would burden you with. I didn't make the connection to Manson the way the press has."

"I'm not interested in your personal life, Major. You're right about that. But I have to look at the big picture, thirty thousand feet. And what I see is a mess, a distraction that could keep you from focusing on your primary mission. Has anyone contacted you to ask what you know about her disappearance?"

"Not yet, sir", Kevin replied. "I'm debating calling the Chairman of the Intel committee and touching base. There's not much I can contribute but maybe I know something that would help."

"That's fine, Major. But don't get involved. I need your full attention."

"Understood, sir. On that note, you should know the French assets lost him in Milan."

"Goddamnit! Again? How is that possible?" The Colonel was livid. Kevin imagined the veins in his neck protruding, throbbing, a rutted brow over his beet red face. He was glad he was forty miles away. But the Colonel had not asked him directly if he was involved in Samantha's disappearance, which assuredly meant he didn't suspect anything. This was a good sign.

"They lost the GPS signal in the train station. It popped up briefly on a train to Rome then disappeared. Nothing since, I'm afraid. We've lost them, Colonel."

"Where are your assets now, Major?"

"On their way to Rome, sir. It's a long shot, but they'll cover the station exits, try to get a visual."

Selbourne was not a happy man. He should never have entrusted the European mission to Falk. That was a mistake, his mistake, and he had only himself to blame. He knew the Major was not a seasoned operative. He would handle the Manson situation himself.

"Concentrate on Florida, Major. Get down there now and make sure it runs smoothly. I'll deal with Europe. How long before the package arrives?"

"Three days, sir. This op is under control, Colonel."

"It damn well better be, son. It damn well better be."

Selbourne ended the call and poured one more cup of coffee. This Manson character was turning out to be a more difficult adversary than he had anticipated. If the man made it back to the U.S. it would be almost impossible to silence him, even harder to quash an inevitable Congressional probe. It had to happen outside the U.S., otherwise the Russian mob narrative wouldn't hold up.

The Colonel carried his coffee into the den he used for an office. He sat down at his desk and put his coffee cup on the large blotter. He opened the center drawer and retrieved a set of keys with which he unlocked the top right-hand drawer and drew it open. In it was a cigar box which he opened and lifted out the top layer of Cuban Montecristo No.2's to expose a cell phone in a hidden compartment below.

Selbourne lit one of the cigars, stretched his legs out beneath the desk, and leaned back in his chair as he dialed the cell phone. A female voice answered, "26 Epsilon 48".

"I need to unleash a jackal", the Colonel stated.

"You're in luck, Colonel", the woman replied with a sexy British rasp. "The Ukrainian just became available."

A broad smile illuminated the Colonel's face as he retrohaled the Monte. "The Ukrainian. Excellent!"

* * *

Gavin waited for Monica to adjust her backpack and start down the gangway of the Anek Lines Superfast II high-speed ferry. The ten-hour ride from Bari to Igoumenitsa had been slightly rough, the rainy weather chopping up the northern Ionian seas, but not so bad either of them became seasick. It wasn't yet 6:00 a.m. but the clouds had begun to part and the morning sun had begun to peek over the eastern hills. Gavin felt like he could exhale for the first time in two and half days.

He hadn't slept well for any of that time, although the soreness of his head and knee wounds had diminished considerably. He credited Monica, in large part, for his speedy recovery. She was dogged and diligent about keeping his wounds clean and changing his bandages regularly. Racecar driver, travel agent, nurse, secretary, translator; there probably wasn't an occupation this woman couldn't do.

At the bottom of the gangway there was a thin old man holding a hand-scratched sign that said "Alex", the code name Chuck had given them to identify Demetri upon their debarkation. Gavin was unsure how familiar to be in such a public location. He nodded as he made eye contact with Demetri who nodded in return then turned and began to walk toward the terminal exit. Gavin and Monica followed in silence.

Outside the port terminal there was a cab waiting. Demetri nodded toward the cab and Monica and Gavin got into the back seat. The cab driver turned and looked at them. "I am Petros. Welcome to Igoumenitsa! Is this your first visit to our beautiful city?" Then he began driving away. Gavin looked out the rear window. Demetri was just standing there watching as they drove off.

"Yes. Yes it is", Gavin replied.

"You can relax, my friends", the man assured them. "I will have you to Demetri's house in fifteen minutes. Tops!"

Gavin wasn't expecting such a friendly exchange after the subdued reception with Demetri. "Thank you, Petros", he offered cautiously.

"Demetri said his mother will help you to get comfortable when you arrive. Her name is Illiana. Sweet woman."

Gavin hoped the man would not talk all the way to Illiana's place. "Good", he said tersely, trying not to extend the conversation.

"So how do you know Demetri?" the man continued.

Obviously, a quiet ride wasn't in the cards. Gavin was thankful the ride would be short. "His brother's daughter is my fiancé", Gavin responded, realizing too late what he had said.

"Your fiancé! Congratulations! That is wonderful. I know Alexandra a long time. Beautiful girl, and smart. You, sir, are a lucky man."

Gavin could feel Monica's stare firmly fixed to his face. This was news. He waited for her to say something, avoiding eye contact, but she sat silent. He hadn't wanted to make it known to anyone he was going to ask Alex to marry him. He called her his fiancé but he hadn't even proposed yet. This was a fine mess.

Petros talked most of the way to Illiana's house but Gavin was happy that he could just listen for the most part. Petros was a conversationalist who barely needed an audience. He obviously liked to hear himself talk but he was a humorous fellow, and amiable, despite his gregarious demeanor.

"Here you are!" Petros said, as he pulled into Demetri and Illiana's short driveway, got out, and opened Monica's door. She reached for her backpack pulling it from the backseat floorboard. Petros quickly took it from her, "I can help you. This way, please."

Gavin followed Petros and Monica into the side patio. Petros set down Monica's bag and knocked on the door. Illiana opened it to greet him. "Petros! Pós eísai?" The two hugged and kissed cheeks. Gavin felt more comfortable about the man as he watched their reaction to each other. It appeared he was a close friend, if not a relative.

"I bring you Alexandra's fiancé!" he announced, moving aside and extending his outstretched arms toward Gavin, his hands palms-up like a circus ring master announcing an act.

Gavin turned beet red. There was no place to hide. He owned this moment, there was no one else to blame. "Illiana! I'm so glad to finally meet you." He extended his arms and Illiana embraced him, warmly but speechless. They kissed cheeks. He backed away about to introduce Monica.

"Alexandra said nothing of getting married while she was here." Everyone could see Illiana was befuddled.

Monica could see Gavin was in over his head. She could relate to Illiana's shock, the news had surprised her, too. But, she needed to come to her boss' rescue before the situation got any weirder than it already was. "Alexandra doesn't know they are engaged yet, Illiana." She smiled and winked. "Hi. I am Monica", as she extended her hand.

Illiana smiled and shook Monica's hand. Then she opened her arms, "Ahh, we hug here", as they embraced and kissed. When they released their embrace she looked at Monica, "When will she know?"

"Soon", Gavin declared. "As soon as I can get back to the States."

Petros backed away waving at Illiana. "Ta léme argótera, Illiana."

"Antio sas, Petros. Efcharistó", Illiana waved. "We were very glad to hear you were alive, Senator. Come in. Come in. You must be very tired after your journey." She motioned for the two to follow her into the living room.

"Very much", Monica agreed. "I am so looking forward to resting in a soft bed."

"And you will", Illiana assured her. "I will fix your rooms shortly. Have you had breakfast?"

"Not yet", Gavin answered.

"Then I will fix for you."

Illiana prepared olive bread and fruit and yogurt while Gavin and Monica showered and changed into clean clothes. They had just sat down at the little breakfast table in the kitchen when Demetri arrived. "I would like to show you something", he beckoned for Gavin to come with him.

Gavin followed him out the door onto the patio. Demetri lowered his voice. "My mother knows nothing of our arrangement. It is better that way."

Gavin assured him that wasn't a problem.

"Rest today. Tonight, I take your pictures and I will give you instructions. In the morning you can leave."

Gavin knew little Greek but he did know 'thank you'. "Efcharistó, Demetri." Demetri just nodded and opened the door for Gavin to return to breakfast.

Illiana was out of the room when Gavin returned. He sat down and leaned close to Monica. "Don't say anything about Demetri providing us with documents. Apparently Illiana isn't supposed to know about it."

Monica nodded in acknowledgement. "Okay."

Illiana returned, "Your rooms are waiting. Go and rest when you are finished with your breakfasts."

"Thank you, Illiana." Monica got up and made her way toward the bedrooms. "Sleep tight, darling", she smiled at Gavin who just shook his head.

"Illiana, I would like to visit Christo's grave if I may", Gavin beseeched.

"Of course you may!" Illiana nodded. "Did you know my Christos?"

"No", Gavin admitted. "I never got the opportunity. I was hoping to ask him for permission to marry Alex but the chance to do that never happened either."

"He understands", Illiana assured him. "Christos spoke well of you." Illiana sat down at the table and cupped her hands around one of Gavin's as she looked into his eyes. "He could tell Alexandra was in love. He would tell me, 'My Alexandra has found another man's heart, Mama. He makes her happy. When she is happy, I am happy also.'"

Illiana stood. "When you are ready I will show you where he rests."

* * *

Gavin and Monica slept most of the day. In the early evening Demetri came to get them and drove them to a small printing shop north of the city. Demetri's print shop was a two-story concrete structure nestled between two apartment buildings along a suburban street. The bottom floor had two two-car garages. The print shop offices were located above the garages.

Demetri drove inside and closed the automatic doors. He invited them out of the car and guided them to an upward set of stairs that hugged the rear wall on the left side of the garage. The enclosed area below the stairwell was secured only by a rickety wooden door with rusted hinges and an old padlock. When he unlocked and opened the door the area inside was dimly lit. It had a damp and moldy smell, the contents were grimy, and the small room was filled with buckets, cleaning supplies, mops, brooms, rags, and an old wooden pallet stacked high with various containers of photo-processing chemicals.

One by one, Demetri removed the containers from the pallet and set them outside the stairwell. Then he lifted the pallet and leaned it against the rear wall revealing a small trap door, round like a manhole cover. With some effort Demetri lifted the trap door then bent down and turned on a light switch inside the dark hole. Light began emitting from the hole and Gavin could see there was a sizeable room below and a ladder leading down into the room, a steel ladder like a fire escape.

"Ladies first", Demetri pointed. Monica looked to Gavin who nodded in approval. She climbed down the thin ladder, Gavin followed, then Demetri.

The room was surprisingly large and Demetri had it packed with state-of-the-art photographic equipment: an off-set press, a digital printing press, multiple inkjet and laser printers, even a computer-to-plate violet laser fotosetter. Gavin recognized several mixed media synthetic materials, micro-porous plastic sheets for forging securitized documents with holograms and hidden identifiers only visible with ultra-violet light. He was no expert, but Gavin could tell this room was a forger's dream.

Demetri pulled down a projector screen and motioned for Monica to stand in front of it. He snapped her picture then did the same for Gavin. "It will be only a minute", he said. In a few moments their photos were being ejected from the photo-processor.

Monica was concerned as she thought about the picture just taken. She hadn't brought either of her wigs. The photo had been taken with her frazzled black locks. "Demetri, should I have taken the photo with one of the wigs?"

"Not unless you plan to wear it", he shrugged. "But why? Your picture looks like you. That is what matters in these things."

She looked at Gavin who seemed unconcerned. "Okay."

Demetri went to a safe, opened it, and removed two manila envelopes. He handed one to each of them. "These are your travel arrangements to the United States. Need I to say, protect them?"

Gavin and Monica opened their envelopes and examined the documents as Demetri explained the contents. "There is a ferry ticket to Brindisi. A limousine will pick you up at the dock. The driver will have a sign which says "Alex" just as before. He will take you to the Aeroporto del Salento. You each have two airline tickets to Rome."

"Why two?" Gavin wondered.

"In case you miss the first flight. The timing is very close. A slow ferry and you might get stuck there. Trust me. You do not want to get stuck at the Brindisi airport."

Gavin and Monica both chuckled. Demetri grinned and scratched his missing ear piece. They laughed even harder thinking he had done so on purpose. It was the first sign he had a sense of humor since they had arrived.

"Your layover in Rome is but two hours, perhaps. Not long. From there you will fly to Havana directly."

"Havana?" Gavin was surprised. He knew Americans were allowed to go to Cuba after President Obama had lifted the embargo. But he wondered, "Why not fly directly into the U.S.? Miami, or Tampa?"

"Facial recognition", Demetri warned. "Chuck thought it better you stay away from airports that might be using it or perhaps testing it."

"What about Rome?" Gavin asked.

"A chance you will have to take", Demetri conceded.

"How long is this trip", Monica asked.

"You will leave here in the morning. It will take thirty-six hours to reach Havana. Tomorrow is Thursday. You will arrive in Havana about 7:30 p.m. Friday evening. You will land at Jose Marti Airport. From there you will need to take a taxi to your casa particular, a private residence in Old Havana. It is an apartment next to the Saratoga Hotel."

Gavin pulled the last piece of paper from the envelope. It was a confirmation for the AirBnB casa particular. "This is for the apartment where we're staying?"

"Yes. The owners are Juan and Ne. Their phone numbers are there. Call them from the airport and they will meet you at the apartment to let you in."

"You said we meet Chuck that evening?" Monica queried.

"Yes. You can use the apartment to freshen yourselves. There will be some money for you there, Cuban currency. You will have time to enjoy dinner before continuing. There are some small restaurants along the Prado."

"The Prado?" Gavin shook his head.

"It is a long tree-lined promenade, a wide European-styled walk separating Old Havana from Central Havana. In its day it was *the* place for the elite to see and be seen. Your apartment is on the same street, Paseo de Marti, just south of the Prado.

Once you have eaten, walk north along the Prado until you reach the Malecón, the famous waterfront roadway. Cross to the water side on the north then walk east along Avenue del Puerto until you see some small fishing boats moored along the sea wall. At 11:30 p.m. a man with a fishing pole and a red baseball cap will come and sit on the sea wall. Ask him if you can charter his boat. He will ask you which boat you are interested in renting. Tell him "Pilar". He will take you to Chuck."

Monica looked at Gavin, "I know this area well. I've been there many times with my father."

"Good", Gavin replied, somewhat relieved that she seemed comfortable with the plan. He knew nothing about Cuba except for the mostly negative stories of a corrupt Communist regime ninety miles from the coast of America.

Monica felt a sense of relief knowing that they at least had a plan for getting home. "Thank you so much, Demetri!" she sighed, as she approached him and hugged his neck. He returned the hug as he reached around and squeezed her butt cheek. Monica was caught off-guard but backed away slowly without making a scene. Better not to bite the hand that's feeding you, she thought. She looked at Gavin who was laughing. She gave him a perplexed look. He just smiled, "Tell you later", he promised, having been told about her uncle's predilection by Alexandra.

Gavin reached to shake Demetri's hand. "Yes. Thank you, Demetri. We owe you. I won't forget this."

Demetri nodded. "Your photos are very good. I will have your passports completed by morning. I am happy to help." He pointed to the ladder leading up to the stairwell closet. "Ladies first."

Monica was about to tell Demetri she'd rather he go first until Gavin stepped between her and Demetri. She handed her envelope to Gavin and quickly climbed out.

"Are you coming, Demetri?" Gavin asked.

"Not now." he replied. "I have to finish here. You should take the car back to the house. I will make other arrangements."

Gavin started to climb out. "See you in the morning then." As he made his way up the ladder he noticed his knee had begun to feel much better. Today had been a pretty good day. With a good night's rest, he felt certain tomorrow would be even better.

* * *

The official position is that the CIA neither trains nor employs assassins. There is even an official denial on their government website. What no one from the agency ever talks about, thus there is never a need to deny, is that the CIA hires assassins; a subtle, but important, distinction.

Sergei Bulavin began life in eastern Ukraine as Petro Honcharuk, "Peter the potter". It was a name he hated from the moment he first learned its meaning. By the age of thirteen he had begun to call himself Sergei, "the protector". He had begun to see himself as defender of the helpless and he was ruthless in their defense.

The agricultural world in which he grew up suited his aspirations poorly. The more he learned of his Ukrainian ancestry, the more he longed for the feeling of independence from oppressive government, and the more he identified with his Cossack roots. He took the surname Bulavin, after the Don Cossack rebel whose army assassinated Prince Yury Dolgorukov sent by Russian Tsar Peter the Great to punish the Cossacks of the Don region for fleeing their serfdom. He identified strongly with the notion that it is necessary to preemptively kill potential enemies rather than chance subjugation to them. Sergei Bulavin was a born assassin, as are most of the successful ones.

Sergei learned early on that the line between the oppressor and the oppressed was not static. Victors, formerly oppressed, easily transitioned to oppressors if their spoils were threatened. In the beginning, it wasn't difficult to find employers for his talent, but it was much more difficult to find the kind of work of which his young conscience would approve. Over time, however, assuaging his conscience became less important than perfecting his skills and abilities, and he learned to rationalize the desire to pursue his craft.

All governments are oppressors, he reasoned. All governments want to eliminate threats from other governments. As long as he acted on behalf of one government against another, or even one agency within the same government against another, the work was conscionable. Oppressors eliminating oppressors, a zero sum game. Sergei had made the natural, albeit psychopathic, transitive progression from idealist to pragmatist.

"You do not include any family history for friends, girlfriends, grandparents, aunts, uncles, nothing!" Sergei scolded Colonel Selbourne. In his thick Ukrainian accent he huffed, "How do you expect me to track down this man with dossiers so weak?"

"You'll have something in six hours", the Colonel apologized.

Colonel Selbourne had not seen the dossiers Kevin had put together for the French assets but, apparently, they had not been sufficient for Bulavin. Within a few hours of sending Sergei updated dossiers, the Colonel received another, more pleasant phone call.

"Your man is in Greece. Igoumenitsa."

"How would you know that?" the Colonel demanded.

"He left his passport and other identifications on dead man's body in Paris. He will need new ones. He has girlfriend with uncle who was forgery expert. Is probably still. He will go there. He may be there now."

"What are you waiting for?" the Colonel snarled. "You should already be on a plane."

"I am", the Ukrainian responded.

CHAPTER 25

D emetri, you must tell me where they are going. I do not have time for
games such as this." The Ukrainian was pointing his small handgun at
Demetri's friend, Petros. "I am sure Petros would not like another bullet
in leg. You can see how uncomfortable he is. Is better you tell me what I need to
know now."

Sergei had shot Petros with his small PSS pistol, an old Soviet gun developed
in the early 1980s. It was not a particularly powerful gun, nor particularly
accurate at longer ranges. The PSS was developed to give Soviet Special
Forces and secret police an almost completely silent option for covert operations
such as reconnaissance and assassinations. It needed no bulky silencer. The
noise suppression was built into its compact design. Sergei's PSS was his
favorite weapon.

The wound to Petro's leg was superficial. Sergei had intentionally shot him in
a fatty portion of his thigh, careful to miss any major blood vessels or nerves. He
was not in the business of killing innocent people, but sometimes an effective
point had to be made to achieve a desired result.

"Demetri! I beg of you! Tell him what he wants to know." Petros was crying,
his blood-soaked pants dripping onto the floor of the second story office of
Demetri's print shop. He was strapped to a chair with his own belt which the
Ukrainian had forced him to remove before binding him to the chair with it.

Demetri had also been strapped to a chair. Both men were seated beside
each other in the middle of the room, facing their captor, arms behind their
backs. Demetri remained silent, staring at Sergei with a blank look of stoicism.
He knew this man, or at least knew of him. The Ukrainian's reputation was well-
known in the circles he used to travel.

"Do you know how difficult is to shoot someone with not damage to
important organ or vessel? If you make me shoot him again maybe he will be not
so lucky next time."

"Please! Demetri!" Petros whimpered.

Sergei's stare turned ugly and mean as he glared at Demetri. "Tell me, Demetri. Tell me now!"

Demetri returned his glare, "They are good people, Sergei. Not your kind of enemy. You have been given false information. I will not help you."

The noise from the second shot was almost imperceptible, but the scream from Petros was loud and shrill as the bullet from Sergei's PSS lodged in his other thigh.

"Does your sweet mother know where they are going, Demetri? Perhaps I should talk with her."

"My mother knows nothing of their plans", Demetri said, now with perceptible concern in his voice.

"Maybe truth, Demetri. But how will I know unless I speak with her, if you will not tell me? You can see I have no choice if you do not cooperate."

Demetri knew he couldn't hold out anymore. His friend was bleeding and in need of a doctor and it was certain the Ukrainian would do the same to his mother if he refused any longer. With tears in his eyes he told Sergei how Gavin and Monica planned to get back to the U.S.

"It would have been much easier on your friend had you cooperated from beginning, Demetri." Sergei stepped around the pool of blood surrounding the chair where Petros sat. He untied the belt binding Petro's hands and cinched a tourniquet around one of his thighs. Then he untied Demetri and used his belt as a tourniquet for Petro's other leg.

Sergei looked at the blood on the floor then at Demetri. "Call emergency services as soon as I leave. Do not try to take him to hospital. He will not make it. Keep him awake if you can."

Sergei had one lingering question in need of an answer. "How will they travel from Havana to Tampa?"

Demetri looked at his bleeding friend, his head bobbing helplessly, ready to pass out at any moment, then back at the Ukrainian. He told him of the man in the red hat with a fishing pole and reluctantly concluded, "A man named Chuck McCrory will pick them up in a speed boat off the northern coast of Havana. He will take them to the mainland."

Sergei looked surprised. Demetri noticed his stunned countenance. "Is this McCrory Green Beret?" Sergei asked.

"Yes", Demetri acknowledged.

"I know this man. You say he is also friend of Senator?"

Demetri nodded. "He is the uncle of the Senator's fiancé."

Sergei turned toward the door to the stairs which led down to the street, then paused briefly before heading down. He held the door half-open as he looked back at Demetri who was already dialing 112, the number for emergency medical services. "Perhaps there is something to what you say, Demetri. Perhaps the people I look for are not, how you said it, 'my kind of enemy'. We will see."

Sergei left the print shop and walked a few blocks down the hill toward the Old Port, admiring the quaint houses along the street and the bright blue waters of Igoumenitsa's harbor. Beyond the port he could see a dozen sailboats being propelled by a salt-laden breeze, their strong masts cast at acute angles to the rolling waves. It was a shame he had had to spend his time here on business. Such a peaceful, beautiful place. As he dialed his cell phone, Sergei promised himself he would one day return and relax here.

"Your man is en route to Havana", he informed the Colonel. "He has twelve-hour head start. I will need very fast jet to be there before he arrives."

As he waited for the Colonel to confirm his request he could hear the sirens of the EMS vehicles coming for Petros. Sergei hoped the man would be alright. He hadn't meant him serious harm. Sometimes he despised this business.

"Ioannina National, 6:00 p.m.? Affirmative, Colonel. I will be waiting."

* * *

Alexandra opened the back door of Muriel's apartment and noticed Grady dragging a large cooler across the sandy, nearly grassless back yard toward the boat Chuck had had him rent in Islamorada.

"Ouch! Ouch! Ouch!" Grady was shrieking as he stopped and sat down on the cooler to remove a row of painful sandspurs from the side of his bare foot.

"Are you okay, Grady?" Alexandra yelled.

"Goddamned sandspurs", he griped. "You can't get rid of 'em. As fast as I rip 'em up they grow back!"

Alexandra giggled as she walked over and sat next to him on the large cooler. "How big is this cooler?" she asked.

"Eighty-four quarts", he replied, pulling the last spur from the top his big toe. "Ouch!"

"I guess you plan on being out there for a while."

"Don't know how long", he acknowledged.

"You don't know, or you won't tell me?" she smiled.

"A little bit of both. Your uncle's big on 'need to know', Allie. I reckon he figures you don't have one right now."

"Can I help you lug it over to the boat?" she offered.

"Sure." Together they lifted the cooler and walked it to the sea wall then stepped down slightly onto the small wooden dock that formed an L-shaped slip.

It was heavier than she expected. She was impressed he had dragged it as far as he had by himself. "Just set it here for the time being", he insisted, as he set his end down on top the sea wall.

"When are you leaving?" she wondered.

"Tonight. I'm not sure what time. Your uncle should be back soon. He'll give me my marching orders."

Alexandra sat down on top of the cooler, turning her back to the sun. The warm afternoon breeze felt good on her skin. She had worn practically nothing but a swim suit for the past week. Before moving to Washington she had a glorious tan which she never really had to work on. It came naturally living in Tarpon Springs. But her tan had been fading since she moved north. Not that there wasn't sun in Washington, D.C., but the long hours she had put in at work left little time to spend catching rays.

She watched as Grady stowed his gear on the boat. Alexandra didn't know much about boats. That had never been her thing. This one looked pretty large to her, but Grady called it a sport fisherman, a twin engine Stamas, twenty-nine feet long with a tower above the flybridge. There was no cabin on this boat. An overnight stay at sea meant sleeping under the stars. Alexandra was sure the tower was to see as far as possible with the high-powered binoculars she had seen him tuck into a cubby hole by the console.

It was obvious this was going to be a reconnaissance undertaking of some sort. Grady had packed several days worth of food, water, and Gatorade plus a sleeping bag, a cot, clothing, some blankets and a couple of folding chairs. But for what? Uncle Chuck had divulged little information about Grady's mission and Grady wasn't offering to fill in the blanks.

* * *

Gavin stared out of the window of the Havana-bound jet at the lush, green farmland of rural Cuba. Prominent red clay roads cut across the landscape in fascinating geometric patterns. He could see that many of the farms had mobile irrigation systems. Visibly distinct circles of green crops gave away their locations.

The pilot had announced the plane's descent into Jose Marti Airport as Gavin was listening attentively to Monica's history lesson about Cuba. As a young girl she had gone there with her father many times and had both friends and relatives there. But when she had become a U.S. citizen she was no longer allowed to travel there legally. Gavin was fascinated with Monica's description of the Cuban Revolution from a totally different perspective than he had ever heard.

"That's not what we were taught in school or read in any text book or newspaper in America. That explains a lot", Gavin said.

"That is because the U.S. Government could no longer control Cuba after the Revolution. They tried to demonize Castro in order to subvert and overthrow his regime but their efforts could not win the hearts of the Cuban people who overwhelmingly supported Fidel. They loved him. Fulgencio Batista had been a dictator, a U.S. puppet for over twenty-five years. The U.S. did not want to see Batista lose power. But when he was defeated by an all-volunteer army of the Cuban people, the U.S. Government realized it had lost all power over Cuba."

"I've always heard that Castro was a cruel dictator and ruled his people with an iron fist, killing his opposition and suppressing freedom of speech and religion", Gavin said. "You paint a very different picture."

Monica had explained that the Cuban Revolution would not have occurred if free elections under the Batista regime had been allowed to take place. In 1953, a young lawyer named Fidel Castro was running as a legislative candidate. Batista cancelled the elections when it appeared he might lose his grip on power over the legislature. In retaliation, Castro and others organized an attack on a military barracks in Santiago. The point of the attack was to make a statement to the government and rally grassroots support for the opposition. Castro was captured and sentenced to fifteen years in prison for his role in the 26th of July Movement, an independence movement similar to America's 4th of July, which would become known as M-26-7.

After Castro's capture, the movement gained strength and the outcry from the people became so strong that the growing grassroots political movement forced Batista to commute the sentences of Castro and many others after only two years.

In 1955, Fidel, his brother, Raul, Che Guevara, and other opposition leaders went to Mexico to plan a guerilla campaign to overthrow Batista. On December 2, 1956, Castro's army of 82 men sailed from Mexico on the yacht Grandma, a rickety 60-foot cabin cruiser designed to carry only 12 people, and landed on the southeast coast of Cuba, not far from Guantanamo Bay. They were attacked by Batista's air force, split in two, and wandered lost in the mountain jungles for several days. Of the original 82 men, only 12 remained when they reformed in the mountains of Sierra Maestra.

The opposition to the Batista regime grew stronger in both the cities and rural countryside. Word spread of Castro's brave revolutionaries in the Sierra Maestra mountains. Initially, hundreds of volunteers joined his army. The people in the countryside helped feed and clothe his men and hide them from Batista's military which was trying to hunt them down.

In trying to suppress the revolution, Batista's government had orchestrated mass human rights abuses, including torture of civilians, with estimates for the death toll at more than 20,000. Because of the abuses they were forced to commit, many of Batista's military began to defect to Castro's revolutionaries. By 1959, Castro's all-volunteer revolutionary army had defeated Bastista's U.S.-supported military regime with the use of guerrilla tactics and the aid of popular uprisings.

"Unless you know the history from a Cuban's perspective" Monica explained, "you cannot understand how the people must have felt to have such a leader. Castro believed in education above all else. You could not join his army unless you were literate. Everywhere his army went they built schools and hospitals and taught the people to read and write. Only 60% of the people were literate when Castro landed in Cuba in 1956. By 1965, just six years after the overthrow of Batista, the literacy rate in Cuba had risen to over 90%. Cuba today is one of the most literate countries in the world, 99.8%, almost everyone can read and write. It is more literate by far than the United States. Only about 86% of Americans can read and write at a functional level."

Gavin was mesmerized at Monica's knowledge of Cuban history. He had been unaware that after the Revolution and the expulsion of Batista, Castro had sought to form diplomatic relations with the United States. But the U.S. Government demanded too many concessions from Castro's young government. It was furious with Castro's refusal to give back the land and businesses, confiscated from Batista loyalists, to the wealthy land and business owners who had supported the Batista regime and fled to the U.S. after it had become evident Batista's dictatorship was over.

"Well that explains why much of the Cuban population in Florida is so angry at Castro. In their minds their families were robbed", Gavin noted.

"They picked the wrong dictator to support", Monica smiled. "Most of the exiles were from the wealthy upper and middle classes who supported Batista. When they fled to the U.S. they thought they would only be gone a short while. The exiles left everything in Cuba: their cars, houses, businesses, farms. They gave them to their families who stayed, believing they would only be in America temporarily and they would eventually get their things back. Surely the United States would put Castro in his place and restore their old government. As we know, the U.S. tried but failed. It is hard to blame the exiles who went from riches to rags for being angry with Castro. But I believe they should be angry at the U.S. Government, not Castro, for propping up the Batista dictatorship for all those years."

"Okay. Castro now controls the Cuban government. It's 1959. The Communist Party in Cuba doesn't form until 1965. So, how did the U.S. let the Russians into Cuba?" Gavin asked.

"I think Castro believed the U.S. would support his new government but instead the CIA tried to kill him. They tried many times in fact. The supporters of M-26-7, the independence movement, are the ones who took control of the government forming the United Party of the Cuban Socialist Revolution, which would later become the Cuban Communist Party. The party was a very idealistic and liberal mixture of anti-Batista, pro-socialist peasants as well as urban workers. This did not sit well with the U.S. Government still angry that American companies had been taken over and nationalized by Castro. So the U.S. Government began to boycott Cuban goods. In retaliation, Castro raised tariffs on America goods, sometimes as much as 50%, even more. When the U.S. suspended the importation of Cuban sugar, Cuba's main source of revenue, it should have been no surprise to anyone that Cuba turned to the Soviet Union for economic help. But I think the U.S. was very surprised."

"So Castro wasn't a Communist when he took over Cuba in 1959?"

"No. No. Remember he started the revolution because Batista wouldn't allow free elections in 1953. Castro was a very liberal socialist at that time, also a deeply spiritual man. But a Communist? No.

Cuba eventually became a Communist nation, but really in name only. Castro began to call himself Marxist-Leninist, but he was a reluctant Communist, at best. When the Russians made overtures to his government to establish major trade and economic relations in 1960, he basically had no choice. It was obvious the United States wasn't going to help him - they were trying to kill him. Without the Russians, the U.S. would surely have assassinated him and retaken Cuba. President Kennedy tried to invade Cuba in April of 1961, the famous Bay of Pigs debacle. The CIA trained a group of disgruntled Cuban exiles and ferried them to Cuba to foment unrest and fight against Castro's regime. They were slaughtered there by Castro's troops."

"So you say Castro wasn't really a Communist but pretended to be one to keep getting economic support from Russia?"

"It's more complicated than that, but yes. Without a major trading partner, no country can survive. The Soviet Union wanted a foothold in the Western Hemisphere and he provided one in exchange for Soviet protection and economic support. Plus, he could thumb his nose at the United States Government for backing Batista and not backing his Revolution. The U.S. had armed Batista's army with small arms, rockets and mortars. This had made Castor very angry with the U.S."

"You said he was deeply spiritual? I thought Castro was an atheist. I was taught he suppressed religion and that the Pope excommunicated him."

"It is true that Pope John XXIII excommunicated him in 1962 because the Soviets would not allow the Cuban government to openly support religious practices. Again, it is not as if Castro had a choice if he wanted Soviet help. So,

214

officially, he had to suppress the church. But he never believed that way. There are pictures of Holy Crosses on some of the walls of his residences. You were never taught that, were you?"

"No. I wasn't", Gavin said.

Then she told Gavin about a letter Castro had written to the father of a fallen comrade while he was imprisoned by Batista in 1954:

'Physical life is ephemeral, it passes inexorably. . . This truth should be taught to every human being – that the immortal values of the spirit are above physical life. What sense does life have without these values? What then is it to live? Those who understand this and generously sacrifice their physical life for the sake of good and justice – how can they die? God is the supreme idea of goodness and justice.'

"To say Castro was an atheist is simply not true. After the Soviets had left, he invited Pope John Paul II to visit. The Pope accepted his invitation in 1998. It was the first time a reigning pontiff had ever visited the island." Monica added, "The people were ecstatic. Every Pope since has visited Cuba.

Within a few months after the Soviet Union collapsed in 1991, he loosened restrictions on the practice of Catholicism. There was no more reason for the restrictions to remain. He stopped calling Cuba an atheist nation and, instead, began to use the word 'secular' when he talked of such things."

Gavin shook his head, "I grew up thinking Castro was an evil, atheistic, communist dictator who lined his enemies up and shot them in firing squads."

"The firing squad stories are true but distorted greatly. After the Revolution, Castro had many captives, prisoners of war, supporters of Batista. He could not just turn them all loose. Many were his enemies but most were just average citizens forced to fight for Batista. Castro needed to find out which of them posed a threat for the future and which could be sent back to their families safely. So, Castro put them all on trial. Can you guess what model he used for those trials?"

"Not Nuremburg?" Gavin hazarded.

"Yes, Nuremburg. It is uncanny how close to the same statistical percentages at Nuremburg his trials also found. Over 85% of the prisoners were sent home with no punishment. Of the remaining who were convicted, most served prison terms from two to five years. Only about 3% were executed, a similar percentage as Nuremburg. Castro used firing squads to execute those who perpetrated the most serious offences. Most people forget that the high command of the Nuremburg trials hanged their victims, desiring them to suffer for their crimes. Allied commanders felt that firing squads were too humane to use as punishment for war criminals. Yet it is from the three percent that Castro executed by firing squad that the CIA and U.S. Government propaganda was initiated."

Monica continued. "I have seen how amazing are the Cuban people. They sing and they dance and they are happy. Some are very poor, but to say that is very misleading. No one is destitute here. Homelessness does not exist. Cuba's health statistics are excellent, better than the U.S. and Canada even. Although poor, Cuba is not like Zimbabwe or Somalia or Bangladesh.

And the people loved Fidel. They did not despise him like the American press falsely reported all those years. But in fairness to the press, that is the propaganda they were told by the CIA and military high command. Still, they should have known better.

Every Cuban child goes to school, every Cuban citizen has free access to medicine and doctors. College is free to anyone who can pass the tests. But students have to serve the government for three years in exchange for a college education. Men have to spend one of those years in military service.

Cuba has one of the most advanced medical systems in the world. All twelve Cuban states have medical universities. Cuba's pharmaceutical industry manufactures some of the most sophisticated drugs in the world, many that the U.S. could use for diabetes, blood disorders and cancer. But the embargo won't allow the drugs into America. Cuba is not stuck in the days of 'I Love Lucy'. It produces almost 70% of the drugs it needs. It is very self-reliant. Most Americans have no idea that Cuban doctors travel all over the world. Their expertise is highly sought after.

Cuba also has more than 300 biotechnology centers. The western Havana facilities alone employ more than 12,000 workers and more than 7,000 scientists and engineers. Almost 2 out of every 1000 people in Cuba are scientists."

Gavin felt the wheels of the plane touch down as the pilot applied the brakes and reversed the thrusters on the giant jet engines. It was nearly dark outside, almost 7:30 p.m. local time. The real test for Demetri's expertise was just ahead of them.

"Almost everything I thought I knew about Cuba seems to be wrong or at least distorted", Gavin confessed.

"Understandably so", Monica replied. "Castro has said 'history will absolve me'. It is starting to do so as Americans are now able to visit Cuba and see for themselves and speak to the people about how they really feel. Cuba is not perfect, but you have to look beyond the propaganda of those with a political agenda to find the real truth."

Gavin nodded in agreement. "That's true everywhere, isn't it?"

The plane rolled up onto the tarmac in front of the gate at Jose Marti's Terminal Number 3. The ground crew outside rolled a set of mobile stairs over to the plane and positioned it at the main doorway behind the cockpit for passenger debarkation. Monica and Gavin gathered their backpacks and walked down the steps and over to the terminal gate. They passed through the gate then stood in line behind gray steel doors until a buzzer signaled for the next person to enter and be interviewed by the Cuban Customs agent inside.

"Would you like your passport stamped?" the agent asked Gavin. With a huge sigh of relief he smiled at her and said, "Yes, please."

"Exit that way", the agent pointed. Gavin pushed open the swinging door to see Monica standing just beyond, a broad smile on her face.

"We made it!" Gavin said in a hushed voice.

"I was so nervous!" Monica whispered.

Gavin put his arm around her shoulders and headed toward the terminal exit. "Let's find a taxi."

The bustling crowd outside the terminal resembled a disturbed ant bed as local taxi drivers and tour bus operators scrambled chaotically to locate their passengers and get them boarded and their luggage loaded. Gavin hailed a 1957 Chevy Bel-Air, candy apple red with a white roof and side panels. Its chrome trim glistened even in the dimming light.

Gavin had never seen so many classic American cars in one place outside of a car show in the States. There were so many it was hard to take them all in. This was like being caught in a time warp, stuck in the Havana of the 1950s.

"That doesn't sound like a Chevy engine", Gavin noted to the driver.

"No señor", the taxi driver acknowledged. "Es Lada."

"What's a Lada?" Gavin asked.

"Russian", the man replied.

A Russian engine in a classic American car! There was just something fundamentally wrong with that, Gavin thought.

As Monica and Gavin's Chevy with a Russian engine pulled away from the terminal, a set of steely eyes followed their journey around the exit loop and onto the main boulevard toward Old Havana. The man behind the eyes adjusted his red baseball cap and began to text a message into his mobile phone... 'Targets acquired.'

CHAPTER 26

In the United States, prohibition lasted only 13 years, January 1920 to December 1933. But the amount of money that changed hands selling illegal alcohol to thirsty patrons of concealed gin mills and secret speakeasies during that short period was staggering. Prohibition had had the unintended consequence of creating a criminal black market greater than the legal market it had been intended to shut down.

During the Prohibition era, illegal liquor smugglers used specially designed "go-fast" boats to transport liquor to the mainland from larger offshore boats coming from Europe and the Caribbean Islands. The go-fasts were long and sleek and heavily powered, designed strictly for speed. Outrunning the Coast Guard was paramount to the success of the "Rum Runners" who supplied the secret bars and liquor stores run by mob syndicates all over the country. And successful they were. Joseph Patrick Kennedy, Sr., father of future President John F. Kennedy, is said to have seeded the family fortune running whisky and rum to the crime families in New York, Massachusetts, Illinois, Florida, and Louisiana.

While many biographical authors have tried to whitewash Kennedy's involvement with crime syndicates during Prohibition, some by labeling it 'myth', his association with mob bosses, Frank Costello of the New York Luciano crime family and Sicilian-American Sam Giancana of the Chicago Syndicate, was too widely known and too blatantly cozy to be dismissed so easily. Giancana called Joe Kennedy "one of the biggest crooks who ever lived". And Costello bragged, "I helped Joe Kennedy get rich."

The crime syndicates supplied bootlegged liquor to every major U.S. city, particularly New York, Boston, Chicago and New Orleans. Gin, whisky and vodka came mostly from Europe, rum mostly from the Caribbean. Shipments of alcohol would be legally transported from England and Ireland to the Bahamas on large freighters. From the Bahamas, the contraband would be loaded onto smaller boats which would then anchor or drift just off the U.S. east coast, outside the three-mile International limit. The speedy go-fast boats would pull alongside the supply ship and load their illegal liquor for the quick trip to shore. At the height of Prohibition, Rum Rows, or long lines of ships just offshore, carried hundreds and sometimes thousands of gallons of liquor. The boats would form small armadas waiting for the go-fasts to come and take their stock.

One of the most prolific rum runners of the era was William "Bill" McCoy. Working out of the Bahamas, McCoy used his schooner, Arethusa, to smuggle well-known, authentic brand names of whiskies and liquors imported from Great Britain. He smuggled only the best. His reputation for quality was so renowned his patron-bootleggers would tell their customers they didn't sell cheap, fake booze like their competitors, but rather "the Real McCoy."

In the 1960s, a new breed of go-fast began to be used to smuggle drugs into the States. Sometimes called "Cigarettes", they were named after inventor and legendary speed boat designer Donald Aronow's offshore powerboat racing team. The sleek racing boats were swift, low to the water, and almost impossible to detect with radar unless the seas were exceptionally calm. Modern go-fast boats still lean heavily on Aronow's design concepts, strongly constructed of fiberglass, carbon composites, and Kevlar. Both V-hull and catamaran designs, aided by 1000 plus horsepower engines, are able to hurl a boat as long as 50 feet to speeds in excess of 100 knots, over 120 miles per hour on calm seas.

Today, Chuck didn't believe a boat that large would be necessary for the trip to Havana, but a boat that fast certainly would. Grady could hear the loping engines of the go-fast idling up the channel behind his duplex. He ambled out to the dock and waited for it to get close enough for Chuck to toss a mooring line to him. Chuck was standing on the bow of the 31-foot Skater 318 catamaran. A stranger was driving. As Chuck threw the bowline to Grady, the driver reversed throttle on one of the twin Mercury 400 horsepower engines and increased throttle on the other as he turned the wheel slightly toward the dock, then away, then straightened the wheel forward. The boat slowed and slid sideways, maneuvering perfectly into position next to the dock. The driver put the engines into neutral as Grady tied the bowline and walked thirty feet to the rear to catch the stern line heaved from the driver.

"Any problems?" Grady asked, as Chuck jumped off the bow onto the dock.

"Nope", Chuck replied tersely. "What do you think of my new toy?"

The girls had followed Grady to the seawall and were standing atop it admiring the new arrival.

"Wow!" they all said in unison.

Cynthia was practically begging. "So, I see six seats, Chuck. Just enough for everyone."

"Sorry ladies. No time. Nunchucks and I will be leaving as fast as we can get Grady set to go. By the way, this is Jimmy Falcon."

"Call me 'Nunchucks'" Jimmy urged.

Everyone exchanged pleasantries. Nunchucks seemed an affable guy, about Chuck's age, maybe a little younger. He was bigger and taller than Chuck with broad shoulders and a slim waist. He had a thick beard which hid most of his face, and long straight hair down to the middle of his shoulder blades. He was wearing a red bandana around his head, presumably to keep his long hair from flapping around in the turbulent currents of the boat's cockpit. Alexandra thought his stature and facial features made him look Native American.

"So is this your boat?" Alexandra asked.

"Yes", Nunchucks nodded. "Offshore powerboat racing is a hobby of mine. This boat is one of my smallest but it's pretty fast. This is a pleasure boat. I don't race it."

Muriel piped up. "This is all very fascinating, Chuck. But can you tell us where you guys are going? Why do you have to keep us in the dark?"

Muriel glanced at Grady. She could see he wasn't pleased with her forthright assertiveness. But he said nothing.

"I can tell you Grady is going to look for a freighter we need to keep an eye on." Chuck smiled at Muriel. "He'll only be gone a day or so. I can't tell you where Nunchucks and I are going, or when we plan to be back."

"Will Gavin be with you?" Alexandra looked deeply at her uncle's eyes hoping to discern some telltale reaction.

He smiled at her, "Allie, that's all I can tell you right now."

Alexandra felt certain that was a 'yes'. But the uncertainty made her anxious.

"I'm boiling up some lobsters", Cynthia informed the newcomers. "Will you guys be here long enough for dinner?"

"Lobster?" queried Nunchucks. "I believe we can." He looked at Chuck for approval.

"I believe we will", Chuck confirmed. "We'll be there in a few minutes. I need to talk with Grady before we head inside."

The women recognized that was their cue to exit the scene. They turned toward the house as Chuck, Nunchucks and Grady huddled on Grady's sportfisherman.

"Got everything you need?" Chuck asked Grady.

"I think so", Grady said. "I'll need to top off the tanks before I head out but I should be good for a week with all the supplies I'm carrying."

"Well, you won't be out there that long", Chuck assured him. "The ship left Miami about 2:00 p.m. this afternoon. If you cast off around 10 p.m. you should intercept them around midnight just north and east of the Dry Tortugas."

"What am I looking for, Chuck?" Grady was unsure exactly why Chuck wanted him to follow the ship all the way from the Keys to Tampa.

220

"When I was at Green Valley Transfer, the guard told me he thought a container was going to Florida. He couldn't remember the name of the place, but he said it sounded like a dog, a Weimaraner. Once I found out the container was going to Tampa I started checking for towns near there close to that sound. There's a small town southeast of Tampa called Wimauma. It's not exact, might not be it. But it's damn close."

"You think they're headed there?" Nunchucks questioned.

"I don't know. But that's all we've got to go on. The question is: How will they get the heroin there? Will they dump the container overboard to be picked up by another vessel? Will they offload the contents before they get to the Port of Tampa? Will they risk taking the container all the way into the port? I don't have an answer to any of those possibilities."

Chuck looked at Grady, "That's why I'm having you pick it up in the Tortugas. We need to have eyes on that ship for as long as we can."

"Not a problem." Grady assured him. "Any feeling for the distance I should keep?"

"The binoculars I gave you will allow you to stay a few miles away and still see what's going on with reasonable clarity."

"How many miles is a few?" Grady asked.

"Three to five. The binoculars have built-in image stabilization that works really well. The tripod you have is gyro stabilized. Once you have the target locked in, the gyro function will compensate for the rocking of the boat. After that, just kick back and watch the tablet. You can pan and zoom with the WIFI control system. We'll have a fairly bright moon tonight. That should help, but it also means they have a better chance of spotting you. Don't try to get any closer. We don't want to take a chance on spooking them."

"Understood", Grady acknowledged. "Will you be in contact range if I spot something?"

"I think so. We pick up Gavin a little after midnight tonight. We may be out of touch until sometime after that."

Chuck looked at Nunchucks. "How fast will that thing get us to Havana?"

Nunchucks' eyes rolled upward as he stroked his beard and calculated the numbers in his head. "The rendezvous point is about 112 miles from here. We should be able to average 65 knots. So, that puts us northwest of Havana in about an hour and a half."

"And the trip back to Tampa? Say, from there to the Skyway Bridge."

"Eh, figure 295 miles at the same speed... four hours, plus or minus fifteen or twenty minutes", Nunchucks concluded. "The forecast is for light winds, 6 to 8 from the southwest over open waters. As long as the waves are in the twos or so we can haul ass. Any bigger we may have to slow a bit."

221

Chuck turned to Grady. "We should be in contact range as early as 1:30 or 2:00 a.m."

Grady nodded, "Good. Alright. So you'll beat me to the Skyway?"

"Sounds like it", Chuck said. "I doubt we'll see you. We'll be hugging the coastline."

Nunchucks was still stroking his beard. "I'd say we make the Skyway about 4:00 a.m. At 20 knots, your target should get there about 8:00 a.m."

"Sounds about right", Chuck concurred.

Nunchucks' cell phone began to ring. He answered it and put it on speaker phone. "Go ahead Billy Boy. You're on speaker. I've got Chuck here and his buddy Grady."

Billy Boy was retired Army Captain William Kendall, another of Chuck's Delta 5 comrades. Bill was organizing the remaining three Delta 5 brothers in case Chuck needed them later.

"Hey Chuckster! We're all set", Bill reported. "Dave, Greg and I are hanging at Winghouse on U.S. 19. What's the plan?"

"You guys are in St. Pete?" Chuck asked.

"Yes sir. Havin' a good old time."

Chuck took a deep breath. He hoped he wouldn't need his former brothers-in-arms but he was really glad they would be around if he did. "First, thanks guys. I appreciate your help."

"No problem", they all said.

"Alright. Nunchucks and I are picking up Senator Manson and a female companion about twelve miles offshore northwest of Havana shortly after midnight. We'll bring them to you at the Skyway rest area. If all goes to plan, ETA your location about 4:30 a.m."

"Okay, Chuck. We'll hang here until they close and then mosey down to the rest stop on the south end of the Skyway. Confirm rendezvous, 4:30 a.m."

Chuck validated the instructions. "Roger that. 4:30 a.m., south side rest stop."

Alexandra had come out to tell the guys that dinner was ready. Their voices had carried well in the quiet early evening and she had overheard Chuck's instructions as she approached. Gavin would be back in just a few hours! Yea! She could barely contain herself. But he wasn't coming here. He was going to Tampa. "Why?" she wondered. Her Uncle Chuck hadn't wanted her to know yet, for what reason she wasn't sure. Though difficult, she mustered a subdued attitude and informed the guys in a low-key voice, "Dinner is ready boys. Come and get it." Then she nonchalantly turned and started walking back to the house as if nothing were out of the ordinary.

The guys hadn't seen her approaching. By the time they had turned to notice, she was already heading back the other way.

"Be there in a minute", Grady responded.

Chuck summed up the conversation. "Bear in mind, gentlemen, this is a fluid situation. Cuba has to go right. And if Grady sees any activity on the cargo ship, that could change everything. You guys should get some rest when you can. Stay sharp. I have no idea what we might run into tonight."

"Not to worry, boss", Chuck could hear Greg say in the background.

"We've got your back", he heard Dave add.

Chuck shook his head. "Stay sober, gentlemen."

"Roger, that." Bill acknowledged.

Nunchucks ended the call then cupped his hand behind his ear. "Did you hear that?" He looked toward the house then back at Chuck with a wide-eyed stare.

Chuck looked around then back at Nunchucks. "What?"

"It's a lobster calling my name... NuuuunChuuucks! Eat me!"

Grady laughed out loud as he climbed off the boat and onto the dock. "I caught those this afternoon", he informed the crew. "You won't get any fresher unless you eat them raw."

Chuck and Nunchucks followed Grady toward the house, laughing and joking. The sun was over the horizon, the early evening clouds taking on a reddish glow. Chuck looked up at the red evening sky with an uneasy feeling he couldn't explain. Red sky at night is supposed to be a good thing. He did take some comfort in the fact his Delta 5 buddies were ready and prepared. There was no better team of men in the world.

* * *

Kevin Falk sat alone on the dock of the Wimauma compound drinking a double shot of Irish whisky and thinking about Samantha Lawrence. He couldn't shake the emotional memory of the moment he twisted her neck and ended her life. He was glad her body had been found quickly. The evening news broadcast had said it had been shipped back to Massachusetts for burial tomorrow. He would like to have been there but the business at hand wouldn't allow it. So far, it appeared no one suspected him of any wrongdoing or involvement in her murder.

The past few days had gone by slowly. The anticipation of tonight's mission had him on edge. Nervousness was unusual to Kevin and he couldn't put his finger on just why he felt so uneasy. But he was confident the team of men he had assembled for this project was dependable and competent. All the test runs and simulations had gone well. Now it was a waiting game as the cargo ship sailed its way around the west end of the Florida Keys and into the Gulf of Mexico. In a few hours, months of planning and preparation would be put to the test.

As Kevin pulled the last swig of sedative from his whisky glass, his phone began to ring. It was Colonel Selbourne. "Good evening, Colonel."

"How are we doing, Major? Everything set?"

"Yes sir. The first set of bags is due to start dropping at 2:00 a.m. Six drops, approximately twenty-two hundred pounds per drop. The last drop will happen a little after 2:30.

"Excellent! How long before you'll have everything bundled up at the House?"

"We're cutting it close, sir. It's three hours from the drop zone to Devil's Elbow. Fifteen minutes from there to the House. The last boat should arrive around 5:45 a.m."

"What time is sunrise, Major?" There was a slight concern evident in the Colonel's voice.

"Sunrise is 6:36, sir. This is a good crew. They'll get back in time." Kevin knew the Colonel was fearful that one of the boats would be spotted on the open waters of Tampa Bay by the Coast Guard or Marine Patrol. "The last boat is scheduled to make Devil's Elbow by 5:30 a.m. We're home free after that. Even if he's a few minutes late it wouldn't be a problem."

"Alright, Major. I'll be down there tomorrow afternoon. I want to see your operation, meet your men."

"Yes sir. You realize the recovery drivers will be gone? They'll be on a plane to Puerto Rico before 10:00 a.m." Kevin wasn't sure the Colonel remembered that the recovery crew would be blindfolded at Devil's Elbow for the trip to the house, a precaution to keep them from knowing where it was located and what it looked like.

"Understood, Major. What time is the truck swap scheduled to happen?"

"Just like Green Valley, Colonel. Our driver will swap trucks with their driver on a deserted side road off State Road 674 near Fort Lonesome. There's nothing out there but phosphate pits, orange groves and a few fish farms. The meet is scheduled to occur at about 1:00 a.m."

"Very good, Falk. Very good."

The phone went dead. Kevin put it back in his pocket. It was time to go inside. The sun was disappearing fast and he was being eaten alive by nearly invisible, pesky little bugs the locals called 'no-see-ems'. They would come out every evening at dusk for a couple of hours, then go away when the sun went down. A curious phenomenon. The itching was almost unbearable. Kevin scratched his legs and ankles on the walk back to the house. One more shot of whisky sounded pretty good.

It would be about three hours before his recovery boat drivers would gear up and head out into the southern gulf to meet the cargo ship from Crimson Hook. They were waiting at a secluded beach house near Marco Island, just south of Naples, for Kevin to give them the go sign.

Kevin could feel his stomach tightening as "go time" drew nearer. Twelve hours from now the first stage of his Afghan Horse operation would be complete. The heroin would be off-loaded from the recovery boats and his lieutenants would be loading it onto a semi-truck for rendezvous with the buyer that night. The recovery boat drivers would be in Puerto Rico by then. He would summon them again when the next shipment arrived at Crimson Hook. It was a good feeling to know he wouldn't have to train a new crew for the next run. After this run he would have a stock of seasoned veterans.

As he entered the house his cell phone began to ring. It was the Colonel again. "Yes sir", he answered.

"I just received a text from our guy in Havana. He has acquired the targets. I thought you might like to know."

"Thank you, sir. That is good news."

Kevin's stomach tightened a little more as the thought of his friend being assassinated tonight melded with his prior thoughts of Samantha. He closed his eyes and tried to squeeze the images of them from this mind. He poured another shot of whisky into his empty glass and quickly downed it. Then he refilled the glass before putting the bottle back in the cabinet. With each swig he felt a little better. Kevin knew tonight would be a long and nervous one. Luckily, there was still plenty of courage left in the half-empty bottle.

CHAPTER 27

The streets of Old Havana were alive with vibrant throngs of humanity. It was almost 9:00 p.m. and Gavin couldn't believe how much nightlife was happening around him. Dancing and singing were everywhere. Musical bands wandered the streets, setting up impromptu sessions on street corners or in alleyways, entertaining passersby who gathered in small excited groups to listen and dance under the stars. Tourists tossed pesos into makeshift tip jars; a hat, a guitar case, a cigar box.

Everyone danced. Mambo, Bolero, Tango, Salsa, especially Salsa. There were so many musical instruments, instruments of all kinds: classical guitars, stand up basses, saxophones, bongo drums, congas, trumpets, violins, maracas, tambourines, clarinets, even trombones. Some were new. Some were old like the gray-haired men who played them. Percussion saturated the atmosphere with the beat of Danzón, the de facto official music and dance genre of Cuba. Gavin could feel the African rhythms fused with European influences. Percussive pulses emanated from the ether defying the body to stand still.

Gavin and Monica stood watching a group of young people Salsa in the ballroom of the Hotel Florida, a popular Salsa night spot. The ballroom had filled quickly, the small dance floor unable to accommodate all the couples who had come to socialize and sip on the Cuban national drink, Cuba Libre, a rum and coke concoction. Revelers were forced to spill out onto the street.

"Do these people ever sleep?" Gavin leaned in to speak directly into Monica's ear.

"The party is just beginning", she winked. "Cuban night life can go into the wee hours of the morning."

"Every night?" Gavin asked.

"As often as not", she affirmed.

Gavin and Monica were on their way to meet the man in the red hat after stopping briefly to rest and refresh themselves at a private apartment in Old Havana. The airport taxi had dropped them off next to the popular Saratoga

Hotel on the southern end of the Prado. Chuck had rented a casa particular for them, a privately-owned apartment next to the hotel.

In 1997, the Cuban government began to allow Cubans to rent out rooms in their houses and apartments for extra income. The proliferation of casa particulars had grown exponentially when AirBnB started to include them on their website for U.S. and Canadian tourists. Literally meaning "private house", casa particular had taken on the vernacular meaning of "private accommodations". Tourists could rent everything from a simple room in someone's home to an entire villa with a swimming pool and other luxury accommodations.

It had been nice to take a shower and change clothes after the long trip from Igoumenitsa. Inside, Chuck had left them enough Cuban money to pay the taxi driver and buy dinner as they made their way to the rendezvous point on the Malecón.

Gavin found it interesting that Cuban CUCs, Cuban Convertible Pesos, exchanged evenly with American dollars - one for one. Even so, Cubans were not supposed to use American dollars or Euros for transacting with tourists. Tourists were expected to convert their native currencies into Cuban currency to do business. Only certain types of banks, Cadecas, were considered safe for tourists to do currency exchanges. It was risky business to attempt exchanges at other types of businesses, even some banks. Scam artists often shortchanged ignorant tourists with similar looking CUPs, a local currency worth only four cents on the dollar. However, Monica had said conversions were safe at the major hotels, most of which offered exchange services.

The aromas of baking bread, cookies, black beans, fried plantains, coffee and myriad spices wafted on the cool evening air. Gavin and Monica ambled leisurely through the quaint neighborhoods on their way to the rendezvous point.

Some of the sights were as unusual as Gavin had ever seen. A man walked by, followed by a Dachshund with a large white rat riding on the dog's back. Another man, painted completely black and dressed like a pirate, was posing still like a statue. As tourists approached he would quickly change to a new position, startling the unsuspecting group. Then he would inch his grog cup, a makeshift tip jar, into plain sight of the now giggling group.

There was plenty of time before Gavin and Monica were to meet the man in the red hat. It felt good to wear fresh clothes and stroll relaxed for the first time in three days. Gavin's knee felt much better and the hike from the casa particular had, so far, bothered it very little.

"Oddly, I feel very safe here", Gavin said. "Not what I expected."

"There is very little crime in Havana" Monica noted. "Not like New York or Chicago where you often wonder if you will be mugged."

"I've noticed there are quite a few well-armed police on the streets. That's a pretty good deterrent I would think."

"Yes!" she laughed. "And we are very near the police station. You are perfectly safe here."

Monica pointed to a street sign. "We should cut over to the children's park", she advised. "This is Chacón Street. It will take us to the Malecón."

Gavin followed, not really knowing where they were, but trusting that she knew where they needed to go. Chacón Street was less than eight blocks long, but one of the more interesting in Old Havana. There were several nice restaurants and apartments, modest guest houses, even a five-star hotel with a jazz bar.

Gavin noticed many of the buildings in Old Havana had little exterior renovation, their weathered outsides belying the modern amenities inside. Such a diversity of architectural styles conflated together made it seem like history had become confused when it encountered Havana. The baroque colonial influences of Spanish and Moorish, Italian and Greek, dated back to the 1600s. Then a progression through neo-classical influences, especially French in the 1800s, added another layer of weird and wonderful to the old city. After the Spanish-American War in 1898, modern American and European influence became more prevalent. Art Deco and Art Nouveau style buildings in the early twentieth century were constructed right next to buildings dating from the 1600s.

Havana's original Capitol building looked strikingly like the U.S. Capitol after which it was loosely modeled. Constructed between 1926 and 1929, the building housed Cuba's Legislature until the Revolution in 1959. After the Revolution it became the headquarters of the Academy of Sciences and, later, the Ministry of Science, Technology, and Environment. The public could tour the first floor's many interesting features, like the world's third tallest indoor statue, Estatua de la Republica, The Statue of the Republic, which dominated the main hall of the Capitolio. Personifying Cuba's nationalism, the beautiful Cuban female model, Lily Valty, modeled for the statue which was cast in bronze and covered in 22 carat gold leaf. Havana was an eclectic conurbation, and it was nothing like Gavin had pictured it.

"I can't believe this!" Gavin exclaimed. "There must be thirty cars lined up here." He was looking at a row of taxis, all of them American classics from the 1950s. Ford, Chevy, Oldsmobile, Buick, Desoto, Chrysler, Dodge, Rambler, even a Canadian Studebaker. The owners stood proudly by their cars which gleamed under the street lights. Some were polishing their cars with pride, wiping away the fingerprints from their last fare. Others stood in small groups talking auto shop and sharing stories of silly tourist encounters. Most spoke English, a decided advantage for drivers who could also act as tour guides for Canadians and Americans, in addition to taking them to their requested destinations.

"There's the children's park", Monica noted. "We want to go this way." She pointed toward the Malecón now in sight.

As he glanced into the park, Gavin could see a large playground with seesaws, swing sets, slides, monkey bars and all sorts of climbing and crawling contraptions for kids to play on. In the middle of the park, a small Ferris wheel spun slowly as parents and kids laughed and shouted from the heights. An old kiddie train circled endlessly on narrow gage rails, decades of red, yellow, and blue paint hiding the rust underneath.

Then, even more classic cars were lined up in the center median of Avenue de Puerto, the Malecón. Gavin and Monica made their way across the four lanes of traffic to the sea wall along Havana Harbor.

"I'm in shock" Gavin confessed. "How did all of these cars survive sixty years here? And they are beautiful! Most of them look like they just rolled off the assembly line."

"On the outside", Monica chuckled. "Car owners in Cuba must be mechanics, especially if they want to operate them as taxis. It is impossible to get parts for American cars because of the embargo. So they make their own parts or modify parts from non-American cars. They do their own bodywork and paint the cars themselves. Often, they barter if they do not have a particular skill. It is rare that a car here has all original parts. As you saw at the airport, our Chevy had a Russian Lada engine. This is more common than not. Russian parts can be legally imported, American parts cannot."

"Why are there so many taxis?" Gavin wondered. "It's obvious the competition is stiff. You have horse drawn carriages, yellow cabs, classic cars, those weird little egg-shaped, three-wheeled rickshaws..."

"Cocotaxis." Monica clarified.

"Cocotaxis? Are those things safe?"

"Not really", she shook her head laughing. "Taxi driving is one of the highest paying jobs on the island. Doctors and lawyers have quit their jobs to become taxi drivers as tourism has increased in the last two decades. A doctor, for example, makes only seventy dollars a month from the government. One taxi ride to the airport pays thirty dollars to a taxi driver."

"Will that change now that the government is loosening restrictions on free enterprise?" Gavin wondered.

"Eventually it has to. But I am sure it will be a slow process. This is a socialist country. Most people here work, but they also depend on government rations and allotments every month to survive just like one-in-five Americans. I don't think most people in the States realize that over twenty percent of the U.S. population, about sixty million people, live on government handouts. Imagine if the U.S. suddenly took away EBT cards or stopped the WIC program or quit providing Section 8 housing. All those people would have to find livable wage jobs, jobs which do not currently exist. It is the same in Cuba."

"Is that our guy?" Gavin pointed to a fisherman along the sea wall. He was wearing a red baseball cap.

Monica looked up and down the wall. There were several other fishermen but he was the only one in a red cap.

"I do not see any others. It must be him", she said.

They approached the man and stood beside him. Gavin began, "Por favor, señor, is your boat available for charter?"

"Which boat did you have in mind?" the man asked, in an accent that was clearly not Cuban or Hispanic.

"Pilar", Monica responded. "We are interested in the Pilar."

"Come with me." The man picked up his backpack and gestured toward an opening in the sea wall with concrete steps leading down to a small cement dock on the water. Gavin thought the man's accent sounded Russian or perhaps some Slavic language. Although he had been expecting the man to be Cuban, the fact he might be Russian wasn't surprising given the close ties between Russia and Cuba.

"Please be seated", the man gestured, waving his hand toward a small motor boat tied to the dock. Not much bigger than a dinghy, the boat looked ancient and questionably seaworthy. The man threw his backpack into the rear of the boat, then jumped in and began to pull the handle of the rope crank on the old rusted motor. After several pulls, smoke billowed out of the two-stroke engine and it sputtered to life. "I will take you to Pilar."

"Thank you", Monica said, as she stepped off the dock into the front of the boat. Gavin got in last and sat in the middle seat.

"My name is Sergei", the Ukrainian informed them. "The seas are somewhat choppy tonight. You could get wet from the splashing waves." He handed them blankets. "These might help. There are life vests below seats. You can put on now if you will feel more comfortable."

"We'll be fine", Gavin assured. "How long will the trip take?"

"Perhaps one hour." Sergei untied the mooring line from the dock cleat and pushed the stern away from the dock. He advanced the throttle on the boat motor. The boat struggled for a short period as the bow rose then began to plow into the lightly choppy waters. As the bow settled the boat's speed increased and it began to plane.

Monica reached below her seat to locate the life vest. The seat was an enclosed bench that spanned the width of the narrow boat. There was a small door to a compartment underneath held shut by a piece of wire wrapped around a nail. It was difficult to figure out how the mechanism worked in the dark. She struggled with the wire momentarily, then it slipped off of its own accord. She opened the door and felt around inside until her hand found the vest. As she pulled it out, another bag came out with it. She untangled the bag from the straps of the vest and started to push the bag back inside until curiosity got the better of her. She opened the cinched neck of the bag, reached inside and removed an emergency flare gun. "Well, at least we can signal for help if this rickety old boat starts to sink", she thought to herself. She shoved it back into the compartment and closed the door.

"Would you like me to help you put that on?" Gavin offered.

"No, thank you. I just wanted it close by."

"Good idea." Gavin opened the compartment below his seat, removed the vest, and placed it next to him on the seat.

The noise of the boat motor made conversing almost impossible. Gavin and Monica sat silent, bouncing up and down, sometimes back and forth, with the gyrations of the boat. Both of them had gotten wet from the sea spray of a few rogue waves and decided to wrap themselves in the blankets to stay warm. There was little doubt the next hour was going to be miserable.

* * *

Alexandra and the women had said goodbye and good luck to Chuck and Nunchucks. They could hear Nunchucks' high-powered engine idling away from the dock. Grady had left almost an hour earlier. All the boys were gone now. Just she, Muriel, and Cynthia were left at the duplex. It was safe to tell the girls what she had overheard earlier.

"You heard them say that?" Muriel asked.

"Yes", Alexandra nodded. "They're picking up Gavin and Monica tonight off the Cuban coast and taking them to the rest stop on I-75 on the south side of the Skyway Bridge."

"Are you thinking what I'm thinking?" Muriel looked back and forth between Alexandra and Cynthia.

Cynthia was hesitant. "Gavin doesn't like surprises and I'm pretty sure Chuck doesn't either. If we show up there uninvited... well, I don't know about this."

"I'm going and nothing can stop me", Alexandra declared. "It may not be the smartest thing I've ever done but a few days ago I thought he was dead. It felt like my life was over. When he steps off that boat I'm going to be there. You girls don't have to come. I'm not asking you to. But I'm going."

"Well, Missy, you're not going by yourself!" Muriel proclaimed. "But we'd better get started right away if you want to be there by 4:30. It's over a six-hour drive from here."

"I don't like it", Cynthia complained, as she followed Alexandra and Muriel out the door.

"Which car should we take?" Muriel queried.

Alexandra didn't hesitate. "We're taking the Chrysler." Muriel's car was comfortable but old. She knew the Chrysler was unlikely to break down. And, it had a full tank of gas. She slid into the driver's seat while Muriel jumped in the back. Cynthia took shotgun by default.

"We're not going to pack any clothes?" Cynthia questioned.

"No time", Alexandra said tersely, as she started the engine and began to put the car in reverse.

"Wait!" Muriel commanded. She got out of the car and ran back to open the door of the duplex. Fifi and Fufu came bounding out of the apartment as Muriel entered. They ran to the car and jumped into the back seat. Muriel was gone for a few seconds then emerged with a small cooler of waters, a pair of dog leashes, and a water bowl. She hurried back to the car, jumped in the back and closed her door. "Let's go!"

Cynthia buckled her seat belt and adjusted the seat back. "I've got a bad feeling about this, Alex."

Alexandra put the car in reverse and backed out of the driveway. "Cynthia! What could go wrong?"

* * *

Sergei stood tall in the stern of the small wooden boat, balancing himself like a gondolier, his hand on the extended tiller of the motor, dodging larger waves, taking the smaller ones head on. The moon was more than half-full and quite bright which made it easier to see than it would have been on a less moonlit night. Eventually, a dim pinpoint of light appeared on the horizon.

"I see something", Monica turned and yelled back to Gavin and Sergei.

"Affirmative. I see it also." Sergei adjusted the motor tiller slightly, putting the bow on a straight-line course toward the light. The light grew brighter as he closed in on it. Within a few minutes the outline of Nunchucks' go-fast catamaran was in sight.

"Please stay in seats when I pull next to other boat. I will tell you when is safe to leave boat." Sergei sat down on the rear seat, reached into his backpack, and quietly removed his PSS pistol. He put it in his jacket pocket. He shifted the engine into neutral and coasted toward the bobbing go-fast.

As the small boat approached, Nunchucks tossed Sergei the loose end of a rope tied to a gunwale cleat on the catamaran. "Pull yourself closer", Nunchucks yelled.

Sergei pulled on the rope until the small boat was within a few feet of the catamaran then tied the rope to a cleat on the small boat's transom. Then he stood facing the catamaran and inquired, "Chuck McCrory! Do you remember me? I was surprised to hear you were still doing work for U.S. government. As you see, I am still doing business also."

Chuck shined his flashlight at the face of the man standing in the small boat. He noticed the man had one hand in his jacket pocket and the other shielding his eyes from the glare of the flash light. The voice was familiar, but not the face.

"You do not recognize yet, Colonel McCrory?"

"Should I?" Chuck moved the flashlight up and down the man's body. 'That voice! I know that voice', he thought.

"Azerbaijan", Sergei helped.

"Sergei! What the hell! What are you doing here?" Chuck was momentarily stunned. It had been almost thirty years since he had seen the young Ukrainian, who wasn't young any longer. It only took a second for Chuck to realize this was not a social call. Sergei was a business man, strictly so. This meeting could not be by chance. The hand in his pocket was not because it was cold. He gave a quick look to Nunchucks that told him be on alert.

Sergei and Chuck had met in the early 1990s in Azerbaijan. The collapse of the Soviet Union had rekindled old disputes between the Armenians and Azerbaijanis. The disputed territory of Nagorno-Karabakh belonged to Azerbaijan, but the population was primarily Armenian. The Karabakh Armenians had revolted, demanded independence, and proclaimed unification with Armenia.

Both Armenia and Azerbaijan had attained independence from the former Soviet Union in 1991. While still part of the Soviet Union, the two countries' ethnic differences had been held in check by Soviet military influence. But in the power vacuum created by the Soviet breakup, full-scale war had broken out between the two nations. By 1993, Armenia, aided by the Russian military, controlled fourteen percent of Azerbaijan territory, forcing the Azerbaijan government to recognize the Nagorno-Karabakh region as an independent third party in the war and begin ceasefire negotiations.

Surrounding countries in the region began to take sides. Many Ukrainians went to Azerbaijan to fight as mercenaries. Sergei had no interest in hand-to-hand combat, but his skills were in demand for other reasons. His familiarity with the Russian KGB had served him well. He had already built relationships with the SVR, Russia's new external intelligence agency, and the FSB, the internal security and counter-intelligence agency born out of the former KGB. Now he saw an opportunity in Azerbaijan to cultivate relationships on the other side, Western Europe and the United States.

Chuck McCrory had been sent to Azerbaijan to provide security while the United States opened its new embassy in Baku, the capital. While his outward duty appeared to be simply that of a military attaché, his more important and surreptitious job was counter-terrorism; working with the CIA to make sure the Armenian Union terrorist group, and other potential trouble makers, didn't disrupt the diplomatic peace talks getting underway in Paris and Baku.

The Armenian Union had formed in Moscow in 1988. The organization provided terrorists with forged documents for their activities in Armenia and Karabakh, and helped move weapons and mercenaries into Armenia, including Russian weaponry. Russia played both ends against the middle, officially supporting the Armenian government while simultaneously selling arms to Azerbaijan. Its public condemnation of the terrorist group's activities was feigned, at best, as was its public position of neutrality on the issue of the Nagorno-Karabakh region. This made it easy for the young, ambitious Ukrainian to establish himself as a paraclete for both sides of the conflict.

It was not suspicious, then, that a young Ukrainian mercenary would side with the Azerbaijanis, as did the Ukrainian government after both countries gained their independence from the Soviet Union. Azeri officers were trained in Ukrainian military academies, and Sergei saw that as an easy way to form friendly relationships with many of the Azeri soldiers who had spent time in his home country. Many of those men eventually worked with the Americans. Even at an early age, Sergei knew the larger his network, the more likely he could stay gainfully employed.

Still an idealist with little international experience, Sergei had found the relationship he had struck up with U.S. Army Lieutenant Colonel "Chuck" McCrory to be an advantageous one, one of student to mentor. Sergei had contracted with the Azerbaijan Secret Police who had been forced to work, however reluctantly, with their American counterparts on covert counter-terror operations in Armenia. While many of his associates found the Americans crude, arrogant and distasteful, Sergei saw them to be a wealth of potential knowledge and experience.

Chuck had long mastered covert skills, and, without actually trying, taught the young Ukrainian not so much the skills themselves, but which skills he needed to develop: keen observation without the appearance of inordinate attention; trusted intuition; split-second decision-making; mastery of role-playing and acting; multi-lingual ability; technical savvy; martial arts and self-defense; and perhaps the most important, the ability to assume false identities.

Coupled with the one God-given ability that can't be taught, intelligence, Sergei had developed a roadmap for his future that would serve him well. He rightly credited Chuck for much of the foundation upon which he had built his career. Sergei wasn't sure this meeting would go well, but it was a meeting he had often thought about, and one that had excited him since his conversation with Demetri. He wanted to see his old mentor one last time, and to thank him... before he killed him.

Sergei smiled at the man holding the flashlight on him, "It is pleasure to meet you again, Colonel."

"I'm not sure I can say the same, Sergei. Your chosen line of work disappointed me greatly when I learned of it."

"Do we not all follow our own conscience? Was your chosen career really so much different from mine?" Sergei asked.

"I can respect a man for following a path he believes in, one where he feels like he stands for something. I can respect that man even if I disagree with his cause. But where is the honor in prostituting yourself to the highest bidder?"

Although obviously rebuked, Sergei did not feel it necessary to take the criticism personally. "That I do not choose to take side in matters has worked well for all who do business with me. It is best if I do not have, as your people say, 'dog in fight'. I am trusted to get job done. I do. You cannot see the honor in that, Colonel?"

Chuck held his flashlight just below the Ukrainian's face. He would have preferred to keep the light in his eyes but keeping watch on the gun in his jacket pocket was more important at the moment.

"What I see is a man with no place to call home; a man with no true purpose in life."

Nunchucks started to slowly back away from the gunwale, sliding toward the front of the cockpit where he kept a handgun in a small compartment.

"Is better you remain still" Sergei warned. "Also, please to keep hands where I can see." Nunchucks did as he was told, but he was livid with himself for not being prepared for this eventuality. He and Chuck had failed to expect the unexpected.

The Ukrainian continued, "Ah, but Colonel, I do have purpose. There is pride to take when mission is completed to satisfaction of client. I am good at what I do. Much of credit belongs to you. I know you understand this."

"What is your mission here, Sergei?" Chuck knew that Selbourne must have contracted him to kill Gavin. But why didn't he do it in Havana? Something didn't add up.

"First is to thank you, Colonel McCrory. With not your tutelage I could not have accomplished so successful career. You are man I admired very much. I needed for you to know."

"Why are you really here, Sergei?" Chuck could sense that it was Sergei's intention to eliminate all of them. He tried to drag the conversation out for as long as possible. Getting a jump on the Ukrainian looked impossible at the moment. Sergei appeared to hold all the cards.

"I was hired to kill Senator Manson and girl", he said coldly and matter-of-factly.

Monica screamed, "Nooooo!", and fell down in the front of the boat, cowering behind the seat. "Please, noooo!" she continued to whimper.

Chuck didn't blink. "So, Selbourne hired you?"

"Very perceptive!" Sergei noted. He began to remove the PSS pistol from his pocket. "And now I can report I have added bonus to assignment. Perhaps he will give to me bonus, also." He raised the pistol at Gavin's chest.

"FffffWhooooosh!!" A missile of brilliant, smoking flame whizzed by Gavin's arm, barely missing him. Gavin jumped in shocked surprise, losing his balance and falling backwards in the bobbing boat. As he caught himself and braced against the side of the boat, he watched the speeding light ball embed itself in the Ukrainian's stomach. The Ukrainian collapsed as his gun went off, silently and harmlessly drilling a hole in the bottom of the boat before it fell from his hand.

The flames grew larger as Sergei fell backwards, arched over the rear seat of the boat, belly up. A fountain of flames frothed from his torso, the fireworks shooting several feet into the air. He writhed and screamed and clawed at his midsection, unable to stop the blaze with his hands. A defeated Sergei looked helplessly at Gavin then at Chuck, unable to comprehend what had just happened to him. With his dying breath his eyes met Monica's. She was no longer cowering behind the front seat of the boat. She was on one knee, both arms extended, the barrel of a flare gun still pointed at him as he lost consciousness.

"Get aboard!" Chuck yelled to Gavin and Monica. The flare was beginning to catch fire to the small boat. Monica dropped the gun and hurried toward Gavin who helped her into the reach of Chuck and Nunchucks. They pulled her aboard the catamaran.

Gavin wrestled with the dead body of the burning assassin, trying to remove his coat jacket and pants before the flames from the flare could overcome them. With water from the bottom of the boat, he damped out the embers around a hole in the back of the jacket where the flare had bore through the man's body. Then he wadded them into a ball and stuffed them into the Ukrainian's backpack and tossed it to Chuck.

"Good thinking", Chuck praised, as he caught the pack and extended a helping hand to Gavin who pulled himself aboard.

Nunchucks perused the clothing and the backpack. In the backpack were two dossiers, one on Monica, the other Gavin. One section of the pack was filled with money, U.S. dollars, Euros, Yuan, Rubles, Francs and Pounds. There were multiple ID's, business cards, and passports from several countries around the world. It was obvious that Sergei had moved stealthfully and comfortably wherever he wanted.

Nunchucks rummaged through the front section of the backpack and found a phone. He opened it and looked through the text messages. The most recent entry was just two words: "Targets acquired". They now had the personal phone number of Colonel Jacob Selbourne. He showed it to Chuck.

"Send a message: 'Targets neutralized'", Chuck ordered.

Nunchucks sent the message. Within moments they received a reply: "Affirmative. The Cayman account reflects your effort."

"That should put him off guard for a while", Chuck said.

"I wish we knew where that Cayman account was", Nunchucks joked.

"I'm afraid he took that secret with him", Chuck half-heartedly lamented.

Gavin and Monica changed into dry clothes and wrapped themselves in the blankets Chuck had brought along. As Chuck and Nunchucks finished rifling through the Ukrainian's gear, Chuck turned to Monica. "Gavin told me you were a strong woman. I think he understated the fact."

Monica gave him a labored smile. "Thank you", she said. But inside she was churning with emotion. She had never killed anyone before. Even though the man surely deserved it, and he surely would have killed her and Gavin, it didn't make her feel any less guilty about taking a human life.

Chuck sensed her guilt and anxiety. He knew how she must have been feeling. "You did what you had to do, lass. The rest of us are alive because you did. Don't dwell too long on it."

Gavin hugged her briefly. "That's twice you've saved my life. You're an incredible woman, Monica."

Monica sat down into one of the four bucket seats in the rear of the catamaran's cockpit and strapped herself in. The seats in Nunchucks' go-fast were cushioned and shock absorbed to handle the pounding of the boat against the waves at high speeds. The seat safety harnesses were constructed like those in a fighter aircraft, able to hold the passenger tightly, comfortably and safely in place even as the craft heaved and bounced and jostled from side to side. She was wondering if she would be able to sleep on the trip back. She suddenly felt exhausted in a way she had never experienced before.

Gavin strapped himself in beside her. He looked over at the burning boat drifting away into the moonlit night. Flames now engulfed the entirety of the small wooden structure. It wouldn't be long before it burned itself to the waterline.

Chuck and Nunchucks strapped themselves into the pilots' seats and Nunchucks set the GPS for a straight line to a waypoint just west of Marco Island. Chuck turned to Gavin and Monica, "This could be a slightly bumpy ride but we should have you back on dry land in a few hours."

"Great!" Gavin gave him a thumbs-up.

Nunchucks pressed the throttles forward and the speedy catamaran immediately jumped on plane. Chuck wondered if Grady had made contact with the cargo ship. His SAT phone hadn't rung yet, but it was possible satellite service in this area could be spotty. The time was approaching 1:00 a.m. As he was debating whether or not to try to contact Grady, the SAT phone began to ring.

CHAPTER 28

G rady White throttled down the sportfisherman and shifted the engines into neutral. He glanced at his watch. It was just before 1:00 a.m. Almost three hours had passed since he left the main channel north of Big Pine Key. At 28 knots on a 320-degree heading, Grady had calculated he should be about sixty-five nautical miles due north of the Dry Tortugas. The cargo vessel he was looking for should have already rounded the Tortugas and set its bearing northward toward Tampa Bay.

Chuck had supplied him with a global satellite internet WIFI system which he switched on and waited for it to auto-sync with the satellite network. The WIFI system created a hotspot he could use with his tablet to locate the current position of the Maruska Alabama using a live shipping traffic application Chuck had installed on the tablet.

Most sea-going cargo and passenger vessels used an automatic identification system, AIS, to constantly broadcast their location to other vessels in the area. It also broadcasted to satellite vessel tracking systems around the world. While radar was the primary method used for collision avoidance on the high seas, AIS could be used to identify the location of vessels well outside of radar range, making it an excellent supplementary method for staying out of harm's way. Grady would use the Maruska Alabama's AIS signal as a backup to Chuck's GPS dart stuck to the shipping container onboard the freighter. As long as the dart's GPS signal and the ship's AIS signal agreed on their locations, it could be assumed the container was still aboard the cargo ship.

Grady opened the app and located the Maruska Alabama. His estimate of its approximate location was dead nuts perfect. The ship was travelling north at a speed of 20 knots just eight miles due west of his position. He opened the GPS tracking app that was following the dart. It, too, confirmed the dart was eight miles due west. Now he needed to get close enough to the ship to get eyes on it without being spotted. Grady turned off the running lights on the sportfisherman and set his heading west northwest. He would run dark for the rest of the night.

In his head, Grady computed the calculations for the speed and bearing that would bring him to within five miles of the cargo ship. Fifteen minutes later he could easily make out the lighted rigging of the two-hundred-foot freighter. Through the high-powered binoculars he could see activity on the deck, but from five miles away in the dark it was difficult to discern exactly what was happening onboard. He would eventually have to move in closer.

The diminishing undulations of the cargo ship's ever-widening wake rippled beneath his boat causing it to toss and roll slightly as the waves passed under him. A ship that size created a four-foot wake that trailed for miles behind it. The seas inside the wake were slightly calmer. Grady slowed the sportfisherman to twenty knots to synchronize his speed with the Maruska Alabama.

Hooking up the binoculars to the gyro-stabilized bow-mounted tripod proved easier than he had anticipated. Now he could relax in the captain's chair, tend to the boat's wheel, and watch the cargo ship's activity on the console-mounted tablet screen. This was actually fun! Grady envied Chuck's ability to get his hands on so many cool, high-tech toys.

It was shortly after 1:15 a.m. when Grady was finally in position to keep an eye on the cargo ship, time to call Chuck's SAT phone and check in. He removed his satellite phone from its cradle and punched the numbers for Chuck's phone.

"Top of the mornin' to ya, Grady!" Chuck answered. "How's it going?"

"I'm all set up. Watching the ship as we speak. It's pretty lit up, Chuck. Good visibility. Not good detail, though. I'm about five miles east southeast of her. That's not going to be close enough. I'm gonna try moving in to three miles. That should increase the detail quite a bit."

"No closer though, Grady", Chuck admonished. "Don't take a chance on being seen."

"Roger that", Grady acknowledged. "So you have the Senator yet?"

"I do!" Chuck concurred. "He and Monica are sitting right behind me. It got a little exciting there for a while. The rendezvous was anything but boring. Monica saved all our butts. I'll tell you about it later."

"What's your twenty?" Grady asked.

"We just left the rendezvous point off Havana. We're on a zero heading right now. We'll skirt the Marquesas in about an hour. Where are you?"

Grady glanced at the GPS navigation system and checked his position. "Uh, it looks like I'm about seventy miles due north of the Tortugas, also a zero heading."

"Doesn't look like we'll see each other, then", Chuck observed. "We're gonna hug the coastline once we make the Naples area."

"Ten four. I'll keep you posted if anything unusual occurs. Safe travels."

"Back at you, buddy", Chuck responded.

Grady turned off the SAT phone and did a quick check of the boat's instruments. Plenty of fuel left, engines cool, oil pressure good. He pressed the throttles forward and increased speed to twenty-five knots. He would close in to three miles and then stay there on vigilant watch. Exactly what he was looking for, well, he had no idea.

* * *

Kevin Falk glanced up at the large clock on the wall inside the steel building at the Wimauma house where in a few hours the recovery boats would be arriving with their loads. It said 2:00 a.m.

The Maruska Alabama had entered the recovery zone right on time. The recovery crew had been waiting on Marco Island to launch their boats. At precisely 1:00 a.m. Kevin had sent word to the team leader of the operation to get underway. There was nothing left to do now but wait.

He was regretting, at least a little, his decision to maintain radio silence for the duration of the operation. It would have been nice to have real-time updates on the team's progress. But caution in an operation of this magnitude was paramount. It was safer to operate in silence.

In three hours Kevin would send his lieutenants to Devil's Elbow to meet the incoming recovery boats. In the meantime, he would try to get some shuteye in the warehouse office. He lay down on the cot in the corner and closed his eyes. The earlier whiskies had left a swirling miasma in his head, but nothing a three-hour power nap couldn't clear it up. He set the alarm on his cell phone to awaken him at 4:00 a.m. Within minutes, he was asleep.

* * *

"What the hell...?" Grady mumbled to himself. The rigging lights on the cargo ship had gone dark. He scrambled to set the binoculars on night vision using the tablet.

"Where is it? Where is it? Where is it?" The binoculars had lost track of the ship when the lights went out. Three miles was too far to use the night-vision capability effectively.

Grady raced to the bow, removed the binoculars from the tripod, returned to the controls, and began to manually scan the horizon for signs of the Maruska Alabama. It didn't take long to spot the ship. A phosphorescent wave of blues and greens glowing in the wake of the ship's bow lit up his night vision image like a beacon, a dead giveaway of the ship's location. He was back on track.

The glowing was caused by bioluminescent plankton. The bow waves of the ship were disturbing the small animals floating just under the surface of the water, causing them to flash brightly. Scientists thought their reaction might have been to scare away predators. Why they glowed didn't matter to Grady. He was just glad they did.

But why had the cargo ship killed its lights? Chuck had told him not to get any closer, but if he was going to be able to see what was going on, he had no choice. As he was about to throttle up and move closer, another plankton glow caught his attention. But this glow was much smaller and sporadic. It would occur briefly, then disappear, then appear again, then disappear.

Grady zoomed in as far as the binoculars would permit on the closet sporadically glowing object. Dimly, he could just make out the shadowy image of a small boat which was much closer to him than the cargo ship, maybe only a mile away. He immediately throttled down and put the boat into neutral. If he could see their plankton wave, they could likely see his.

Grady focused the binoculars on the approaching glow which kept coming closer and closer. Eventually he could clearly make out the outline of the small craft which appeared to be a recreational fishing boat with a single crewman aboard. The boat was now less than a half-mile from him. Grady killed his engine in case the noise of his boat could carry that far on the light breeze. He wasn't sure he could outrun the other boat if he was spotted, best to just drift quietly for a while.

The small boat zoomed on plane again and came right toward him at high-speed. Uh, oh! They had spotted him! He reached for the ignition switch, ready to turn the key, when the speedy boat slowed then stopped dead in the water and turned broadside to him, barely a quarter of a mile away.

Aided by the bright moon light, Grady's night-vision binoculars afforded him the best look he had had yet of the darting craft. It was an open fisherman Contender, about the size of his boat. As clear as day he could see a Hispanic man in the bobbing boat lift a heavy floating bag over the port gunwale and onto the shallow deck. Grady was fairly sure he knew what was in that bag. He could clearly see the man maneuver the bag into a fixed position and secure it to the inner sidewall of the boat. Then the man reversed course and sped back toward the freighter at high-speed.

As the glowing bow wave of the Maruska Alabama moved away to the north, Grady remained idle in the lightly undulating seas. Intermittent luminescent streaks of light flickered here and there well behind the larger craft. Obviously, there were multiple small craft like the one he had encountered doing the same thing, he assumed. It was impossible to estimate how much heroin had been off-loaded from the large ship. But judging from the amount of activity going on ahead of him, it was a sizable amount.

Grady took a deep breath and released a huge sigh of relief. It was only by divine providence that he hadn't been seen. Now he knew how the drugs were being off-loaded from the freighter and how they were being hauled to shore. What he didn't know was where the contraband was being taken.

Following the Maruska Alabama didn't seem necessary any longer. He could track one of the smaller vessels to find out where the drugs were going. Unfortunately, neither the GPS nor AIS signals could aid him further. From here on, he would have to keep one of the small boats within visual range, a feat that might or might not be possible, but one that surely would be dangerous.

The boat he was following drafted lower in the water than he would have expected for an open fisherman, even though it was moving across the surface at a pretty good clip. It must have been loaded down quite a bit. Keeping up with the over-loaded boat was not going to be a problem.

Should he report the situation to Chuck? Or should he wait until he had a better idea where the smaller boats were headed? He was afraid Chuck might tell him to stand down or back off and wait for support. Grady didn't want to lose track of the only boat left in sight. So for now, he would follow the lagging craft at a safe distance and inform Chuck later when he had a better feel for where the boats might be going.

* * *

Muriel Goldman sat restlessly fidgeting with her necklace in the back seat of the Chrysler 300, her mind churning with questions until she finally blurted out, "Alex, how did we get into this situation? I mean, why are there people trying to kill you and Gavin?"

Alexandra drew a deep breath. The answer was complicated and she wasn't sure how deeply Muriel actually wanted her to go with an explanation. She would start with the simplest answer: "Because we know too much, Muriel."

"What is too much? What, exactly, is it you know that would make them want to kill you?"

"We know what they're doing. We know where they're doing it. We know, at least partially, who's doing it. We think we know why they're doing it. If we can figure out how they're doing it, we can go to Congress and the Justice Department and expose them. But we need evidence, not accusations or speculation. Right now all we have is a conspiracy theory for which they have deniability because we have insufficient proof. They can't afford to let us uncover that proof."

"I'm scared", Muriel admitted.

"We all are", Cynthia assured her.

Muriel reminisced, "The CIA was always looked upon with reverence and admiration when I was growing up. They were saving us from the Communists and helping the rest of the world protect itself from evil dictatorships and such. They were the good guys in white hats. Weren't they?" She was questioning her long held beliefs.

"They've simply outlived their usefulness, Muriel", Cynthia stated. "When a government feels it has to spy on its own citizens, it means it is scared of its people, what they think. It is paranoid that its sway, its hold on power over the population, is at risk. That is a very dangerous tipping point for a country to be at. The next logical step is the suppression of its people's rights and freedom."

"This is the United States", Muriel said. "That could never happen here. Besides, they're only spying on us to find the evil people... terrorists and such."

The Constitutional lawyer in Cynthia was sympathetic with Muriel's naiveté. The average person had no idea what went on in the seamy underbelly of the world of espionage. Nor did they care. Nor, perhaps, should they. It was their elected officials' job, Congress's job, to oversee the various agencies and bureaus and insure they didn't overstep their bounds or abuse their authority. But over the last few decades, politics had become polarized to the point it was impossible for Congress to cooperate in an effective way, thus allowing domestic spying programs to operate like the wild, wild, west inside the CIA and the NSA and, to a lesser extent, the FBI.

In the late 1990s, the NSA had begun to "bulk collect" data, that is, spy on every citizen in the United States. The NSA collected so much data that it was forced to build a one million square foot facility in Bluffdale, Utah, to house it all. NSA cyber analysts had secretly developed the capability to turn on the cell phones and tablets and laptops of anyone whose information they had collected and watch them or listen to their private conversations - no warrant, no FISA court approval. They were able to get away with it because no one yet knew that they had the capability, never mind that they were already utilizing it.

Agency heads like the NSA's James Clapper would look Congressional committee members in their eyes and blatantly lie about the extent of their agencies' illegal collection methods and abilities. Men like John Brennan, who headed the CIA as Director of National Intelligence, was caught red-handed spying on members of the Senate Intelligence Committee, Congress itself.

No one knew these men were doing it until Wikileaks released its Vault 7 trove of evidence about the CIA's domestic spying tools and capabilities, and Edward Snowden blew the whistle on the NSA's similar set of domestic spyware in June of 2013. The evidence undoubtedly proved NSA Director Clapper to be a boldfaced liar. And while lying to Congress is a punishable federal offence, no one in the administration or Congress at the time seemed to care. Thus, no one was ever tried for their crimes, much less went to jail.

Did Snowden's revelations or the Wikileaks' exposé enrage the public? Did it encourage them to rise up and yell and scream and protest in front of the agencies that had betrayed their national trust and violated their Constitutional rights? In a word: No.

Instead, the public sheepishly followed the lead of the CIA's and NSA's damage control specialists, including Clapper and Brennan themselves, who spent a couple of weeks on national and international television and editorialized in the major newspapers and magazines about the incredible harm Snowden's and Wikileak's traitorous acts had done to national security.

The hubris of the National Intelligence agencies was on full display and few people noticed it for what it was. Of the few who did, even fewer cared enough about their Constitutional rights to complain. By the end of the news cycle, the agencies had effectively minimized the damage to their abilities to continue operating illegally and secretly by creating the image of two dastardly demons bent on destroying American democracy. Edward Snowden had been erroneously branded a traitor and accused of being responsible for single-handedly weakening the security of an entire nation. And the NSA went back to bulk collecting data from every Facebook post, Snap chat, Twitter tweet, phone call, Google search, and text message... and still no one cared.

"We're not going to make it by 4:30", Muriel warned, seemingly content to drop the subject.

"I can't go any faster this time of night. I'll get a ticket for sure." Alexandra was already doing eighty-five miles an hour as the women headed north on I-75 toward the Skyway Bridge.

"How much further?" Cynthia queried.

Alexandra wasn't sure. "We're in Fort Myers. Maybe a hundred miles? An hour and twenty minutes?"

"Then we'll probably be late", Muriel noted. "It's 3:30 now, sweetie."

"What else can we do?" Alexandra was frustrated but there was nothing to be done.

"I say we call your uncle", Cynthia offered. "He may get mad but at least they'll wait for us if they know we're almost there."

Muriel agreed. "We should call him, Alex."

"The emergency phone is in my purse." Alexandra handed her purse to Cynthia. "Uncle Chuck is the only contact in it. Call him."

"You want *me* to call him? This trip was your idea!" Cynthia's sarcasm caught Alexandra off guard. Was she joking or serious?

"Because I'm driving. Besides it was *your* idea to call him", she shot back.

"Oh, for heaven's sakes, you two! Oy vey!" Muriel reached over the back of the front seat and grabbed the phone from Cynthia's hand. "He's not going to kill us."

"No, but he might wound us", Cynthia retorted.

Alexandra looked at Cynthia and just shook her head.

Muriel opened the phone and selected the contact number for Chuck. She put the phone on speaker and the girls listened as it rang and rang with no answer.

"Are you sure you called the right number?" Cynthia asked.

"Try it again", Alexandra advised.

Muriel manually entered the number this time instead of selecting the contact button. They counted the rings, ...seven, ...eight, then silence. "There's no way to leave a message?" Muriel asked.

"You're leaving one now", Alexandra informed her. "Don't hang up. Uncle Chuck, this is Allie. We're on our way to the rest stop by the bridge. We'll be there about 4:50 a.m. Please wait for us if you get this message. Okay, you can hang up."

Muriel ended the call. "He doesn't use a 'Leave a Message' message?"

"No", Alexandra said. "Not on a burner. No traces, not even a voice."

"Why didn't he answer?" Muriel inquired.

"I was wondering the same thing", Alexandra confessed. "It's not like Uncle Chuck to ignore the emergency phone." The women could sense Alexandra's concern and it made them nervous as well. Alexandra looked over at Cynthia and quietly mouthed, "Something's not right."

CHAPTER 29

Kevin Falk's cell phone began to alarm. It was 4:00 a.m. His head was still fuzzy and he had awakened in a funky, depressed mood. In thirty minutes the recovery boats would start arriving at Devil's Elbow. That should have been a joyous occasion and one that made him feel successful and proud. But all he was feeling was a sense of loss for the woman he had murdered and the friend he had betrayed. He shook himself awake and forced the negative thoughts to the back of his mind. There was business to do.

"Any word from the lookout, Sergeant?" Kevin yelled to his first in command.

Sergeant Robert Eller was a former Marine Gunnery Sergeant mustered out of the Marine Corps after he had killed a man in a bar fight in Tijuana, Mexico. It had been an accident, but the problem was, Eller wasn't supposed to be in Mexico. He was stationed at Marine Corps Base Camp Pendleton in California and had no authorization to leave southern California much less permission to leave the United States.

Kevin had met Eller in Afghanistan in May of 2010 when Eller's unit, Combat Logistics Battalion 5, had been deployed to support the Obama Administration's escalation there. The escalation was in support of the Bush Administration's now ten-year occupation of Afghanistan, aptly called Operation Enduring Freedom, emphasis on enduring.

It all went south for Eller when he and two buddies got a three-day pass and started their short leave off with a few drinks in a small bar in Oceanside. Sometime in the wee hours of the morning the suggestion that Tijuana hookers sounded like a good idea took hold of their anesthetized minds and forced them down I-5, across the border, and into a derelict drinking hole called Adelitas.

All had gone well until a shoving match between Eller's buddy and a Navy Ensign came to blows forcing Eller to intervene. When he cold-cocked the belligerent Navy officer, the man fell and hit his head on the corner of a table. Two weeks later the Ensign died in a San Diego hospital of complications from head trauma. Five months and a court-martial later, Eller was sentenced to two years in the brig and separated from the Marine Corps on a bad conduct discharge.

The sergeant's military bearing and devotion to duty had impressed Kevin in Afghanistan. Eller seemed like a natural born leader, and, with no one to lead now, it had been an easy recruiting job to get him to join Kevin's Florida operation, the closest thing to a military environment the sergeant would ever see again.

"Just talked to him, sir. Nothing happening yet", Eller responded.

"I want to know the moment the first boat makes rendezvous at the Elbow."

"You will, sir", the Sergeant yelled back.

Kevin stretched as he left the metal building and walked back over to the house. As he opened the screen door his cell phone began to ring. A quick look confirmed his assumption.

"Nothing yet, Colonel", he answered.

"Alright, Major. I'm anxious to report this thing up the chain. Let me know as soon as you have something for me."

"Will do, sir."

Kevin grabbed a banana from the fruit bowl on the kitchen table and peeled it as he walked out the back door toward the creek. It was dark out but the bright moon illuminated the yard along the creek bank and a delicate fog left an iridescent glow on the mangrove trees, their leafy lunar reflections on the slow-moving water nervously shimmering like a lacey rainbow on an uneven breeze.

The secluded area along the tributary creek was hidden from the main section of the river by a slight bend and a distance of several hundred feet. The trees and shrubs along the main part of the river were dense enough that the property near the house and the docks couldn't be seen by passing boats.

There were two docks extending out from the creek bank, one on each side of the newly constructed boat ramp. The creek was thirty feet wide at the docks, more than wide enough to maneuver the 28-foot Contenders onto the concrete ramp. This far upriver the creek was still subject to the tides from the bay but the effect was only a foot or so, not enough to prevent the shallow draft Contenders from being able to make the short trip up the creek to the obscured property.

Shortly before Kevin had awoken, Sergeant Eller had dispatched a 21-foot Boston Whaler to Devil's Elbow. Onboard, seven of Eller's men waited for the Contenders to arrive. It was planned that as each Contender reached the elbow, one of the men in the Whaler would take command of it. The recovery driver would be hooded, his wrists bound with zip ties, and he would be hidden from view for the trip further upriver to the compound. Once all of the Contenders had arrived, the last man would bring the Whaler back to the house keeping an eye out up and down the river for anyone or anything that looked suspicious.

Kevin had made the calculated decision that this part of the operation was relatively safe from ambush and didn't require much precaution or protective armament. Only two of the men in the Whaler would be visible. They would appear to be armed only with fishing poles in case local residents happened by in the wee hours of the morning. Should that happen the plan was for the armed men to duck and hide while the phony anglers smiled and waved at the passing intruders.

Once the shipment was on land, however, it became more vulnerable to attack. Back at the dock, every man would change into Marine commando-style battle dress and protective gear with body armor. Each man was issued a Beretta M9 sidearm and an M4 assault rifle. Their head gear allowed them to communicate with each other, Eller, and Kevin. All of the men were ex-Marines, handpicked by Eller and trained extensively to guard the expanse of the property quietly and stealthfully. Six of the men would take up guard positions around the perimeter of the property. Eller and the remaining man would unload the heroin from the boats and transfer it to the ship container on the transfer truck.

Kevin tossed his banana peel into the creek and watched it drift away toward the Little Manatee. He searched briefly for some sort of meaning in the departing Musa skin, but nothing came to mind. Still, he stood there until it had drifted around the bend and out of sight. As he turned back toward the house Sergeant Eller was approaching.

"Contact, Major. The first Contender has arrived. It'll be here any minute."

Kevin smiled at the Sergeant. "Good. You know what to do."

"Yes sir."

Minutes later Kevin could hear the Contender idling upstream. The large twin engines made a distinct resonance as they pushed their way into the creek mouth. It was only a moment before he could see the bow of the boat rounding the bend.

Kevin walked out to the far end of the dock closest to the house and stood observing as Eller backed a heavy-duty pickup truck and boat trailer down the ramp and into the water next to the dock on the far side. Eller got out and waited on the dock for the driver of the first heroin-laden vessel to idle alongside and align his boat with the float-on trailer. He gave the driver a thumbs-up and in a second the driver had accelerated the heavy Contender up and onto the trailer.

As the driver killed the outboard engines and toggled the switch that lifted them out of the water, Eller walked down the ramp and secured the trailer's wench cable hook and safety chain to the boat's bow eye. Then he returned to the pickup truck and pulled the heavy boat and trailer up the ramp and out of the water. He swiftly exited the truck and removed the bilge plug and let the boat drain for a few minutes. The driver hopped down from the boat and prepared to don his battle gear in preparation to take up his assigned sentry position.

Kevin was feeling much better, happy with what he had seen. The precision with which his men had operated was excellent. The long hours of practice, preparation, and training were paying off. Five more boats and the hardest part of Operation Afghan Horse would be complete, the concept proven. No doubt the Colonel would be pleased, too.

Sergeant Eller pulled the dripping boat and trailer through the large overhead door and into the metal building and parked it where it could be easily unloaded. He placed a hook ladder over the side of the boat and summoned the hooded recovery driver to it. The nervousness of the man was evident as he helped him off the boat and over to the detainee detention room, a small secured room with a single indirect-entry door and no windows. The man sighed with relief when Eller removed his hood and cut the tie wraps from his wrists. He tried to reassure the man, "The rest of your team will join you shortly. You did great. You'll be well rewarded, I assure you."

Kevin had been skeptical of the Sergeant's recommendation that the hoods and wrist restraints of the recovery drivers be removed as soon as possible. But he had relented when Eller had proposed a secure detention area inside the metal building with no possibility of the detainees seeing the house or any other part of the compound. "Give them a couple of beers, a pool table, and some magazines. Let them relax after the mission and decompress, chat with each other, build a camaraderie. They won't hesitate the next time you call on them." Kevin knew the Sergeant was right.

The first boat had arrived without a hitch. Over a ton of heroin was inside the building and already being loaded onto the transport truck that would be swapped with the buyers in less than twenty-four hours.

Kevin opened his cell phone and called Selbourne's number. Finally, he had some good news for the Colonel!

* * *

The light breeze which had kept the open waters of the gulf relatively calm the last few hours had begun to pick up. A few white caps had formed, cresting atop a light chop that bounced the boat around slightly. The moon had fallen toward the horizon but the skies were mostly clear and the stars could still be seen hovering delicately above the few clouds that wafted on the upper winds. In the distance Grady could just make out the yellow, illuminated suspension cables of the Sunshine Skyway Bridge which spanned the mouth of Tampa Bay.

Following the recovery boat that he had spotted back at the Maruska Alabama had proved a simple task so far. The night vision binoculars had worked excellently which had allowed Grady to keep an eye on and a constant distance between his boat and the heroin-hauling Contender. It was time to call Chuck and check in.

Grady removed the SAT phone from the cradle on the console and punched the keys for Chuck's number. The phone wouldn't respond. It appeared to be dead. The battery seemed okay and nothing looked broken. The phone simply wouldn't work. He fiddled with the buttons for a few minutes and removed and reinstalled the battery. Still nothing. Son of a bitch!

If he was close enough to a shore tower his cell phone should work. Grady retrieved his backpack and searched the pockets until he felt the phone. It was fully charged according to the power level indicator. He called Chuck's emergency cell phone number and waited. After several rings the call went straight to voicemail, no prompt to leave a message, as he'd expected.

"Chuck, it's Grady. My SAT phone's out. Don't bother trying to call it. I'm in pursuit of a 28 or 30-foot Contender loaded with contraband. Some kind of bags were tossed off the freighter and picked up by several smaller boats. Not sure how many. I'm following one of the boats. It is now ...," he checked his watch, "4:34 a.m. We're about to pass under the Skyway. This guy is obviously headed into the bay. Call me with instructions. Otherwise, I'll remain in pursuit. Grady out."

It wasn't like Chuck to not answer the emergency number. It gave Grady an uneasy feeling. Not being able to communicate with the team made his reconnaissance that much more dangerous. So far, he had been able to stay far enough behind the Contender that he was comfortable it didn't know it was being followed. But in the confines of the bay, he would eventually be forced to track closer to the target which would make it more difficult to remain inconspicuous. The fact that the Tampa Bay shoreline was well-lit in many areas added to his unease.

Ten minutes after passing under the Skyway, Grady raised his binoculars to check on the boat's progress. The Contender was leaving the main channel. It had bore starboard at the 6D marker, apparently heading for the channel near Little Cockroach Bay, the entry into the Little Manatee River. Interesting. He reached for his cell phone and called Chuck again. He had forgotten to tell Chuck he had turned on the GPS tracking app on his cell phone. Without the SAT phone, his cell phone's GPS was the only way for Chuck to track his location.

* * *

The Sunshine Skyway Bridge was a continuous concrete cable-stayed bridge built in 1987 across the mouth of Tampa Bay. Its modern looking twin-sail design had always fascinated Chuck. He marveled at its beauty as Nunchucks began to slow the go-fast and line the catamaran up to enter the main channel underneath the longest clear-span concrete bridge in North America.

At night the bridge's stays were lit up by dozens of flood lights. The lights illuminated the sunshine-yellow cables which supported the 1200 feet of roadbed that spanned the main channel beneath it. Cable-supporting pylons at each end of the span reached 345 feet into the air in the center of each sail, resembling the huge masts of a majestic tall ship. At the tip of each mast was a large red beacon blinking a warning to low-flying aircraft to keep their distance.

While the current marvel of construction had had a relatively boring thirty-year history, except, perhaps, for the 135 suicide jumpers who had each paid a dollar to leap from the lofty toll road, such could not be said of its predecessor. The original Skyway Bridge had been built in two spans at different times, two similar bridges that paralleled each other. The first was constructed in 1954 replacing a ferry that carried travelers from the southern tip of St. Petersburg to the northern edge of the Bradenton/Sarasota area.

But growing traffic demands by the late 1960s, plus non-compliance with Interstate Highway regulations, necessitated a second bridge be built alongside it. In 1971 the second bridge was completed, effectively doubling the number of commuters able to travel over, rather than around, Tampa Bay.

Chuck had been home on leave in 1980 and recalled turning on the television on the dismal morning of May 9th to learn that the southern span of the Skyway had collapsed. A Japanese-built freighter had collided with one of the bridge's support piers, one not meant to take the brunt of an outsized cargo ship. The impact collapsed the bridge, plunging 1400 feet of steel girders, supports, and roadway into the angry waters below.

A ferocious Florida storm had formed quickly that morning off of Egmont Key, outside the mouth of the bay. It ambushed the 608-foot phosphate freighter, Summit Venture, as it tried to navigate the narrow channel under the bridge. Sixty mile-per-hour winds lashed the freighter forcing it out of the channel and sending it crashing through a support column holding up the massive steel overpass. In the blinding winds and rain, six cars, a blue pickup truck, and a Greyhound bus failed to see the missing roadbed and plummeted over the edge of the broken span, falling 150 feet onto the deck of the freighter and into the churning waters below.

252

Thirty-five people lost their lives that morning. Only the man in the blue pickup truck survived. Chuck remembered reading that the man had died of bone cancer just a few years later after having suffered from survivor's guilt for most of that time. The pilot of the freighter, John Lerro, received death threats for months, his wife left him, his dog was stolen, beaten and urinated on. It was little consolation for Lerro when he was eventually exonerated and his pilot's license restored, for less than a year later he was diagnosed with Multiple Sclerosis and died just a few years after that.

Nunchucks cleared the bridge span and veered starboard toward the rest area on the southern causeway. Three and a half miles and they would be back on dry land. "I'm not sure how close I can get to the seawall over there." Nunchucks knew that the area around the rest stop had large jagged rocks and oyster beds close to the seawall.

Chuck was more familiar with the terrain than Nunchucks. "There's a spot we can tie up across from the restrooms. Put the bow on the wall and we'll use a stern anchor to hold us perpendicular."

"Roger that", Nunchucks agreed.

As the catamaran idled up to the rest area, the rest of the Delta 5 team was already waiting by the guardrail. Chuck threw out the stern anchor, making sure it secured itself to the sandy bottom, then handed the loose end of the rope to Gavin. He grabbed a thirty-thousand candle-power lantern from the locker under the console and climbed onto the bow signaling Nunchucks directions through the shallow but brightly-illuminated water until they were close enough to the seawall to toss a bowline to one of the men onshore. When the mooring line was secured he signaled to Gavin who pulled the anchor line taut and tied it off to a stern cleat.

"Gracias a Dios!" Monica said, as she crossed herself.

"Amen", Gavin added. "Dry land is going to feel awfully good!"

Chuck jumped onto the seawall and hopped over the railing. Gavin followed, grabbing the extended hand of Greg who shook it after Gavin caught his balance. "Welcome to America, Senator."

"Thank you...uhh" Gavin said with hesitation.

"It's Greg, sir."

"Thank you, Greg. It's good to be home."

Nunchucks helped Monica onto the bow of the catamaran and she gingerly made her way forward until she could reach Gavin's hand. He pulled her to the railing then helped her over it.

"Has anybody heard from Grady?" Gavin asked.

"Oh shit!" Chuck jumped back on the boat and retrieved the SAT phone and his cell phone. "I'll try him again. He should have checked in by now." He dialed the SAT phone and waited for a response. Nothing. "He's not answering his SAT phone. I'll try his cell."

Chuck swiped his cell phone face to open it. No response. He swiped it again. The phone was off! How had it gotten turned off? He racked his brain. "When would I have turned it off? When would I have turned it off?" It didn't matter. He pressed and held the power button until the phone came alive. Then he waited for the start function to awaken it.

"How long has it been off?" Nunchucks asked.

"I'm not sure. I don't remember turning it off. Maybe I sat on it wrong. I don't know."

When the home screen popped open Chuck looked at the phone message icon. Four! Four messages were on his emergency phone.

"Goddammit!" he blurted.

Chuck quickly opened the first message: *"Don't hang up. Uncle Chuck, this is Allie. We're on our way to the rest stop by the bridge. We'll be there about 4:50 a.m. Please wait for us if you get this message. Okay, you can hang up."*

"What the hell!" Why was Allie coming here? Then it hit him. It was hard to blame her. "Gavin you're going to have a visitor in a few minutes."

"I am? Who?"

"Allie's on her way. Somehow, she knew you were going to be here. She must have overheard us talking at Grady's place. I swear to God, nothing gets by that girl!"

Gavin smiled. "Shame on her!"

Chuck just shook his head as he checked the next message: *"Chuck, it's Grady. My SAT phone's out. Don't bother trying to call it. I'm in pursuit..."* Oh no! Grady was following one of the boats and it had been over an hour since he left this message. The guy had no weapons, no way to protect himself if he was spotted. Chuck could kick himself for not realizing his phone had been off. He would have told Grady to lay back and wait for support.

The next message was good... Grady had called to tell him the boat he was tracking was headed for the Little Manatee and that he could be tracked by the GPS app on his cell phone. But it was the last message that sent a shiver down Chuck's spine. He played the message over again, and a third time.

Chuck looked around at the Delta 5 who had gathered around him when he put the message on speaker. It was Nunchucks who spoke first. "This ain't good, man. This is not good."

CHAPTER 30

It was nearing low tide as Grady negotiated the easterly turn at Marker 6D and set his course toward the channel along Little Cockroach Bay. The recovery boat was still in sight from a safe distance but soon it would be in the river channel where he would be forced to move in closer. Grady didn't know this area of Tampa Bay very well. He called up a navigational chart on the tablet, NOAA chart 11416, to try to get a better idea where his target might be headed.

The mouth of the Little Manatee River was a shallow delta, the entrance to the navigable portion of the river difficult to maneuver. Grady would be approaching the river mouth from the south following the Cockroach Bay channel markers northward along the coastline. The main channel into the river reversed almost 180 degrees, winding its way back to the south and zigzagging several hundred yards before entering the main river flow. Although the channel was well marked it was slow going. No Wake zones impeded high speed travel. This is where the reconnaissance would become the most dangerous. To keep the other boat in sight he would have to speed up and get close enough that it would be able to see him as easily as he could see it.

The sun would not rise for another half hour but the skies had already begun to lighten. It was now impossible to remain invisible. There were a few other boats moving about, mostly crabbers and shrimpers getting ready to start their days. Their presence would help but his recreational boat would stand out among the others which were obviously working boats. Regardless, he had to move in closer. There were no other alternatives.

The one thing Grady knew for sure now, was that somewhere up this river there was a piece of property with a large stash of heroin. If he could keep the Contender in sight until it made landfall, he would know where that was.

Grady increased the illumination on the tablet displaying the navigational chart he was using to find his way into the shallow, irregular river mouth. It showed that red channel Marker 14 ended the string of navigational aids that led into the main river flow. He had tried to stay about a half mile behind the

Contender which had caused him to lose sight of it once it passed Marker 14. But from there the Contender only had two choices of routes. It could hug the coast to the north along Shell Point, above the Negro and Chicken islands, or it could turn south cutting between Whiskey Key and Goat Island. Since the tide was low, Grady believed the Contender would choose the deeper course, the northerly one, especially since the Contender was drafting so deeply with its heavy load. He sped up slightly and veered onto the northerly route.

A light fog had begun to form along the river. Visibility had become more difficult as the fog had become more dense. Grady throttled back to a slow idle as he approached Devil's Elbow, a double 90 degree turn in the river. For the first time he was unable to see what was ahead of him, no clue what lie around the bend. Caution would dictate turning around and trying to contact Chuck again before proceeding. But caution was something Grady hadn't practiced a great deal in his life.

As he rounded the port turn into Devil's Elbow an excited voice came from a shallow cove in the mangroves. "Allí, amigo, el hombre que me siguió!"

"You're sure he's the one who followed you?"

"Sí señor, era él."

Grady knew immediately this situation spelled trouble. He regretted not having contacted Chuck earlier with an update. Now it was too late. Or was it? He removed the cell phone from his pocket and palmed it by his side then looked down to press the only contact in his list. When the message recorder silently connected he laid the phone on top of the console and yelled to the men, "Dis be da Devil's Elbow? I be lookin' for da Devil's Elbow."

Grady knew exactly where he was located from the navigational chart, but he hoped the cell phone would pick up the conversation long enough to leave a clue for Chuck about his position and his situation. The uneducated accent had been a kneejerk reaction but maybe it would help persuade the men he was just an innocent old black man out fishing. Would it work? Who knows? But it certainly couldn't hurt.

There were three men and two boats from what he could make out through the fog. Both boats drew closer and Grady could see two of the men were carrying weapons, big ones. One of the boats was the Contender he had followed, the other a smaller Boston Whaler. The man in the Whaler appeared to be in charge. His weapon, an M4 assault rifle, was pointed at Grady. "Who are you?" he asked. "Why were you following this boat?"

Grady had instinctively raised his hands when he saw the man's gun pointed at him. "I wadn't followin' nobody. I don'ts even know dat guy. I be lookin' for da Devil's Elbow. Sposed da be some kinda fine fishin' in da turns. Snooks, reds. I don't be followin' nobody."

"Keep your hands where I can see them", the man in the Whaler admonished.

"I don't gots no weapons on here. Jussa fishin' pole o' two."

"Check him out, Bobby", the man in the Whaler ordered as he pulled alongside Grady's boat. The man named Bobby hopped aboard and immediately frisked Grady. Nothing found, he signaled with a head shake that Grady had no weapons on him. He moved to the console: A cell phone, a tablet with a chart of the bay on it, a pair of high-powered binoculars and a satellite phone.

"What are you doing with a SAT phone?" he asked Grady.

"Dat be a friend's phone. It don't work. He leff it here."

The man fumbled with the phone for a minute then sat it back on the console. He walked back to the rear of the boat, opened the large cooler and rummaged through it. "Why are you carrying so much food in here? You plan on being gone for a while?"

"After I leaves da Elbow I be goin' to da middle ground."

"By yourself?"

"I cain't gets nobody to go wimme. I has to go by mysef. My wife won't go wimme. Nobody."

"Yeah, well, I don't doubt that. Crazy old fool. Nobody goes to the middle grounds alone. That's a hundred miles out!"

The man in the Whaler was growing impatient. "What do you think, Bobby?"

"I think he's clean. But, man, we can't let him go now. He's seen too much."

"Alright. We'll have to take him back with us. Take your man back and let Eller know what happened. I'll stay here and watch him until you return. Bring somebody back with you to get his boat. And bring another hood and some ties."

"Yes sir", the man acknowledged.

As the Contender idled away upstream, the man in the Whaler ordered Grady back to the cooler in the stern of the boat and had him sit down on it. Then he lashed the Whaler to Grady's boat and idled both boats into a small mangrove cove on the side of the riverbank, out of the sight of any river traffic.

The fog had begun to burn off as the dawn light grew brighter. This was not how Grady had pictured the mission going to this point. For the first time since he left the military he had started to feel the juices flow from his commando training. Could he overpower this guy should the opportunity arise? It was obvious the man was former military by the way he carried himself. He was younger and stronger. Grady knew that if he did try, it would have to be under near-perfect conditions and he would have to get it right the first time.

The sun was beginning to peek through the gathers of Spanish moss titivating the tall pines and oaks above the mangrove-lined riverbank. A narrow beam of sunlight illuminated the cell phone sitting on the console. Grady stared at the phone. He knew it was tracking every move the boat made in real-time, and the gunmen were going to take his boat back to their hideout, so they had said. Not the brightest move on their part, but one he certainly welcomed.

Shifting himself on top of the large cooler, Grady leaned back and adjusted his hat, shading his eyes from the sun. He folded his arms behind his head and rested the back of his head on the transom. Sooner or later the Delta 5 would come looking for him. He just hoped he was still alive when they found him.

* * *

"Where are you, Allie?" Chuck had called Alexandra back to check on the ladies' progress.

"We're just passing Bradenton, near 64, Uncle Chuck."

"Okay. Get off at the next exit, 301, in Ellenton. Make a right. There's a motel on the river. Wait there. We'll meet you soon."

"Alright. Bye."

"I wonder why he wants us to go to the motel?" Muriel pondered. "Maybe they aren't at the rest area any longer?"

"Maybe. He didn't say and I didn't ask. Uncle Chuck doesn't like to be questioned when he's barking orders."

"Neither does Gavin", Cynthia noted. "Must be a military thing."

"Sucks for you, Cynthia", Alexandra chided. "Gavin knows better than to give me orders." The girls all laughed.

"There's the river. The exit is on the other side. Remember, you want to go right", Muriel said, making sure Alexandra didn't miss the exit. "Don't dally, honey, if you know what I mean."

"I'll drop you at the door", Alexandra chuckled.

Alexandra pulled up to the door of the motel and let Muriel and Cynthia out while she parked the car underneath a street lamp near the entrance. Fifi and Fufu were whimpering something about being eager to stretch their legs. Alexandra strapped their leashes on and was about to walk them to a grassy area when a white van sped into the parking lot and abruptly pulled up next to her car and parked. She was slightly startled when three strange men quickly jumped out and stood like sentries around the van. The man who had gotten out of the front passenger door reached back and slid open the side door of van. As he did, Monica stepped out. Right behind her was Gavin.

"Oh my God!!" Alexandra screamed. She quickly hugged Monica. "I'm so glad you're safe. I was so worried."

Tears began to flow down the cheeks of both women. "Oh, Alex. I was so scared sometimes. But Gavin was my rock. Thanks be to God he was there." Alexandra hugged her more tightly.

Gavin stood beside Monica until the girls had released their embrace. Then he waited as Alexandra stood transfixed, just staring into his eyes. "I thought you were dead", she whispered.

"I know", he said. "It was best you didn't know."

"I was so scared. I don't think I could go through that again."

Muriel and Cynthia had returned. Muriel took the leashes of the dogs from Alexandra's hand and backed them away.

"You won't have to", Gavin assured her. He wrapped his arms around her as she put her head on his shoulder and softly sobbed. Happy tears. Tension-releasing tears. He cupped her face in his hands and lifted her lips to his. It was an awkward but romantic kiss as she laughed and cried at the same time.

"You're hurt", she said, when she noticed the dressing on his temple.

"It's okay. I'll be fine."

"I love you, Gavin Manson."

"I missed you, Alex. I missed you so much."

"Alright break it up, love birds. The clock is ticking. You can do that later." Chuck had arrived with Nunchucks. They had driven Nunchucks' boat around from the rest area to the motel and docked it on the waterway. "Everyone inside. Let's get checked in. We're going to need to formulate a plan asap."

Muriel looked around for Grady who was nowhere in sight. "Where's Grady?" she asked Chuck.

Chuck stood silent for a moment, a concerned look in his eyes as he struggled with how to break the news to her. "He's with the bad guys" is the way he chose to phrase it.

* * *

It was late afternoon by the time Colonel Selbourne arrived at the distribution compound. He had caught a hop from Langley Air Force Base to MacDill where he rented a car for the roughly one-hour drive to Wimauma. This was his first trip to the Florida facility and his first look at Kevin's new operation.

Selbourne's first impression of Wimauma was just as Kevin had described it: nothing but cattle, palmettos, orange groves and fish farms. He had a little trouble locating the driveway to the property, which was good. Unexpected visitors would be unlikely. An inconspicuous barbed-wire gate protecting an old rusted cattle gap was the only giveaway to the location of the narrow drive that wound its way back to the creek side where the house was located. This place seemed damn near perfect.

The gravel drive serpentined its way through dense woods, a mixture of tall pine trees and huge live oaks covered in Spanish moss. Many of the majestic oaks were probably hundreds of years old, judging by their huge and gnarly configurations. As he made his way toward the end of the quarter mile drive, the Colonel noticed that it had been altered slightly. The Major had added a chicane at the end of the drive, obviously to keep unauthorized eyes from seeing any activity happening in the facility until the last moment the road entered the large yard area. Smart, very smart, he thought. As he approached the chicane the Colonel noticed a guard posted at its entrance. There were five other sentries posted around the property someplace. He was curious to find out where.

Kevin's Mustang was parked outside the back door of the house. The Colonel drove up beside it and turned off his engine. As he exited his vehicle he saw Kevin coming down the back steps. The Colonel had expected to be greeted with an upbeat attitude. After all, the Major had just successfully smuggled six tons of heroin into Florida. Instead, the first words from the Major's mouth were unsettling.

"I believe we could have a problem, Colonel. The entire operation may be compromised."

"What are you talking about, Major? You didn't mention any of this on the phone this morning."

"No sir. I wasn't aware this morning."

"Aware of what?" the Colonel demanded.

"Come inside, sir." Kevin escorted the Colonel over to the metal building and into the detention room. The recovery drivers were gone. They had been detained only shortly in the morning before being driven to Tampa International Airport to board a flight to San Juan, Puerto Rico. Instead, a metal chair bolted to the floor in the middle of the room caught the Colonel's attention. Strapped to the chair was Grady, his arms tied behind him with zip ties, his feet bound together in front of him. A black hood covered his head which was slumped over to one side. He appeared to be unconscious.

"Who is this, Major?" The Colonel's face was souring, the veins in his neck beginning to bulge.

"His name is Grady White. That's all I really know, sir. We've been interrogating him since early this morning. He's told us nothing."

"How do you know his name, Major? Grady who?"

"Grady White, Colonel. I met him briefly at the airport in Baltimore. That's how I knew who he was. I ran into the Senator's Chief of Staff and his girlfriend when I was there. I offered them a ride home but this guy showed up and they went with him. I'd never seen him before. No idea who he was, or who he is."

"Have you run fingerprints, anything?"

"Yes sir. That's how we learned his last name is White, from his military records. Former Green Beret. He was mustered out of the Army in '75. Then he goes dark."

"What do you mean 'dark'?" The Colonel was incredulous.

"He's off the grid, sir. No driver's license, never voted, no traffic tickets, no address we can find. The man is a ghost."

"So he's connected to the Senator somehow?" Colonel Selbourne was beginning to share the Major's concern. "How did he get here?"

Kevin explained how his men had run into an old guy claiming to be fishing in the river and brought him back to the house as a precaution.

"Eller had him detained in here when he called me to come take a look. I recognized him immediately. He knows a lot more than he's telling. But nothing I've tried so far has gotten anything out of him. I was getting ready to waterboard him, sir."

"Don't waste your time, Major", the Colonel directed. If he was Green Beret it could take days to break him. "We only have hours. There's been a change of plans."

"What's changed, sir?"

Grady had come to while the men were talking. He had groaned slightly, his head throbbing from the beating he'd been given by Kevin. The hood over his head kept him from being able to see what was going on but he recognized Kevin's voice. He had no idea who the other man was until Kevin addressed the man as Colonel. This had to be Colonel Selbourne! Grady put his head back down and tried to remain as still as possible, hoping the men would think he was still passed out and continue to talk freely. But the men had apparently heard him waking.

"Let's talk outside, Major."

"Keep an eye on him, Sergeant", Kevin ordered as he gestured for the Colonel to follow him out of the detention area and into the main bay of the metal building.

"Well, this is quite the operation." Colonel Selbourne looked around inside the building. The six Contenders were lined up side by side on their trailers at the end of the building nearest the detention room. On the far end were Kevin's office and a maintenance area for mechanical upkeep and repairs. In the middle of the bay was a flatbed truck with a 10-foot shipping container loaded on it. "I take it the heroin is in there?" he asked, pointing at the container.

"Yes sir. The truck is gassed and ready to make the swap whenever we get the go sign."

"Well, therein lies the problem, Major. There's not going to be a swap tonight."

"I don't understand, sir."

"The buyers called me yesterday and tried to renegotiate the deal. They low-balled me knowing we have to move this stuff out of here as soon as possible. They're gambling we don't have a backup buyer", Selbourne explained.

"What did you do, Colonel?" Kevin had trouble believing what he was hearing.

"They're coming here tonight to pick up the heroin directly once the Bitcoins for the renegotiation are in our possession. Their wallet will be on a BitCoin thumb drive. Once we verify the stick is legitimate... Sayōnara, gentlemen."

Kevin couldn't believe what he was hearing. "You're letting them come here, sir? You're not serious? Why would you let anyone know where this operation is located? I don't think that's wise, Colonel."

"Relax, son. I said they were coming here. I didn't say they were leaving." A broad smile across the Colonel's face told Kevin that the Colonel had no intention of making the location of his operation known to anyone. He had misunderstood the Colonel's use of the word sayōnara.

"What do we do with the container, sir?"

"I've lined up new buyers for tomorrow. I used tonight's profits to give them a pretty good discount for operating on such short notice. We'll have to hold on to the shipment for one more day but tomorrow we make the Fort Lonesome swap just like we had planned to do tonight."

"And this Grady White guy?"

"Send him offshore fishing tomorrow along with tonight's visitors", the Colonel laughed.

Kevin smiled. He liked the idea. Tonight they would kill the buyers and the black guy. In the morning he would send Eller and another man to scuttle the old man's boat and dump the bodies into the Gulf of Mexico thirty or forty miles offshore. Shark food. Simple enough.

The Colonel didn't seem to be as worried about the old man as he was. In Kevin's mind, there were too many unknowns. Gavin was dead but still this guy shows up? How had he known about the shipment? Obviously, the old man couldn't be working alone which meant there must be others out there looking for him. Kevin's team would need to be on high alert until tomorrow's swap was completed.

CHAPTER 31

"C huck! Take a look at this. These are the photos I took this morning."

Greg displayed photos of the property around the distribution compound where Grady was being held. A mobile projector displayed the reconnaissance photos he had taken onto the wall of the motel room. Chuck, Gavin, and the other Delta 5 gathered around.

"These SAT photos are the latest I could get on short notice. They were taken two days ago. The comparisons were taken five months ago."

"Looks like the house existed", Chuck observed. "But the metal building and the docks, and, that must be a boat ramp - they're all new?"

"They looked new to me", Greg confirmed.

"They've made some changes to the drive, too", Nunchucks added.

"These are two days old?" Chuck wanted verified.

Greg nodded.

"Did you have any trouble moving around the property?" Nunchucks asked.

"Negative. These guys all appear to have been regular Marines. I don't believe any of them are Special Forces."

"Well, that's a load off my mind", Nunchucks admitted. "How pretty are they?"

"They're all wearing old school IBAs except for one guy with an MTV."

"How many?"

"Eight, plus Falk and another guy I didn't recognize. They weren't fully geared."

"Camo?" Chuck asked.

"M81," Greg responded. "But before you get too relaxed, they're sporting M4s, they all have Marine issued 9mm Berettas and FLC vests stuffed with ammo. They expect trouble."

"Must be hot in those suits", Dave chuckled. "It's a shame it's not August." Everyone chuckled with him.

"Yeah, well, it would be August for us, too", Chuck chimed in. "Be thankful for small favors." Everyone nodded in smiling agreement.

Chuck continued, "Alright. Listen up. We move out at dusk. Communication and night vision gear are prepped in the van. That's our biggest advantage, gentlemen. We'll own the dark but don't get cocky. I have tactical command. Move on my orders only. Your call signs are numbers only." He pointed at each member. "I'm one, Nunchucks - two, Dave - three, Greg - four, Bill - five."

"You're not leaving me behind," Gavin insisted, staring into Chuck's eyes with fervor.

"Alright, Senator. You're six. I have an extra weapon and comm gear but I don't have body armor for you. Lay back until we secure the premises." Gavin wasn't happy about not being a part of the assault but he knew arguing with Chuck at this juncture was counter-productive.

"Pop the latest SAT photo back up", Chuck instructed. He pointed at two wooded locations along the drive where Greg had noted posted sentries. "D-man and Gregster: neutralize the bad guys here and here. Do it quietly, please." Greg and Dave gave an acknowledging nod. "Then move to the back of the house and take up positions here and here", pointing to two corners of the house where their backs would be to the woods but they would be able observe the yard and the steel building beyond.

"Bill, you're with the Senator. Take care of the two guards on the side road. Gavin, let Bill handle that alone. You're not equipped. Then, both of you make your way through the woods in back of the house. Position yourselves behind Dave and Greg, here and here."

Greg's recon had identified that Grady's sportfisherman and a Boston Whaler were tied up to the docks. Chuck's pointer was indicating two positions next to the creek where the boat ramp and docks could be observed without their being seen. "Make sure nobody gets to those boats."

"Roger that", Bill nodded, as he locked eyes with Gavin who gave an assuring nod to both Bill and Chuck.

"Greg's best assessment is that Grady is in the steel building. I'm going with that. Nunchucks and I will set explosives on the power lines and the backup generator as soon as it's dark enough. I will remotely blow the power lines and backup generator. Everyone move immediately when it goes dark. Be sure you've double checked your night vision gear *before* the lights go out. I wouldn't ordinarily say that but some of you are old and haven't done this shit in a while." Everybody laughed.

"We're all old!" Nunchucks jibed.

"Speak for yourself", Gavin piped up. "I'm half the age of you old codgers."

"Alright, tighten up." Chuck reasserted control over the laughter. "Dave and Greg will clear the house. Nunchucks and I will take the metal building. Any questions?"

For the first time each man could feel the reality of the situation setting in. No more jokes. No more kidding around.

"We've all done this before. Instinct *will* kick in. Trust it. Watch your six and the man's next to you and we'll put these bastards in their place tonight." Everyone nodded.

Monica knocked on the door and Bill wandered over to let her in. "We are going to the restaurant across the street. Alex wants to know if any of you would like to go with us."

"Sure!" Nunchucks said. "This old body needs all the nourishment I can give it."

"Yeah, I'll go." Bill spoke up.

"Me too", others joined in.

"Hang on, hang on!" Chuck grunted. "These are the coordinates for the gate to the property and the yard between the house and the building. Put them in your GPSs." Chuck projected the coordinates onto the wall. Everyone quickly entered the locations into their handheld navigators before heading out.

"Lead the way, Muchacha!", Nunchucks bellowed, as he put his arm around Monica and escorted her out the door. "Does this place have habanero wings?"

* * *

Kevin stood alone on the boat dock staring out over the creek at the sandy bank on the other side. A raccoon had ventured out at dusk and was foraging along the water for its evening meal. Its bandit eyes made it appear cartoon-like, not real somehow. That was how this whole operation had started to feel. Not real.

The change of plans that Selbourne had initiated made him uncomfortable and nervous. He couldn't put his finger on quite why but something just didn't feel right. He trusted Selbourne. The Colonel was his mentor for God's sake. But the idea that the buyers, complete strangers, were being invited into the compound to be slaughtered didn't sit well with his sensibilities. Why not meet them in Fort Lonesome, kill them there? Why invite them here? What if they told somebody where they were going? The open-endedness was disquieting and disturbingly uncalculated for Kevin's liking.

"10 p.m.", came a voice from behind him. Kevin turned to see Colonel Selbourne ambling up to the dock. "It's a *Go*, Major. 10 p.m."

"We'll be ready", Kevin assured him.

The Colonel shook his head and huffed, "Sorry little bastards think they can fuck with the CIA."

"Should I put a guard at the gate to let them in?"

"No", the Colonel replied. "If they can't figure out how the goddamn gate works, fuck 'em. Keep your boys inside the tree line, out of sight. I don't want any neighbors to report seeing militiamen roaming around with guns or some such bullshit." The Colonel removed a handkerchief from his pocket and wiped his brow. "Still goddamned hot here in October. When does it cool off, Major?"

"End of the month, November gets better."

"Your guys know what to do?" the Colonel asked.

"Yes, sir, they've all been briefed", Kevin assured him.

"Good. Nothing to do now but wait." The Colonel turned and headed back toward the house. Sergeant Eller was approaching. They nodded as they passed one another but no words were exchanged. The Colonel never spoke to any of Kevin's men, only to the Major.

"Everyone is in position, sir", Eller informed Kevin. "Baker is guarding the guy in the detention area, Smith and Hudson are covering the exterior of the house and the building, Brownrigg and Crawford have the drive. Copeland and DiPalma will watch the main road."

"What about you?" Kevin asked.

"I will stay with you and the Colonel... just in case, sir."

"Thanks, Sergeant. Good work."

"Just so you know, sir. I moved Brownrigg closer to the gate, just inside the trees. When the visitors enter the property he'll wave them thru and report in. If anything looks suspicious he'll give us a heads up."

"Good idea, Sergeant. Let the men know the visitors are scheduled to arrive at 10 p.m. Tell them to stay alert."

"Yes sir."

Kevin was impressed he hadn't had to instruct his Sergeant how to deploy his men. Eller was a smart cookie. Too bad the Marines hadn't seen it. Too bad for them, that is. Good for him. Eller was a natural born leader.

As Eller walked away, Kevin looked back toward the creek bank where the raccoon had been. There was a family there now, mom and three little ones. Male raccoons aren't involved in raising their young. The mothers teach their babies everything they need to survive. He felt a slight sorrow for the siblings, no father in their lives. But he knew it wouldn't stop them from being successful. It hadn't stopped him.

* * *

"I don't like this. Just sitting here makes me jittery." Cynthia stood up to pace the short length of the motel room, her bare feet almost silent on the newly carpeted floor. Alexandra and Muriel watched her nervously stride back and forth as they sat with their backs to multiple pillows leaned against the headboard of the king-sized bed. Monica was sitting in the hard desk chair, her feet propped up on her backpack. They all felt the same thing Cynthia did.

Alexandra had turned on CNN and she was waiting for the Breaking News that was promised after the commercial break. "There's nothing we can do right now. The guys seemed prepared and in good spirits. Uncle Chuck says they're the best at what they do."

"Did", Muriel corrected her. "What they did. It's been years since any of them did anything like this."

"Alright. Still. I'm sure it's like riding a bike to these guys." Alexandra tried to reassure Muriel, put a positive spin on the situation. "You could see they all keep themselves in great shape. Not a beer belly among them."

"I know", Muriel admitted. "But I can't help worry. What if something happened to Grady? I lived a great life with Arthur. He was a wonderful man and a dear husband. But when I met Grady it was like becoming a kid again. He makes me feel so young and so special. I wouldn't know what to do without him."

"Muriel!" Alexandra scolded. "You're not going to lose him. Stop talking like that."

The commercial break was over and the CNN anchorman broke into the evening broadcast with the headline of the hour:

"Missing Senator, Gavin Manson, is a suspect in an Afghanistan heroin smuggling operation."

"What are they talking about?" Monica screamed. "He is risking his life to try to stop the smugglers." She was livid. "Fake News!! Those people will say anything. La verdad no les importa!!"

"Shhh! Listen", Alexandra hushed.

Anchor: "So, Gabe, what do we know about this bombshell revelation involving Senator Manson?"
Reporter: "Bombshell is an interesting way to put it, Wooly. Our anonymous sources tell us the bombing in Paris was a false flag to cover up the fact that Senator Manson and a man named Habib Karim Saffari, the former Minister of

267

Agriculture for the Nimruz province in Afghanistan, were in business together to smuggle heroin into the U.S. Apparently, there was a falling out between the two. Manson had Saffari killed in an explosion at a small restaurant in Paris where the two had secretly met, obviously to put Saffari into a situation where he could be murdered by bomb."

Anchor: "Incredible! And does your source know how long this relationship had been going on?"

Reporter: "He didn't say, Wooly. But the implication was that it had been going on quite a long time."

Anchor: "What about the location of the Senator? Have we learned anymore about his possible whereabouts?"

Reporter: "I'm afraid not. Speculation is that he is still hiding out in Europe. There have been numerous reports of sightings but, so far, Senator Manson has been able to elude European authorities."

Anchor: "Great work, Gabe. Amazing work. CNN viewers heard it here first. For those of you just joining us, our sources tell us that Senator Gavin Manson has been implicated in a drug smuggling operation out of Afghanistan. Stay tuned to CNN for the latest developments. Back to you, Sandy, in our Atlanta headquarters."

Alexandra shook her head and turned the TV off.

"Oh my God!" Cynthia exclaimed. "Those lying bastards! They have to know it isn't true. Why would they put that on the air?"

"They don't like his political party?" Muriel offered.

"It's CIA disinformation", Alexandra explained. "It probably came from Selbourne himself. The CIA knows the media outlets will run with anything they're told from a deep state source. The network will retract it later, maybe with an apology, maybe not. But it's all about ratings. CNN probably suspects it's not true. But the attention is too much to pass up. Gavin says the fourth estate is broken. It's hard to argue with him when you see something like this."

"Well, they're not going to get away with it", Cynthia said sternly.

"What can you do about it?" Alexandra asked.

"I'm calling Mike." Cynthia pulled her cell phone from her purse. "Damn it!" she shrieked. "It's dead. Whose phone works?"

"I have the emergency phone", Alexandra offered. "But let's think about this first."

"Alex, what's to think about? We need to get ahead of this BS! Right now! Mike is in Orlando on a story. I saw it in the Post this morning. He can be here in an hour."

"Yes!" Monica agreed. "Alex, it is a wonderful idea. Mike will report the truth."

Alexandra looked at Muriel who shrugged her shoulders. She pulled the phone from her purse and handed it to Cynthia.

"Would it be better for Mike to go to the place where the guys are?" Monica asked with a devilish smile.

"It would if we knew where that was", Cynthia agreed with a puzzled look. "Do you know where that is?" she coaxed.

"Alex, do you have the key to Chuck's room?" Monica held out her hand knowing full-well she did.

Alexandra hesitated. "Whoa, ladies! Did you not see the guns and equipment the guys had? This is not a game. It's not safe to follow them this time. It's dangerous and foolish."

"But you heard the news, Alex", Cynthia countered. "They accused Gavin of treason, conspiring with international criminals. Doesn't that make your blood boil?"

"It does", Alexandra agreed. "But it doesn't convince me that following the guys into battle is a good idea. We're not prepared for anything like that."

The lawyer in Cynthia began to argue her case. "We don't have to follow them into battle. I'm not saying that. But we should be closer to the action. Who knows how some of the cable networks might want to spin the situation once they become aware of it? Especially since they've already taken a public position that will have to be retracted? What I am suggesting is that we call Mike and put him in position to write the first report on whatever takes place. Just the facts, ma'am. No spin. The straight truth."

Alexandra handed the key card to Monica and the girls followed her next door and into Chuck's room. Monica turned on Chuck's computer and then the projector he had attached to it. Upon the wall were projected a pair of GPS coordinates, longitude and latitude, superimposed on an aerial view of the Wimauma house on the Little Manatee River.

Cynthia snapped a photo of the coordinates of the property's entry gate and texted it to Mike's phone. Then she called Mike's mobile number.

"Mike, honey, it's Cynthia. I need you to look at the GPS coordinates I just sent to your phone. -- Mike! Yes, I'm fine, honey. I'm alive and I love you, too. We can do this later, baby. You have to meet me in an hour. It's important. -- I'm trying to tell you where. Cierra la boca y escucha! -- I know. I know. I love you, too. Listen to me. Senator Manson is alive and I know where he is. -- Yes. You can't tell anyone. Come straight to the coordinates I sent you. -- Okay, put them into your GPS and we'll meet you there. -- Right now. Go! Go! Go! -- Sí, yo también te amo. Hurry, baby!"

Cynthia ended the call.

"I think he loves you", Monica grinned.

Cynthia smiled and danced in place, high stepping and shimmying with her arms pumping like a boxer pummeling her opponent's mid-section. "One hour!" she squealed. "Let's get out of here!"

The girls filed out of the motel and piled into the car, Fifi and Fufu running loose in the back seat of the Chrysler 300. Alexandra cranked the engine and implored, "Does anybody know exactly where we're going?"

"I do", Monica said from the back seat.

"Cynthia, get in the back. Monica trade places. You're my navigator. Where to?"

"Right on 301", Monica instructed.

"Would you like to drive?" Alexandra offered.

"No!" Monica said firmly. "Oh mi Dios, no!"

CHAPTER 32

This satellite image shows the entrance right there." Monica was pointing at the inconspicuous barbed-wire gate protecting the graveled driveway into the compound.

"Where's the guys' van?" Muriel wondered.

"Maybe they drove it inside", Cynthia offered.

"They more likely left it somewhere out of sight... like we need to do." Alexandra suggested, "Let's park down the road where we can see the gate and wait for Mike to get here."

"Uh oh!" Cynthia gasped. "Who is this?"

The piercing headlights of a large black Mercedes illuminated the interior of their Chrysler 300 as it drove up in front of them next to the gate where they were parked. Two men in expensive-looking Italian suits exited rapidly and approached them on both sides. Alexandra thought briefly of trying to flee but changed her mind when she noticed both men brandished handguns.

"We're lost. That's our story", she told the ladies as she rolled down her window to the approaching stranger. "Hi! Can you tell me if this is the gate to the Nordstrom's house?"

"Nordstroms?" she heard Cynthia whisper. "That's the best you could come up with?"

The gunman produced a flashlight and adroitly peered around inside the car shining the light at each of the women's faces and running it up and down their bodies. Fifi and Fufu jumped up and down and yapped at the stranger while hugging close to Muriel's lap.

"I'm afraid you will have to come with me", the gunman insisted. "Get out of the car, please."

Alexandra made an effort to persuade the man to change his mind. "Sir, what is this about? We're just looking for the Nordstrom's. We just..."

"I won't ask you again", the man said firmly, with a raised voice that meant business.

"Put your hands behind your heads", he barked as the girls exited the car. "Line up over here", he ordered, the beam of his flashlight pointing along the ground directing them to move to an area beside the gate. The gunman addressed his cohort, motioning toward the women's car with a jerk of his head. "Keep the dogs in the car", he told him.

"Please leave a window cracked", Muriel implored.

The rear passenger-side window of the Mercedes began to lower and the women could see a single shadowy figure inside. "Put them in the truck when it arrives and bring them with you."

"Yes sir", the second gunman said.

The driver opened the gate wide then returned to the Mercedes. He slowly drove across the cattle gap and followed the gravel drive toward the compound house. The tires of the large black vehicle forced coarse crunching noises from the pebble strewn lane. By the time the Mercedes had disappeared into the woods, a large box truck had arrived.

"What's this?" the truck driver asked the gunman standing guard over the women.

"They were parked by the gate when we pulled up. The boss said to bring them along."

"Yeah? Okay", the truck driver shrugged. He climbed down from the cab, made his way to the back of the truck, and raised the heavy overhead door.

"Get in ladies", the gunman ordered. He marched them over to the truck and instructed the box truck driver, "Help them up."

Alexandra yanked her arm from the driver's grip and stepped up onto the short two-step ladder by herself. She grabbed the handle on the side of the truck and pulled herself up and into the bay. As she turned to aid Muriel, a sudden movement behind the driver caught her attention. Before she could make sense of it, the gunman was lying on the ground gasping, bleeding from the throat and mouth with loud gurgles which caught the attention of the driver. As he turned, Chuck was already upon him, knife drawn. Within seconds the driver's body was being dragged across the hard scrabble and laid in the drainage ditch next to the other man's now lifeless corpse.

Muriel began to scream.

"Cállate!" Monica urged, "Shhhh!", and forcefully put her hand over Muriel's mouth holding it firmly in place as she whispered, "It's okay. It's okay. Be quiet Muriel! Be quiet." When Muriel had settled, Monica released her grip. Alexandra and Cynthia were shaken but composed.

"Good job!" Chuck praised. Then he angrily admonished the group in a low but forceful tone, "What the hell are you doing here? You could have gotten yourselves killed! You're lucky I saw you pull up to the gate when I did."

Cynthia started to explain, talking excitedly. "We're waiting for Mike. He'll be here soon. CNN reported Gavin was smuggling heroin from Afghanistan. We thought an honest reporter should be here when you guys..."

"Okay. Okay." Chuck cut her off. "Pull your car over into that field behind those trees and wait. Stay down, keep out of sight. When you see Mike, flag him down and bring him over there with you... and keep quiet! Someone will come get you when it's safe. Do not! I repeat, DO NOT leave that spot until you're told! Understand?"

Alexandra nodded as she ushered everyone back into the Chrysler. Chuck watched from the gate making sure she had hidden the car from sight. He started toward the box truck just as his earpiece squawked, "Unit 1, we have eyes on a black Mercedes entering the yard - two bad guys."

"Copy that", he responded. "Unit 2, have you neutralized your bogies?"

"That is affirmative, Unit 1", Nunchucks responded. "Bound and gagged."

"Good work, Unit 2."

Chuck had hesitated to inform the rest of the Delta 5 what had just transpired. It wasn't necessary for them to know and he thought it best if Gavin remained unaware that Alexandra was here.

"All Units, be advised I have commandeered the bad guy's truck. I will be bringing it up the drive." Chuck wanted to be sure everyone knew he had command of the box truck so no one would mistake him for one of the bad guys. One-by-one they each acknowledged, "Copy that, Unit 1."

Chuck climbed behind the wheel and slowly drove the truck up the drive toward the house. As he neared the chicane Nunchucks stepped out beside the drive ahead of him. Chuck slowed as he pulled alongside, reaching over to push open the passenger door. Nunchucks jumped onto the moving running board and pulled himself up and into the passenger seat.

"Units 5 and 6, report." Chuck queried the status of Bill and Gavin. He was particularly concerned about their responsibilities since he had asked Bill to handle both road guards.

"Bad guys under control", Bill responded. "Units 5 and 6 in position."

"Roger that. Any problems?" Chuck asked.

"Negatory. The Senator actually took down the second man. The man's a ninja, Chuck!"

Chuck smiled. "Copy that. Units 3 and 4, how about it?"

"Targets neutralized. One man seriously wounded, the other will have a headache but he's alive. Units 3 and 4 in position."

"Roger, that", Chuck replied. Everyone had taken care of their bad guys. So far the mission seemed to be going to plan. He informed Nunchucks of the women's presence then filled him in on his own progress. "We've got to take this truck in or we lose tactical advantage. I had time to set the power line explosives but when the women showed up there was no time to set the secondaries."

"Okay, man. Let's just do this", Nunchucks agreed.

The team needed to know they may or may not need night-vision gear.

"All units, I will blow the main power lines for effect", Chuck announced, "but be advised the lights will probably come back on. I repeat, the lights WILL come back on. There are no explosives on the main generator. Acknowledge."

"Roger that", all acknowledged.

The Delta team had eliminated the six perimeter guards. Only five visible men remained in the yard near the house. Greg's reconnaissance had identified one more man who was yet to be accounted for. There was no way to know if there were others. For the moment, Chuck had to assume the missing man was guarding Grady either in the house or the steel building.

He put the truck in gear and slowly continued up the drive and through the chicane. Rounding the final turn he could see the black Mercedes had parked next to the house alongside Kevin's Mustang. The five men were gathered together, four of them engaged in what appeared to be a heated discussion. The fifth, Sergeant Eller, was standing away from the discussion, his weapon held in ready mode. No one gave the truck a second glance as Chuck pulled it into the yard. He strategically parked so the cab of the truck remained in the shadows, he and Nunchucks' faces difficult to make out.

Chuck did a doubletake when he noticed who was with the two men from the Mercedes. He expected to see Major Kevin Falk, but Colonel Jacob Selbourne was a real surprise. "I'll be goddamned!" Chuck exclaimed. "Look at this! I thought we would only have a smoking gun linking this operation to the CIA. But what we have here, my friend, is *in flagrante delicto.*"

This was truly a pleasant surprise. CIA director's rarely got their hands dirty. This must have been an incredibly important operation to justify the presence of such senior management.

"Unit 3, do you have eyes on the group gathered by the house?" Chuck queried.

"Affirmative", came the reply.

"On my mark, neutralize the man in uniform."

"Roger that", Greg replied.

Chuck set the expectations for the coming confrontation. "All units, listen up. I want the rest of the men alive. Repeat alive. Do not kill Falk. Do not kill Selbourne or the other two gentlemen."

"Copy that", everyone responded.

Chuck reached into a retention pocket on his IBA and removed the remote detonation switch for blowing the incoming power lines. He armed the switch and then began:

"Blowing the power on my mark, 3, 2, 1..." Chuck pressed the switch on the detonator. He and Nunchucks flipped their night vision goggles into position and jumped down from the truck. Two shots rang out from the corner the house and the uniformed Sergeant slumped to the ground.

BOOOOM! BOOOOM! The ground shook from the two explosive charges and the lights around the yard went off as Chuck and Nunchucks ran toward the disoriented men. Nunchucks tossed a concussive flashbang which further added to their confusion. Within a few seconds the backup generators had kicked in and the lights gradually began to illuminate the yard again.

The men from the Mercedes had fallen to the ground face down and put their hands on the back of their heads. They had obviously done this before.

Chuck barked out orders, "Unit 2, restrain the men on the ground then wait for my orders. Units 3 and 4, clear the house. He noticed the Colonel dashing toward the parked cars. "I'll take Selbourne."

Kevin had recognized immediately what had happened. He dropped to the ground next to the old house and began to crawl underneath it. His mind was racing, his ears were ringing, but he knew he had to crawl as fast as he could underneath the house toward the docks. His hastily formulated plan was to exit the crawl space on the far side and shoot his way, if necessary, over to one of the boats.

Selbourne had headed the opposite direction. He tried to get to the Mercedes hoping the keys were in it. He did and they were. He started the engine and shifted the car into reverse. With one hand on the steering wheel and the other on the seat back, Selbourne turned to face backwards, his foot on the accelerator, and began to quickly back the car. Chuck ran toward the front of the vehicle and pumped two quick shots into the front tires and then a short burst into the radiator. A steam cloud rose from the seams in the hood and the holes in the engine grill.

Selbourne stopped and turned to look out the front windshield. He had heard the shots but did not yet realize from where they had come or the damage they had done. Chuck had now positioned himself at the driver's window, his rifle raised at the Colonel's head. "You're not going very far", he warned the Colonel who could see the steam billowing up from the engine compartment.

Selbourne knew he was right. He shut off the engine and put his hands on the steering wheel. Chuck ordered him out of the car and removed the keys from the ignition.

Greg and Dave had finished clearing the house. "House is clear", Greg advised. That meant Grady and the other guard must be in the metal building.

"Unit 4, secure and restrain the man by the Mercedes", Chuck ordered as he held his rifle on the Colonel. Dave ran over to the Mercedes and hastily cuffed the Colonel with plastic restraints. Then he walked him over to the other men being detained and sat him down on the ground next to them.

"You and Greg keep an eye on these guys and don't let anything happen to Selbourne", Chuck ordered. "Nunchucks come with me."

Greg and Dave stood guard over the captured men as Nunchucks jogged with Chuck toward the metal building.

"By my count there should only be one man inside", Chuck told Nunchucks. "But we can't make that assumption. We go in by the book", he ordered. Nunchucks nodded. As they approached the exterior door of the building, Chuck turned the knob slightly. It was unlocked.

"Take the lead", Chuck commanded as he yanked the door open wide and Nunchucks took a long stride through the door, careful to maintain his balance. It had been decades since he had practiced clearing operations but Nunchuck's muscle memory was still there. The efficiency of his motions was automatic, the economy of his movements subconscious. He scanned the bay area... empty. He glanced into the office area. "Clear", he announced loudly.

Chuck had entered right behind him and scanned the opposite end of the building. The lights were still on in the main bay. He could see another door on the far end of the bay. The six boats parked at the other end were problematic but the odds of a man hiding in a boat with a canvas cover on it seemed unlikely though Dzhokhar Tzarnaev, the younger of the brothers responsible for the Boston Marathon bombing, did cross his mind. More likely someone was guarding Grady on the other side of that door.

"Clear", he called to Nunchucks.

Nunchucks turned to see Chuck pointing at the door at the far end of the bay. They started together toward the door, cautiously, quietly, they inched their way over.

* * *

Grady was tired and hungry. His face and head hurt. He had taken a significant beating, evident from the amount of blood soaked into his clothing and the large congealing pools on the floor below him. He could barely remember the beating, which wasn't a good sign. It probably meant he had a concussion.

He looked around the room as best he could. A single swag lamp with a metal funnel-shaped shade hung over the workbench in front him. The lamp cord hung from a metal roof beam twenty feet above the bench. It wasn't a bright lamp and the shadows from the dim light cast a creepy eeriness over the room.

Grady's chair was bolted to the floor. There would be no moving it around to try to find a way to escape. Even if he could wrestle himself free of his bindings there was a powerfully built guy sitting in a chair next to the workbench reading a Sports Illustrated magazine. In his weakened condition, Grady knew it would be impossible to overpower the man.

Still, he tried to assess his situation. The man was dressed in battle gear. He had removed his IBA, his body armor, and put it on the bench next to his M4 assault rifle and a 9mm Beretta. It was apparent these guys were serious and well-armed. He hoped Chuck and the guys were prepared for such formidable opposition.

"Do you people feed your prisoners?" he asked the husky guard.

"They're probably just going to shoot you anyway. What do you care if you eat or not?" the guard replied, never looking up from his magazine.

"I'm hungry", Grady insisted. "At least I should die comfortable."

"Let me finish this article and I'll go see if they'll let you eat."

"What time is it?" Grady asked.

"A little after ten."

"a.m or p.m.?"

The guard looked at Grady with a puzzled stare. "p.m.", he said.

"How long have I been here?" Grady asked.

"Two days", the guard told him. "They must have beat the shit out of you, old man."

Grady groaned from the pain as he tried to move around in the chair to make himself more comfortable. He was a little worried that it was taking so long for the guys to come find him. Maybe the phone's GPS hadn't worked. Maybe this place was too fortified. He ran through several negative scenarios in his mind before he stopped himself. "Of course they'll come", he murmured out loud.

"What?" the burly one asked.

"I was just saying they'll come", Grady repeated.

"Who'll come?" the guard asked. "What are you talking about old guy?"

"My friends", Grady answered.

"You're dreamin' man. Ain't nobody coming for you", he laughed.

BOOOOOM! BOOOOOM! Two giant explosions rocked the area outside the building and shook the ground underneath Grady and the guard. Grady knew immediately who and what had caused the explosions.

The light over the workbench went out. The room went pitch black and Grady couldn't see anything. Outside he could hear a commotion and brief sporadic fire from automatic weapons. He knew the Delta 5 team was here.

"What the hell!" he heard the guard say in the darkness. Then he could hear what sounded like a diesel engine start up and the light over the workbench gradually came back on. The guard was scrambling to put his body armor on.

"I wouldn't bother with that if I were you", Grady said in a calm relaxed tone that caught the guard by surprise.

"Oh yeah? Why is that?" The man stopped momentarily to engage Grady.

"Any minute some men are going to come bursting in here and kill you. And there's nothing you can do about it."

"Seriously, old man?" The burly guard was incredulous.

"Cut me loose and I'll see that you live", Grady offered.

The guard grabbed his Beretta from the bench and holstered it in a weapons retention pocket on his IBA. Then he picked up his M4 rifle and ran the strap over his shoulder. He flicked off the safety and moved toward the exit door of the detention area. Turning back he looked at Grady, "You must think I'm a fucking idiot."

"Just trying to help", Grady said.

Before the man could turn back around, a brilliant flash and a great explosive bang went off right beside him. He was thrown against the wall behind him, his ears ringing so loudly he became disoriented and unable to hear. The bright flash had rendered him unable to see so he instinctively tried to fire in the direction from which he felt the explosive had been thrown. He went to raise his rifle but was thrown off-balance when Nunchucks stunned him with a double tap, two rapid shots to his armor protected chest. Nunchucks immediately fired a second double tap to his head and the man slumped lifelessly to the floor.

Grady had also been disoriented by the loud flashbang Chuck had tossed into the room. He hadn't seen Chuck and Nunchucks work their carefully choreographed clearing operation. His eyes had been closed from the pain of the explosion. His ears were ringing and still hurt incredibly. He barely heard Chuck yell to Nunchucks that the room was safe. "Clear!"

Chuck made a beeline for Grady and began to remove his restraints.

"Are you okay?" he asked Grady.

Grady could see Chuck's lips move and understood what he was asking even though he could hardly hear him. He nodded. "I'll be alright."

"Stay here. We'll be back", Chuck assured him. "Stay right here."

Grady rubbed his eyes and shook his head as he watched Chuck and Nunchucks leave the way they had come. His balance was off and it was difficult to stand. He lifted himself slowly from the chair to which he had been tied for two days. His legs were wobbly and it hurt to move. Grady stood for a while holding onto the chair. It felt good to stand. He listened for gunfire but wasn't able to hear any, his ears still loudly ringing.

As he began to feel more stable he moved toward the door bracing himself against the wall as he walked. He stared at the dead body of the man who had guarded him for the last few hours. The man's weapons were lying beside him, useless to him now, just as Grady had warned him.

"You should have taken my advice", Grady whispered to the lifeless corpse as he stepped over it. He warily peered around the edge of the doorway and scanned around the inside of the main bay of the metal building. Then he looked back down at the dead man and scoffed, "You'd be alive now if you had."

* * *

The flashbang hadn't affected his sight. Kevin had been looking the other way when it went off. But his ears were ringing and the hearing loss was disorienting. His eyes hadn't adjusted to the lack of light and the moon wasn't up yet. He could barely see in the pitch blackness. He told himself not to panic. Then suddenly the lights came on again.

The unanticipated explosion, coupled with the electric failure, had set off alarm bells in Kevin's head. Something bigger than disenchanted drug dealers was happening. He wasn't sure what it was but he instinctively knew he had to extricate himself from the situation, and quickly. He moved hastily, crawling underneath the house toward the opposite side.

The old wooden house he had crawled under had been built in the 1940s. The hardwood oak floor was elevated three feet above the ground, a common construction method in those days where the wiring and plumbing remained exposed for ease of repair and maintenance. Kevin quickly scrambled beneath the house as he made his way toward the opposite side. He moved with alacrity through the cramped crawlspace. Thick cobwebs collected on his face and neck as he pushed through the musty length, but he took no time to remove them. Lizards scurried to get out of his way, some missing their tails from close encounters with marsh egrets or one of several feral cats which roamed the premises. He was barely aware of the caustic smell of rat urine and feces which permeated the fetid air in the narrow opening beneath the house. Although it was dark under the old building, he focused on the light coming from the far side where he intended to make his exit. It took only seconds to reach the outer edge of the house. Kevin stopped to survey the surroundings, keeping back far enough in the shadows to avoid being seen if anyone was looking.

Kevin had a clear line of sight to the dock and boats. He needed to make an immediate decision which boat to commandeer. The Whaler. It was smaller and more maneuverable on the narrow river. It could also traverse shallower water. He knew the keys were in it, he had watched Eller moor it earlier in the day. He reached to remove his pistol from the holster on his side but the holster was empty. "Shit!" He turned to look behind him. It was nowhere in sight. There was no going back to look for it. Kevin leaped from under the house and bolted for the dockside.

"It's Kevin!" Gavin shouted, jumping up from his prone position and racing toward the boats to intercept him. He realized he would not be fast enough to reach the boats before Kevin. But it would take some time for Kevin to undo the lines and start the engines. He tried to quicken his pace but the extra effort helped little. His knee was stiff from lack of use and his slight limp was holding him back. Still, he was faster than Bill who lagged considerably behind.

Kevin had untied both mooring lines and was trying to start the engines by the time Gavin reached the dock. Gavin quickly unstrapped his weapons and dropped them on the dock. Chuck had said he wanted the man taken alive. So did he.

The Whaler had drifted several feet away from the dock. Kevin turned the ignition key and the twin engines roared to life. As he engaged the throttles forward, Gavin leaped toward the back of the moving boat. He landed short of the stern with his feet dangling in the water while his arms managed to reach over the side, his hands finding a grip in a hollow opening inside the gunwale.

Gavin tried to pull himself aboard but Kevin turned the boat sharply and jammed the throttles full-forward throwing him backwards. His arms had already tired and he was out of breath from the long run to catch the escaping boat, but he hung on to the gunwale opening, waiting for the boat to slow enough to again try to pull himself aboard.

The creek was too narrow at the docks for Kevin to maneuver quickly. He reversed the engines and aligned the boat down creek toward the river. Gavin's arms were jelly but he couldn't let go. He struggled to throw one leg up and over the gunwale but as tried to pull his body up the side, Kevin again pressed the throttles forward. Gavin's leg fell from the side of the boat and he was left hanging with only the aching grip of his hands and arms inside the gunwale.

Kevin sped up. Gavin's body twisted and turned beside the boat as it bounced and skipped along the top of the water. Kevin veered toward the shallow bank of the creek attempting to graze along the edge of the protruding mangrove branches, hoping a limb would grab his friend and rip him from the side of the boat.

The thin limbs and leaves of the mangroves scraped Gavin's body, tearing the skin on his ears and face and neck and shoulders. He turned his head toward the rear of the boat to keep his eyes from being gouged out by the passing branches. He wished Chuck had had body armor for him.

Kevin had grown impatient. The limbs were not throwing Gavin off. He veered the boat deeper into the bank to catch more substantial limbs. As he did, the propellers started to chatter along the creek bottom and the boat began to slow and spin out of control. He had dug the props too deeply into the sandy creek bottom. The stern of the boat bounced up and down and the bow was thrown up onto the bank. The fast-moving Whaler came to a sudden and abrupt halt and the engines died, the props stuck in the muck along the shoreline.

The abrupt halt threw Gavin forward. He lost his grip on the gunwale and felt himself toppling head over heel through the shallow water bouncing along the shore. He landed in a sitting position waist deep in the water, disoriented from the topsy-turvy ride.

Kevin hurriedly attempted to restart the engines but the props were stuck too deeply in the sandy shallow muck. He grabbed a boat oar and hurried to the stern to try to push the boat back into deeper water. He kept one eye on Gavin who was still sitting on the edge of the bank, slow to gather his wits. After several attempts Kevin managed to push the stern back into the creek, freeing the props from the muddy shore.

Gavin had sat and watched as Kevin struggled to free the boat's propellers from the creek bank. As he sat on the shallow bank he tested his limbs one-by-one. Everything seemed to be okay, nothing broken. His arms were like jelly and they ached from the turbulent ride but otherwise he was alright. The disorientation was quickly subsiding and he knew he needed a second wind. He was out breath and nearly exhausted but he was coherent enough to realize he was still running on adrenalin. If he was going to be able to stop Kevin from escaping he would have to do it before the adrenalin wore off.

The Whaler was now floating freely in the creek. Kevin had dropped the oar on the deck and returned to the console to restart the engines. Gavin took a deep breath, rose quickly, and dove into the water. He swam straight for the dive platform on the back of the boat and managed to climb up on it.

The engines roared to life again and Kevin looked back at them briefly. In the short time his back had been turned, Gavin had already cleared the transom and was inside the rear cockpit.

"I'm not letting you get away" Gavin shouted, his conviction evident in his voice as he rushed toward Kevin. Kevin picked up the oar and swung wildly at Gavin's head. Gavin ducked and protected himself with his arms. The oar struck him in the hand and deflected into the gunwale.

The pain from the blow was intense but Gavin managed to grab the end of the paddle and hold on to it. Kevin yanked back and forth trying to wrest the paddle from Gavin's grasp. With a final firm pull he freed it from Gavin's hands, drew it back low like a spear and lunged at Gavin's neck and face. Gavin reached out defensively, deflecting the oar again with his hands, each blow as painful as the last. Kevin lunged at him a second time and a third time until Gavin lost his balance. He fell backwards towards the stern of the boat, slipping as he fell, and came to rest sitting on the deck with his back against the transom.

"There's no place to go, Kevin. Even if you escape from here, there's no place to hide. It's over."

Kevin stared down at his old friend sitting on the deck of the boat. The words coming from his mouth were meaningless. He was wrong. It wasn't over. The man was supposed to be dead. He was supposed to have died in Paris; he was supposed to have died in Havana. Instead, he would have to die here. And NOW!

Gavin could feel himself weakening, the adrenalin no longer helping him. He sat resting against the transom, his chest heaving from deep breaths as his mind raced to find a way out of the danger. He could not muster enough strength to continue the battle. If he had to stand right now he knew he would not be able. His arms and legs felt like mush. Gavin breathed deep and continued to talk, to try to gain more time to recover from his weakened state.

"Why, Kevin? You're not a criminal at heart. I've known you too long. You're a patriot. What was the purpose of all this?"

The glaze in Kevin's eyes softened to a glare as he looked at Gavin with disgust. "This country is going to hell in a hand basket. And people like you are leading the charge to its self-destruction. You think your stupid legislation will change anything? Make the world a better place? Bullshit! When was the last time you voted to fund the defense budget? I know your record. You're a goddamned peace freak."

"I vote my conscience, Kevin. If I thought the military would spend it on defense, instead of empire building, I would gladly vote to appropriate. Well, wake up, Kevin. The world hates us. Not because we're free, like some of my colleagues would say, but because they're tired of being bullied. Tired of being told how they should run their own countries. How they should be more like us. That's the bullshit, man."

"You're a fucking isolationist then", Kevin said angrily. "You think those towel heads in the Middle East are capable of running their own governments? You were there. You saw it. If it weren't for the U.S. they would still be living in tents and driving camels to work every day."

"Those towel heads did just fine without our help for centuries. Unfortunately for them, everything changed when *our oil* was found underneath *their sand*. Do you really think we're over there to spread democracy and help them to be better global neighbors? You know goddamn well we're not. We're there to protect the financial interests of the Halliburtons and the Schlumbergers. And we'll bomb every city and change every regime that dares to stand up to us. Peace freak?

No, Kevin. I'm just doing my part to make sure we mind our own goddamned business."

Kevin was unfazed by Gavin's diatribe. "Operations like this aren't going away just because you managed to stop this one. The CIA, the NSA, and programs you don't even know exist will keep on fighting the good fight. If Congress won't fund them they will fund themselves, just like we did. They won't just quit. They won't just close up shop. The safety and security of this nation is too important to entrust to the holier-than-thou hands of people like you, cowards who aren't willing to spend the blood of a few to protect the many."

"You're delusional, Kevin. You're not protecting anybody like this. You're endangering the lives of millions of people by bringing these drugs into the states and turning them loose on the streets. And not just the people who'll use them, but their families and friends and coworkers. My brother died because of people like you and North and Selbourne. You're being used by people interested only in wielding power, not saving the country. You are their willing tool, their fool. You can't see that?"

"Your brother died because he was weak, Gavin. Because he didn't have the strength, the intestinal fortitude to push through the pain without a crutch. Your brother was a weakling just like you."

Kevin reached around the side of the center console and removed a spear gun from the rod holders. He dropped the oar and cocked the gun quickly, then pointed it at Gavin's chest. Gavin was still weakened but he knew he had to go on the offensive or die. He no longer knew Kevin Falk. The man who stood over him was a stranger, a stranger bent on killing him, a stranger with a fishing spear pointed directly at his heart.

"Don't do this, Kevin. You're not a murderer", Gavin beseeched. He leaned forward lunging and reaching for the oar. Kevin stepped on the handle of the oar with one foot and kicked Gavin in the mouth with the other. Gavin was thrown backwards against the transom but he clung to the paddle end of the oar until the handle slipped free of Kevin's foot. Gavin raised it quickly, swinging the handle at the tip of the spear gun knocking its aim off mark.

Kevin held fire. He backed up slightly, out of range of the oar, and re-aimed at Gavin's chest. Gavin leaned forward just as Kevin pulled the trigger. He swung the oar again as the spear left the gun. Gavin saw the spear point glance off the oar's paddle as he fell back against the transom. Then he felt the pain, the burning, searing pain of the spear point as it passed through his right shoulder. He scrambled in desperation to stand but he was unable. The spear had lodged itself into the wall behind him, pinning him to the fiberglass transom.

"Don't bother begging for your life. I have no mercy left to give", Kevin screamed. Then he began to whimper. "I loved her, Gavin. She was the best thing that had ever happened to me. But she was weak, too."

For a moment Gavin couldn't make sense of what Kevin was saying. Who was he talking about? Then it struck him. "You killed Sam? Why, Kevin? Why would you do that?"

Tears began to stream from Kevin's eyes. He pulled another spear from the rod holders on the side of the console and loaded it into the gun. He gripped the rubber hoses that launched the spear and pulled them taught to cock the gun. "She threatened to tell your committee about Crimson Hook. I couldn't let that happen. She would have ruined everything."

"So you killed her?"

"I didn't want to. What choice did I have? She would have ruined everything", Kevin sobbed.

Gavin knew his life was over. He was exhausted and there was nothing left to do. He had tried to pull the spear from the transom but it wouldn't budge. He was pinned with no way to escape. But he wasn't going to beg for his life. He wouldn't have whether or not Kevin had told him not to bother.

Kevin raised the spear gun and pointed it at Gavin's chest. "I'm sorry", he said. "I wish it didn't have to end this way. I really do."

This time Gavin made no effort to move. He closed his eyes and waited for the inevitable pain to come.

POW! POW! POW! Shots rang out from the shoreline, their reverberations disrupting the damp stillness of the quiet night, sending slumbering sea birds fleeing to new safe havens. Gavin opened his eyes as Kevin fell forward firing the spear gun as he fell. The spear point whizzed by Gavin's head and buried itself into the transom next to his ear. Kevin's body fell face-forward to the floor in front him. His head bounced with a thud as it impacted on the unforgiving deck. His body writhed and shuttered for a few moments, then fell limp.

Gavin stared at Kevin's face. It was a face he recognized but it belonged to a tortured soul he no longer knew. Kevin's eyes had not yet closed but there was no more life in them. His long-time friend was dead.

Gavin looked over toward the bank of the creek from where the shots had rang out. The moon had begun to rise and its faint light illuminated the silhouette of the man who had fired the shots. He didn't recognize the face of the man who was turning to walk away while others rushed onto the boat to help him to safety. He wouldn't find out until later that it was Grady White who had saved his life.

"Get this boat back to the dock", Chuck ordered. "And somebody find a bolt cutter and cut him away from the transom. Don't try to remove the shaft. Leave it in until the paramedics can look at it."

Grady stopped and looked back toward the creek. He watched in silence as the Delta team took command of the boat and tended to Gavin's shoulder. Chuck slowly drifted over and put his arm around his buddy's shoulder as he reached down and gently removed the pistol from Grady's hand. No words came to him so he just stood there with Grady for what seemed an eternity.

Grady finally turned and began to walk slowly back toward the house. "My fuckin' face hurts bad, man."

CHAPTER 33

Captain C.H. Davis founded the little town of Wimauma, Florida, in 1902. He had helped build the 55-mile stretch of railroad halfway between Turkey Creek and Bradenton. Davis derived the name of the town by taking the first letters of the names of his three daughters, Wilma, Maude, and Mary.

It was after midnight when the sleepy little rural community was awakened by the sound of sirens coming from all directions and news helicopters circling overhead the property of the distribution compound. Out on the main road, cable news satellite trucks were setting up in the field across the road from the barbed-wire gate to the property. The gate had been barricaded and was being guarded by several Hillsborough County Sheriff's deputies. A dozen law enforcement vehicles from a half-dozen agencies surrounded the gate, lights flashing.

Chuck had asked Mike Ramirez to take responsibility of liaison for the press corps gathered outside the gate until the law enforcement agencies were able to put together a joint press task force. Most of the cable news networks were on-air reluctantly retracting earlier erroneous reports. They had obtained the reports from CNN sources. The retractions had been made necessary after Mike had revealed the truth concerning the role of Senator Gavin J. Manson in the international drug smuggling operation which had just been busted.

Around 12:30 a.m. a black Cadillac SUV pulled into the yard. Two portly agents of the DEA got out and looked around at the busy scene of CSI teams, FBI and CIA agents, other DEA agents and local law enforcement.

"Who's in charge here?" barked DEA Special Agent in Charge, Richard Wichart, in an authoritarian tone that let everyone within earshot know that he thought he was.

"Who are you?" Chuck demanded, even though he recognized Wichart from other high-profile drug busts in Florida where Wichart was the TV spokesperson for the agency. Usually he was standing next to the governor or other high-ranking officials as they would all take turns sharing the photo op and informing the public of the great job they were doing together. The fact that they did little of the work themselves was of minor consequence. It was the face time that mattered most and Richard "Dick" Wichart's political ambitions couldn't have been more well-timed than by being the lead agent on the biggest Federal drug bust since the 1990s. He was going to get lots of face time on this case.

"Special Agent in Charge, Wichart. Who are you?"

"Chuck McCrory, U.S. Army Special Forces, retired. The man to my left is James Falcone, also retired Green Beret. The man on the gurney here is Senator Gavin Manson." Chuck smiled at Gavin.

Wichart's head snapped to look at the Senator's face. He hadn't recognized him at first. It WAS the Senator. This was too good to be true. He reached out to shake the Senator's hand. Gavin was unable to shake with his right arm so he extended his left.

"Oh, sorry Senator", Wichart apologized. "I didn't realize you were wounded. What the hell happened here?"

Chuck, Nunchucks and Gavin filled the Agent in on much of the detail regarding the CIA's smuggling operation and the information that had led them to this location. They conveniently left out the fact that three other buddies had helped with the takedown. The involvement of the other Delta 5 members was potentially illegal and the less anyone knew of their existence, the better. Wichart was skeptical that only four men could have accomplished this alone.

"McCrory and I had been tracking them ever since", Gavin concluded. "We called you when our surveillance tracked the operation to this place. Unfortunately, they spotted us and we were forced to engage them before you arrived."

Wichart turned to Chuck, "How many bad guys here, McCrory?"

"Fourteen. Two CIA, one of them is dead, a Major Kevin Falk. The other is an active CIA director, Jacob Selbourne."

"Colonel Jacob Selbourne?" The Agent seemed surprised.

"Yes sir. One in the same", Chuck confirmed. "You know him?"

"Yeah, sort of. I ran into him on a trip to Afghanistan back in the early 2000s. I remember he seemed more interested in protecting the poppy growers there than taking them down. Struck me odd. Makes sense now."

Chuck continued, "Two buyers, tied up over there." He pointed. "Two lieutenants for the buyers, both killed, eight for the sellers. Three of them are dead, one wounded."

"And the four of you disposed of all these men and captured the rest by yourselves?" Agent Wichart was doubling down on his incredulity.

"We're all Special Forces, Agent", Gavin interjected. "This rag tag bunch didn't really put up much of a fight... except for this piece of metal in my shoulder."

Wichart sensed their story was bullshit. But he also knew enough not to impugn the word of a sitting Senator, especially one that was about to become a national hero and help him get his face on national television.

"Right. Well, good work Senator."

A medevac helicopter was arriving, about to touch down in a remote section of the yard. Agent Wichart held on to his hat as he raised his voice above the noise to talk to Chuck.

"I'll need a full report, McCrory. It's either that or a debriefing in my Miami office."

"A report sounds doable to me, Agent", Chuck smiled. "Can you give me ten days?"

"You've got three", Wichart replied, as he started to walk away barking orders to his subordinates. "Agent Burns! Get your ass over here!"

"Five it is, then", Chuck yelled over the noise that had started to die once the helicopter had touched down.

Alexandra, Monica and Cynthia had gathered around Gavin's gurney. Alexandra was holding Gavin's hand while the four of them conversed.

"Alex, I can't reach my pocket with this arm. Would you get something out for me?" Gavin implored.

"Sure, honey." Alexandra reached into his pants pocket and felt around but there seemed to be nothing there.

"It's small", he said. "Try deeper."

Alexandra found the object, a small box.

"Open it", Gavin said. She gasped as she opened it. It was a diamond engagement ring with a rock the size of Montana.

"I've been carrying it since Igoumenitsa", Gavin grinned. "Take it out and give it to me", he said, holding out his good hand.

Alexandra complied. Tears began to well in her eyes as she braced herself for what she knew was coming.

"Alexandra Katsaros, will you marry me?"

Alexandra stood silent for a long moment that dragged into two. The emotion had left her speechless.

"Oh my god", Cynthia gasped. "Say, Yes!!"

"Yes!" Alexandra finally blurted. "Yes, yes, yes!" She held out her hand and Gavin placed the ring on her finger. With tears streaming, she bent over and kissed him, clumsily trying to find an arrangement of lips, hands, and arms that didn't hurt his ailing shoulder. Gavin grimaced but the slight pain was every bit worth it.

Monica jokingly lamented, "I have lost my lover forever." The girls laughed and cried as they held Alexandra's hand and admired her new ring.

"Congratulations!" the couple heard from behind Alexandra. They turned to see Grady and Muriel approaching, Fifi and Fufu in tow.

"Thank you!" Gavin and Alexandra both said simultaneously.

Gavin looked at Grady. "And thank you, Grady. I've no words."

Grady appeared uncomfortable as he reached over and shook Gavin's left hand. "None necessary, man."

"How you feeling?" Gavin asked him.

"Woozy as hell. My jaw and my face hurt pretty bad. They gave me something for the pain. I'll probably see you in the hospital. Muriel's driving me there now."

"Want a helicopter ride?" Gavin offered.

"Thanks, but no thanks. I'll be fine."

A nurse checked Gavin's IV bag of Ringer's Lactate while two paramedics started to move everyone away from Gavin's gurney and prepare him for the short helicopter trip to Tampa General Hospital.

"We're going to give you a slight sedative for the pain, Senator. Try to rest", the nurse advised.

"Is there room for us?" Alexandra asked the nurse, pointing to herself and Cynthia. The nurse looked at the paramedics who both nodded in the affirmative.

"No, not me", Cynthia deferred. "Mike and I will make our way back to D.C. from here. I'll see you guys when you get back to Washington... unless you need me for something in the meantime, Senator."

"Nothing, Cynthia. Take your time on the way back."

"Thank you, sir."

The paramedics wheeled Gavin over to the helicopter and lifted him into the emergency bay. "Wait!" Gavin ordered one of the paramedics. "Get that man's attention." He pointed to Chuck.

"So, Chuck", Gavin yelled over the helicopter's rotors. "I'm going to need a best man."

"Well, I guess Grady killed your first choice", Chuck muttered to himself. Then he walked over to the helicopter and leaned in, "Do I have choice?"

"No."

"Alright then", Chuck acquiesced. The two talked for a few moments before Chuck backed away and returned to where Monica had been waiting alone. He smiled and asked her, "Would you like to ride back to Tampa with me, young lady? You're kinda stuck here it looks like."

"But you don't have a ride either", she observed.

"Oh, actually I do, lass."

As Gavin's medevac helicopter rose out of sight, another copter descended into its place. "I've booked us a couple of rooms in a nice hotel in Tampa. I'll take you to visit Gavin tomorrow."

Monica hugged Chuck. He put his arm around her shoulder and gave her a fatherly hug as they began walking toward the helicopter. "By the way, Gavin just told me that the first thing he wants you to do tomorrow is call your father and let him know you're alright. And see if he feels up to coming to Washington for a visit."

"That would be wonderful!" she exclaimed.

Chuck took her by the hand and they ducked and ran through the rotor wash to the idling helicopter. As he helped her aboard, he heard a loud voice from behind them. "Five days, McCrory!"

"Seven max!" he yelled back, and closed the helicopter door.

EIGHTEEN MONTHS LATER
Key West, Florida

The late afternoon sun was nearing the horizon, the festive revelers below it still blissfully basking in its fading but warm and welcoming rays of spring. On the beach, photographers were taking pictures of Gavin and Alexandra and the happy and joyful wedding party.

The wedding ceremony had been as beautiful and exciting as Alexandra had hoped and wished. The guests had been asked to dress casually in island attire and the wedding party only slightly better than the guests. Alexandra and Gavin had dressed quite formally except for their bare feet. She wore her mother's dress and he a black tuxedo. Everyone was in awe of the contrasting fashions which were striking and extraordinary.

Chuck had performed double duty, giving away the bride and serving as Gavin's best man. Cynthia had been a dazzling maid of honor, and Monica's sister's children, little Ernesto and his younger sister, were as cute as buttons in their show-stealing roles. The newlyweds had danced their first dance to the Carpenter's "Because We Are in Love", the emotional lyrics summoning multiple tissues from tiny formal purses.

Formalities completed, the guests were all seated comfortably around the Tiki Bar pavilion or milling around out on the beach. Everyone enjoyed watching the happy couple casually mingle with their guests, sip champagne, and enjoy the special moments they would cherish for the rest of their lives.

"I love beach weddings!" Cynthia proclaimed. "Alex always said she just wanted a casual beach wedding. This was the best thing ever. I'm going to hate dressing formally for weddings now."

"I cannot believe how beautiful she looks in her mother's dress! Ella es muy hermosa!" Monica extolled.

"She's more than beautiful", Cynthia concurred. "She's radiant. And you are so right! That dress! It fits her perfectly. Can you believe Illiana is such a seamstress?"

"I have never been to a more wonderful wedding", Monica lavished. "You have your work cut out for you, Cynthia."

Cynthia held out her hand and showed Monica her engagement ring for the fourth time in thirty minutes. "I know", she agreed. "The bar is set pretty high for Mike and me, isn't it?"

The girls laughed as Muriel approached. "Hola, Chiquita!" Monica welcomed. "Where have you been? We couldn't wait for you. The call of the margarita was too strong."

Muriel laughed. "That's okay, honey."

"Come sit over here", Monica beckoned. "I will get you something from the bar. What would you like?"

"Thank you, Monica. How about a rum runner?"

"De nada. I will be right back."

Cynthia made room for Muriel at their table. "We were just saying how incredible Alex looks today."

"I've never seen her more radiant", Muriel agreed.

Cynthia reached over and touched Muriel's hand. "That's exactly what I said! I'm just glad her dress got here in time. You know Chuck flew to Igoumenitsa to pick it up for her?"

"And her grandmother", Muriel added. "Don't forget about Illiana. He picked her up, too."

Cynthia and Muriel were still giggling as Monica returned with another round of margaritas and a rum runner. "What's so funny?"

"We were just talking about Illiana", Cynthia replied. "Speaking of which, has Demetri pinched anybody here yet?"

The girls laughed and clinked their glasses in salutation to the occasion.

"So, have either of you congratulated Gavin yet?" Cynthia asked.

"About the wedding or the legislation?" Muriel implored.

"The legislation."

"Yes, I did", Monica nodded. "The Samantha Lawrence National Drug Reform Act. It squeaked through by only a few votes but it is the law of the land now. I am so proud of him! And to honor Samantha that way. He is an amazing man."

"Here, here!" Cynthia saluted Monica's sentiment. "He didn't get everything he wanted, but I think it's a good start. At least the tacit abolishment of the War on Drugs should slow down the incarceration rate and channel some of that money to prevention and rehabilitative services. That's the goal anyway."

"Don't hold your breath", Muriel advised. "I've been around too many years, honey. Until young people vote the cronies out of Washington and establish realistic term limits, I assure you, nothing will change. Money has a siren stench. And there are no keener noses than the ones on career politicians."

Cynthia admitted, "You're probably right, Muriel. But Gavin won't be one of those. He told me yesterday he won't be running for reelection next year. He said his work is done in Washington."

"Really?" Muriel asked. "What does he plan to do?"

"I'm not sure exactly. But I think he plans to start a watchdog organization that blows the whistle on individuals or companies that fail to comply with his legislation."

"That won't pay much", Muriel said cynically.

"Probably not", Chuck said, as he and Grady strolled up and sat down with the ladies. "But that's one of the things I admire the most about our groom. He just doesn't give a shit about the money. I don't get it. But the world needs more politicians like Gavin Manson, that's for sure."

"He's not really a politician", Grady judged.

"No, I suppose you're right. Maybe that's what makes him such a good one", Chuck conjectured.

"Did he offer you a job in his new adventure?" Grady asked.

"Well, of course he did."

"What'd you tell him?"

"I told him to go screw himself."

Everyone laughed. The girls got up to find another drink and mingle among the crowd. In the corner of the pavilion, tropical music had started to emanate from a local group of quite talented musicians. Chuck recognized it was the same Reggae band he and Muriel and Grady had seen the night he first learned Grady could dance. Diehard dancers had kicked off their shoes and established a makeshift dance floor near the band, gracefully gliding barefoot in the sugary evening sand.

"How was your trip to Igoumenitsa?" Grady asked.

"Bittersweet. I hadn't had time to think much about Christos passing until I got there. It hit me pretty hard. But on the other hand, it was really nice to meet Demetri and Illiana. It made me feel good to bring them back here for Allie's wedding."

"I'm sure Christos would be smiling right now." Grady put his arm around his good friend's shoulder and shook it gently.

"It's getting loud here, Grady. Let's drag a couple of chairs out to the beach."

"Alright. Let's do it."

Chuck and Grady carried their chairs out to the edge of the water and sat facing the setting sun. They had each brought three beers with them to cut down on trips to the bar. Chuck raised his bottle toward Grady and saluted, "Here's to you, man. This wedding wouldn't be happening if it weren't for you, my friend."

Grady clinked bottle necks with him. "You know my nightmares have gone away."

"No shit! No, I did not know that. That's great, man!"

"Yeah, Muriel is damned happy about it."

"I bet."

"So how's Gavin's shoulder?" Grady asked.

"He says it's almost good as new. Not sure I believe him. But the man doesn't complain. I admire that."

"Yep. Me, too."

Some of the dancers had journeyed their way to the water's edge, dipping their toes in the salty solution as they two-stepped to the beat of Bob Marley. Beyond the dancers, on the distant horizon, the settling Florida sun had finished brushing the sleepy clouds with hues of pastel pink and orange while the first few twinkles of starlight emerged from the departing dusk.

"Red sky at night..." Grady observed with obvious pleasure.

Chuck smiled as he leaned back and folded his arms behind his head, with the apparent approval of Mona Lisa.

"Sailor's delight, Grady. Sailor's delight."

Visit **www.AfghanHorse.com** for information and insights into the making of this novel.

Click on NOVEL LOCATIONS to see pictures and images of many of the locations of the scenes in the book.

Printed in Great Britain
by Amazon